THE FALL OF THE ORC

FINLEY FENN

Edited by Eris Adderly
Cover artwork by Qaisan
Cover design by Sylvia at The Book Brander
Supported by the generous members of the Orc Sworn Patreon

The Fall of the Orc

info@finleyfenn.com

Sign up at www.finleyfenn.com for bonus stories and epilogues, delicious orc artwork, complete content guidance, news about upcoming books, and more!

ALSO BY FINLEY FENN

ORC FORGED

The Sins of the Orc

The Fall of the Orc

ORC SWORN

The Lady and the Orc

The Heiress and the Orc

The Librarian and the Orc

The Duchess and the Orc

The Midwife and the Orc

The Maid and the Orcs

The Governess and the Orc

The Beauty and the Orcs

Offered by the Orc

Yuled by the Orcs

THE MAGES

The Mage's Maid

The Mage's Match

The Mage's Master

The Mage's Groom (Bonus Story)

AUTHOR'S NOTE

Dear reader,

Thank you so much for picking up this MM tale!

If you're new to my orcs, welcome! This book is a great starting point, and reads as a total stand-alone. But if you're familiar with my other books, this one happens about two years before the beginning of my Orc Sworn series.

The Fall of the Orc tells the tale of how two enemy warriors fight through their differences to find love, trust, and peace. However, this means it also takes place during wartime, and includes some darker themes, including depression, PTSD, and suicidal ideation. If you'd like a full list of what to expect, please visit this book's page on my website at finleyfenn.com.

Thank you again for reading, and hugs from Orc Mountain!

Yours,
Finley

To Katie at Romantically Inclined Reviews
for all her generosity and enthusiasm, and for encouraging me to
finally write this book.
I am forever grateful!

This book was made possible by the incredible support of my
generous friends on Patreon.
You honour me, my kin!

1

Aulis Gerrard was going to die.

He grunted as his shaky hands swung up his broadsword, just in time to clang against the orc's huge, sweeping axe-blade. The impact strong enough to set him staggering, the pain reverberating up his shaking arms, jarring his teeth, his skull. While the dread kept wrenching louder, deeper, in ominous accord with the thunder of his heartbeat.

He was finally going to die. After thirty years of sweat and luck and sheer damned stubbornness, this would be the end. His body cleaved apart by a cruel orc's axe, thanks to the fool command of quite possibly the most arrogant, dim-witted commander in the realm.

No retreating this time, General Livermore had ordered the regiment, before they'd set out—again—for the orcs' camp. *You take their base, or don't come back.*

But it was their third attempt that week, after months of similar futility, and the men were hungry, weary, and deeply unwilling. And as the next-highest-ranking officer left standing in this godsforsaken outpost, Gerrard had been tasked with outfitting and mustering the regiment, and leading the charge. Inspiring his exhausted men to do this, to risk their lives for this, one more time.

So once they'd caught sight of the orcs—a solid wall of muscle and steel at the edge of the foggy clearing—Gerrard had drawn his trusty broadsword, and sprinted straight toward them. Again making for the biggest, most brutal orc in the line, a scarred, massive, grey-skinned berserker with a gigantic double-bladed axe, and a harsh, craggy face.

The orc's grim expression hadn't changed as he'd swung his axe to meet Gerrard's sword, or as the clangs and shouts of pitched battle rose around them. But that bulky grey body moved with ruthless, inhuman power, his axe-swings focused and vicious, blocking Gerrard's blade again and again and again. Forcing Gerrard to work harder and harder, to dodge and weave and strike, seeking in vain for an opening, an advantage, a weakness.

But there was nothing but noise and sweat and frustration, and the relentless steel barrier of the orc's infuriating, ever-present axe. And though Gerrard was unquestionably faster, lighter on his feet—and he'd gotten in a few good strikes on the orc's bare arms and chest—the orc still hadn't once faltered. That massive axe just swinging again and again, coming closer every time, driving Gerrard deeper and deeper toward sheer, staggering exhaustion.

He was going to stumble, and then he was going to die.

The certainty kept rising with every swing, every strike, every shudder of Gerrard's wavering blade in his numb, weakening hands. And his brief, searching glances through the fog around him didn't find anyone else faring any better—the orcs were gaining ground, and several of his men had already fallen, curse it, *curse* it—

He should be retreating. He should be turning, hollering for his men, and running for the safety of the outpost, like any responsible lieutenant would do. There was no point in killing an entire regiment over a stupid skirmish, over a stupid camp with only a few dozen orcs, on a stupid command from a stupid general. It was tactically useless, it did nothing to stop the orcs' incessant raiding, and it meant nothing—*nothing*—to the legions of powerful orcs still hunkered down in that damned Orc Mountain, sixty leagues to the southwest. Orc Mountain couldn't be taken, it was an impenetrable rock fortress, and this war was a cursed fucking *blight* of endless fighting and disease and death.

And even if Gerrard survived this battle, this deadly orc—there would be another, and another, and another. There would be more pointless deaths of his men, his friends and colleagues, upon his own conflicted commands. For the gain—the bragging rights—of arrogant, unthinking fools like Livermore.

And for what? Gerrard's thoughts demanded, as the orc's axe again clanged against his sword's edge, shattering more dizzying exhaustion in its wake. For what. For the naive, stupid ideals he'd once held? His thwarted dreams of someday becoming the youngest general in Preia, and making much-needed reforms that might actually help his men, rather than dragging them to their deaths? Or maybe, more likely, for the coin he'd be paid, if he ever made it back north to the city? For the shitty food and conditions, or the too-familiar gnawing hunger? For the quick fumbling fucks with other tired bodies in the darkness, out in the mud and dirt?

Or for the challenge of it, his distant memories pointed out, as he dodged sideways, and managed to duck beneath the next swing of the orc's huge axe. He'd always revelled in competition, in pushing the limits of his own skill and strength and endurance. In the unparalleled thrill of knowing he'd bested a worthy opponent. An opponent just like... like this.

But in this moment, as the grim-faced orc's axe again

crashed against his wavering blade, Gerrard couldn't even seem to find a vague, far-off satisfaction in the battle itself, or the ever-decreasing hope of victory. Because even then, if he did somehow rally and regroup, and crushed this orc beneath him—then what? He would slice this powerful grey body apart, drain all its blood into the earth, watch the life fade from those hard, glinting eyes. And the orc's empty face would join all the others that crowded Gerrard's dreams at night, woke him up in cold sweats, his heart fighting to escape out his throat. While he was still trapped here in hell, trapped serving the realm's worst general, staring down the truth of all his own dreams shattered at his feet.

No. There was no point. No fucking point, but stupidity, and greed, and misery. None.

He was going to die, and that was all.

So when the orc raised his axe again, Gerrard didn't move. Didn't bother trying to lift his own leaden blade. And instead he just stood there, tall and proud and despairing, as the orc's axe swung straight for his throat.

2

Gerrard's death should have been quick. Quick, and clean, and relatively painless, his head sliced from his shoulders in one sharp, decisive stroke.

But instead, it was—pain. Agony, flashing white through Gerrard's skull, as the orc's huge axe-blade wrenched up and sideways, and the flat of it crashed against his shoulder.

It sent Gerrard flying, his body slamming into the muck with shocking force, smashing the breath from his lungs, the sword from his hands. While the agony kept wailing, spewing out in stark dizzying streams, in ragged, desperate gasps from his mouth. He was still breathing, why was he still breathing, what the hell had happened, what the—

The orc. The orc had done it. He'd turned his blade, spun it up at the last possible instant, and—and in doing so, he'd kept Gerrard alive. And now he was standing here, looming over Gerrard in the fog with his huge shoulders heaving, his axe still bobbing in his massive clawed hands.

And—wait. Wait. Maybe the bastard wanted to play with Gerrard first. Maybe this was just the start of it, and this orc was going to make Gerrard's death slow and excruciating, make an example, a mockery, for the rest of them. And Gerrard had witnessed humans—his own damned superiors—doing the exact same thing to orcs, so why was he even surprised, what the fuck had he been thinking, what had he done—

And for perhaps the first time in this hellish day, this entire hellish mission, there was—fear. Fear, creeping cold and terrible up Gerrard's spine, closing around his throat. He'd always wanted his death to be fast. Painless. And now he had to face more agony, more misery, more humiliation, while all his own doomed men witnessed it. And somehow, watching *this* orc do it would make it even worse. He'd been a brilliant fighter, a worthy opponent, who hadn't spoken a single word of mockery or shame. And now—now—

Now Gerrard was—trembling. Quivering in the mud at the orc's feet, like the defeated useless failure he was, while the orc just stood there, and watched. Watched, his huge shoulders heaving, as something shifted, changed, in his grim black eyes.

Something almost like... pity.

Gerrard's mortification surged up alongside the terror and grief, his body reflexively curling in tight. Bracing, waiting, dreading, until—

The orc dropped his axe, and lunged. His massive deadly bulk lurching for Gerrard's cowering form, his hand swinging out, its black claws aiming for—

For Gerrard's waist. That huge arm slipping around him, grasping him, and then—dragging him up. Setting him onto his shaky, staggering feet. Upright. *Alive.*

And close enough that they could be... embracing. Close enough that Gerrard could smell the orc, could feel his rapid breaths, could have leaned forward and tasted his scarred, sweaty grey skin...

Gerrard flinched all over, but for a brief, horrifying instant, he couldn't seem to move. Could only seem to stare up at the orc, his breath heaving, his heartbeat still clamouring in his throat. What the hell. What the fuck was happening. Did the orc want to cut him down like this, maybe make him fight again, force him to keep at it until he collapsed from the exhaustion and then—

"Go," the orc hissed, his deep voice barely audible amidst the shouts and clangs echoing through the fog around them. "Run, human."

Go? *Run?* Gerrard couldn't understand, couldn't follow, couldn't possibly look away from the orc's grim, glinting black eyes. The eyes that still spoke of that damnable pity, or even regret, and—

"I said, run!" the orc growled, his eyes suddenly alight with rage, with pain. "Run, you stubborn man, before I *destroy* you!"

And that—that, Gerrard understood. The awareness shooting bright and blinding through his shaky body, his streaming thoughts. Run. *Run.*

But first, he... nodded. Nodded, ducking his head toward the orc, as if in obedience. In deference. In *gratitude*...

And then he shoved away and staggered off, screaming for his men as he went.

3

The fallout, of course, was hellish.

"I told you not to retreat again!" General Livermore hollered, his beady eyes bulging as he paced back and forth in his large canvas commander's tent. "You disobeyed a direct order, Lieutenant!"

Gerrard's frustrated exhaustion was already tilting toward recklessness, toward rage—and he heard his cursed mouth laugh, even as he reflexively rubbed at his shoulder, felt the pain flash and judder beneath his hand. "Tell me, General, what would you have preferred?" his tired voice demanded. "For all of us to die out there, and leave *you* here unprotected and alone, so the bastards could come for you next? You think they'd have trouble breaking through the gate or the palisades, without any guards? You think they'd be kind to you, while they kill you?"

Gerrard's scrambled thoughts had lurched back to that moment with the orc, to his own shameful terror at that threat of a slow, painful death. And for an instant, Livermore's pale, twisting expression echoed just how he'd felt in that moment, when he'd been cowering and trembling in the dirt before the orc. Raw, hunted, exposed. Weak.

"You weren't supposed to die," Livermore snarled, a little too late. "You were supposed to *win!*"

Gerrard laughed again, the sound scraping painfully in his still-ringing ears, as his exhausted body sagged heavier onto the hard wooden stool beneath him. "We were outmatched, and outnumbered," he shot back. "Those orcs had better weapons and better defense, they're better at fighting in shitty conditions like this, *and* they're probably better fed, too. And like I've been telling you all week, there's no tactical advantage to taking that camp! What's in it for the men? For me? Why even fucking *bother*?!"

It came out sounding plaintive, pathetic, almost pleading—and Gerrard probably deserved the deluge of shouting from Livermore that followed. The stream of justifications, the tired blather about honour and pride, about defending one's home and women and children from those cruel, evil, conniving beasts, who would plunder and pillage and torture in the night, and steal helpless women away to bear their deadly sons, until the entire realm was laid to utter waste beneath the horde's brutal rampaging feet.

Gerrard only half-listened, his body sinking heavier onto the stool, while his overtired brain made useless, silent objections. He had no home. No family left to defend. He'd never had the slightest interest in taking a wife, which meant that children were some abstract, far-off impossibility. Beyond his soldiers, and his occasional bedmates—which were already few and far between these days, because he didn't fuck subordinates—Gerrard had no one to protect, to support, to care for. No one who cared in return.

And despite all Livermore's ranting claims about the cruel deadly orcs, that orc today *hadn't* been cruel. He'd fought clean and fair. He could have easily killed—or tortured—Gerrard, but he hadn't. Instead, he'd helped him up. Sent him away. Saved his life.

He'd... *pitied* him.

And the more Gerrard thought about it, the more humiliating it all became. Not only had the orc roundly defeated him, but he'd watched him cower and shiver at his feet. He'd made Gerrard weaker than he'd perhaps been in his life, and then he'd let him keep living, out of pity. As if Gerrard had been some innocent, easily overwhelmed greenhorn, rather than an experienced lieutenant, a veteran of almost fifteen years' standing, with countless kills and victories to his name. And Gerrard was one of only a few dozen active lieutenants in the well-respected Preian army, and he'd been personally promoted by the army's High Commander, the extremely influential Duke Warmisham himself. And Warmisham was one of the realm's wealthiest, most powerful noblemen, and...

And in the face of the orc's pity, what had Gerrard done? He'd bowed his head. He'd... *deferred* to the orc. *Thanked* him. And then he'd run off, and... and...

"Where's my sword?" he croaked, cutting off Livermore mid-rant. "Did I have it, when you dragged me in here?"

Livermore's mouth pursed, his beady eyes narrowing, and Gerrard's gaze wildly darted around the tent, while yet more shame thundered through his ribs, his skull. Had he left his weapon on the battlefield? What, at that blasted orc's feet? As some kind of fucking *prize*?!

"Why should I know where the hell your own weapon is?" Livermore snarled back, crossing his arms against his pristine blue uniform. "You probably left it on that battlefield for the orcs, when you directly disobeyed my orders, and deserted your post like the incompetent *coward* you are!"

Gerrard couldn't hide his flinch, his bitter hiss through his teeth. And that was triumph in Livermore's eyes, victory, as he stalked closer, looming over Gerrard's slumped, exhausted form on the stool. "You failed me, and your men," Livermore's grating voice continued. "At least two of them are dead, and many more are injured! And as punishment for your shameful behaviour, I'll be writing to Duke Warmisham and Head Command at once, and demanding they strip you of your rank, as well as your pay for this abject *failure* of a mission!"

What? No. No. Gerrard's body snapped to horrified stillness, his eyes shocked wide on Livermore's face. The coin he could handle, but—his rank? That vaunted title of Lieutenant, the palpable proof of all his dedication and determination and damned hard work—Livermore was just... taking it away? Just like that?

"But—you can't," Gerrard stammered, his breath hitching. "Sir. I've served for fifteen years. Half my life. I've led dozens of battles and skirmishes, and won many more than not. We couldn't have won today. We couldn't. I almost *died*."

But the weakness was clearly consuming him, crushing him from the inside out, because he was fucking begging. Just like a coward, like the innocent, overwhelmed weakling the orc had thought him to be. And Livermore thought it too, Livermore was smirking at him, knowing full well Gerrard had been defeated, yet again.

"I'll hear no more of your insubordination, Gerrard," Livermore said crisply. "If anything, you should be bowing before me, and thanking me for not having you bound to the palisades and *flogged*!"

Gerrard stared at Livermore with dull, disgusted disbelief— as if this prick would even *try* it—and for a hurtling, miserable instant, he almost wished he was back on that battlefield, standing before that massive orc. And instead of just giving up, waiting for his death, he should have kept fighting. Made it look like he was still fighting. And only then should he have dropped his guard, let the orc's axe kiss his throat, make it all go away...

But it was too late. It was all too late, there was no point, he'd failed, he'd failed. And unlike the orc, Livermore wasn't worth it. Livermore sure as hell wasn't getting his acknowledgement, his gratitude. His shame.

So Gerrard rose to his feet, as steadily as he could, and reached to grasp the distinctive silver lieutenant's badge on his still-aching shoulder. Yanking it off with a sharp jerk, and letting it fall to the earth beneath his feet.

"Have it your way, then," he gritted out, as he strode for the door. "I'm done."

4

Gerrard should have known he wasn't done.

At least, not yet. Not with the cluster of his familiar, muddy, bloody men, waiting for him outside the tent. Well over a dozen of them, all looking to him for guidance, for reassurance, for support.

So Gerrard ignored his aching shoulder, his ever-creeping exhaustion, and instead clapped them on the back, praised their skill and valour and quick thinking, and reminded them to rest and recoup, and that future days would be better. And then, in a burst of bitter rebellion, he stalked over to the near-empty supply-wagon, and dragged out the last barrel of salted meat, and a full keg from Livermore's personal supply of ale. Earning a tired round of cheers from the assembled men, and even a few weepy, grateful smiles.

But that was the easy part. The harder part was trudging over to the med tent, surveying the newly wounded on their rickety cots, speaking false empty words of hope and healing and victory. And then, far quieter, discussing the much grimmer reality with Officer Ekene Bassey, the regiment's chief medic, and leaving firm directions about preparing the paperwork to send north, in hopes of ensuring the proper payouts to families were made.

Gerrard couldn't bear to go around back to see the bodies—thankfully they'd been recovered from the field, at least—and instead headed for his own cramped canvas tent, near the edge of the camp. And once he'd stripped off his bloody, grimy armour and uniform, he collapsed his aching body down onto his hard sleeping mat, and finally let his eyes flutter closed.

But despite the all-consuming exhaustion, sleep was a long time coming—and once Gerrard did drift off, it was fraught and fitful, poisoned with dark, desolate dreams. Visions of death, of pain, of weakness and failure and futility. Of loss.

And worst of all were the visions of that orc. That grim grey face, that relentless swinging axe, the way his arm had felt around Gerrard's waist, pulling him up. The way he'd smelled, rich and warm and sweet. And the astonishing depth of that growling voice, rumbling into Gerrard's belly, his bones.

Go. Run, you stubborn man, before I destroy you.

But maybe the orc had still destroyed Gerrard, after all. Destroyed his pride, his position, his rank, all his victories and accomplishments. Curse it, the orc had even taken his sword. The sword Gerrard had picked out after his very first promotion, his slim chest swelling with pride, with hope.

It's a damn good blade, the armourer had told him, with an approving glint in his eyes. *A bit big for you, though, boy.*

I'll grow into it, had been Gerrard's reply, cocksure and full of eagerness. And though he'd indeed grown into the blade, that innocent hope had been so unfounded, so foolish. Useless. A waste.

Gerrard didn't know how long he lay there, tossing and turning on his mat, fighting off the misery and dread. But when he finally sighed and blinked his tired eyes open, the surrounding darkness had slightly brightened, slipping into the slowly creeping dawn.

And with the light, somehow, there was a new awareness. A new, decisive determination, quiet but resolute, at the back of Gerrard's thoughts.

He'd failed with Livermore. He'd failed with the orc. He'd lost his rank, his men, his purpose. His pride. His hope.

So what the hell else did he have to lose? Why not go down doing whatever the hell he wanted, and seek out his victory—his vengeance—however he pleased?

And—he shoved up on his mat, gazed blankly at the dim light through the crack in his tent's flaps—why not try to take down Livermore with him? Why not... why not try to take down the *orc*?

Something fizzled and crackled in Gerrard's chest, more life than he'd felt since that battle yesterday—and with it, there was even a cursed stirring in his damp, filthy trousers. Yes. *Yes.* He would hunt down the orc, and kill him, regain his sword and his honour and his pride.

Or else—or else he would die trying. He would go out the way he'd been meant to. Fast, quick, impaled on the end of a worthy warrior's blade.

So Gerrard ducked out of his tent, and readied himself as quickly as he could. Washing his hands and face, choking down a bit of dry bread, and then swiping a far inferior replacement sword from their makeshift armoury. And after one last look toward the still-sleeping camp, he turned for the forest, and left his life behind him.

5

It didn't take long to reach the muddy, trampled battleground, or the orcs' camp beyond it.

Or rather—where the orcs' camp had been. They were... gone?

Gerrard cursed under his breath as he prowled around the clearing at the top of the hill, kicking at the remnants of fires, the charred bones from game and fowl, the large patches of flattened vegetation. The orcs had gone. They'd won, and then they'd *gone*.

And rather than the triumph Gerrard should have felt at this unexpected discovery, he felt—thwarted. Enraged. The orcs had hunkered down here for weeks on end, goading Livermore into ordering all those attacks, wasting all those men—and now that Gerrard wanted the brutes to be here, they'd packed up and left? Just like that?

Gerrard cursed aloud this time, and glared at the thick forest all around him. The southern Preian forest was notoriously difficult to navigate, full of brush and swamps and muck, and of course the orcs had gone straight off into it. Of course that great grey bastard had gone into it. Of fucking *course*.

But Gerrard wasn't being deterred at this, not now. And after another moment's glaring around at the abandoned camp, he strode toward the trees. Following the clear path the orcs had left behind, the greenery visibly crushed beneath muddy booted footprints.

It was slow, tedious tracking, but Gerrard doggedly kept going, picking his way through the muck and brush. And as he went, his still-furious thoughts swarmed over his plans. His vengeance.

He would track the orcs. Stay very quiet, keep a careful distance. And then he'd watch, and wait until the orc was alone, and attack.

And this time—he hunched his shoulders, gripped at his sword-hilt—he'd do his damnedest to kill the inhuman swine. He'd watch the light fade from those ugly orc eyes, and then he'd hack off that huge hideous head, and take it north. He'd take it all the way to Preia's capital city, and straight to Duke Warmisham himself.

Gerrard had personally met Warmisham on multiple previous occasions, most recently at the ceremony when he'd been granted that lieutenant's badge. And while Warmisham seemed just as smug and spoiled and self-centred as every other noble Gerrard had ever met, he also hadn't missed the... *interest*, there. The way Warmisham's speculative eyes had run up and down his tall, uniformed body, lingering with obvious appreciation. With... opportunity.

The realization had only irked Gerrard at the time, not only because Warmisham's own laws technically prohibited such liaisons between men, but also because Warmisham had recently remarried, in a grand public to-do. And it was so typical—and so damned enraging—for a rich titled commander to be playing house with a pretty young wife, while also fucking his way through his subordinates.

But. It also gave Gerrard an opening. A way to get directly to

Warmisham. He could easily find the right people, and drop the right hints. Allude to a highly memorable past liaison, one that had been thoroughly enjoyed by Warmisham. One that Warmisham would very much like to repeat.

And once Gerrard had Warmisham alone, he'd do everything he could to make his case. He'd hand over the orc's head as a personal gift for the vaunted ducal mantel. He'd tell as many graphic tales about Livermore's gross incompetence as he possibly could. And if it came down to it, he would even grit his teeth, and fuck Warmisham into oblivion, too. He would demonstrate—very vividly—why it would be in Warmisham's best interests to keep him around. To let him keep his hard-won rank as a lieutenant. Maybe promote him to commander, or even general.

And if it turned out that Warmisham liked it the other way—liked to get off to high-ranked soldiers begging on their knees—well, Gerrard would force his way through that too, and then avoid Warmisham for all the rest of his days. He would do whatever the hell it took to crush that cursed orc, and to crush Livermore, and get his pride back. Get his life back.

He kept repeating that thought as he slipped ever deeper through the trees, as the grey sky above—predictably—began pelting raindrops onto the thick foliage above him. He would do anything. Anything.

And if he failed, if that damned orc jumped out from behind a tree and killed him—well, then so be it. There was nothing else anyway. Not even that fear from the day before, that terror of a slow agonizing death. Because if the orc had wanted that, he could have had it. He could have had it so easily...

But he hadn't. Instead he'd saved Gerrard, insulted him, *destroyed* him. And where the hell even was the orc, how much ground had these blasted orcs travelled already, if Gerrard had to track the bastard all the way to Orc Mountain he was going to be *very fucking irate*—

"Ach, human," cut in a voice, a deep, devastatingly familiar voice, rumbling low in Gerrard's belly. "You seek this, I ken?"

Gerrard whirled around, his heart leaping into his throat, his hand already closing on his borrowed sword's hilt—because it was him. The *orc*. Huge and grey and grim, and brandishing Gerrard's stolen, priceless sword in his big clawed hand.

Gerrard's breath choked, his gaze holding to that sword—*his* sword—and then darting up and down the orc's massive, muscled body. He seemed even bigger than before, despite wearing only a pair of cropped, badly fitting trousers—and in the brightening morning light, Gerrard found himself noticing many more details than before. The rich sheen of the orc's pearly grey skin. The thick shaggy mess of his loose dark hair. The heavy dusting of yet more dark hair across his powerful chest and calves and forearms. The way the muscles shifted in his hard abdomen, and those broad shoulders. And—most distracting of all—that distinct shape of an over-large *cock*, rounding out the front of the orc's grubby trousers.

Gerrard forced his gaze upwards again, and suddenly he felt even more enraged than before, the fury surging wild and stark in his chest. He would have his vengeance. He would.

"You bastard," his voice hissed, all on its own. "That sword is *mine*."

And in return, the orc—*smiled*. His beady eyes crinkling as his grim mouth broadened into something bright and horrifying, full of menace and mockery and sharp white teeth.

"Then come, human," he said, almost a purr between them. "And win it back from me."

6

Gerrard didn't wait. Didn't hesitate.

He lunged forward with as much speed and power as he could muster, his borrowed weapon light in his hand, his focus narrowing on the orc's huge, shifting body. On the way the orc was holding his stolen sword, how he would probably block, what he was likely to do next...

The orc swung up that sword, met Gerrard's with a loud, shirring scrape, but Gerrard was already leaning into the impact, and using the momentum to spin away. Sweeping his blade around toward the orc's bare shoulder—his actual target—and crowing aloud at the sharp, satisfying sensation of steel striking bone. At how the orc grunted and shifted backwards as blood sprayed, and pain—and then appreciation?—flashed across his glinting black eyes.

But Gerrard couldn't spare a moment, a breath, and he was already rushing in again. Aiming for that too-obvious bulge in the orc's trousers this time, but the bastard lurched away just in time, his sword belatedly catching Gerrard's, knocking it sideways. And again Gerrard charged in, now aiming up toward the orc's neck, and missing it by just a hair.

He could see the orc's expression shifting again, sinking into that familiar grim focus, and this time he parried properly, if still a little too late. Giving Gerrard just enough time to duck in again, drawing a thin red line against the orc's torso. Flashing another flicker of pain across the orc's eyes, and surging more deep satisfaction—or even a strange, reckless triumph—into Gerrard's chest, into his racing heartbeat.

"Bet you're missing that axe right now," his voice spat, as he tossed his mediocre sword to the other hand, and managed to land another strike to the orc's opposite shoulder, spraying out another satisfying arc of bright red blood. "Not nearly as good with a sword, are you?"

Damn him, what the fuck was he doing, he wasn't here to rile up this orc, he was here to kill him—but then he almost lost his footing at the sight of the orc... smiling. Smiling, again, with all those sharp teeth, and perhaps less mockery in his dark eyes than before.

"Ach, no," the orc's deep voice replied, as if—as if in *agreement* with Gerrard's mockery. "But I thought this should be more... fair."

More fair. As though the orc was pandering to Gerrard, condescending to him, laughing at him. Taunting him, the way one might taunt an excitable little kitten, and Gerrard's fury surged again, tangling with mortification, with something much like despair. And he couldn't at all identify the sound that escaped his mouth, a bitter bark of rage, or pain, or... or grief.

"Fuck you," he shot back, as he lunged in again, knocked aside the orc's attempt at parrying, and again made impact, against the orc's thigh this time. "*Fuck. You.* If you wanted to be fair, you"—he gulped for air, charged in again—"you should have damn well killed me yesterday, when you had the chance!"

The orc again grunted as he shifted backwards, avoiding

Gerrard's strike—but his big head cocked sideways, his eyes oddly intent on Gerrard's face. "This was not—*fair*," his deep voice countered. "This was you—giving up."

Giving up. Gerrard instantly recoiled, fiercely shaking his head as another miserable barking growl escaped his throat— and when he ran in again, the orc's parry seemed almost distracted this time. "You gave up, human," he insisted. "You wished to fall upon your own sword, but have this blame—this guilt—fall upon *me*. You ken this is *fair*?"

The words caught and bloomed in Gerrard's chest, powerful enough that he staggered backwards, gasping for the suddenly thin air. And wait, he'd left an opening, the orc should be rushing in, he should be taking the opportunity, destroying Gerrard where he stood—

But again, the orc—didn't. And he'd even lowered the sword, his big body pacing sideways, and Gerrard reflexively matched it as his breaths heaved, the sweat now streaking down his hot face. This brute. This *beast*. This—

"You are too good a warrior to be cut down thus," the orc's deep voice continued, and Gerrard distantly noted that his bare grey chest was heaving too, streaked with blood and sweat. "Mayhap the most skilled human I have ever faced in battle."

Gerrard was still panting for air, for comprehension, as his feet kept pacing opposite the orc, both of them now moving in a slow circle. What the fuck was this. The orc was flattering him, trying to trick him, to catch him and then crush him underfoot, and—

"Rubbish," Gerrard croaked back, wiping at his sweaty face with a strangely shaky hand. "You're just trying to—"

What? Curse him, what? He couldn't seem to think, couldn't look away from the orc's hard, glinting eyes. Or from where the orc was now shrugging, rolling his huge sweaty shoulder.

"Why should I speak false in this?" the orc replied, his voice flat. "You have shown yourself strong, swift, skilled with a blade, sure on your feet. You are quick to learn your foe, to find his weakness, and wield this to your gain. And"—he shrugged again—"you showed yourself a good lieutenant to your men. You came for me alone on each charge against us, so they would not need to face me. And you retreated, each time these past days, when you saw your men falling."

Oh. Something again shifted, swelled, in Gerrard's heaving chest—and then it escaped, in a sound much like a laugh. "Doesn't mean anything," he growled back. "I still failed. My commanding officer raged at me. Stripped my rank, and my pay, too. Even threatened to have me *flogged*. After fifteen fucking *years*."

He twitched at the sound of those damning words, escaping his own cursed mouth. This orc was an enemy, a smug mocking swine, and Gerrard shouldn't be telling him anything, anything—

But then, to his genuine astonishment, the orc curled his lip, and snorted. The sound deep and guttural, and almost... incredulous. Contemptuous.

"Your commander is a fool, if he chastised you for this," the orc shot back, the disdain glinting in his eyes. "You ken he ought to be glad to have a brave and skilled lieutenant to lead his battles, and spare his men from needless death. But"—the orc's thick brows furrowed as he mightily frowned—"wise commanders are as rare as gooseberries in winter, ach?"

Gerrard's still-pacing steps briefly faltered, catching on a loose stone at his feet. The orc was—commiserating with him? *Agreeing* with him? And—far more importantly—he was implicitly condemning his *own* commander, too, right?

"Who's your commander," Gerrard demanded, without thinking. "Borek? Or Slagvor?"

It had been a guess, based on the look of the orc and his band—there were multiple orc clans, and they usually fought with their own kind—and Gerrard was distantly satisfied to see the orc's thick brows snap up, the surprise clear on his rugged face. "Ach, Slagvor," he replied, and then shook his head, his eyes again narrowing. "And how do you know this?"

Now it was Gerrard's turn to shrug, because any half-decent officer should take the time to learn his enemy—but even so, the triumph seemed to bubble higher, warmer, in his belly. "You look like a Bautul," he said, with a curt wave toward the orc's harsh features, and his broad, bulky form. "And fight like one—you, and your band. And Borek and Slagvor are the Bautul's captains, aren't they? The ones who keep sending you over here to raid and camp and skulk about, and strike fear in the hearts of Preia's peasantry? Or whatever the hell this is?"

Gerrard's hand waved irritably at the forest around them this time, because as much as he loathed Livermore and his fool orders, the orcs' actions were frequently foolish and enraging, too. It made no strategic sense for an armed orc band to be camping here on a random hill in Preia, sixty leagues away from their impenetrable Orc Mountain. There were no nearby orc settlements to supply with their raids, there were no important human strongholds here to take, no tactical advantages to win. Truly, it felt just as meaningless—just as directionless—as the human lords' actions against the orcs. Just more moving of pieces on a board, for someone else's gain.

And surely Gerrard was reading into it now, seeing what his traitorous brain wanted to see, but it almost looked like the orc had winced, his steps stiffer and slower than before, his big shoulders hunching. And if Gerrard was smarter, he'd have taken the opportunity to rush in, to strike with all his strength—but instead, he was watching. Waiting, for the orc's answer.

"Ach, this is Slagvor's doing," the orc finally said, his voice very steady, his eyes held to Gerrard's face. "He seeks to flaunt our strength and victories against Duke Warmisham here in

Preia, and thus to gain the favour of the Captain of Orc Mountain."

The Captain of Orc Mountain. That particular bastard was named Kaugir of Clan Ash-Kai, Gerrard well knew, and Kaugir was without question the most notorious face of this endless war. And while Gerrard had long ago learned that it wasn't necessarily the faces one needed to blame—it was the entire grinding apparatus built around them—he still couldn't deny a shudder, rippling up his back. Even if half the tales about Kaugir were true, he was a raging despot who treated his own orcs like chattel, and made Duke Warmisham look like a sweet-faced summer child.

"How lucky for us all," Gerrard belatedly hissed, earning a grim nod from the orc in return—and only then did he realize the depth of what this orc had just told him. The orc had identified his own commander. He'd divulged his commander's goals. He'd hinted—no, he'd admitted—that his captain's commands were also a farce, designed to gain the favour of a far-off superior who would probably never need to face the fallout, let alone look death in the eyes himself.

This orc was—betraying his own. To Gerrard, to an enemy. And for what? Wait, was he—was the orc going to kill him now? The orc had to kill him now, right?

"And now you're going back to report to Slagvor?" Gerrard demanded, pushing now, but what did he have to lose, after all this? "Tell him you were victorious? That you sent us all running and squealing back to our outpost, licking our wounds?"

The orc didn't even bother trying to deny it—why would he, because it was all true—and he shrugged as he gave a half-hearted whirl of Gerrard's sword in his hand. "And mayhap show off this blade, also," he said coolly. "Tell the tale of how the fair-faced warrior ran screaming from me, and forgot his weapon on a battlefield."

Gerrard blinked, stared—and suddenly the rage was seething again, drowning out any bizarre sense of understanding, of affinity. Curse this taunting condescending prick, that was Gerrard's sword, Gerrard's property, and how *dare* this orc use it to mock him like this.

Gerrard roared as he rushed forward again, his far inferior sword aiming straight for the orc's abdomen. But the enraging brute easily knocked Gerrard's blade aside this time, and he even had the gall to laugh, the sound deep and rolling, shuddering in Gerrard's belly.

It only seemed to flash his rage higher, and he funnelled his focus into fighting, into gaining every possible advantage he could. Striking again and again for the orc's exposed skin, sneaking past his guard, using his superior speed and dexterity to duck and jab and weave. Avoiding nearly all the orc's strikes in return, some of them damned close—so close that it took Gerrard far too long to realize that the orc was... holding back. He wasn't hitting him. On fucking *purpose*.

"Come on!" Gerrard snarled, between his panting breaths, as the rage hitched even higher, tinged with something too close to despair. "Fucking hit me, you great arrogant *swine*!"

The orc hadn't liked that, his bushy brows dropping, nostrils flaring—so Gerrard kept at it, lunging forward again, swinging his sword far more wildly than was wise. "Hit me, you ugly beast," he gasped, the words thick and bitter in his throat. "You coward. Can't take out a single human who's fighting with a worthless borrowed sword? You're that weak? That much of a failure? What's your clan going to think of that?"

The displeasure—the discomfort—flashed higher in the orc's eyes, and Gerrard somehow laughed, and lunged in again. "What do the Bautul think of cowards?" he rasped. "What does Slagvor think of cowards? What do you think he'll do, once he finds out the truth about you?"

Yes, yes, it was working, it was—and without warning, the

orc... snapped. Roaring as he hurled the sword aside, and charged straight toward Gerrard. And there was only a breath to register it, to swing up his blade—but the orc's broad forearm easily knocked it away, and Gerrard flew backwards, crashing onto his back on the earth. The air spewing from his lungs, the pain flashing white behind his eyes, and for an instant, it was like he was back on that bloody battlefield, tossed like a useless doll onto the earth at the orc's feet...

But this was worse. So, so much worse, because the orc was still here, right here, his massive body heavy on top of Gerrard's, crushing him beneath its weight. And when Gerrard kicked and shoved, he only met hot, solid, sweaty flesh, and then found the truth of a huge powerful hand, clamping around his neck.

"You foolish, reckless human," the orc's deep voice growled, far too close, and when Gerrard's eyes refocused, the orc's harsh grey face was looming over his, his black eyes bright with rage. "You wish this much to die?!"

And as Gerrard wretchedly gasped for breath, blinked up at the orc's furious face, he found that... he couldn't seem to deny it. Couldn't seem to stop the helpless, shameful words—the weakness—from jostling into his throat, escaping, becoming truth...

"I'm going to die anyway," he croaked. "Sooner rather than later. You know it, I know it. I would just rather it be—on my terms. Would rather it be"—he dragged in breath—"*you.*"

You. What the fuck was he saying, what was he betraying, he didn't think this, he hadn't thought this, had he? This hadn't once occurred to him, when he'd spoken to Bassey, when he'd deserted the outpost that morning, when he'd left his entire life behind. When he'd come up with that utterly ludicrous plan to hunt down and defeat a gigantic, obscenely powerful orc in single combat, and take his head to Duke Warmisham...

"I'm so damned sick of this war," he gasped at the orc,

without thought, without even hearing it. "It's such a useless endless *waste*, full of shit and misery and slaughter. But you—"

The orc was still hovering over him, pinning him down, staring at him with those glinting black eyes—and maybe it was still working, maybe Gerrard could still get what he wanted from this, after all. "You're a brilliant fighter," he rasped. "Fought fair and clean, without any rubbish. Didn't try to trick me. Didn't capture or torture me, when you should have. Would have made a good show for Slagvor, you know? Gotten you a promotion, maybe."

The orc's breaths seemed to be heaving harder, despite the stillness of the rest of his huge body crushing Gerrard into the earth. And Gerrard might have even smiled, desperate, delirious, up into the orc's harsh, staring face.

"So if you kill me now," he whispered, "that works for us both, doesn't it? Gets us both what we want?"

But to his whirling distant surprise, the orc... shuddered. His glinting eyes closing, his lashes thick and black against his sweaty grey cheekbone. And his mouth was twisting, his nostrils flaring as he inhaled, the breath hitching into his huge swelling chest...

"Foolish human," the orc breathed, his voice dark and low. "I do not wish to kill you. I wish to..."

His eyes fluttered open, his gaze heavy and strange on Gerrard's, and Gerrard stared back, unblinking, as a long, slithering black tongue slipped out, and brushed against the orc's lips. And Gerrard should have been recoiling, cringing away, but he was still just staring, frozen, transfixed. Waiting, breathless, as his own lips parted, as...

As the orc bent his shaggy head, and... *kissed* him.

7

ulis Gerrard was kissing an orc.

What the fuck. Curse him, curse this orc, curse the entire world, what the *fuck* was he doing.

But he was still—doing it. His mouth caught on the orc's, *in the orc's*, as the orc's hot huge tongue slid between his lips. And why was Gerrard gasping against it, why was he opening more, and even—even nudging his own tongue back against it. Feeling the undeniable truth of the orc's conquest, his victory—and instead of the shame he should have felt, there was only a strange, dazed resignation.

The orc had won. Fair and square. And he hadn't wanted to kill Gerrard, he'd wanted... *this*. This orc—this huge, brilliant, powerful fighter—wanted *this*. From *him*.

And surely, that was another insult. Another shameful, towering failure. A failure of Gerrard's skill as a fighter, his worthiness as an opponent, his entire damned goal in coming here. Ending with him being crushed to the earth beneath a gigantic orc, while the orc's hungry tongue plundered into his throat.

But it was still here, still happening, and Gerrard had even gasped into the orc's mouth, his sweaty, shaky body reflexively arching up to meet the solid wall of muscle above him. And oh, the way the orc growled back, rumbling it into Gerrard's tongue, his throat, as his heavy hips ground downwards. Making Gerrard suddenly, shockingly aware of that bulge in the orc's trousers—or rather, not just a bulge now at all, but a long, thick, demanding ridge, prodding hard and hungry into Gerrard's belly.

And most appalling of all, Gerrard's own body was... prodding back. He was already swollen to full mast in his trousers, and what the fuck was this, why was he grinding up harder, why was he fully thrusting his own tongue back into the orc's mouth. Tasting the strange musky sweetness of him, unlike any human's mouth he'd ever known—and in return, that was another growl from the orc, higher-pitched this time. Sounding pained, shocked, maybe even... helpless.

A brief, bizarre flare of triumph bubbled in Gerrard's belly, and without warning, a hoarse noise escaped from his own mouth, almost like a laugh. A laugh that the orc swallowed with a sharper, deeper growl of his own, a harder grind of his hips into Gerrard's groin—and Gerrard met it again, arching up again. As if he was countering it, challenging it, again prodding the orc, pushing him to—to—

The orc groaned again, and then yanked himself away, back from Gerrard's mouth. Staring at him with stunned, glittering black eyes, his mouth swollen, his sweet breath shuddering into Gerrard's face—

And in a dizzying flash of movement, the orc grabbed Gerrard by the hips, and bodily wrenched him over. Shoving him onto his hands and knees in the dirt, leaving him scrabbling for balance, for breath...

And then—Gerrard gasped—he felt the orc's hand on his trousers. Catching on the waistband, and then—yanking the fabric down to his thighs. Revealing Gerrard's bare arse, exposing him fully to the cool open air.

Fuck. *Fuck.* Of course that was what this bastard wanted, what he expected from this. He was an orc, an *orc*—and why wasn't Gerrard fighting it. Why wasn't he punching and shouting and wrenching away. The orc hadn't tortured him, surely he wouldn't force him to take this, either... right? And oh, hell, that was a big warm hand, brushing tentatively against Gerrard's exposed arse...

A suggestion. A... question.

And Gerrard's answer was—unthinkable. It was his head rapidly nodding, as his bared, suddenly trembling body shoved back into the orc's touch, his offer. Saying, blatant and shameful, *yes. Yes. Fucking do it. Take it. Take your damned victory.*

The orc's groan was thick and guttural behind him, the sound of shifting fabric and leather far too loud, until—Gerrard gasped—something touched him. Something hot and new and alive, seeking its way into his bared, exposed crease. Something that was already slick, swollen, dripping wet, and wait, that was *orc-seed* making it wet like that, and what the fuck was Gerrard doing, what was he—

Pushing. Pushing back against it, onto that blunt slick tip, feeling the pain whisper and flare as that hot flesh jabbed its way inside. Only a little, but enough that Gerrard could feel it juddering, could hear the orc's answering moan, choked and urgent in his throat.

"*Ach,*" the orc breathed, and that was the touch of his big hands, both of them blatantly gripping Gerrard's arse now, pulling him wider, like the presumptuous bastard he was. And Gerrard should have been fighting it, and maybe he was, he was. By willing himself to relax, to open—and to push back further. To swallow more of that huge, prodding, throbbing flesh inside him, to wring another guttural, helpless-sounding groan from the orc behind him.

"Ach, human," the orc moaned, his hands spasming against Gerrard's skin. "You cannot—you cannot want—may *harm* you—"

Gerrard's growl escaped on its own, his body shoving back harder, as more glorious burning pain blossomed around the orc's relentless invasion. "Fuck—you," he gasped. "I can take it. I know what I fucking want."

It was so clearly false, based on everything else he'd said and done this past day—and the orc's low answering laugh should have felt like an insult, especially with how his giant throbbing prick was now gouged halfway into Gerrard's upraised arse, and still sinking deeper. But those big warm hands were rubbing up and down Gerrard's sweaty flanks, as if in appreciation, in... approval.

"Stubborn human," he murmured, as that pole in Gerrard's arse swelled fuller, sank a little deeper. "This is not your first time, ach?"

Gerrard was not answering that, was not going to betray— or even recall—how much he'd once liked this kind of thing, especially with men markedly bigger and stronger than he was. But these days, there were very few such men to be had, even if Gerrard could bring himself to trust them enough to do this— and besides, he'd had more than enough submission and weakness and defeat of late to last the rest of his days. So why was he doing this, why why why—

The orc's big hands were still stroking up and down Gerrard's sides, almost as if to soothe him, reassure him, as that hard cock kept pushing deeper inside, slow but sure. That oozing orc-seed slicking the way with unsettling ease, so that the only remaining resistance was Gerrard's own taut, stretched-open flesh. Now clamping reflexively against the orc's shuddering strength, but the orc kept driving deeper, opening Gerrard wider, splitting him apart, as the pain flashed and burned. His rim so tight and strained, his body utterly pinioned, pierced, until—

Until the orc's hips met him. Touched, pressed, flush, skin to sweaty skin. The orc was fully inside him, an orc, an *orc*. And Gerrard's chanting, chattering thoughts were shouting, scrambling, not at it being an orc, but just at—at how good it felt. So damned good. So strong that there was no room for anything else, no shame or fear or despair, just this, just this—

"Fuck me," he gasped, ordered—and that was another hoarse, helpless moan from the orc as he... obeyed. Drawing himself out a little, and then sinking in again. Driving a choked groan from Gerrard's mouth, betraying both pain and pleasure—but oh, the orc was doing it again, and again. Moving smoother, swifter, with every stroke, until he was pumping in and out in a steady, staggering rhythm, his heavy bollocks slapping against Gerrard's skin, while Gerrard's moans pitched louder, higher, fuck, fuck—

His shaky, tingling hand fumbled beneath him, yanking his trousers down further, grasping himself in a tight thrusting fist—and suddenly the thudding pleasure caught, roared up into ecstasy, as he sprayed out onto the dirt. His whole body arching with it, shouting with it, clamping him over and over against the orc, against this invasion, this... relief. This brief, hanging, impossible quiver of rightness, of... of *peace*.

Behind him, the orc's body was pitching double, his hands catching on either side of Gerrard's on the earth—and he shouted, loud and pained and desperate in Gerrard's ear, as he spasmed all over, and poured out his pleasure, too. Flooding Gerrard full of him, full of what seemed to be an appalling amount of seed, pumping out again and again and again. While Gerrard's frantic, frenzied thoughts drew up the whispers, the tales, of the sheer quantity of an orc's spend, and Gerrard had never once wondered about that, let alone imagined taking a full load inside him... right?

But he was doing it, he'd done it, and it was already over, already inside him. And the orc's huge, heavy body had sagged down onto him, crushing him fully into the hard ground beneath him, and Gerrard should have finally found the will to resist, to fight. Especially the strange, hitching sensation of the orc's hot sweaty face, gently nosing at his neck, easing down into the crook of his shoulder, until...

The orc *bit* him. Bit him, breaking the skin, flashing out pain beneath sharp slicing teeth. And too late, Gerrard spasmed and gasped, his body snapped to stillness, his eyes shocked wide—

And finally, finally, he fought. Shoving up against the orc's overpowering weight, wrenching away from that clamp of teeth in his skin. And though he felt the skin ripping, tearing, flashing up more pain, he didn't care, he just needed to get away away *away*—

But that meant getting away from the orc's huge cock inside him, it meant yet more pain, and a loud, humiliating squelch as he broke free of it. And then the unmistakable, horrifying feeling of hot liquid, escaping from inside him, streaking down his thighs—and though he reflexively fought to clamp it off as he leapt up, yanked up his trousers, that meant the seed was... still there. Still there, inside him, and his trousers even felt noticeably snugger around his usually slim waist. Because—he shot a brief, mortified glance downwards—he was... bloated. Swollen. As if he'd gone off and eaten a massive damned feast.

And curse the orc, because he was looking, too. Holding his dark, greedy eyes on Gerrard's rounded belly as he slowly rose to his feet, not even bothering to pull up his own trousers. And therefore shamelessly, blatantly showing Gerrard what had just been jammed inside him—a huge, ponderous, veined grey orc-prick, streaked with a mess of white, and still oozing more shiny, viscous seed from its blunt, glossy tip.

Gerrard stared for an instant too long, his heart slamming

in his chest, his mortification jolting even higher. What the fuck, what the fuck, what the *fuck*—

And before the shame could swallow him whole, Gerrard whirled around, away, back toward the trees.

He needed to run.

8

Gerrard needed to run. Needed to escape. Needed to pretend for all the rest of his days like this had never fucking happened, never, never, *never*—

"Wait," cut in the orc's voice, deep and urgent, as something hard and powerful clamped around Gerrard's forearm. "Wait, warrior!"

Gerrard jerked to a stop, hissing through his teeth, but he didn't turn back toward the orc, didn't otherwise acknowledge this devious cheating bastard. And he could hear the bastard's shaky breaths, suddenly, could feel the air shuddering against the torn, painful skin of his still-exposed shoulder.

"You ought to—take this," came the orc's rough voice, as something hard nudged at Gerrard's clenched fist. "Tell your brothers how—how you won it back from me."

Gerrard's gaze snapped downwards, toward where—oh. His sword. The sword the orc had stolen, and wielded against him. And now the orc was just—handing it back? As some sort of pity prize?

But despite the shame still crushing Gerrard all over, he snatched for the sword, gripped its hilt tight. Felt the familiar ridges of wrapped leather beneath his palm, the weight and strength of solid steel in his shaking hand.

"Tell your brothers how you hunted me, and fought me," the orc's low voice behind him continued. "Tell them how you brought me to my knees, and conquered me. Ach?"

Gerrard's shame skittered sideways, pitched with bitterness, with disbelief—and against all his better instincts, he whipped back around, and glared at the orc's watching eyes. "I don't need your pity in this, orc," he spat. "Or your damned fucking *lies!*"

He couldn't at all read the orc's expression, or the little twist on his hard mouth. "These are not *lies*," he countered. "Every word of this is truth. You ken a good Bautul warrior should ever allow his enemy to steal back a fairly won battle-prize? Let alone *tasting* a human man, or"—he grimaced—"granting one his fresh seed? His *scent*?"

Gerrard kept glaring back—what did he mean, his *scent*—and then his traitorous gaze reflexively dropped to that still-appalling sight at the orc's groin. Prompting the orc to grasp his trousers, roughly yanking them up, even as his other hand gripped tighter to Gerrard's arm, gave it a hard little shake.

"I granted you my scent, human," the orc hissed. "And now, any orc who scents you shall know this. They shall know what I have done. They shall know how I have betrayed my own kin with you!"

His voice sharpened as he spoke, laced with frustration, with urgency, with... dread. And for an instant, Gerrard could only seem to blink at the orc's face, while those preposterous words jangled through his skull. Orcs did have powerful scenting abilities, he knew, but surely it wouldn't extend that far... would it?

"And what'll the other orcs do to you if they smell me," Gerrard snapped, not that he cared, he *didn't*. "What's Slagvor's punishment for blowing your load into a man."

He was still carefully watching the orc's face, and that grimace still looked uneasy, almost... afraid. "I... I do not know," the orc said, quieter. "Some kind of death, I ken."

Some kind of death. Suggesting, all too clearly, that it wouldn't be the simple kind of death. The straightforward kind. The kind Gerrard had come here seeking, and—he swallowed as he held the orc's eyes—surely the kind the orc would want, too.

"So what brings that about, then," Gerrard demanded, without at all meaning to. "Another orc catches a whiff of me? At what range? For how long? Do I need to be alone, or can they smell it in a skirmish, too?"

The orc grimaced again, and rubbed his free hand at his eyes. "It hangs upon the orc's scenting skill," he replied thickly. "For most Bautul, this close"—he waved aimlessly between them—"would be near enough to scent. The further away you are, and the more scents there are around you, the less clear this becomes, but..."

He didn't finish, his eyes now blankly fixed beyond Gerrard's head, and Gerrard kept standing there, staring, while his heart kicked erratically in his chest. "So won't they smell me on you, too, then?" he asked, his voice still too sharp. "Will they take one whiff of you, and haul you up before Slagvor to be tortured to death?"

He didn't miss the shift in the orc's eyes at the mention of Slagvor's name, or the telltale spasm of that hand still gripping his arm. "It is not always easy to tell blood from other human scents," the orc slowly said, as his gaze darted to Gerrard's torn, still-stinging neck. "Most of all if it is not seed, and not put... *within*. I shall need to tell them we fought at close quarters, and I spilled your blood, and..."

His uneasy gaze flicked down to Gerrard's sword, and Gerrard reflexively drew it closer, tighter into his side. "And then... maybe you can say I ran away screaming again," he supplied, his voice bitter but steady. "Like the weak little coward I am. And while I was at it, I threw the sword into a river. Or maybe into a crevice or something. Something too small for you to get at."

The orc blinked, as well he should, because damn it, Gerrard wasn't—helping him. Trying to help fix this. Was he?

"And I can carry another weapon for a while," he continued, to the orc's still-blinking eyes. "Until your smell on me fades, at least."

The orc's astonishment abruptly shifted, into something much like gratefulness—but then he winced, and shook his shaggy head. "But... my scent, human," his deep voice replied, very quiet now. "This shall... not fade from you, with time. Not ever."

Wait. The orc's scent wouldn't fade from him. Ever. *Ever*?!

Gerrard startled and gaped at the orc, as something clutched and curdled, deep in his bloated belly. "Ever?" he demanded. "Wait, so you mean to say I can *never* get this close to an orc again? Unless I want Slagvor to torture you to death?!"

The orc winced again, and Gerrard's irate disbelief lurched higher, his hand gripping tighter at his sword. "How the fuck do you expect me to manage that?" he continued, even louder. "I'm a soldier, you prick! This is my calling, my livelihood, my *life*!"

The words rang out between them, too bare, too exposed—and suddenly the memories were surging, flooding Gerrard's face with yet more chagrined, mortified heat. Yes, that had been his life—but he'd left it behind. He'd rushed out here like a fool. And he'd all but begged the orc to kill him, to take him away from this stupid pointless war, this ever-deepening despair. And when the orc had decided to take his victory from Gerrard's arse instead, Gerrard had willingly knelt and welcomed it. Begged for it. Just like the acclaimed successful lieutenant he was, right? Fuck. *Fuck*.

He braced himself for the orc's judgement, his pity, his well-deserved mockery—but to his distant surprise, the orc still just looked... unsettled. Uncertain. And his big hand tightened again on Gerrard's arm, drawing him a little closer, almost near enough for their chests to touch.

"I ken you must do as you need, human," the orc slowly said, his deep voice very even. "And do not think of me or my fate in this, should you not wish. But"—his breath heaved, his fingers spasming against Gerrard's arm—"I ken it may do you good, to stop fighting for a spell. To tell your brothers this tale of how you defeated me, ach—but mayhap also tell of how you gained some grievous hidden wound from me. And then..."

His voice faded, his mouth contorting, but as Gerrard kept staring, unblinking, the orc drew in breath, and fixed him with a sudden, ghastly frown. "And then, seek to rest, human," he continued, harder. "Seek to rest, and eat, and watch, and be *prudent*. Seek to better wield your wisdom and your cunning in this, in place of your recklessness."

Be *prudent*. In place of his *recklessness*. Those damnable words dragging Gerrard's mortification even higher, burning in his cheeks, because this accursed orc was—chastising him. Admonishing him. Condescending to him, as if Gerrard was some rash foolish child, about to thoughtlessly abandon his life, to come up with some harebrained scheme, and rush off to his death. Or, as it had turned out, to be bent over and pounded by an orc, and...

And he couldn't stand it, couldn't bear it, any more than he could bear the bulge in his belly—and before the orc could say another single horrible word, Gerrard wrenched away, and ran.

9

Gerrard's long, tedious trek back to the outpost offered him far too much time to think.

What the hell had he done. What the hell had he been thinking, to rush out here alone like this. To sprint headlong toward... his death.

But the more he brooded over it, trudging tiredly through the brush and muck, fighting to ignore the still-present ache in his shoulder, the distinct burning in his arse—the more he couldn't keep denying it. That damned enraging orc had been right, curse him. Gerrard had *wanted* to fall on his own sword. He'd wanted the orc to do it for him. He'd wanted a swift, merciful death, at the hand of a worthy foe.

And maybe—maybe the truth of that shouldn't have even been a surprise. Everything had grown so much... darker, of late. Heavier. This war was useless, pointless, with no end in sight, and where did that leave a lieutenant like Gerrard? On the front lines, watching his men die, dreading his own inevitable end. And maybe it was no wonder he'd gone seeking it out, wanting it on his own terms. He'd always liked doing things, being in control of things—and yes, he could admit, maybe it made him thoughtless, sometimes. Foolish. Reckless.

He winced and cursed under his breath, as the orc's craggy face again loomed in his thoughts—and fuck that hypocritical bastard, because he'd been foolish and reckless, too. He'd been the one to fuck Gerrard full of his—his *scent*, even if it might get him killed. Even if Gerrard would now carry that scent forever. *Forever.*

And what the hell kind of rubbish was that? That great fool brute had apparently marked Gerrard, *permanently*, and for what? He'd risked his own position, his own entire *life*, for a few moments' relief in the damned dirt? With an enemy lieutenant? A human he saw as foolish and reckless and—

You are mayhap the most skilled human I have ever faced in battle. You have shown yourself strong, swift, skilled with a blade, sure on your feet. You are quick to learn your foe, to find his weakness, and wield this to your gain. You showed yourself a good lieutenant to your men...

Gerrard cursed again, and irritably hacked his sword at a clump of brush blocking his path. Surely the orc hadn't... liked him. Hadn't groaned and shuddered as he'd opened him wide and plunged inside, as his huge bollocks had slapped rhythmically against Gerrard's skin...

Ach, human. You cannot want—may harm you—

There was a shameful stirring in Gerrard's trousers, and even as he kept hacking at the path ahead, his other hand slipped to his waist, feeling the still-distinct, still-strange swell of it. The orc had... filled him. *Wanted* him. Enough to forever mark him. Enough to risk his own life over it.

It didn't make sense. None of it made sense. Especially how, despite the utter disaster this entire day had been, Gerrard had almost begun to feel more... settled. More clearheaded, somehow, or even calm. More than he'd felt in weeks, or maybe months, or years. And had it been that long since he'd had a good hard pounding like that? Maybe... maybe it had?

But no. *No.* Gerrard was not thinking about that. Was not thinking about the inexplicable pleasure he'd found in it. Or that brief, fleeting feeling of rightness. Of... peace.

And most of all, he was *not* thinking about how he'd begun to limp as he neared the camp, dragging his foot, clearly favouring his left side. And even yanking at his grimy uniform's neckline a little, pulling it further down, displaying the grisly ragged remnants of the orc's bite in his skin.

"Lieutenant!" called a familiar voice, Corporal Allan Cosgrove's voice, as Gerrard limped his way into the camp. "You're back! What happened? We thought you—"

Deserted, Cosgrove had clearly been about to say, and his plump face flushed with red, his chagrin flashing across his round blue eyes. And for an instant, Gerrard eyed Cosgrove, weighing him—he was a jovial, hardworking junior officer, who often spoke longingly of his wife and young daughter back home. And, more importantly, he was also a notorious gossip, who made no secret of his rising frustrations with Livermore. So maybe—an ally. An opportunity.

"Oh, no, nothing like that," Gerrard said, as easily as he could, with a cheerful clap to Cosgrove's meaty shoulder. "Just went out on an early morning adventure. Took a few turns I didn't expect, that's all."

Cosgrove's blond brows rose, his curious eyes darting to Gerrard's visibly wounded neck, and Gerrard huffed a light, self-deprecating laugh. "That huge orc with the axe stole my sword yesterday," he said. "So I tracked him down, and fought him in single combat, and won it back. The bastard put up a good fight, so I'm sorry to say I didn't finish him off—but I got some good intel out of it, though."

Cosgrove's eyes had gone even rounder, the shocked awe unmistakable on his face, and Gerrard gave another laugh, followed by a genuine wince. "Got myself pretty banged up too," he said. "Bastard even *bit* me. I'm headed for the med tent next."

Cosgrove rapidly nodded, his eyes still very wide, and Gerrard limped off toward the med tent, feeling strangely, grimly satisfied. It wouldn't take long before the tale of his heroic exploits filtered around the outpost, ideally with a few embellishments thrown in, too. Hopefully enough to quash whatever rubbish Livermore had claimed about his unexpected absence, and hopefully enough to make the tale of his injury believable, too.

"Mind if I camp out here for a while, Bassey?" he asked, as he limped into the large tent, which still had a half-dozen wounded soldiers convalescing inside. "Got myself pretty beat up today."

Bassey's brown face frowned up from where he'd been tending to one of their wounded, and he strode over toward Gerrard at once. "What the hell happened to you, Lieutenant?" he demanded. "Rumour was you left?"

Gerrard gamely told the entire tale again, making rather more of a fuss about various injuries than was warranted. And when Bassey's too-clever eyes began hinting at suspicion—not a surprise, because he was a damned good medic—Gerrard took a breath, and took a chance.

"And look, if you want the full truth," he began, quieter, glancing around at the seemingly unconscious soldiers nearby, "I also met up with... a man from Head Command. One of Warmisham's household guard. And he told me they've been hearing some tales about Livermore's... ah... *difficulties* here in the south. And they want us to... lie low for a while, while they sort things out on their end. File the paperwork, that kind of thing."

Bassey, of course, knew all about paperwork, not to mention the depths of Livermore's utter incompetence—and

Gerrard was deeply gratified by the flash of understanding, or maybe even determination, across his deep brown eyes. "Of course, Lieutenant," he said firmly. "And I'm placing you on bed rest here for the foreseeable future. At least a week. And also"—his eyes narrowed again as they caught on Gerrard's neck—"did that orc *bite* you?"

Gerrard shrugged and waved it away, and in return Bassey harrumphed, and went to fetch a rag, and a basin of clean water. "You might as well try cleaning it," he said, "but there's something strange in orc-bites. From everything I've seen, it's likely to scar like that. Permanently."

Permanently. The word seemed to thud into Gerrard's belly, and he had to swallow hard, and will down the abominable twitching in his trousers. So not only had that orc permanently marked him with his scent, but he'd done it with his *bite*, too? And had he known it would scar? Surely he'd known, right?

"Thanks, brother," Gerrard belatedly said, reaching for the rag, while Bassey jerked a nod, and strode off. Leaving Gerrard to clean the bite in silence, wincing not at the pain—in truth, it already seemed considerably less painful than it should have been—but at his own fool choices in this. Letting that orc bite him, mark him, and... influence him.

Stop fighting for a spell. Tell of how you gained some grievous hidden wound. Be prudent. Seek to better wield your wisdom and your cunning...

But curse it, Gerrard was still doing it. Still lying meekly here in the med tent, nursing his wounds, pretending not to notice how one of his ostensibly sleeping wounded men was now watching him with cautious, curious eyes. Having surely overheard everything Gerrard had just said to Bassey, and now even more rumours would begin to spread and simmer, as they always did in such close quarters. And then...

"Gerrard!" snapped a voice, one Gerrard had been fully expecting, and he sighed as he shifted around on his cot, and found himself facing none other than General Livermore. Who was looking typically enraged, his pointy face flushed, his shoulders stiff and high and square in his spotless blue uniform.

"Why the hell are you lounging around in here?" Livermore demanded. "And where the hell did you run off to this morning? You were supposed to be on duty!"

Gerrard didn't need to pretend to look bewildered, though he also attempted a dismissive shrug. "Well, you demoted me yesterday, didn't you, sir?" he said blandly. "Stripped me of my rank and my pay, and my duties here. So there was no reason not to go off after that orc bastard myself, and at least get my sword back."

He patted the sword still at his side, feeling his shoulders slightly relaxing with the truth of it there—and watched with inward satisfaction as Livermore shot an uneasy glance around at the other soldiers in the tent. "I did *not* strip you of your duties, Lieutenant," he retorted. "Or any other such nonsense. I told you I was writing Head Command about your failures, and letting Warmisham do as he willed with you!"

Ah, yes, of course, and Gerrard barely bit back his snort as he twitched another shrug. "Wasn't how I heard it, sir," he said, clipped. "So I'm not about to be flogged after all, then? And do you still have my lieutenant's badge?"

There was a beat of uncomfortable silence, and Gerrard could feel the other injured soldiers' attention, now, eagerly listening to every incriminating word. And even Livermore had grimaced, glancing again around the tent, and then waving Gerrard toward the door. "We'll discuss this in my tent, Lieutenant," he snapped. "Now."

But Gerrard shook his head, and shot a regretful glance over toward Bassey, who was industriously writing something in his notebook, while clearly also listening, too. "Sorry, sir, but

I've been badly injured, and need to stay put here for at least a week," he said. "Medic's orders."

Livermore barked an incoherent noise of outrage, and again launched into one of his usual tirades about Gerrard's immeasurable failures, and the abominable disruption of him acquiring such an inconvenient injury. And instead of trying to argue or defend himself this time, Gerrard waited in blank, stony silence, allowing Livermore to rant and rave before a captive audience of all these watching men. Men who had all been wounded far worse than Gerrard, all of it beneath Livermore's own inept command.

"So are you saying we're not allowed to get injured, then?" Gerrard finally asked, clipped, before he could stop himself. "Or we're just not allowed to do so at a time that's inconvenient for you?"

It earned him another round of wild ranting condemnation, but perhaps it had been worth it—because when Livermore finally ran out of air and left, Gerrard didn't miss the men murmuring to each other, their eyes on him gone sympathetic, or even appreciative. And when Gerrard twitched a knowing smile back, and maybe even a roll of his eyes, several of them snickered in return—and even Bassey's mouth was quirking as he kept writing away in his notebook.

It left Gerrard lying there, breathing a little too fast, while his frantic brain belatedly caught up with everything he'd just said, and what he'd just done. Faking his injuries. Making up that tale about an investigation. Openly questioning and undermining his commanding officer. Bringing his men to his side...

Was he... was he starting a rebellion against Livermore? A *mutiny*?

But no, no. Full-on mutiny was a public, messy business, bad for image and morale, and very likely to lead to sweeping, brutal punishments. Punishments that wouldn't only affect

Gerrard, but his men, and possibly their families and children, too. And his men had already borne far too much of Livermore's rubbish these past months. They needed a rest too, and most of them were already overdue for leave, weren't they?

That unpleasant reminder seemed to settle Gerrard's determination even deeper, harder in his gut. There was a damned broad spectrum between obedience and mutiny, and Gerrard was sick to death of obeying. Of despairing. Of being weak and defeated. And before he walked mindlessly into his death again, he could at least try. Could try to learn his foes, find their weaknesses, wield that knowledge to his gain. He just needed to be prudent. Wise. Cunning.

He made a face, and forcibly shoved that presumptuous orc bastard out of his thoughts—at least, until he cleared his throat, and glanced sideways at Bassey again.

"What have you heard of the orcs' Captain Slagvor, Bassey?" he asked, without at all meaning to. "You've been on a few missions in these parts, right? Hear any tales about him?"

Medics usually heard all the best gossip, Gerrard knew, and he wasn't surprised to see Bassey nodding as he glanced up again. "Well, by all accounts, Slagvor's even more vicious than the rest of them," he replied flatly. "Takes joy in causing pain, and making a mockery of the wounded. On one mission a few years ago, we had to retreat and leave the wounded behind. Our commander at the time ordered them killed, for their own sakes."

His voice was clipped, clinical, but Gerrard could easily envision the sheer sickening horror of it, and his contrary thoughts again flicked back to the orc. *Some kind of death*, he'd said. *Do not think of me or my fate in this, should you not wish...*

Gerrard's hand tightened on the sword at his side, and he forced himself to cast backwards, to draw up everything he'd himself heard of Slagvor. Huge, vicious, merciless, a brutal fighter. Not unlike the tales Gerrard had heard about the rest of the Bautul clan in general, perhaps...

"Have you ever heard of any weaknesses, on Slagvor's part?" Gerrard asked Bassey. "Or have any men you've treated ever gotten close to him? Fought him in person?"

"If they did, they didn't survive," Bassey curtly replied. "But from what I've heard, he'll often send out bands without him—like the one we've been fighting here—or if he's present, he'll camp at the rear and watch. Make his lieutenants do all his dirty work."

Well, that all sounded unpleasantly familiar, and Gerrard's thoughts were again on the orc, who was clearly one of those lieutenants. And he did not care about the orc's problems with his own rubbish commander... did he?

"Don't suppose you've heard any of those lieutenants' names?" he asked now, too casually. "Especially the ones usually sent to these parts?"

Bassey shook his head, and Gerrard sighed and sank back onto his cot, frowning at the tent's canvas ceiling. No. He wasn't supposed to care about any of this, about that damned condescending orc. He didn't need to know his name. He needed to focus on himself and his men, on resting and watching Livermore, and...

He groaned and flopped onto his front—and then hissed through his teeth, because his belly was still... rounded. Swollen. And he should be going out to the latrine to deal with it, why wasn't he going to deal with it, why was he just shifting over to his side instead, squeezing his eyes shut...

Sleep came easily this time, and Gerrard drifted in and out of it, for what felt like a good long while. And when he fully awoke again, the tent was quiet and dark, illuminated only by a silvery shaft of moonlight, shining through the tent's flap.

Gerrard gazed at it for a while, keeping his thoughts intently blank, waiting for sleep to swallow him again. But the longer he lay there, the more awake—and the more antsy—he felt. He needed the latrine, he needed to wash up, he needed to just—do something. Anything.

He carefully shoved up on his cot, wincing—his shoulder was still wickedly sore, and he was not thinking about that burn in his arse, or how the swell in his belly had considerably diminished while he'd slept. And instead, he focused on keeping quiet as he snatched for one of Bassey's clean rags, and crept out the door. Escaping the tent without incident, and then heading first for the latrine, and then the closest proper creek, maybe a half-league away from the camp.

The creek was rocky and shallow, its bubbling water flashing merrily in the moonlight, and Gerrard eagerly knelt and drank, and then stripped off his grimy clothes, and began washing all over. Hissing at the feel of the icy water on his various injuries—not to mention his arse—but damn, it felt good to be clean, and he waded in a little deeper, ducked his head into the frigid water. And then arched back up to whip the water off, because his hair was getting too long these days, and...

A sound. A sound, curse it, a twig cracking, far too close. Someone was here, hiding, *watching* him, on the opposite bank. And fuck, had Gerrard destroyed all his plans with his recklessness already, betrayed his stupid injury ruse for a stupid bath, and—

Wait. It wasn't a soldier, or even a human at all. It couldn't be. Not with the sheer size of that bulk, now shifting forward into the moonlight. Not with the huge curve of that distinctive axe, glinting sharp and silver over a broad scarred shoulder...

It was the orc.

10

The orc was back.

For an instant, Gerrard froze all over, standing waist-deep in the creek's rippling water, while his heart kicked and galloped in his chest. The orc had come back, just like he'd...

Like he'd... what? Surely neither of them had held any delusions about another meeting, after all that? Surely Gerrard hadn't... wondered, even a little, if the orc might return? And surely, curse him, he hadn't come out here alone on purpose, and stripped bare, and frolicked in a fucking creek?

No. No. Absolutely not.

"What the hell, orc," he croaked, his voice far too loud in the darkness, even amidst the sounds of the bubbling creek around him. "Aren't you supposed to be off cozying up to Slagvor, and pretending I don't exist?"

But his heart was still thumping, his attention fully on the orc's shadowy bulk, waiting for his answer. Watching as the orc shifted forward toward the bank, his axe-blade flashing, his broad bare chest burnished and gleaming, his grey skin almost silver in the moonlight.

"I wished," came the orc's deep voice, "for a rematch."

A rematch. The words caught in Gerrard's chest, and then escaped in a choked, disbelieving little laugh. "You *won*, orc," he replied, too thick. "What the hell do you want a rematch for?"

The orc didn't immediately respond, and too late, a distinct, breathless alarm blazed through Gerrard's chest. This could be a setup. The orc could have been found out by Slagvor, and then sent back out to expose Gerrard, to kill him. Or maybe he'd thought better of all this himself, and wanted to get rid of the evidence—and that would be the smartest solution, wouldn't it? Especially for someone who'd so firmly advised Gerrard to be prudent? Cunning?

And even without any of that, this was still damned dangerous. If anyone found Gerrard naked in a creek with an orc, he'd be finished for certain. Charged with treason, and hauled up before Head Command, before Duke Warmisham, maybe even before an angry mob. It only took one wrong witness, one sleepless soldier out for an evening stroll...

Gerrard couldn't risk this again. He couldn't.

He was already backing away in the water, his eyes darting over his shoulder toward his sword, still lying uselessly with his clothes on the bank. And what had he even been thinking, to come out here alone like this, this orc was a death-trap and Gerrard was indeed a reckless thoughtless fool, and—

And then the orc dropped his axe. The heavy steel thudding into the soft earth of the creek's bank, while the orc himself lurched closer. His big body hunched, stiff, his skin still shimmering silver in the moonlight.

"It was a joy to spar with you, warrior," his deep voice said. "And I shall not wound you or kill you. I swear this, before the Goddess of Bautul. She is our goddess of the moon, who even now watches over us."

His big hand had come to his broad chest, closing in a tight fist against it, and his shaggy head lifted, tilting up toward the light of the full moon. Showing Gerrard his hard, craggy profile, his hooked nose and heavy jaw, the massive bulk of his heaving chest and shoulders. The way he looked almost... earnest. Reverent.

Gerrard swallowed, dragged for words, for rational thought. "You were the one who told me not to be reckless," he countered, too sharp. "If even *one* of my men catches me out here with you, I'm done. *Forever.*"

The orc's gaze dropped back to Gerrard, his heavy brow furrowing. "There are no other humans within scenting distance," he said. "And no other orcs, also. You ken I would have come to you, otherwise?"

Oh. Right. The orc could smell these things. And he wouldn't want to get caught, either, would he? He wouldn't take unnecessary risks. He would be cunning. Prudent.

Gerrard twitched a shake of his head, searched for some kind of answer—and found that he could only blink in the moonlight, his heart hammering in his chest. His bare body shivering in the cold water, now, needing to do something, anything, and...

He moved. Not away from the orc, not toward the opposite bank, with his sword, his clothes, his safety. No, his treacherous feet were moving toward the orc. Toward the silty bank, as the water around him grew shallower and shallower. Showing his abdomen, his bare hips, the surely shrunken sights dangling at his groin...

"Fine," he snapped, though his voice was hoarse. "But if you kill me, or betray me, I'm haunting you forever. With your goddess as my witness."

He couldn't have said why he tacked on the last bit, given his usual lack of interest in distant unhelpful deities—but he didn't miss how the orc's expression shifted in return. Looking uneasy, or maybe even alarmed, as he shot a brief, searching glance up at the watching moon—but then his chest hollowed, and his eyes darted back to Gerrard again. First to his face, and then dropping down to his bare chest, his abdomen, his groin. Holding there for a long, thudding moment, before slowly sweeping back up again.

Gerrard grimaced, his cheeks flushing hot, but he was doing this now, for better or worse. And when his bare foot kicked at a good-sized stick, lying there on the bank, he snatched it up, and settled into his usual fighting stance. But naked, barefoot, with a stick as his weapon.

It was absurd, utterly preposterous—but the orc still wasn't laughing. Instead, he shook his big body a little, and then glanced around, and swiped for a stick of his own, before settling into his already-familiar fighting stance, too. His weight shifting low, his eyes wary and watchful on where Gerrard was already circling sideways, eyeing him, seeking an opening...

Gerrard rushed forward at full speed, aiming straight for the orc's bare torso. And though the orc snapped up his stick to block it, it was a little too late, and Gerrard used the impact to twist his own stick up. Slipping above the orc's guard, just enough to jab the stick's blunt end into his sternum.

The orc blinked, glanced downwards—and Gerrard couldn't stop the sudden, triumphant grin from flashing across his mouth. A grin that seemed to make the orc falter again, his eyes almost dazed on Gerrard's face, and Gerrard took the opportunity to rush in again. This time swinging lower, and striking the orc's bulky thigh with a satisfying *thwap*.

"Even slower today, I see," he said, far more cheerfully than was warranted, as he spun in again, managed another strike to the orc's other side. "You tired, orc? Drunk? Hung over? Or..."

Or did Slagvor somehow get to you, he nearly asked—but then he bit off the words, just in time. Because he didn't want to talk about Slagvor, he wanted to keep watching and dodging and dancing around the orc like this. Wanted to feel the inexplicable exhilaration thrumming higher through his chest, sparkling in his limbs. And he wanted to keep the orc looking at him like that, like...

"Ach, I am only... diverted," the orc grunted back, as he belatedly jerked up his stick, blocked Gerrard's swing for his neck. "You are..."

His voice hitched as he knocked away Gerrard's next strike, and his eyes had unmistakably dropped to Gerrard's groin again. Looking almost... appreciative, curse him, as his nostrils flared, and his big chest filled with his breath.

"What, orc?" Gerrard demanded, and he didn't want to hear it, did he? "Faster than you? Better with my stick?"

The orc visibly startled, his eyes now darting between Gerrard's face and his groin, and Gerrard fought down the bizarre blend of chagrin, disbelief, and amusement swarming in his chest. He was teasing this bastard, goading him with this, and—he grunted with satisfaction—jamming his stick into the orc's undefended belly, and grinning as the big brute gasped, and actually staggered a step backwards.

"Definitely better with my stick," Gerrard's taunting, traitorous voice continued, as he darted in again, closing up the ground he'd gained, pushing the orc backwards toward the creek. "You like being poked with my stick, orc? Like having a human prick into you?"

The orc betrayed an actual groan at that, oh hell, and Gerrard heard himself laugh aloud, the sound bright and appallingly merry as he dodged in again. Swinging for the orc's hip this time, and noticing—without at all wanting to—that the orc was already hard, of course he was, his absurdly oversized bulk tenting out the front of his trousers. Enough that Gerrard felt his own dangling cock stirring, and he gritted his teeth as he dragged his gaze back up, focused on charging in again, pushing the orc further toward the creek. And not—*not*—thinking about the implications in this, the heated, hovering possibility that the orc still wanted that, wanted him, and...

"Lost your voice, too, then, orc?" Gerrard taunted, husky now, as he landed another hit to the orc's side. "Can't admit that you're about to be defeated by a human. A naked and *injured* human, at that, with only a stick to poke you with. Or maybe"—he winked—"two sticks, if you want to count this one, too?"

His audacious hand had actually slipped down to grasp at his own exposed, half-hard shaft, circling around the damnably heavy length of it—but it was working, the orc was faltering, staggering, staring at the sight with wide, hazy eyes. And it only took one more too-close rush in, Gerrard's bare foot hooking behind the orc's calf, his good shoulder charging hard into that solid chest, and—

The orc blanched, tilted, swiped out toward Gerrard—but he was too late, too off-balance, and finally his huge body tipped backwards, toward the rippling creek. Crashing into it with a gigantic, deeply satisfying splash, spraying Gerrard all over with streams of chilly water—and as the orc frantically floundered to find footing again, he even lost hold of his stick, which bobbed uselessly away down the creek.

Gerrard wiped the water from his eyes as he watched, his mouth twitching—and then he threw back his head, and laughed. Laughed like he hadn't laughed in years, his entire body shaking with his guffaws, his hand clutching at his convulsing abdomen. The sounds ringing and rippling with the bubbling water around them, and suddenly there was the most bizarre urge to just jump into it, to tackle the orc's flailing body beneath him. To claim his victory any way he wanted, and maybe the orc would... let him. Maybe he would bend over and...

And then the orc surged up. Rushing straight toward Gerrard's laughing, undefended form—and now Gerrard was the one staggering backwards, landing heavily in the shallower water at the creek's edge. While the orc was the one looming over him, crushing him into the bank, and glaring down at him with hard, glittering black eyes. With fury. With cold, terrifying rage.

Gerrard's smile instantly faded, his laughter breaking off into silence, draining into the rapidly rising darkness. Because—*fuck*, he was a fool. He'd won, fair and square, just like he'd wanted, just like he'd planned...

And for that, now he would die.

11

Gerrard couldn't stop shivering as he stared up at the orc's furious face, his heartbeat distantly screaming in his chest.

Fuck. Fuck, this had been stupid. Reckless. Thoughtless. To rush straight into a foolish risk like this, to somehow forget that losing—and very likely dying—was still the only logical outcome. This wasn't a fun game between friends, this orc was his sworn enemy, and this was war, it was life and death. Gerrard knew better, he did, and why the hell had he even come out here, what had he been thinking...

He kept gazing helplessly up at the orc, waiting, bracing for the inevitable blow. For the orc's huge hand to start punching him in the mouth, maybe, or clamping around his neck. It wouldn't even take long, so why was the bastard staring at him like this, dragging it out like this, please...

And then the orc's eyes squeezed shut, and his shaggy head dropped. Dropped toward Gerrard's bare, heaving shoulder, because he was going to bite him again, maybe leave him to bleed out here in the creek—

When the orc... kissed his neck. Kissed at just where he'd

bitten Gerrard the day before, and left that mess torn into his skin. And it did still sting a little, prickling under the unexpected softness of the orc's warm lips and tongue, and Gerrard couldn't move, couldn't think. What was this. What was happening. He should jump up, he should run, or maybe he should just keep lying here, maybe it would still be relatively quick and painless, and...

"Ach, human," the orc murmured, his voice cracking. "There is no need to look thus, or scent thus. I shall not harm you, or kill you. I swore this to the *goddess*."

Gerrard's flailing thoughts could scarcely follow the orc's meaning, let alone the strange intensity in his voice—or the way that big, dripping body shuddered over him, pressing him heavier into the shallow rushing water beneath them. "You are only... too much, warrior," the orc continued, hoarse. "With your skill, and your cunning, and your laughter, and your— your *scent*—"

His voice faltered, his face nudging deeper into Gerrard's neck, and Gerrard could feel him inhaling, his broad chest slowly filling. And then again, and again, as if the orc was truly smelling him, drawing him in, and... liking it. Liking it enough that his hips were grinding down, that huge ridge at his groin now prodding hungrily into Gerrard's belly.

Gerrard swallowed, felt the orc's mouth kissing again, lingering on his wounded skin with a fervent, focused attention. Almost as if to lick the bite clean, despite the bubbling water still swarming around it. And somehow, foolish, *foolish*, Gerrard felt himself relaxing a little, his breath exhaling, his eyes fluttering closed. Sinking into the impossible feeling of the orc's hot mouth, how it had begun trailing down his shoulder now, to where... to where it hurt again. Because right, that was where the orc's axe had slammed into him the other day in the battle, and—Gerrard glanced sideways—it had apparently grown into a massive black bruise. A bruise that the orc was intently kissing, his mouth moving so careful and gentle over it, his lashes long and dark against his hard cheekbones.

Gerrard's heart skipped a beat as he watched, but he didn't move, and the orc didn't stop. His mouth skating over the bruise again and again, until the twinges of pain had seemed to... fade, somehow. And only then did the orc shift away again, his lips slipping downwards. Moving slow and deliberate over the wet chilly skin of Gerrard's chest, lingering on every single one of his welts and scrapes, until...

Until those lips found Gerrard's *nipple*, and sucked it inside. The sheer sudden sensation making him choke and gasp, his body arching up into the press of the orc's weight—and that was the feel of the orc's soft chuckle, rumbling into his ribs, before his mouth pulled off again. But that long, sinuous black tongue kept caressing, curling against that rigid pink nub, and Gerrard gazed blankly down at the sight, while his heartbeat lurched faster in his chest. He wasn't still doing this, wasn't wanting this, wasn't watching the orc's mouth licking across his chest to his other nipple, sucking that in deep too...

But it was still here, still happening, and Gerrard distantly noticed that his hands had found the orc's broad shoulders, gripping against smooth shifting skin. While the orc kept licking and sucking and lavishing him, not just his nipples, but now down his abdomen, to his belly, curling into his taut navel, the sharp hollows of his hips, closer, closer...

Gerrard's own cock was fully hard now, its ruddy length straining up eager and shameless, bobbing toward the orc's hot, clever mouth. And yes, yes, the orc's swirling, sinuous tongue was seeking ever closer toward it, licking into the coarse hair at its base, caressing against Gerrard's bulging, aching bollocks. And then that slick black tongue slowly, leisurely twined itself around the full girth of him—*fuck*—and began slipping up the length of his swollen, spasming shaft. And Gerrard was bucking, moaning, his hand clutching at the orc's thick black hair, needing him to put that hot wonderful mouth all around him, to swallow him whole—

But then the orc jerked up, back, away. His head shaking, his eyes squeezing shut, as if he'd suddenly remembered what he was doing—and as if he regretted it. Hated it. Had stopped himself, just in time.

The darkness swirled again in Gerrard's chest, stark and bitter and cold. Damn it, why the hell did he keep getting dragged into this? How the hell did this orc keep doing this to him? This bastard was fucking with him, he apparently didn't even *want* this with him, and Gerrard dropped his inexplicably prickling eyes, and fought to shove himself up, away. He was going to get dressed and then he was going to leave, and forget any of this had ever happened, forever...

"Ach, wait, warrior," came the orc's voice, sudden, frantic—and he was here again, catching Gerrard's wrists, holding him in place. And now Gerrard and the orc were both kneeling together in the shallow rippling water, both breathing hard, and Gerrard's brief, baleful glance up at the orc's face found him looking... urgent. Alarmed.

"You ken I would," the orc's voice said, almost a croak. "I only—I cannot risk even a *drop* of a man's seed on my skin, let alone my tongue. Most of all a man such as you. A warrior. An *enemy*."

Gerrard blinked at the orc, at his wincing mouth, his surprisingly earnest eyes in the moonlight. "The scent and taste of fresh human seed," the orc's rushed voice continued, "is so strong, and so sweet, it should—it would at once speak of this to any orc who scented me. And thus, to Slagvor, also."

Oh. Right. *Right*. The scenting again. And as Gerrard kept blinking at the orc's pained, shimmering eyes, he felt his own body relaxing, his shoulders sagging. While something damnably like commiseration, like relief, shuddered through his chest.

So the orc... *had* wanted it, then. He just... hadn't wanted to risk getting tortured by Slagvor over it.

"Uh, spunk doesn't taste sweet, orc," Gerrard belatedly replied, his voice rough, because it was all he could dredge up, curse him. "Tastes like something rotten, you mean."

The orc frowned back toward him, his shaggy head tilting. "Ach, no," he countered, husky. "For many orcs, the fresh seed of a human man is mayhap the richest, sweetest, most wondrous taste in all the realm. Not that we oft like to admit this, you ken."

Gerrard was gaping at the orc again, at how his mouth was now betraying an amused, regretful little grimace. As if he really had meant that, as if he knew it from *experience*—and that was not, *not*, jealousy, simmering low in Gerrard's belly.

"So you've done this before, then, have you?" he demanded, too sharp, too accusing. "What, do you have a regular habit of seducing and sucking off human men, in between bouts of killing us?"

The orc grimaced again, and shook his head. "I have not before had a man thus," he replied thickly. "But I have heard the tales. And ach, I can *scent* you, warrior."

His voice had deepened, his big hand giving a frustrated-looking wave up and down Gerrard's bare body, and Gerrard could only seem to stare back at him, breathing hard. Damn it, he was a mess, he couldn't again be feeling *relieved* by this. He should be fighting this, extracting himself from this ludicrous situation, rather than kneeling naked with an orc in a creek, and...

"But should you wish to test this," the orc continued, his eyes shifting, glinting with meaning on Gerrard's face, "mayhap you shall allow me to taste you... elsewhere?"

Elsewhere. Gerrard fought down the bizarre leap in his chest, felt his eyes widening on the orc's face. But he didn't move, didn't argue, just kept waiting, silent and staring, as the orc's big hand found his bare hip, and... tilted him. Moving Gerrard, just like he had the day before, shifting him sideways and around on his knees. And Gerrard still wasn't fighting it, was just letting the orc turn him, and bend him over, his huge body hovering close behind him, so he could...

Lick him. Oh, fuck, the orc was *licking* him, just there, that long slippery tongue delving deep between his bare arse-cheeks. Seeking that tight knot of heat with dizzying accuracy, and twining swift and shameless against it, *into* it. While Gerrard choked and jolted all over, because this could not be happening, this orc's tongue was not inside his—his—

The sound from his own mouth was almost a mewl, because oh, the orc was already working harder, deeper. Flicking and twisting that long slippery tongue, hitting that perfect spot again and again, flaring out staggering sparks of furious sensation deep into Gerrard's very core. What was happening, this could not be happening, he was kneeling in a creek with an orc's *mouth* latched to his hole, and an orc's unthinkably long *tongue* buried inside him?!

But it was still happening, still here, still swarming Gerrard with impossible pleasure, drawing helpless, humiliating sounds from his mouth. And he was already shuddering, trembling on his hands and knees, to the point where one of his hands slipped on the rocky creek bottom—and the orc abruptly lurched back, away, his own hands gripping at Gerrard's heaving sides, holding him in place.

"Is this yet—pain for you, warrior?" came his deep voice from behind Gerrard, laced with undeniable concern, with *alarm*. "I did not ken how much you were—ach. I did not wish to—*wound* you with my prick, this day past, as I did."

Gerrard's sudden rebellion kicked and seethed in his chest, and his head snapped around to glare at the orc. No, damn it, no. This bastard was coddling him again, as if he was a weak, reckless little kitten who couldn't bear a bit of rough handling now and then. And suddenly the hazy unreality of this confounding situation was again flickering away, fading beneath the mortifying truth of it. He was on his knees for an orc in a creek, this poisonous prick was his sworn *enemy*, this could easily ruin his *life*, and—

But before he could scrabble away again, the orc's hands gripped tighter at Gerrard's hips, his sharp claws painfully digging into bare skin, holding him still. And the orc's gaze glinted on his, steady and challenging, as he dropped a clawed hand to his own wet tented trousers, and shoved them downwards.

It released the full length of his huge orc-prick, bobbing out heavy and veined and silvery between them, leaking a thick string of white from the glossy tip. And already the orc was shifting it closer, deliberately lining it up with... with Gerrard's exposed, waiting crease. With where he still felt wet and wide open from those shameless ministrations of that hot filthy tongue, and Gerrard wrenched all over at the feel of that blunt slick head settling against him. Finding its place. Prodding just a little inside...

But the orc was still watching, waiting. His grip even slightly softening, his heavy brows raised. Very clearly giving Gerrard a chance to refuse, to run, to escape—but curse this orc, Gerrard didn't want to escape. He just wanted—he wanted—

"Then take your defeat, human," the orc hissed, all hot, deadly, wonderful promise. "And welcome your enemy's prick up your rump."

12

Yes. Yes. That was what Gerrard wanted. His enemy's prick. There. *Now*.

And then yes—oh hell—it was here. The orc was here. That hot hard flesh pushing forward, digging inside Gerrard, splitting him apart. The feeling far too strong, and yes, admittedly painful—but Gerrard was already lost in it, needing it, howling helplessly toward the moon as the bastard punched himself to the root, buried bollocks-deep in Gerrard's arse.

It felt even bigger than before, invading him from the inside out, pinioning him in place like a giant vengeful spear—and then the orc started pumping. Far harder and faster than the day before, enough to make Gerrard's teeth chatter, his hands sliding in the silty creek bed. The sensation so staggering, so impossibly overwhelming, hurling away the rest of his existence, coiling it down to this, just this.

And he could only bow his head, grit his teeth, and take it. Let the orc have his victory, let him keep using him, having his way with him, and Gerrard cried out again at the truth of it, the bare, brutal ecstasy of it. He was being conquered, ravished, powerful hips slamming hard, as slick swollen flesh gouged in again and again and again. And as a big, warm hand slipped down between his shaking thighs, fingers closing with proprietary ease around his hanging swinging bollocks, and squeezing tight—

Gerrard shouted as he sprayed out, his release pulsing into the rippling water beneath him with long, sustained jerks. While behind him, the orc faltered and groaned, the sound rumbling rich and low—and then he stiffened all over, and shot out, too. His rigid invading flesh kicking up again and again as he emptied his grinding bollocks, pouring himself deep inside Gerrard's spasming grip, while Gerrard arched and moaned and... took it. Accepted it, as his defeat.

He was still shaking when the orc finished, when that softening heft yanked out with a slick sound, and a reluctant-sounding hiss—but then, without warning, the orc was gone. His touch, his hands, his cock, his warmth—all just *gone*, and Gerrard whipped around, fighting back the damnable plunge in his chest. Not again, what the fuck was it now, this prick couldn't be—

Afraid? Yes, wait, that was fear in the orc's eyes, in his big body, as he rapidly lurched backwards in the creek, his wide eyes fixed on... the water. The water that was bubbling and swirling around Gerrard, still with... with noticeable large splotches of Gerrard's *spunk* in it.

The alarmed awareness swarmed Gerrard all over, his breaths coming fast and shallow as he watched the evidence slowly swirling away, eddying down the creek. Damn, that had been stupid, and careless, and reckless. *I cannot risk even a drop of a man's seed on my skin*, the orc had said, and here Gerrard had blown his load in water right beside him? That definitely had to be something the other orcs could smell, right? Something Slagvor could smell? Something that could get them both killed?

"And you call *me* reckless, orc," Gerrard said, fighting to keep his voice steady. "Is—is Slagvor gonna smell that on you?"

He rapidly searched the orc's face in the moonlight, watching as his eyes squeezed shut, his breath shuddering out thick and hard. "I... hope not," he replied, hoarse. "I hope I caught this in time, I..."

His mouth twisted, showing Gerrard a glimpse of sharp white teeth, while yet more miserable comprehension plummeted in Gerrard's belly. "Is—is Slagvor already suspicious of you?" his hollow voice asked. "Did you already see him yesterday, after we...?"

He didn't finish, but the orc clearly followed it easily enough, his shadowy eyes blinking open again. "Ach, I saw him," he replied. "But if he scented aught of you upon me, he did not betray any hint of it, so I hope..."

He shook his wet head, his chest heaving, his clawed hand running through his messy hair. And Gerrard swallowed as he watched, as he again read those signs of unmistakable fear all over the orc's form. This damned orc, who'd fought him—and fucked him—with such relentless, dizzying power, was afraid of Slagvor. Truly, genuinely afraid.

"So it's that bad, is it?" Gerrard's empty voice asked, not wanting to know, but needing to know, all the same. "What Slagvor would do to you, if he smelled me on you?"

A distant part of him was again sifting through his own likely fate, if his treason was discovered by the likes of Livermore—the destruction of his livelihood, his accomplishments, maybe even his freedom, or his life. But he still couldn't seem to find this kind of fear in it, not like this, not like that look in the orc's eyes.

"It is not so much what Slagvor would do to *me*," the orc replied, his big shoulder jerking. "It is what he—and his orcs— would do to *you* first, whilst making me watch this."

Oh. A cold shiver slithered up Gerrard's back—yeah, there

it was—and his hand clutched in vain for the sword that was no longer at his side. While Bassey's ominous tale from earlier twisted in his belly, echoed in his ears. *The general at the time ordered them killed, for their own sakes...*

"But Slagvor did not scent you upon me," the orc continued, harder now. "He did not, and he will not. I will wield all my power to make sure of this, human. And henceforth"—his jaw flexed in his cheek—"for as long as I am able, I shall seek to keep my Bautul kin well away from here. I shall be sure it is only me who scouts near here, so that no other orcs shall catch scent of you. Ach?"

Oh. Gerrard was already nodding, exhaling, with something almost like gratitude—but wait. Wait. Hadn't he said...

"What do you mean, other Bautul might scent me while they're scouting?" he asked, and his heart was suddenly thundering, echoing in his ears. "I thought you said—you said they needed to be close to smell your scent on me, right? Close enough to touch? So I just need to play up my 'injuries', and stay out of any skirmishes until we're done here?"

He winced at the unmistakable panic in his voice, and he could see the orc wincing too, his hand rubbing at his grim face. "I... I thought this to be truth," he replied, slower now. "This is how it would have been, if you were an orc, or even a woman. But I did not foresee how... deep my scent would go, upon you. It is as if you were... steeped in it. As if you kept my seed safe inside you, until your very flesh drank and swallowed it whole, and grew fatter upon it."

Gerrard's throat spasmed, his cursed hand now dropping brief but betraying to his waist, to where it again—again!—felt rounded. Swollen. Even more than yesterday. Because damn him, he really had gone and... kept that seed there yesterday, hadn't he? He'd slept all night with it still inside him, and he'd only gone to clean himself up this morning—but by then, it had already been mostly... deflated. *Swallowed*, into his *flesh*. *Permanently*. And fuck his stupidity, fuck his life, he was a fucking reckless mess, and now this great bastard had gone and—

"So you thought it would be a good idea to do it *again*?" he demanded. "To make me reek even stronger of you, no doubt? Without even fucking mentioning this to me first? What the hell, orc!"

The orc grimaced, his big hand still roughly rubbing at his face. "I did not... plan to take you again, when I came to you this night," he replied heavily. "I wished only to tend to you, and be sure you were well. But you wished for my rough handling, and my hard ploughing, so..."

Gerrard's mouth was hanging open, the furious humiliation burning in his cheeks, prickling behind his eyes. "You lying, condescending bastard," he hissed. "You only told me you wanted a rematch! And I didn't tell you I wanted *shit all* from you, let alone—"

He finished with a frantic wave of his hand between them, as a sound much like a roar barked from his throat. While in return, the orc's heavy brows furrowed, a hard little curl lifting his lip.

"Ach, do not deny this to me, human," the orc hissed, flat and curt. "I can scent you. I can see you, and taste you. You did not wish for kindness or tending from me. You wished for me to overpower you, and take all I wished from you, so you can tell yourself you should never hunger for an orc! You again"— his voice hardened, deepened—"wished for your own blame, and your own guilt, to fall upon *me*!"

It almost felt like the orc had struck at Gerrard again, punched that huge fist into his undefended, seed-swollen belly, and he had to gasp for air as he fought for some kind of response. This arrogant prick was wrong, he was so, so wrong, and Gerrard wanted to shout at him, wanted to throw all this rapidly rising despair back at his damned distracting face, still shimmering silver in the moonlight—

"Yeah, well, maybe I also just wanted a rematch," he finally replied, his voice strangely small, as he dropped his gaze to the creek, and began to move his cold, leaden feet through it, toward his sword, his clothes, his safety. "And I fucking *won*, even if *you* didn't want to admit that, either. And maybe if you'd have just let me have my win, I'd have felt differently about it, yeah? Maybe"—he jerked a shrug—"maybe I'd have felt like you saw me as... an equal. Not just an enemy to defeat."

He couldn't seem to meet the orc's eyes now, even as he went to push past him in the water, heading for the bank. But wait, the bastard was in front of him, blocking him, yet again. And when Gerrard shot him a brief, baleful glare, the orc was shaking his head, his eyes squeezed shut, his expression almost... pained.

"Ach, human, I follow," the orc said, rushed and thin. "But—Bautul do not—lose. Not to humans. We should *die* first."

Gerrard blinked at him, once—and then a hard, bitter laugh choked from his throat. "Oh, right then," he drawled. "So what, next time I need to kill you with my stick first? Try to drive it into your heart, maybe, or gouge your eyes out? That's the only way I get to win, is it? And then I get to take your dead body as my victory prize?"

The orc's face was still contorted with pain, his head shaking, but his eyes had blinked open again, holding heavy on Gerrard's own. "If you take my *alive* body thus, human," he hissed back, "we *both* die. Ach?"

Gerrard swallowed, fought down yet more unwilling comprehension, more twisting despair in his chest. "Right," he said thickly. "Right, then. So"—he squared his shoulders—"that's it, then, yeah? We're agreed?"

There was an instant's silence from the orc, and Gerrard

couldn't look at him anymore, couldn't fight through the mess of misery in his gut. This had been so stupid, reckless, pointless all around—and there was no good end. No good way out, for either of them. None.

"So we're done here, orc," he said, over the clutch in his throat. "I won't be seeing you again. Good luck, and goodbye."

13

Gerrard truly meant it this time. Meant to leave this cursed confounding orc behind forever, and never set eyes upon him again.

Until a deep noise rumbled from the orc, and he lurched to stand close before Gerrard in the water. "How is this?" he hissed, far sharper than before. "What is *done* between us, human?"

Gerrard twitched and glowered up at the orc's hard face, as an incredulous laugh escaped from his throat. "What's done?" he demanded. "Everything is done, orc! Everything! We're enemies. We're on the opposite sides of a war. This is risking both our livelihoods, and our *lives*. It's risking setting a demented orc *despot* on our heels, so he can maim and torture us for laughs! It's stupid, and—and *reckless*! Like you said!"

The orc grimaced, opened his mouth, but Gerrard's own mouth was still spouting off, rash and breathless. "And on top of that," he gasped, "you just told me you didn't even *want* what I just gave you back there! And maybe I don't want—*rematches*—with someone who can't even admit I won, let alone someone who won't let me be in charge now and then! So what is even the damned point?"

He held the orc's eyes, his teeth gritted, his chin raised and defiant. And he didn't move when the orc came another step toward him, his gaze shifting, unreadable on Gerrard's face...

And then those big clawed hands suddenly reached for him, and clutched him close. That shaggy head ducking into his neck, as the orc hauled in a slow, dragging breath, the sound far too loud in Gerrard's ear.

"The *point*, warrior," the orc whispered, "is that you have already won. I have already fallen, and you have taken... *all.*"

What? Gerrard froze in the orc's arms, his heart juddering erratically in his chest, as those bizarre, impossible words echoed through his skull. *I have already fallen, and you have taken... all.*

It was a... confession. An admission of defeat. Of... of...

Gerrard couldn't seem to breathe, suddenly, not amidst the thick, thudding stillness, or the swarm of protests surging his thoughts. *You don't know that, orc,* he should have said. *You barely even know me. Two reckless, risky tumbles in the woods, and now you're making confessions? Admitting... admitting...*

"I wished for what you gave me, warrior," the orc's voice croaked, even quieter, against Gerrard's neck. "I wish for all you might ever give me, ach? I have never—*never*—before tasted aught such as this, between us."

Oh. Gerrard's breath was still locked in his throat, but he was shivering, now, because the orc was—*kissing* him. Kissing at that same place he'd bitten, as his hands slid around Gerrard's bare back, drew him closer. Drew him into the danger, the chaos, the mess, all the many, many reasons not to do this, everything Gerrard had just shouted at him. Their work. Their lives. Slagvor. Treason. Death.

But Gerrard... wasn't fighting it. Wasn't pushing away. Was even tilting his head to give the orc more room, as he felt his eyes fluttering closed, his shoulders sagging lower, his own hand snaking around to settle against the hollow of the orc's spine. Almost as if in... capitulation. In... *agreement*.

Damn this orc. *Damn* this orc.

"Fucking reckless," he groused, hoarse, into the orc's chest. "Gonna get us both *killed*."

The orc's breath shuddered out, together with a low, unsteady little growl. Sounding much like laughter, or like relief—but he just kept on kissing, again and again. Almost desperate, now, as if he couldn't bear to stop tasting Gerrard, couldn't stand to let him go.

I have already fallen, and you have taken... all.

"What's your name?" Gerrard's voice finally rasped into the silence, in lieu of all the much better, much wiser things he ought to have said. "Titan the Man-Tamer, maybe? Or Dreadnought the Doomed?"

And damn, the way the orc laughed again, soft and almost affectionate, his big body vibrating all over, his breath warm against Gerrard's skin. "I am Olarr," he murmured. "Olarr, of Clan Bautul. And you"—his voice shifted even lower—"are Lieutenant Gerrard, ach?"

Right. Of course the orc had already known that, he'd had that advantage over Gerrard, too, and Gerrard made a face the orc couldn't see. "*Aulis* Gerrard," he said, maybe just to be contrary, maybe. "Though only my mother ever called me Aulis, so..."

The orc's lips kissed him again, even softer than before. "Aulis," he repeated, slow, like he was turning it over, turning it into an intimate, lingering caress. "It suits you, warrior."

Gerrard swallowed, and only halfheartedly attempted to dredge up some argument, or some reasonable explanation for why he'd given the orc that, too. Given—*Olarr* that. Olarr. Olarr, of Clan Bautul.

"Yours sounds like a good proper orc name, right?" his

cursed voice asked instead, a little stilted. "From your father's side?"

He'd heard of a few orcs carrying human names, no doubt a considerable source of shame among them—and he was vaguely surprised by the feel of another low chuckle into his neck. "Ach, but my father's first choice would have been *Athalbriktr*, after his own father," the orc—Olarr—replied. "But my mother would not hear of this, so in the end, they settled upon Olarr instead."

Gerrard blinked, because for all he knew, most orcs' human mothers didn't stick around long enough to name their orc sons, let alone argue with their fathers over it. But that might have been wistfulness in Olarr's sigh, in the hitch of his breath. "My mother was a wise woman," he continued. "At least, until the day she ran into a pitched battle to save a runaway orcling. I ken it was not the men who killed her"—another chuckle, dull and distant this time—"but our own Bautul kin."

Oh. It took Gerrard's overwhelmed brain a moment to digest all that, his eyes blinking blankly into the moonlight. Olarr had known his mother. Olarr had been raised by his mother, and had clearly grieved her death—by friendly fire, of all things, yet another all-too-frequent outcome of this useless war. And in truth, why hadn't Gerrard guessed at any of this until now? The orc's common-tongue was excellent, and he obviously had an—affinity for humans. Along with an irrational tendency to rescue them on battlefields...

"Your father still alive, then?" Gerrard asked, his voice a croak. "Fighting alongside you, maybe?"

Olarr shook his head against Gerrard's shoulder, and Gerrard distantly noted that he was resting its full weight there now, the shaggy hair tickling his skin. "My father died many summers past," came Olarr's reply, very steady. "In yet another battle."

Gerrard didn't miss the clear implication in that—it had

been men, men like him, who had killed Olarr's father. And Olarr was still standing here like this in a creek, compromised and alone with a human, with his head on the human's shoulder.

I have already fallen, and you have taken... all.

Gerrard shoved that thought away, even as he felt his own hand stroking a little against the orc's bare back, his fingers spreading wide. "My parents are both gone, too," he said, offered, his voice hollow. "Ma when I was maybe ten, of lung sickness. Pa was a sailor, but didn't even get to die in battle. Ship foundered and they all drowned. They wouldn't give the death payout to a kid, so a year or two later, I joined the army myself."

He huffed a bitter little laugh as he spoke, because that particular injustice still rankled, all these years later—he hadn't been old enough to get his own father's rightful inheritance, but he'd been old enough to sign up, to walk straight toward his own death without the slightest administrative obstruction. And he could feel Olarr's head abruptly lifting now, could feel the weight of his gaze on his face.

"They would not even hold this in trust for you?" he demanded, his voice harder than Gerrard might have expected. "Their own warrior's orphaned *son*?"

Gerrard shrugged, shook his head, and blinked at the sound of Olarr's growl, surprisingly harsh. "You humans," Olarr hissed. "Throwing away your priceless sons for *naught*. I hope you have now addressed this cruelty, at least? It cannot yet be thus, amongst you?"

Gerrard couldn't help another bitter little laugh, betraying the army's absolute and ongoing failures in this, and calling to mind his own constant efforts to make sure the death paperwork was filed properly, and that next of kin were found. And that someone, somewhere, followed up with the children at some point, and made sure they were getting at least part of what they deserved.

"And you cannot address this yourself?" came Olarr's next question, even more disconcerting than the last. "You are a lieutenant, are you not?"

Gerrard's bitter laugh sounded more like a sigh this time, his thoughts snapping back to Livermore. If Livermore was half competent, he might be able to advocate for reforms, and make meaningful progress—but Livermore cared only for his own status, his own reputation, his own coin. While Gerrard was stuck doing most of the actual work, cleaning up the messes, filing all the damned paperwork.

At least... until now. Until this orc had faced off against Gerrard's despair, and Gerrard had finally gone and... done something. Wielded his cunning, instead of his recklessness. Faked his injuries. Lied to Livermore. Made up that preposterous tale about Head Command investigating him. In hopes of... of...

"Well, there isn't much I can do right now, trapped down here in the middle of nowhere like this," Gerrard's quiet voice ventured, tentative, *treasonous*. "But if things were different, I think I could actually have a decent shot at getting a big promotion. I've won a lot of battles, made a lot of lucky calls, and gotten a good amount of goodwill with the higher-ups, yeah? My last commander, before Livermore, used to say that if I didn't get myself killed first, I'd probably become Preia's youngest general in a generation."

He couldn't quite hide the pride snaking into his voice—or the wry little laugh, because Slagvor probably would kill him first now, right? "And if I did ever better my own situation," he continued, steadier, "I'd do my damnedest to get our men out of here, forever. And I'd try to clean up some of the army's mess, too. Try to push for real reforms and benefits for soldiers. Make life better for them, and their families."

He blinked at the sound of the words, at his own voice speaking them, because how long had it been since he'd even thought about all that? How long since he'd thought past the endless battles, the endless slog of shit and misery, to all those foolish naive dreams of what he would do, if he ever had the chance? And oh, he did *not* need Olarr to kiss him for it, did not need that warm clever mouth easing with obvious approval up his neck, sharp teeth skimming at his earlobe...

"Ach, I ken you would," came Olarr's murmur, hot and far too tempting. "I ken you could wield your cunning to gain this, Aulis. You could gain aught that you ever wished."

Aught that you ever wished. Gerrard's breath shuddered in his chest, the heat suddenly pooling to his groin—and it was enough to jolt him to awareness again, his eyes snapping open. The moon had clouded over at some point, leaving the night far darker than before, and when he drew a little backwards, he could no longer make out Olarr's face, his eyes.

But those tempting, honeyed words were still echoing uneasily through Gerrard's ears, endorsing his treachery against Livermore, encouraging it. As if this damned disruptive orc hadn't already done enough, and set that looming threat of Slagvor upon them both? And was Gerrard really going to keep committing more treason, digging himself even deeper, just because an orc suggested it? Treason that would ultimately benefit... who?

"Look, I really should go," he said, his voice rough. "I'm supposed to be laid up in the med tent. They'll start wondering, if I'm gone too long."

Olarr's nod was instant, his hands dropping from Gerrard's back, his body moving sideways. Letting Gerrard go, without even trying to argue, and Gerrard shoved down the inexplicable disappointment as he strode to the bank, and dried off and dressed as quickly as he could. Not looking back toward Olarr the entire time, but he could still feel the weight of his attention, his watchfulness, his uncertainty. Maybe even his own disappointment, too.

And curse him, but once Gerrard had strapped his sword to his side, he spun and stalked back to Olarr again, fixed his eyes on his shadowed face—and then realized he couldn't at all find what to say, amidst the swarm of possibilities now burning through his thoughts. *Can I truly trust you, orc? Can I really believe you'll keep Slagvor away, and keep my treason secret? You wouldn't betray me, would you? Or break a vow to your goddess?*

Or even worse, *What happens next? Will I see you again? When? Soon?*

"So what do *you* want, then," Gerrard finally heard himself say, too clipped. "What's your goal in all this, Olarr of Clan Bautul."

There was an instant's stillness, a tilt of Olarr's shaggy head up to where the moon had been. "I wish to come to you again, Aulis," he said, very low. "Mayhap in a few days, once I am sure of Slagvor. And then, should you wish, I should welcome another rematch with you. And should you defeat me again"—he drew in a breath—"I shall seek to... *let you be in charge.* Should you yet wish for this."

Let you be in charge. It was an exact quote of Gerrard's accusation from earlier, and it flashed a dizzying, undeniable thrill of heat up his spine. This orc would really—allow that? Really give him that? After everything today?

"But it cannot be your prick," Olarr continued, flatter now. "Or your seed. Not yet."

Not yet. But that was another promise, another tantalizing temptation dangling before Gerrard's traitorous, treasonous eyes. Most of all when Olarr leaned in a little closer, and took another long, shuddering inhale against the crook of Gerrard's neck.

"But I ken you can think of other ways, Aulis," he purred,

"for you have shown yourself to be a prudent, cunning human, ach?"

Gerrard groaned aloud, elbowed Olarr hard in the ribs— and for his trouble, Olarr nipped sharp teeth at his throat, his big hand slapping Gerrard's arse through his trousers. And despite everything, all the lingering darkness and doubt, Gerrard was grinning as he drew away, shaking his head. Feeling suddenly lighter, warm, alive, like anything was possible. Like maybe they really could live through this, even just until next time...

"Oh, I'll show you cunning, orc," Gerrard drawled back. "You just wait and see."

14

For the next few days, Gerrard indeed put his cunning to the test.

He began by running a thorough review of the outpost and the regiment, including the state of their goods and supplies, and their current standing orders. Most of his information was gained through Cosgrove, under the guise of wanting to stay busy while being laid up, but his fellow injured soldiers in the med tent soon began to weigh in too, many with far more candour than Gerrard had ever heard from them previously.

No, Livermore didn't send for more supplies. No, he didn't want to pay that smith what he asked, so the arms weren't repaired. No, we didn't pay those farmers for their grain, either. No, we don't have enough stakes to repair that break in the palisade. No, his last steward didn't quit, he was discharged. No, that other one deserted. No, he didn't request cavalry units. No, we don't have any fruit left. No, he just screamed at me when I asked. No, no, no, no.

The more Gerrard heard, the more furious—and genuinely sick—he felt. He'd spent all these months in this godsforsaken outpost focusing on his own assigned goals as a lieutenant—

keeping his men in order and in good fighting shape, gaining accurate on-the-ground intelligence, carrying out all these advances against the orcs, and yes, filling out all the paper-work. Which left Livermore to direct their strategy, to communicate with Head Command, and to ensure the outpost was properly supplied and fed—but clearly, Livermore was catastrophically failing at all of it. While apparently also telling Head Command that they were making great gains down here against the orcs, and their efforts were even coming in under budget, too.

It was rubbish, utter stinking reeking *rubbish*, and Gerrard roundly cursed his past self for not noticing more. For not realizing just how bad life had gotten for everyone in the outpost, on all fronts. He should have been more prudent. More cunning. Should have let himself take a rest, and take the time to see it.

But now that he had seen it, he was doing something about it. He was making a plan. And somewhere along the way, he'd gradually settled on two major priorities. First, to keep caring for his men, to do a better job of keeping them healthy and safe—which included keeping them the hell away from any future skirmishes with the orcs, for as long as fucking possible. To make sure there were no more offenses, no more attacks, no more pointless, preventable deaths.

And secondly, and even more difficult, was to get rid of Livermore. Not to kill him, if at all possible—Gerrard still had no stomach for a full-on mutiny, let alone more blood on his hands—but to find a way to permanently remove him from this camp, if not the rank of General altogether. Livermore was unfit, incompetent, and it was vastly unjust to allow him to be in command of anyone, throwing away their lives and their wellbeing without a second thought. Livermore needed to go, and Gerrard was going to do his damnedest to make it happen.

He still didn't have a solid plan around how to actually

achieve that, but for now, he was focusing on that first goal, and his men. First was a proper calculation around how long their remaining stores of victuals would last—not long—and next was overhauling their usual training regimen to focus on hunting and foraging for food, and repairing the broken palisades, shoring them up against attack. And next—trickier but not impossible, with Cosgrove's help—was pinning down Livermore's usual communication schedule with Head Command, and making plans for his own... interceptions.

And finally, several days later, at the great expense of his own pride, Gerrard hopped on crutches over to Livermore's tent. Where he gritted his teeth and offered a profuse apology for his previous untoward behaviour, and attributed his lamentable disrespect to what Bassey had now identified as a severe blow to the head. Which, naturally, would require at least another week of rest on Gerrard's part.

Livermore was highly affronted by Gerrard's continued convalescence, but since there were no other uninjured high-ranking officers to lead any attacks—and no other orcs in the general vicinity to attack in the first place—his ranting and raving had no real point. So Gerrard only half-listened, occasionally nodding and mumbling vague apologies, while also taking particular note of where multiple letters lay strewn on Livermore's writing-desk, along with his quill, ink, and personal stamp.

It was another small step forward, another flicker of hope in his chest, and Gerrard was almost smiling as he hopped across the camp again, heading back toward the med tent. At least, until he noticed—something new. Something lying on the ground just outside the tent, directly in his path.

A stick. A stick that hadn't been there before.

Gerrard stared at it for an instant too long, his heart kicking in his chest, his hand gripping the familiar sword-hilt at his side—and he fought to steady his breaths as he glanced up, and rapidly glanced around him. It was just a stick, it didn't mean anything, and...

Another one. Another stick, of a similar size, lying just inside the palisade. Leading... south.

Gerrard's heart was still blaring, wildly beating against his ribs, and after another furtive glance around him—no one in sight was paying him any notice—he turned and headed for the outpost's gate instead. Hopping along as quickly as he dared, and then heading around the palisade, toward where the stick had been—and yes, yes, here was another one, lying innocuously on the packed earth. This one now pointing south, too, leading straight into the forest.

Gerrard hopped along faster, faster, until he was well into the trees, and finally he snapped the crutches up into his hand, and began briskly walking instead. Covering ground as quickly as he could, and fighting to ignore the spinning and churning in his thoughts. The eagerness. The anticipation. The... *relief*.

Because despite his best efforts to shove the orc—Olarr— out of his awareness these past days, it had proven almost impossible not to think of him. And Gerrard had found himself repeatedly running through his memories of their encounters, reviewing them in intensive, obsessive detail. Recalling not only how Olarr had fought, how he'd blocked and struck and parried—but also, far stronger, how Olarr had looked at him. How he'd touched him, tasted him, taken him. How he'd... tended to him, licking his wounds again and again. Treating Gerrard like a helpless, precious little princess, who needed to be fussed and fawned over.

And Gerrard hated that rubbish, hated all of it... right? And he had not once thought of it while he'd stroked himself off, these past days. He had not thought about Olarr bending him over, Olarr's hard flesh invading his, Olarr's hot mouth kissing and caressing over his skin, worshipping him. Almost as though he *cared* for him...

But no, no, that was ridiculous. They barely knew each other. And far more importantly, Olarr was still an enemy. He still couldn't be trusted, and there was still a very real chance that this could all be some elaborate orc ruse meant to compromise Gerrard. To draw out his treason. To destroy him.

But even so, it hadn't stopped Gerrard from counting down the days since that night in the creek, and growing more and more irritable with each day that Olarr hadn't returned. And it wasn't stopping him from rapidly searching the trees up ahead, while the anticipation kept wheeling through his chest. Olarr had to be here, he *had* to be...

And yes. *Yes.* A shift of silvery grey up ahead, a telltale crackle of twigs underfoot. And suddenly—there—Olarr was here. *Here.* Standing big and stiff and square before Gerrard, his huge axe gleaming on his back, his body again bared to the waist.

Gerrard's breath caught, exhaled in something much like relief—and now he couldn't seem to look away. Couldn't stop his eyes from eagerly running up and down, catching on the breadth and strength of Olarr's bare chest, the hard ridges of his abdomen, the bulk of those powerful thighs. And perhaps most compelling of all, the unmistakable swell in those trousers...

Gerrard guiltily yanked his gaze back up to Olarr's face, to where those dark eyes were already holding his. And now shifting with a strange, glittering intensity as Gerrard walked closer, closer, closer. His heart thudding erratically, his throat swallowing, his mouth opening—

"Still alive, then?" he asked, hoarse, maybe because it was the least dangerous of all the stupid things he'd been about to say. "Slagvor didn't find out about us yet?"

Olarr's eyes shifted again, his shoulder jerking a shrug, as he briefly rubbed a hand at his nose. "No," he replied, the word thick in his throat. "Not yet."

Not yet. Gerrard twitched, made a face, because that meant Slagvor *would* find out, sooner or later. Which also meant they should stop this, they shouldn't be risking this again. It was dangerous, it was deadly, it was going to ruin both their lives. And if they were wise—prudent—they would both leave now, and never, ever come back...

But Gerrard wasn't leaving, and Olarr wasn't, either. He was still just standing here, an arms-length away from Gerrard, and... looking at him. Looking at him, at his hair, his face, his uniform, his neck.

"I am glad to find you so hale and hearty, warrior," came his gruff voice. "You look and scent... good. Better than last time."

Oh. Gerrard shot a brief, uncertain glance downwards—his belly was thankfully flat again, though he'd indeed eaten better these past days, too, after all his hunting and foraging directives. But wait, no, Olarr had to mean—the wounds. The injuries.

"Yeah, well, about that," Gerrard said back, a little too quickly. "My wounds from last time all healed up way faster than they should have, yeah? My medic even asked if maybe I'd found some kind of magical secret ointment."

He barked a short, betraying laugh at the memory of Bassey's consternation, while before him, Olarr's brows snapped up, and his big body lurched closer. His hand very carefully reaching to the neck of Gerrard's uniform, drawing it down to the side, and exposing the skin of Gerrard's neck. Where Gerrard knew that the messy, bloody orc-bite had now become a large, impressive-looking scar, its jagged teeth-marks gleaming white and smooth against his skin.

Gerrard could hear Olarr's sudden intake of breath, together with a sharp swallow in his throat—but he otherwise didn't move. Just stood there, blankly gazing at Gerrard's neck, and it distantly occurred to Gerrard just how many times he'd kissed it, last time they'd met. So, so many times, as if he really had wanted it to heal, wanted to care for him...

"Was it some kind of... orc-magic, then?" Gerrard asked now, his voice only slightly hitching. "Or just..."

Olarr was still staring at it, his swallow again convulsing in his throat. "I do not ken I bear any magic," he said, quiet. "But I have heard tales of this. How an orc's kiss can oft be a gift of the goddess toward men."

Oh. The goddess again. Gerrard reflexively glanced up toward the bright blue sky above them, while Olarr bent forward, slow and dazed, until his mouth again found Gerrard's neck. His warm soft lips skating against Gerrard's healed skin, as his breath deeply inhaled, and then exhaled in a sound much like a groan. And then again, and again, while Gerrard just stood there and let it happen, his eyes fluttering, his heart thumping hard against his ribs.

"Thought you wanted a rematch," Gerrard said, his voice a croak—and curse him, because Olarr instantly reeled backwards, his grey face visibly flushing in the bright light, his lips pressing tight together.

"Ach," he replied, with a jerky nod. "Ach, warrior, if that is all you wish."

His eyes were downcast, his steps rapidly backing away, and without even realizing it, Gerrard lurched toward him, gripped a hand at his rigid forearm. "Who said that's all I wanted?" he asked, before he could possibly stop it. "It's just—if you actually still want a good fight from me, it's not gonna be *after* we—"

He finally caught it there, clamping his fool mouth shut, but Olarr had already glanced up again, the comprehension flashing across his eyes, sagging his taut shoulders. "Ach, then, I follow," he said, with a twitch of a smile. "And I wondered if this time, mayhap, we could take this... below ground, where it is safer?"

Below ground. Gerrard blinked, glanced up at the bright sky—and then toward the close clusters of trees all around them. It wasn't the best sparring spot, to be fair, and yes, anyone could be hiding and watching in the trees, but... *underground?*

"It shall only be us," Olarr said quickly. "And should this alarm you, I shall bring you up again at once."

Gerrard couldn't hide his wince, because the bastard was coddling him again, and this time, he damn well deserved it. So he jerked a nod, gave an irritable wave of his hand toward—wherever—and thankfully, Olarr turned at once, and strode off. Leaving Gerrard to follow him a short distance through the trees, toward a rocky little incline, where Olarr promptly began pulling up what appeared to be a flat, heavy-looking boulder. Or rather—Gerrard stared—a secret *trapdoor*, revealing a yawning dark chasm beneath it.

Gerrard had heard of hidden orc-tunnels, of course, but he'd never before seen one, let alone been inside one. And he was distinctly grateful when Olarr's warm hand caught his, and drew him toward what appeared to be a set of rough, uneven stone stairs, disappearing down into the darkness.

Gerrard carefully followed Olarr downwards, the air noticeably cooling as he went, and soon found himself standing on solid, packed earth, in a narrow underground tunnel. And once Olarr had shut the trapdoor above them, he led Gerrard deeper down the tunnel, and into what appeared to be an actual underground *room.*

It was lit with a faint flickering glow, thanks to an iron lantern hanging on the wall, and it was walled with earth all around, including a smooth, dry dirt floor. It was also surprisingly wide and open, without any furnishings to be seen—except for the far corner, where there was a large grey fur spread on the floor. Along with a basket, a full waterskin, and a pair of identical wooden *swords.*

Gerrard blinked at it all for an instant too long, his breath hushed in his throat, because had Olarr—brought this? Planned this? Set up some kind of... assignation? With—wait, was that a *picnic basket*?

Gerrard's sharp glance toward Olarr found him purposefully looking away, that flush again staining his cheeks. Suggesting that yes, yes, this was exactly what he'd done. And Gerrard couldn't think of a single thing to say in return, and he walked with jerky steps over to the fur, and plucked up one of the wooden swords.

"These are nice," he said, his voice too loud in the silence. "You make them?"

It took Olarr an instant to respond, but then he rapidly shook his head. "No, I borrowed them," he said, his gaze still fixed somewhere beyond Gerrard's head. "From the Bautul fighting-pit, at home."

At home. Gerrard's eyes snapped wider, and he only distantly noticed his hand flipping the sword-hilt, testing its weight. "Wait, you went all the way back to *Orc Mountain*?" he demanded. "How many days' journey is that, from here? Four? Five?"

Olarr shrugged again, though he still wasn't meeting Gerrard's eyes. "Ach, mayhap three, for orcs, with a full band," he said. "And less than two, alone."

Oh. So not only had Olarr spent three days trekking halfway across the realm to Orc Mountain, but then he'd turned around and made a two-day trip straight back here again. And hell, that must have been exhausting, and no wonder he'd been gone so long, and... and had he done it all just to see Gerrard again? Surely not?

Something hot was sparkling in Gerrard's chest, simmering in his belly—and before he'd quite realized it, he'd set the wooden sword down again, and begun... undressing. Unbuttoning the front of his uniform jacket, stripping it off, setting it on the fur. And then kicking off his boots, too, and his trousers, and his undershirt. Leaving himself fully naked, except for—he swiped it back up from the fur—the wooden sword in his hand.

And all the while, Olarr just kept watching. Watching, his expression gone entirely, intentionally blank—but Gerrard knew better now, he did. And he didn't miss how the flush had deepened in Olarr's cheeks, or—yes—that still-growing swell, tightening the front of his trousers.

"So now, my cunning captain," Gerrard said, his voice damnably husky, as he tossed the second sword over toward Olarr. "Will you come fight me? Show me just what you came here for?"

Olarr caught the sword with a swipe of his hand, a dangerous flash in his eyes—and before Gerrard could take another breath, Olarr raised the blade, and attacked.

15

This time, the fight was brutal.

Olarr's strikes were focused, relentless, almost furious—and as Gerrard frantically dodged and parried and danced away, it occurred to him that maybe he'd pushed this a little too far. Not only by teasing Olarr with that too-flattering title *captain*, but also by making it clear that he'd followed all Olarr's surprisingly thoughtful efforts on his behalf. And maybe, most of all, by how he'd undressed for Olarr like this. By making it so blatantly clear that he was using his body to his advantage, knowing full well that Olarr wanted it. Olarr was... diverted by it. Olarr had lost, last time, because of it.

But even so—Gerrard grunted as he whirled sideways, just in time to escape Olarr's next massive swing—Olarr damn well knew it, too. And last time, Gerrard had taken him by surprise with it, so this time he wasn't. This time he was laying it out up front. Being more... fair.

"Been practicing, have you?" he asked, breathless, as he finally got in a passable hit to Olarr's arm. "Finally figured out how to use a sword properly?"

He'd fully intended the double meaning in his words, waggling his eyebrows as he ducked and weaved beneath Olarr's merciless attacks, but Olarr wasn't smiling. He just kept charging in, swinging again and again with single-minded strength, and curse it, that comment of Gerrard's had clearly been taking it too far, too. Taking aim at not only Olarr's fighting skill, but also his virility, his dominance. While even hinting, maybe, at what they both knew was at stake this time, between them.

Should you defeat me again, Olarr had said, had promised, *I shall seek to let you be in charge.*

So Gerrard shut his mouth, gritted his teeth, and watched Olarr with his full focus, anticipating the next attack, dodging and blocking as quickly and efficiently as he could. While mentally overlaying all his memories from their last matches, all that time he'd spent lying in that cot and obsessing this past week. He needed to use his speed, needed to conserve his stamina, to tire Olarr out. Then he needed to knock him off-balance, somehow, and deliver the final blow.

And for that, Gerrard had fully planned on a repeat of last time—running his mouth, while blatantly flaunting what was on offer—but now he found himself revising that plan, too. Instead sinking his actions into a somewhat predictable pattern of movement, parrying and striking and dodging, until he could see Olarr settling into it, too. And yes, Olarr was slowly getting winded, the sweat beading across his broad chest, his swings not quite as sharp as before. And Gerrard kept repeating that pattern, parry strike dodge, again and again and again, until—

He charged. Rushing forward with all his speed and strength, ducking under Olarr's arm, slamming straight into his upper body, while digging his sword into the earth behind Olarr's foot. It was the exact same move he'd done last time in the creek, but Olarr again hadn't been expecting it, and Gerrard crowed his victory as Olarr tripped backwards, and slammed flat onto the fur behind them. Very narrowly missing his picnic basket, and Gerrard swiftly shoved it to safety with his sword before dropping to his knees over Olarr, and pressing his blade flat into Olarr's neck.

"Got you," he gasped, both hands pushing on the blade, now, because this bastard was not taking this away from him this time, he was *not*. "My win, orc."

Olarr's big body was heaving beneath him, his face shiny with sweat, his eyes glittering on Gerrard's with something not unlike fury. Because he damn well hadn't wanted to lose this one, that had been very clear—but he'd lost all the same, and Gerrard had won it with no taunts, no games. Just good hard fighting, and if Olarr had been pulling his strikes all that time, well, too bad for him. He'd fucking lost, to a human.

"My win, Bautul," Gerrard said again, flatter this time, his mouth pressing thin. "Right?"

Olarr still didn't reply, his eyes still flashing with that anger, that rebellion—and Gerrard's own rebellion flared higher as he shoved the blade harder into Olarr's thick neck. "Right, Olarr?" he demanded. "You remember what you promised me?"

He could see Olarr's jaw flexing, could feel how his body stiffened—but then, oh hell, a nod. A curt, angry, bitter little nod, as Olarr's sweaty, shaggy head turned away, his eyes squeezing shut.

"Ach, human," came his reply, hoarse beneath the press of Gerrard's sword. "Do with me as you wish."

16

*D*o *with me as you wish.*

It seemed to scatter something, shake something awake, deep in Gerrard's chest—and he blinked down at Olarr's face again, at the tightness in his jaw, his eyes, his mouth. At the way he looked... braced, somehow, rigid and coiled all over, as if anticipating some harsh, painful blow.

As if he was... dreading this.

Gerrard blinked again, as his thoughts skipped back to that match, to the way there'd been no ease in it, no fun this time. Because Olarr had been like this then, too. Fighting against this, dreading it, maybe even *fearing* it.

And why the hell would Olarr fear Gerrard, surely Gerrard couldn't actually *hurt* him, right?—but wait, curse him, he was still looming up naked over Olarr, pinning him to the ground, driving the flat of his wooden blade into his neck with both hands. Digging it in so hard his fingers felt numb, and Olarr's grey skin had gone pale on one side of the blade, and red on the other, and—

Gerrard belatedly yanked the sword away, shoving it aside with a shaky hand—but wait, Olarr's hand had gripped his wrist, his eyes catching blank and strange on Gerrard's face. "Use it, should you wish," he said thickly. "Or your steel blade. I shall not... fight back."

Wait. What? Gerrard stared down at him, blank and unmoving, while Olarr's chest filled and emptied. "You won, human," he continued. "I swore to... submit, as you did to me. It is only... fair."

Fair. It took Gerrard another instant to find his breath, and it came out in a laugh, loud and incredulous. "You think I want to—to hurt you?" he demanded. "To... punish you? What, in retaliation for last time?"

Olarr's expression was unreadable, now, but he slowly nodded, his chest again hollowing. "Why should you not?" he said, very steady. "We are enemies. I stole your win from you last time, and then took what I wished from you—as I did the time before, also. And then, even when I promised you freedom with me, I yet forbade you from using your prick or your seed. So why should you not wish for... other pleasures, instead?"

Other pleasures. Like roughing Olarr up? Like taking revenge, using *steel* on him? And damn it, had that truly been what Olarr had meant last time, when he'd teased at Gerrard about using his cunning? Olarr had volunteered for that, expecting this? And then he'd done all that travelling, done all that work and plotting to get himself back here, to bring an actual *picnic*, knowing he might be facing Gerrard's brutal beating in return? For his *pleasure*?

"You ken orcs also heal far easier than you humans, even without any tending," Olarr continued, speaking faster now, and then he snapped his own arm to his mouth, and—*bit into it.* Hard enough that Gerrard could hear it, could see the blood spattering across Olarr's cheek—and as Gerrard stared, still frozen, Olarr turned the arm back toward him, showing him the bite-marks. Not dissimilar to the ones he'd made in Gerrard's own neck, but the blood trickling out from Olarr's grey skin was already slowing, thickening, and… stopping. Healing.

"So there is no need to—hold back," Olarr's voice continued, rough and low. "I wish to grant you—all that you wish. All that you deserve."

Damn him. *Damn* him. And Gerrard couldn't stop looking at Olarr's arm, at his uncertain face, at that dread and resignation still simmering in his eyes. *You have already won, and taken all.*

"Oh, *captain*," Gerrard whispered, a low croak in his throat, as he bent down, and pressed a brief, fervent kiss to Olarr's neck, to where he'd shoved that hard wood into his skin. "Slagvor hasn't fucked with you that badly, has he? How could you *possibly* think I would—"

He couldn't even finish, pressing more urgent, frantic kisses against that ugly red line he'd left on Olarr's throat. Even though he could see it already healing, too, fading back into grey, he just kept kissing, tasting, trailing his tongue against it. Feeling the way Olarr twitched and swallowed, the sound so loud and close, because he really had thought that, he maybe still thought that, and…

"You really think I'd go straight to steel, if I can't use my prick on you?" Gerrard breathed, as he kept kissing, kept tasting, drinking up the musky sweetness of Olarr's shivery, sweaty skin. "What kind of rubbish cunning is that? Not the kind you'd tolerate in your bed, is it, captain?"

He'd pulled back enough to angle a brief, searching look at Olarr's face, because he wouldn't… would he? Or maybe he would, based on how he'd purposefully glanced away again. Or maybe—Gerrard studied him for far too long—maybe he hadn't been given a choice in the matter.

"Well, if you have, fuck all those fool pieces of stinking *carrion*," Gerrard growled, with more viciousness than he meant. "And when you overthrow Slagvor, I hope you'll kill them all, too."

Olarr's gaze darted back to Gerrard's face again, uneasy and searching this time, because they hadn't once spoken about that degree of treason, had they? And maybe it had been a lucky guess on Gerrard's part, or maybe... maybe Olarr had already said it, if not out loud. Maybe he was still saying it, by lying here beneath Gerrard's naked body like this, next to a damned picnic.

And wait, Gerrard had almost forgotten about being naked, and his half-hard bare cock was pressed against the waist of Olarr's trousers—so he belatedly groped sideways for his nearby undershirt, and stuffed it down between them. And then, after a brief twitch of a smile at Olarr's stunned-looking eyes, he bent down, and fastened his mouth back to Olarr's sweaty, salty-tasting neck.

And this—not steel, not pain—was what had kept Gerrard hard and awake for so many of these past nights. This uninterrupted opportunity to taste Olarr, to touch him, to taunt and tease and tantalize him. To trail hungry fingers down that broad chest, to feel the rapid thud of that heartbeat, to stroke over the stunning strength of those shoulders and biceps. To feel all this raw power, tamed and quivering beneath him, caught in his thrall, awaiting his command.

He angled another glance up at Olarr's face, at where Olarr was still staring back down at him, his eyes still dazed, disbelieving. And Gerrard kept touching him, kept stroking, as he cocked his head, gave him a crooked little smile. "This all right?" he asked, husky. "You'll tell me if you don't like something, right, captain?"

He didn't miss Olarr's full-body shudder at that meaningful word *captain*—damn, that had been a good guess on Gerrard's part—followed by a jerky nod, his dark eyes oddly bright.

"Ach," Olarr whispered back. "Ach, warrior. Whatever you wish."

Well. Gerrard let his smile tug a little wider, almost jaunty, revelling at the way Olarr shivered again as he stared—and then he bent down, and again set to work. Stroking that huge, powerful body all over as he kissed and lavished his way down, just the way Olarr had done to him last time. But Gerrard was taking it even slower, dragging it out, making it last. And even the first light brush of his tongue to a deep grey nipple had Olarr groaning, arching up into it, and Gerrard chuckled as he eased off again, keeping it light and teasing, keeping Olarr unsettled, hungry, desperate for more.

He took even more time kissing down Olarr's hard belly, trailing his tongue into the ridges of his scarred abdomen, tasting the musky salt of his navel. Feeling the roughness of thick hair against his tongue, now, and Gerrard's eyes fluttered as he slowly kissed lower, lower, lower. Until he ran into the waistband of Olarr's trousers, and he rapidly untied them, yanked them down to his thighs, and kept kissing. Intentionally avoiding the too-close bulk of Olarr's cock—now lying thick and straining against his belly—in favour of trailing his hungry mouth down Olarr's hip, to his hair-dusted thigh. Skirting dangerously close to those bulging bollocks, enough that Olarr jerked and spasmed, his steady gasps deepening to groans. And in another burst of reckless craving, Gerrard yanked down one of Olarr's trouser legs, all the way, until he could pull it off his large foot altogether, and spread those big, trembling thighs wide apart.

But Olarr still wasn't resisting or protesting, not in the slightest, and Gerrard's searching glance up at his face found it still deeply flushed, his eyes shimmering, his black tongue brushing out again and again. Looking almost rapt, reverent, as Gerrard shot him another jaunty grin, and slowly slid his wandering hand down below those heavy bollocks, seeking into his hot, hairy crease.

"Still good, captain?" he breathed, as he found what he was looking for, as his finger nudged up against it. "Should I keep going?"

Olarr's nod was instant, still frantic, his eyes even brighter—and Gerrard rewarded him by slipping his other hand up to circle around those big heavy bollocks. Cradling them, caressing them, as his seeking finger kept nudging, prodding, pressing. Waiting for Olarr to give this to him, to welcome this from him—and yes, yes, there it was, his rigid shaky body intentionally bearing down, opening up, letting him inside. Suggesting, again, that this wasn't new, and Gerrard fought down that awareness as he settled his finger a little deeper, just enough to keep Olarr open, to make him feel it.

"Good, captain," Gerrard murmured, with another flash of a smile up at Olarr's face. "You feel so good. Look so good. Such a good orc, aren't you?"

Olarr arched and gasped again, his silken heat tightening around Gerrard's finger, so Gerrard kept at it, slipping a little deeper, while gently squeezing those bulging weights in his other hand. "Such a good, strong, cunning Bautul," he continued, hoarse. "So good at getting your man on his knees for you, aren't you?"

And fuck, the way Olarr bucked and moaned at that, his eyes shocked even wider on Gerrard's face—yes, yes, this was it—and Gerrard let his smile go wry, rueful, as he let his hand slide up from those full bollocks, toward that huge, straining grey shaft. Toward where it instantly responded to Gerrard's barest touch, throbbing and dancing against his fingers, and spurting out little splatters of white against Olarr's hard belly.

"Yeah, you have me right where you want me, don't you, captain?" Gerrard continued, even huskier. "On my knees for you, working you over, lusting after this gorgeous cock of yours. Remembering how good it felt inside me."

Olarr nearly howled this time, his big hands now in tight fists at his sides, as his gaze wildly darted between Gerrard's face, and Gerrard's hand on his cock. On how Gerrard had finally, finally circled his fingers around that full, straining shaft—*damn*—and guided it straight up, so he could blatantly admire the view.

"Fuck, this felt so good," he continued, his voice rasping between his own gasping breaths, as he slowly, reverently, began stroking it. "Never felt anything like it in my life, captain. Your big, fat Bautul cock spreading my human arse wide open, shoving around in my insides, making me fit you—"

Olarr's whole body was jerking, now, his hips powerfully pumping up to meet Gerrard's stroking hand, and Gerrard let him do it, watched the utterly impossible sight of it, while his finger began slipping in and out of that clutching heat, fucking along with it. "And then pouring me full," he choked. "Dumping out all that good Bautul seed into my belly. Emptying these big bollocks for me, fattening me up on you, until—"

Olarr's cries hitched deeper, harder, his huge body thrashing beneath Gerrard's touch, even as that silken heat finally fully opened, relaxed, swallowed his finger deeper inside—and Gerrard only had an instant, a breath of pure instinct, to lurch down toward that pulsing, dribbling cock, and suck it deep inside his mouth.

Olarr sprayed out with a roar, flooding Gerrard's mouth with a sudden, shocking surge of... *sweetness*. Yes, sweetness like maple, like fucking *honey*—and Gerrard's initial disbelief rapidly plunged beneath the overpowering, all-consuming urge to swallow. To aim that fat spewing head straight into his throat, so he could suck down every last drop of it. And fuck, it was good, it was the best fucking thing Gerrard had ever tasted in his life, and he moaned as he sucked out more, as Olarr bucked helplessly up into his mouth, as he distantly felt his own cock locking, shuddering, and—

Gerrard cursed as he yanked off, backed away, catching his own shaft tightly in his hand—but it was too late, damn it, *damn* it, and all he could do was aim it down, away, between his legs. Shaking all over as the pleasure wracked and roiled through him, crushing him in wave after wave of it, as the dregs of Olarr's load splattered across the fur, and their mingled groans echoed through the room.

It took far too long for Gerrard to catch his breath again, to find his brain again—and suddenly there was only fear, sharp and sickening, as he scrabbled backwards, away. Away from where he'd left a vivid wet spot on the fur, and—he nearly choked—and on Olarr's trousers. On where they were still bunched on Olarr's leg, dangling against his knee.

Olarr had belatedly stiffened too, his eyes following Gerrard's, his body shoving up—and in a flurry of motion, they were both yanking the trousers off, taking care to keep the wet spot away from Olarr's bare calf. And once Gerrard had tossed the trousers safely away, across the room, Olarr bent toward his knee, dragging down a long, searching inhale—and then his shoulders heavily sagged as he exhaled, the relief shuddering all through his form.

"Ach," he said, his voice cracking. "Ach, this did not sink through. Thank the *goddess*."

He'd even put his fist to his chest, his shaggy head bowing to his unseen deity, and Gerrard twitched a shaky nod, rubbing hard at his eyes. Fuck, that had been close, again—and so damned stupid. Why the hell were they even doing this, risking this again? Why had Gerrard ever thought it would be a good idea to go anywhere *near* Olarr without trousers on? And worst of all—Gerrard darted a brief, wincing glance down toward his own belly—what the hell had he been thinking, to go and swallow Olarr's load like that? To fill himself with it, again, because—

Because yes, curse it, his belly looked just as rounded, just as compromised, as before. His new little paunch sitting just slightly higher this time, his stomach feeling excessively full—and now he could feel Olarr's attention on it, too. No doubt remembering all that rubbish Gerrard had said in the midst of that, and why had Gerrard given him that, either, still given him the *victory* in it, and...

"Aulis," came Olarr's voice, scraping up Gerrard's spine—and suddenly there were hands clasping both of his, squeezing them tight. Wanting Gerrard to look at him, but Gerrard wasn't, he couldn't.

"Ach, this was—this was so—so good of you, warrior," Olarr's voice continued, rapid and hushed. "So—kind, and so noble, and, ach, so—cunning. To grant me such gifts, when you ought to have only taken what you wished from me. This is—this was—"

His voice broke into his deep, dragging breaths, and finally Gerrard risked a glance upwards. To where Olarr was blinking back toward him, his grey face sweaty and flushed, his eyes glittering bright.

"I ken it is not easy for you, warrior," Olarr choked, "to grant your power to me thus. But in this, you only keep gaining *more* power over me, ach? You make me fall all the harder at your feet. Until"—his breath shuddered, his voice dropping—"there shall be none commanding me but *you.*"

Oh. Gerrard swallowed hard, fought to ignore the way those impossible words caught, kindled, in his gut. It was another confession, another admission of defeat, of loyalty, of *treason*—even after Gerrard had gone and debased himself like that, had said all those appalling things, had knelt before an orc, and sucked his full load down his throat. And he didn't even suck cock, he hadn't for years and years and *years*, it was supposed to taste rotten, and...

"So will you please stay here for a spell longer?" Olarr asked, his voice still thick, his hands clenching against Gerrard's wrists. "Please, Aulis?"

His eyes were still pleading, and he even brought up one of Gerrard's hands, gently kissing his sweaty palm, as though he was some fair, timid maiden at a ball. And Gerrard should be refusing, should be shoving him away, salvaging what was left of his pride, and...

And instead he was... sighing. Sighing, his shoulders sagging, as he watched Olarr kissing him, felt those warm lips and tongue caressing over his skin. Wanting him. Maybe even... worshipping him. *There shall be none commanding me but you.*

"Yeah, all right," he said, the words a betraying waver in his throat. "I'll stay."

17

Olarr's relief was like a light, brightening his eyes, flashing a broad grin across his mouth. And then he eagerly spun on his knees toward the basket he'd brought, yanking it over toward them with slightly trembling hands.

"Do you hunger, then, warrior?" he asked Gerrard, still smiling, though for an instant, it looked almost shy. "Or mayhap you wish for aught to drink?"

Gerrard took a breath, and then heard himself huff a laugh, thin and rueful in his throat. "I think I've had enough to drink for now, thanks," he said, as he shot a wry glance down at his waist. "But food, yeah, sure, maybe a bit."

Olarr's grin flashed even broader, his eyes glimmering with amusement, maybe even appreciation, as they followed Gerrard's gaze to his belly—and then he yanked out a small steel platter from his basket, and carefully began setting out food upon it. "I have brought dried meat, and cooked tubers, and carrots, and berries," he said quickly. "We do not now have a garden or a working kitchen at home, so I have gained what I could for you, ach?"

His voice had gone a little uncertain, his gaze uneasy on the platter of food before Gerrard, because this was another admission, wasn't it? Olarr had done all this himself, because he'd wanted to please Gerrard with it. And curse him, but Gerrard was already reaching for a piece of dried meat—venison, maybe—and taking a large, overconfident bite.

"It's—great," he said as he chewed, though in truth it was very tough, and rather charred, too. "Thanks, Olarr."

He could see more obvious relief in Olarr's shoulders, the tug of another smile at his mouth. "Ach?" he said, again almost shy. "Without the kitchen, it is rare that we cook meat, so I ken I have near forgotten how to do this. I feared it might not be fit for you to eat."

Gerrard smiled and waved it away, and even took another over-eager bite. And then managed to find the wherewithal to ask Olarr what had happened to Orc Mountain's kitchen, and the garden, too.

He'd half-expected Olarr to dodge the question, but to his vague surprise, Olarr took a breath, and gave him a surprisingly comprehensive answer. Mostly incriminating Orc Mountain's vile captain Kaugir, who apparently—much like certain other useless leaders Gerrard knew—had chronically devalued and undermined the importance of proper sustenance for a strong fighting force, until his warriors had been left to fend entirely for themselves.

"It has meant that only the strong amongst us become stronger," Olarr said, now frowning darkly down at his own meat, "whilst the weak or wounded are left to suffer, most of all if they have no close kin left to care for them. It is short-sighted and cruel, and breeds much anger and grief amongst us."

Gerrard blinked at Olarr's candour, at the blatant treason he was again laying out between them—but then again, they'd already come this far, hadn't they? Lying to their superiors, fornicating with the enemy, sharing a damned picnic. Why the hell not be honest, too? Especially since Olarr surely knew, by now, that Gerrard wasn't going to betray him in this? Even though—a distant rational part of Gerrard could still admit—he still shouldn't just be recklessly trusting Olarr at his word, either. Olarr could still betray *him*. Right?

"So what are *you* doing about it, then?" Gerrard asked, or maybe challenged, around another bite of his tough meat. "I can't see you just sitting back and watching your clan suffer like that?"

There was a flicker of surprise in Olarr's eyes, but he was already nodding, letting out a sigh. "Ach," he replied heavily. "Captain Kaugir has a son—Grimarr, of Clan Ash-Kai—who has long been working against this. He has been seeking out allies across all five clans, and gathering forces to his side. If any of us have the power and cunning to defeat Kaugir, and end this war"—another heavy exhale—"it shall be him."

Huh. This Grimarr orc wanted to defeat Kaugir... and end the war. He wanted to *end the fucking endless war.*

"And you mean to say you're *allied* with him?" Gerrard demanded, sitting up straighter, his eyes wide and intent on Olarr's. "*You* want to overthrow your horrible Captain Kaugir, and end the war, too?"

Olarr's eyes had gone wary, now—and no wonder, because this was yet another whole level of treason, wasn't it?—but he nodded, slow and careful. "This war has not been kind to any of us," he said, his voice hard. "And mayhap to the Bautul most of all. We are wielded like chattel, sent off to the dregs of the realm"—his big hand irritably waved around them—"and commanded to fight and kill men like *you*, without question or complaint. Whilst orcs like Kaugir sit safe in the mountain, and hoard all our gains and glory—and ach, all our food—for themselves."

He was almost growling by the end, the anger glinting in his eyes, and Gerrard felt his hand reflexively reaching to grip at Olarr's bare knee, giving it a firm, familiar little shake. He knew. Fuck, he knew. He could have spoken it all himself, and meant every damned word.

"So what's with bastards like Slagvor, then?" he asked, searching Olarr's eyes. "He's Bautul too, right? Why does he keep going along with Kaugir's commands? What does he get out of it?"

Olarr's eyes shifted, back into something much like surprise, and his hand gingerly slid toward Gerrard's own knee, spreading warm and heavy over it. "Kaugir is cunning enough to keep Slagvor close," he replied slowly. "We have already lost many Bautul, and mayhap a third of those yet living have run from our home, and now live deep in the south. So of the Bautul captains that remain here, Kaugir has granted them great power and plunder and rewards. And"—his lip curled—"the promise of much more, with each new victory against the men."

Right. So this Kaugir bastard had paid the Bautul leaders off, then. Bribed them to sacrifice their own clan members, the ones who'd stayed and been loyal, for their own selfish gain.

"So are you... a spy, then?" Gerrard asked, still searching Olarr's eyes. "Or... or more? Are you supposed to be finding a way to slip a knife into Slagvor's ribs when nobody's looking?"

He'd twitched a half-teasing smile as he spoke, but Olarr's face was grim now, his breath hitching in his chest. "It is not... not so easy, for orcs," he replied, low. "For any blade or poison betrays the scent of its wielder, and thus risks instant vengeance, and death. There are few ways to kill another orc in secret, and even fewer that make this seem... by chance. Most of all"—his brows furrowed—"when the orc does not fight in pitched battle, and instead sits safe at the rear, and commands the rest of us."

Right. Gerrard remembered Bassey mentioning that about Slagvor too, and he made a face as he considered it, his head tilting. "So if close combat incidents are out, then," he said slowly, "what about range attacks? A crossbow, maybe? Would the scent still carry on the bolt, even if the bowman didn't load it himself?"

That surprise again flicked through Olarr's eyes, but he gave a slow, resigned shake of his head. "Ach, the scent might be safe, thus," he said, "but should *you* wish to be the bowman in a tree, whilst a full raging orc-band seeks to sniff you out, and avenge their captain's death?"

Right. Gerrard made a face, and found his thoughts oddly skipping, his hand tightening on Olarr's knee. "But maybe it would be worth it," he said, his voice thin, "if it saves your entire clan from... this? From being sold out to a horrible captain, and slowly starved to death?"

Olarr's mouth twisted with a sharp, sudden bitterness, his head slowly shaking. "But you ken, human," he said, "it is never an easy death, ach? Most of all if this... bowman... had close kin or lovers to witness this. And to know that they—and any others they care for—may be next."

His voice had gone very quiet, his eyes fixed blankly to Gerrard's hand on his knee. To where Gerrard had somehow begun absently stroking, feeling the coarse hair sharpen and soften as his fingers slid up and down. While his eyes kept searching Olarr's face, and something new dipped, plunged, in his over-full belly.

"That happen to you, then?" he asked, hoarse. "Someone you loved?"

Olarr's swallow was too loud, too incriminating, plunging even deeper in Gerrard's gut. "Ach," he said finally. "His name was Harja. He was one of our strongest fighters, and he sought to kill Slagvor by calling him to a Bautul duel. No true Bautul would refuse a call such as this, ach? And if Harja failed, it ought to have yet meant a clean and honourable death. But instead"—Olarr drew down a ragged breath—"Slagvor... made this last. For a full night, and a full day."

His eyes had gone blank, now, gazing unseeing at the opposite wall, and suddenly Gerrard just felt sick, and wretched, and cold all over. "Fuck, Olarr," he said, his voice a croak. "That must have been—*fuck*. I'm—so sorry."

Olarr jerked a shrug, but his eyes were strangely bright, now, blinking at the wall. "Ach, it was many summers past, now," he said, heavy. "And Harja well knew the danger in this, and would listen to naught that I said or begged upon it. He was never one to be... prudent."

He'd choked a bitter laugh, his mouth crumpling, contorting. "But by the goddess, I shall have my vengeance," he continued, a low growl in his throat. "No matter how long this takes, ach?"

Gerrard's hand had stilled on Olarr's leg, his fingers strangely numb, and he belatedly twitched a jerky-feeling nod. "You will," he said thickly. "You know you will, Olarr. Your"— he took a shaky breath—"Harja will be so proud. Cheering you on from your goddess' side."

And he meant it, meant it so hard it ached, and why did it ache so much? Why was he blinking away the sudden prickling behind his eyes, swallowing down the thick lump in his throat. And curse him, why was he even still here, he was supposed to be convalescing in the med tent, Bassey would no doubt already be making excuses for him, but they'd only hold out for so long, and...

"And look, sorry, but I—I need to go," Gerrard abruptly said, without meeting Olarr's eyes. "They'll be waiting, and I..."

He what? What, damn it? He needed to go, because they were waiting, because he couldn't bear to be here an instant longer. Because was he—was he some kind of—*consolation fuck* for Olarr? Some kind of pity prize, a reckless, imprudent warrior to replace the one he'd lost? Or maybe—maybe he was even part of Olarr's vengeance against Slagvor? Slagvor had killed Olarr's true lover, his Bautul orc lover, so in return Olarr would go off and fuck his human enemy instead? Get that human to kneel for him, to praise him, to debase himself for him?

Never felt anything like it in my life, captain. Your big, fat Bautul cock spreading my human arse wide open, shoving around in my insides, making me fit you—

Gerrard's hands shook as he yanked on his undershirt, and swiped for his uniform. Not looking at Olarr as he pulled it on, even though he could feel Olarr watching him, could almost taste the sudden tension juddering in the air between them. And fuck, no wonder, because Olarr had just told him something so personal, so horribly, sickeningly vile, and now Gerrard was just—just—

"Sorry," he said thickly, with a brief, chagrined glance toward Olarr's oddly pale face. "I just..."

He couldn't finish, again, and he spun and lurched unseeing for the exit, for the tunnel that led to the trapdoor. And how the fuck did it even open, why the fuck had he thought it was a good idea to come down here, and—

And now Olarr was here, striding after him into the tunnel—and he was even still entirely naked, because Gerrard had gone and ruined his trousers. And Gerrard couldn't think, couldn't hide how fast he was blinking, as Olarr silently handed over the crutches—curse it, he'd almost forgotten them—and then he stepped past Gerrard, and shoved up the trapdoor.

It flooded them both with light, so bright Gerrard had to cover his eyes, but it gave him an excuse to wipe at them, to brush the appalling wetness away. And maybe Olarr hadn't seen it, or had he, because he cleared his throat, and came a step closer.

"Ach, Aulis," his low voice said. "I... I did not wish to make you scent thus. If there is aught I have done wrong, I hope you might... speak to me of this."

It was too much, too damned much, and Gerrard shook his head, attempted to wave his hand—but now Olarr had caught it, and again brought it to his mouth. "Or if you ken I yet long for Harja," he said slowly, his breath wavering against Gerrard's skin, "you mayhap ought to know that I have had—other lovers, since this. But none have ever... called to me, as you have. None have ever gained my... my trust, in this. My fealty."

His trust. His *fealty*. And was he lying, he had to be lying, Gerrard was still his enemy—so why was he looking at Gerrard like that, his dark eyes pleading, almost sad. And why was Gerrard's hand slipping up to that heaving chest, just needing to touch him again, just for a moment...

But it was still too much, too close, too heavy to bear—and Gerrard spun and sprinted away. Away, up the stairs and out into the sun, as fast as he could run, before Olarr could see him weep.

18

Gerrard spent the rest of the day in a towering foul mood. Avoiding his men, glaring off at nothing, and even snapping at Bassey when he'd asked where he'd run off to all afternoon.

"Sorry, Bassey," Gerrard mumbled afterwards, rubbing at his eyes. "Was just—trying to work off some steam after that meeting earlier with Livermore. Overdid it a bit."

Bassey seemed to accept this without complaint, and even blandly pointed out that Cosgrove had come by looking for Gerrard, on what he'd said was an important matter. Which very nearly had Gerrard snapping again—why was he only hearing this now?—but he gritted his teeth and thanked Bassey as steadily as he could, before hopping back out on his crutches to find Cosgrove.

It turned out that a letter had come from Head Command for Livermore, a few days earlier than expected—and that the runner was staying the night, and returning with Livermore's reply in the morning. But—Cosgrove's blue eyes looked rather panicked—Livermore had already finished his response, and the letter was currently sitting sealed and ready to go on his desk.

Gerrard couldn't deny an instant's panic at this, too—but no, curse it, he'd spent the afternoon sparring with an orc, and he could be cunning when he damn well needed to be. So after a few moments' considering it, he sent Cosgrove off with specific instructions, and then slowly hopped back in the direction of Livermore's tent. Taking his time getting there, and then calling out to Livermore through the flap, asking if he might have another moment. And at Livermore's irritably snapped assent, Gerrard ducked inside, and...

"General Livermore!" came Cosgrove's frantic holler, from across the camp. "Your horse got loose! He's running off due west this instant!"

Livermore leapt up and dashed past Gerrard at once, pale eyes blazing with rage—just as Gerrard had fully expected, since the bastard had always cared more about his horse than any of his men. And with Livermore safely occupied and out of the tent, Gerrard strode over to the desk. Swiping up the letter that had been lying there, and then slicing off the wax seal, and rapidly scanning the letter's contents.

It turned out to be mostly more predictable rubbish about the regiment's various recent successes against the orcs, but— damn him—Livermore had also included a detailed description of Gerrard's failures and inconvenient injuries, along with an official request for his demotion. And after staring at Livermore's cramped writing for an instant, Gerrard crumpled the letter in his fist, and snatched out a brand-new sheet of parchment.

His new letter was short and terse, copying Livermore's terrible penmanship as closely as possible, and it requested food, medical supplies, relief units, and proper leave time for any men who were overdue, while also flatly pointing out that given their current limitations, further offenses against the orcs were now impossible. And with his heartbeat now thundering in his ears, Gerrard blew the ink dry, folded the parchment just the way Livermore had done, and used Livermore's stamp—still lying carelessly on the desk—to press on a new seal.

He left the letter precisely where the previous one had been on the desk, and hopped out of the tent with as much innocence as he could muster. Luckily, there still seemed to be general chaos coming from the west side of the camp, so Gerrard headed back to the med tent, and gratefully collapsed onto his cot again.

But despite the apparent success of the entire business, Gerrard's foul mood only seemed to worsen as he stayed there in the cot, frowning up at the tent's canvas ceiling above him. He'd been... prudent. Cunning. Just how he'd intended. Or, rather, just how Olarr had intended. Just how Olarr had suggested, endorsed, encouraged...

It was all crashing back in again, clouding and swarming Gerrard's thoughts, because damn it, now he knew why Olarr had wanted him to be prudent and cunning. He knew what this meant for Olarr. What Olarr had faced, what he'd suffered, what he'd lost. What that sick bastard Slagvor had stolen from him.

The images of it—the horrifying possibilities of it—were now streaming behind Gerrard's eyelids, and he dug his palms into his eyes, hard enough that he saw stars. Fuck, it was vile. It was downright evil, and Olarr had been forced to bear it, to keep serving Slagvor, fighting and killing for Slagvor, for *years*.

And when Olarr had told him about it today, what had Gerrard done? He'd shut down, and jumped up, and left. He'd just fucking left, because—he dug his palms in harder—he'd gone and made it about him. About whether Olarr truly... *cared*... for *him*.

Gerrard dug his palms in harder, biting back his groan, because why did it even matter? Why did it matter if Olarr actually cared, or whether he was using Gerrard as a replacement, or a pity fuck, or vengeance, or—or anything else? They'd only met a handful of times, they still barely knew each other, *none have ever called to me as you have...*

Gerrard fought to shove that away, to shove himself over in the cot, to sleep—but now there were visions from the cave, of how Olarr had looked at him, gasped for him, trembled all over for him. And how Gerrard had smiled down at him in return, and kissed him all over, and... and comforted him. *Oh, captain. You feel so good. Look so good. Such a good orc, aren't you?*

It had felt like more weakness, more failure, but the more Gerrard considered it, glaring up at the ceiling, the more self-serving that felt, too. Was it really weakness to show kindness, affection, to someone who kept showing him so much kindness in return? Someone who—unlike so many men in Gerrard's past experience—had kept coming back, even once he'd gotten what he'd wanted? Someone who'd saved Gerrard's life, and brought him a damned picnic? Someone who'd even tried to reassure him today, in the midst of him being a complete and utter selfish arse?

It was well past sunset now, and the camp had gradually quieted, suggesting that Livermore's horse had been retrieved—and before he could think better of it, Gerrard shoved himself up, off the cot. Earning himself a narrow sidelong look from Bassey, but he didn't comment, and Gerrard nodded back as he snatched up his crutches—and the nearby lamp—and hopped out of the tent.

He was going back. He needed to go back.

The trek back through the forest seemed to take so much longer this time, even once Gerrard had thrust the crutches up under his arm, and broken into a jog. Following the same path as closely as he could, climbing over rocks and roots, shoving through foliage, while his breath came shorter and shorter, his heartbeat ringing louder and louder in his ears.

Olarr had to still be there. He had to be. He would have needed at least a night's rest before turning around and heading back again, right? And the cave would be an ideal place to stay... right?

But there was no obvious sign of Olarr, no huge grey bulk lurking in the trees, and Gerrard was now twitching at every crackle and rustle, the urgency wheeling higher in his heaving chest. Olarr had to still be here, he had been just right around here, somewhere, *somewhere*—and yes, yes, that was the rock, the trapdoor, and Gerrard lunged for it, fought to yank it up—

But it wouldn't budge. It was either too heavy, or had some kind of latch on it, curse it. And Gerrard groaned aloud as he wrenched at it, kicked at it, hurled his stupid useless crutches down against it.

"Olarr!" he heard himself shout, his voice hoarse. "Olarr! Are you still there?"

There was no answer, no response, and something wild and dangerous welled inside Gerrard's chest, threatened to escape. What if Olarr had left. What if he'd left for good, and he never came back...

"Olarr!" Gerrard shouted, even louder than before. "Open up, damn it! Open up, wake up, I need to talk to you!"

There was still no response, and Gerrard kicked at the rock again, felt the dangerous weight in his chest juddering higher, quavering in his throat. "Please, Olarr," he croaked. "Please, I—"

But then—a sound. Heavy. Behind him. And Gerrard whipped around, raised his lamp—and yes, yes, it was Olarr. Olarr, with his full pack in his hand, and his huge axe slung on his back. And—Gerrard's eyes dropped, held—both wooden swords hanging off his belt. As if he'd been *leaving*.

Gerrard gulped, twitched all over—and then lurched forward, nearly tripping on his feet. Until he was standing there before Olarr, his eyes blinking hard, his throat swallowing again and again.

"I wanted—" he began, but the words wouldn't come, sticking hard and painful in his throat. "A—a rematch. Please."

He waited for a frozen, hanging moment, his eyes still blinking, fixed to Olarr's shadowy face. While the weight again plunged in his chest, the misery surging even higher, about to escape—

"Ach, then, human," came Olarr's voice, quiet and resigned. "If that is all you wish, we shall fight."

19

Gerrard knew he was going to lose this time.

Olarr hadn't taken him back into the cave for the match, but had instead dropped his pack and his axe where he stood, and silently tossed Gerrard one of the wooden swords. Meaning that they'd be fighting out here, in this cramped little clearing, with only the light from Gerrard's lamp, and a faint gleam from the waning half-moon above them.

But the terrible visibility didn't really matter, and neither did the awful terrain, with the roots and stones scattered everywhere—because from the first swing of his sword, Gerrard had known he was just too damned tired to win this. Too unsettled. Too frantic and unfocused to think, to plan, to be cunning.

And instead, he was just—reacting. Blocking and parrying, desperately fighting to keep moving, to stay upright, to avoid the trees and rocks all around. All while keeping his eyes on Olarr in the shadowy light, working to follow his swings, to stay the hell out of his way.

But Olarr just kept coming, swift and merciless, his eyes gone strangely blank, almost empty, as he charged and stabbed and lunged. As Gerrard ducked, blocked, spun behind that tree, scrambled away, until—

He tripped, on a root. Staggered sharp and sideways. And Olarr's sturdy wooden sword, which had been sweeping for Gerrard's blade, instead swung straight for Gerrard himself, and struck him full and brutal across the chest.

The impact flashed agony all through Gerrard's body, slammed the breath from his lungs—and he was soaring back, flying toward a tree behind him. Hitting its solid trunk with another dizzying, disorienting crash, as a choked little whisper escaped from his throat, and his head snapped back, about to strike into—

Olarr. Olarr's hand. Olarr's whole body, suddenly hovering close and hazy before Gerrard's eyes. And now his big hands were hauling Gerrard away from the tree, drawing him downwards, gently setting him on the soft damp ground. While Gerrard's lungs kept dragging for breath, the pain still screaming through his chest, flashing white behind his eyes.

He only distantly felt those warm hands running all over him, rapid and panicked, yanking off his tunic—but when they gently brushed over that angry new welt across his chest, Gerrard reflexively curled up, fought to turn away. His mouth betraying a thin, helpless croak as water streamed from his eyes, his body spasming against the hard earth.

But wait, wait, those hands were here again, making Gerrard lie flat again, so—so something could—kiss him. So *Olarr* could kiss him, oh, his warm lips and tongue sliding soft and urgent across Gerrard's chest, caressing against the wound he'd made in Gerrard's skin, already oozing out dark red blood.

Gerrard's pain again croaked from his mouth, sounding far too much like a sob—and he only distantly heard the odd sound from Olarr's mouth in return, almost as if he'd sobbed, too. As his kisses came faster, even more urgent than before, his tongue sweeping again and again and again, lancing fresh pain all through Gerrard's trembling body.

But as the moments slowly thudded past, it distantly occurred to Gerrard that perhaps the pain wasn't quite as vicious as before. And the wound didn't seem to be bleeding anymore, either, and Gerrard slowly felt his breaths returning again, his watery vision gradually refocusing. Taking in the sight of the moonlit sky above him, the trees around him, the... the orc, bent over his sprawled body, still kissing and licking at his chest with frantic, desperate urgency.

"Think it's—all right now," Gerrard heard himself wheeze, his voice not his own. "Don't think—anything's broken. Should be—fine. Thanks."

Olarr replied with a thick, unsteady growl, and a glance up at Gerrard's face that looked almost appalled. "This is not *fine*, human," his deep voice hissed. "I—I did not think. I fought you here in the dark, where you could see naught around you. And thus"—he hauled in a dragging breath—"I wounded you, warrior. I could have *killed* you!"

Oh. Well. That. Gerrard's gaze slid back to the sky, his eyes blinking again and again, as his breaths kept heaving through his chest. "Wanted you to hit me," he gasped, and did he mean that, he did. "Deserved it. Was so—so shit to you, today."

Olarr made that growling sound again, and he lurched up to look at Gerrard, staring at him with hard, disbelieving, wet-looking eyes. "You did not—*deserve* this, Aulis," he said, and Gerrard couldn't at all read that waver in his voice. "And you were not—*shit*. You were—*wondrous*."

Fuck, maybe Gerrard was more grievously injured than he thought, because he'd surely misheard that—right? Or had he, because Olarr abruptly reached for his face, cradling it in both hands. And his hands were... shaking, as his too-bright eyes caught on Gerrard's, and shimmered as they held.

"You were *wondrous*, Aulis," he rasped. "I have

never—*never*—had a lover do such things. Say such things. I shall never, ever forget this, in all my days, and now I have—I have—"

He was rapidly blinking, his black lashes fluttering again and again, and he shook his head, bit one of his sharp fangs at his lip. "I have harmed you," he choked. "I have near killed you. *Ended* you. *Ach.*"

He sounded genuinely distraught, the raw intensity in his voice catching, shuddering, deep in Gerrard's chest. And it distantly occurred to Gerrard that he should be arguing this, that one bad blow from a wooden sword wasn't going to kill him, and that Olarr was making a big fuss over nothing. Gerrard was a lieutenant, he'd faced worse dozens of times, he didn't need coddling, or...

Or did he. He'd been such a reckless mess today, running off the way he had, and dumping all his own rubbish onto Olarr. All his own... fear. Fear of being betrayed. Hurt. Weak.

Gerrard swallowed hard, drew in a breath, glanced up at the shining light of the half-moon above them. While his still-tingling hand slid up, found Olarr's broad, sweaty back—and then began stroking, up and down. Feeling the rigid strength in it, the tension in the hard packed muscle beneath his skin. The way it also spoke so powerfully of... fear. Of concern. Of...

Olarr's breath caught at the touch, his eyes snapped strange and arrested on Gerrard's face, and Gerrard swallowed, twitched a small, wavering little smile in return. Wanting to say, about to say, so close...

"Just glad you're still here, captain," he said, hoarse. "And you still won, yeah? Aren't you gonna take your prize?"

It still wasn't all he should have said, but it was something. And it set Olarr's eyes shifting again, as his breath hitched, and that familiar cock shuddered and swelled beneath the front of his trousers, hardening against Gerrard's thigh.

Gerrard was still wearing his own trousers, and he rapidly

shoved down the waistband, wincing at the feel of a pointy rock beneath him—but wait, Olarr had swiped sideways, for his pack, and yanked something out of it. The—the fur. And then he lurched up to his feet, heading toward where a large, flat boulder was encircled in a ring of nearby pine trees—and once he'd spread the fur on the boulder, he came back for Gerrard again. Lifting him up with palpable care, and carrying him over the short distance to the rock. Settling him down on the fur's plush softness, before gently pulling off his boots, his trousers.

Gerrard's lamp had gone out at some point, so it meant that he was now fully bared in only the faint moonlight, gleaming white and silvery on his skin. And despite the bizarre unreality of this—of being undressed, spread out by an orc beneath the moon—he still felt his body relaxing, his breaths deepening, as Olarr's warm hands began slowly, purposefully caressing him. Sliding down from Gerrard's face, stroking against the bare skin of his neck, his shoulders, his arms. And then slowly slipping down his front, carefully skirting around his wound, before easing up again. As those shimmering, still-blinking eyes held to Gerrard's face, watching him, searching his response, maybe even seeking his permission.

But Gerrard just gave another small smile back, his tongue brushing his lip, because oh, how this looked, how it felt. This huge, powerful, deadly orc on his knees for him, touching him as though he was starving for it, and looking at him with such strange, fervent light in his eyes. Such... reverence.

The pleasure was already drowning out the lingering pain, and Gerrard's breaths were coming even deeper, his body relaxing heavier against the fur. And though a distant whining unease was still there somewhere, rattling deep in his skull, Olarr's touch, Olarr's reverence, was so much closer. So much stronger. Shouting at Gerrard, swarming him all over with a strange, settled certainty.

He wanted this. Wanted to keep trying this, fighting for this. Wanted to accept what Olarr kept telling him, the way Olarr kept doing this. Kept looking at him like this, touching him like this, pressing all those impossible words deep into his wounded skin.

I have already fallen. None have ever called to me, as you have. You were wondrous, Aulis. I shall never, ever forget this.

And maybe—maybe Gerrard hadn't really let himself believe it, until now. Lonely soldiers talked that way, sometimes, after a taste of physical contact that wasn't battles and fighting—but it didn't mean anything, because your body could just as well be anyone's, anything with warm hands and a heartbeat. But Olarr hadn't gone for anyone else, he'd kept coming for Gerrard, multiple times now, and...

"You haven't fucked anyone else, right?" Gerrard's cursed voice croaked, all on its own. "Since we started this?"

Olarr blinked, drew a little backwards, and Gerrard was already wincing, bracing himself, stupid, *stupid*—but wait, Olarr was shaking his head, his hands still caressing, stroking, so warm and gentle against Gerrard's skin. "No," he whispered back. "None have called to me as you do, ach?"

Right. That again. And somehow Gerrard was smiling again, as relief shuddered through his still-sore chest. "Same," he said, quiet and certain, over the increasingly distant nattering in his skull. "Just—you."

And now it was Olarr smiling, a brief quirk of flashing approval, or even appreciation. "Ach, I ken," he replied, just as quiet. "I have scented this, upon you. You now reek of *me*, warrior. *Only* me."

He'd even shot a brief, smug-looking glance down at Gerrard's belly—which was still slightly rounded from earlier, damn it—and instead of the weakness and humiliation Gerrard should have felt, he was rolling his eyes, and kicking at Olarr's leg with his foot. And then arching up further into

Olarr's touch, into that hard, hungry ridge still prodding into his thigh...

"You gonna do it again, then, captain?" he asked, spreading his hand against Olarr's arse. "Make me reek even stronger of you? Fatten me up on you?"

And fuck, the way Olarr's breath choked, his nostrils flaring as he glanced downwards, his wide eyes now blatantly lingering on Gerrard's belly. No doubt imagining how he'd look after being filled from both ends, curse him—and the smug bastard was already yanking himself out of his trousers, his swollen, shuddering grey length hovering huge and hungry over Gerrard's groin. But as Gerrard arched up again, grinding into the still-stroking press of Olarr's big warm hands, he still couldn't seem to find the energy to protest. He was doing this. He wanted this. Wanted Olarr's touch, his pleasure, his care.

And yes. Yes. That was care, in the way Olarr's hands slid down to Gerrard's thighs, gently grasping them, tilting them up and back. The way that slick, pulsing head settled against Gerrard's tight heat, waited for him to soften in return. And oh, the way Olarr's reverent eyes rapidly darted between Gerrard's face, and the sight below his upraised legs. Where he could feel himself slowly, slowly, stretching wider and wider as that fat, slick, pulsing orc-prick gently breached him, and began easing its way inside.

It felt even bigger this way, like a whole damned horde gaining ground breath by breath, and splitting Gerrard apart. Occupying him, conquering him, setting up camp and pitching fucking tents, while he surrendered, opened, welcomed them in. Letting in more, and more, and more, until they were every-where, it was everything, buzzing and brawling and jabbering inside him, foreign and loud and bright and strange. Packing in tighter, ramming in thicker and deeper, until—Gerrard keened, convulsed all over—he was full. Full, closed off, wedged to the brim, with hard strength pressing flat all around his entrance, locking the gates tight behind that blunt, brutal invasion.

Gerrard gasped and arched again, shuddering against the battering ram breaching him—and then... felt the ram shiver in return. Felt the entire force wavering, not only inside him, but all over him. Because Olarr had fallen to his elbows over Gerrard, and his huge, powerful body was... shaking. Trembling with what looked like uncontrollable spasms as he gasped desperately for air, as his bright, shimmering eyes rapidly blinked down at Gerrard's face. Looking at him with that same reverence, that affection, that... care.

And then it all shifted, spun up and around and sideways, and it occurred to Gerrard, with yet more shuddering certainty, that he had Olarr's entire force... trapped. Surrounded. Locked and held and conquered, deep inside his body, his heart.

I have already fallen, and you have taken... all.

Gerrard arched and moaned again, clamped hard against the strength inside him, revelled in his victory—and when Olarr gasped again, the sound almost a sob in his throat, Gerrard grasped for his head, yanked it down, and kissed him. Finding that hot mouth, making it his, and yes, yes, it was his. Groaning as it instantly opened, yielded, giving up its tongue, its breath. And Gerrard took it, tasted it, gloried in it, in the way it moaned and trembled for him. And in how that huge body trembled under his touch, too, gooseflesh prickling out at the barest brush of his fingers, scattering across smooth, sweaty silver skin.

"So good," Gerrard gasped, into Olarr's mouth, rocking up against him, swallowing that battering ram even deeper inside him. "You feel so damn good, captain."

Olarr's groan was instant, guttural, and yes, yes, he was rocking now too, wedging himself even deeper, burying himself within Gerrard's waiting grip. "Ach," he gasped back, between heavy breaths. "Y-you also, warrior."

Gerrard kissed him again for that, his blunt fingernails lightly scraping against Olarr's neck, his back—and oh, Olarr liked that, the shudder wrenching all the way up his big body, escaping in another heated, helpless-sounding moan. So Gerrard did it again, again, until Olarr was writhing and kicking and howling over him, inside him. That invading pole swelling and straining as his hips frantically plunged, as the triumph and the ecstasy caught and flashed and soared, so close, so—

"Up, captain," Gerrard gasped, into Olarr's mouth, just in time—and Olarr lurched up, away, still howling as he kept ramming into Gerrard's hole, and as Gerrard finally took his own ruddy, aching length in hand. Pumping it up once, twice, while Olarr choked and stared, and then matched the movements with his own shaky furious thrusts—

They shouted as they came together, the release flying between them, flaring into sharp, shattering bliss. Olarr bucking and spasming as he emptied his bollocks deep into Gerrard's innards, as Gerrard's own load spurted up across his chest, his neck, even his face. Spraying all over him, making a sticky mess of him, but—a distant rational part of him pointed out—at least it hadn't seemed to go anywhere near Olarr. And instead, Olarr was moaning again, his cock inside Gerrard still erratically spasming, as his heavy-lidded eyes fluttered, and he bent over Gerrard's spunk-splattered chest, and inhaled.

Gerrard had almost forgotten how to breathe, and he belatedly hauled in a breath too, his own eyes fluttering as he watched. As Olarr just kept hovering over him in the moonlight, breathing in slow and deep, while his spasms inside Gerrard gradually weakened, and then quieted altogether. And Gerrard could feel the thick invading flesh slowly softening, too, shrinking, surrendering. Until it finally slipped out of him, away, as if it truly had been defeated. Conquered, by Gerrard's body, Gerrard's pleasure.

At least, until Gerrard realized what Olarr was looking at, now. What he was... smelling, with such quiet, stilted reverence. It was his own damned belly, which now looked appallingly plump, rounded—because Olarr had indeed gone and flooded it full from both ends. Fattened Gerrard up, just as Gerrard had asked. Just as he'd... wanted.

And despite a brief but concerted attempt, Gerrard still couldn't seem to find even a whisper of the humiliation, or the shame. He'd wanted that. He'd had a hell of a lot of triumph in that. And as strange as it was, he suddenly felt almost... light. Content. At ease.

"Yeah, keep looking, you great arse," he groused, kicking at Olarr's leg, though there was barely any heat in his voice. "You love it, don't you. Making it look like you put a damned *baby* in there."

Olarr's glance upwards was swift and warm, the amusement kindling across his dark eyes. "An *orcling*," he corrected, husky and hot. "A hearty, hale Bautul orcling, mayhap."

Gerrard scoffed and kicked at him again, though a smile was twitching at his mouth, too. "Well, too bad, captain," he shot back, "because there's no orcling in there. There's only"— he made a face, but said it anyway—"a seedling. An *orc-seedling*. Get it?"

Olarr stilled, blinked at Gerrard for an instant—and then he threw back his shaggy head, and laughed. The sound low and rich and rolling, rumbling deep into Gerrard's gut. And suddenly Gerrard was laughing too, shaking his head, grinning so hard his face hurt. "You just wait, you prick," he managed, between chuckles. "Until my orc-seed-ling is born. You won't be so happy then, will you?"

Olarr laughed even harder, his guffaws now roaring through the open air, and there were even tears streaking down his cheeks. The sight of it making Gerrard laugh harder, too, the joy so bright and warm and pure between them. Enough that he very nearly reached for Olarr again, needing to pull him close, to wrap him into his arms—

But no, no, wait, curse it, the scent. *Slagvor.* And Gerrard couldn't even risk touching Olarr now, not with his own spunk spattered all over him like this, and he felt his mirth abruptly fading as he yanked a little backwards. And he could see Olarr reflexively reaching for him in return, as if wanting him close, too—and then wincing as he realized it, as he sank back to his knees on the fur-covered stone.

"Ach, warrior," Olarr said, almost a groan, but his eyes were still so warm, so soft, on Gerrard's face. "I am so glad you came back here tonight. And"—he winced again as his gaze dropped to Gerrard's chest—"yet so sorry, for this wound."

Gerrard waved it away—it only ached a little, now, and it had been damn well worth it—but found his thoughts catching, already festering, in places they had no business being, and...

"*Do* you want—a real orcling, though, Olarr?" he blurted out, before he'd come close to stopping it. "Like—with a woman?"

Olarr blinked, tilted his head, while Gerrard's heart suddenly kicked, pattering in his chest. Fuck, this hadn't even occurred to him before, but orcs all longed for sons, didn't they? For a *hearty, hale Bautul orcling,* Olarr had said. And for that, like all orcs, Olarr would need a human woman. And even if he truly did care for Gerrard, Gerrard could never, ever give him that, and—

"I do not wish for a woman," Olarr said, speaking quickly, now, as his body shifted over to sit beside Gerrard's on the fur, his big hand carefully slipping up to spread against Gerrard's dry back. "My hunger has always been toward—toward strong, skilled, well-formed warriors like you. And I should gladly choose this over any orcling, ach?"

Gerrard shot him a sharp, searching look, as that uneasy

whispering refrain lurched back into his thoughts—they were enemies, they still barely even knew each other—but now Olarr was mightily frowning toward him, his brows furrowed, his claws slightly pricking into the skin of Gerrard's back.

"I would, warrior," he insisted. "Ach, why should I ever wish to bring an orcling into this war? This would only grant me more fear and failure. More threats of loss and grief, waiting to be wielded against me."

His eyes darkened as he spoke, his frown twisting into genuine bitterness, surely thinking of Harja, of Slagvor. And Gerrard felt his own unease shifting, settling, as he let out a breath, and leaned a little closer into Olarr's side.

"Right," he replied, thick. "I get that. I just—you'd be a good father, yeah? I wouldn't want you to give that up, for... for someone like... *me.*"

His voice had gone very quiet, and well it should, because that was damned presumptuous, to assume Olarr really cared... that much. That this—whatever the hell this was, between them—would ever extend beyond fights and fucking, beyond taking their pleasure while it lasted. Because chances were slim that they'd even both survive this endless war in the first place, and...

"Ach, I should not regret this," Olarr said, giving Gerrard a firm little shake. "Though you have not said, Aulis"—his forehead furrowed—"whether *you* should not regret this? Do *you* not wish for a son? Or a daughter?"

Gerrard blinked, made himself consider the question—and maybe Olarr had the right of it, because even the thought of bringing a helpless, needy child into this war felt utterly absurd. And the thought of needing to court a woman, to settle down and marry a woman, was even more alarming, and—

"Hell, no," Gerrard said, with a convulsive little shudder. "If I ever did get to a place where I wanted a kid in my life, I'd just go—find one. An orphaned army kid like I was, maybe. One who could use the help."

He'd been speaking without really thinking, the words tumbling from his mouth, and he was vaguely surprised to see Olarr nodding, and giving him a slow, approving smile. "Ach, I ken you would," he said, his voice soft. "This is what we should do, then."

What we should do. We. Those words clamping and coiling tight in Gerrard's gut, because it was even more presumptuous than what he'd said… right? But curse it, no matter what either of them said, it was never going to happen. It was a fantasy, a stupid ridiculous delusion, to think of someday living in a simple little cottage together, sparring and training together, going off on missions together. Raising a son together…

Gerrard swallowed, so loud he could hear it, and felt his head tilt sideways, settling onto Olarr's shoulder. "Think we need to survive the next week first," he said, his voice a rasp. "You're probably off again for a while, right? Back to Slagvor?"

He couldn't seem to look at Olarr, but he could feel Olarr's shoulder rising and falling against him, could hear the weight of his breaths. "Ach," he replied. "But I could come to you again, when next I can. Should you yet… wish for this."

Gerrard did dart a look up at him now, brief and incredulous. "You have to ask?" he said, before he could stop it. "Of course I want it. I need"—he caught it just in time—"a rematch."

He didn't miss that shift in Olarr's eyes, not unlike the look he'd worn when Gerrard had first come here tonight. When Olarr had thought, maybe—more comprehension flashed across Gerrard's thoughts—that it really had been just about the rematch. Or the challenge of it, or the escape, or the treason, or any of the other dozen things Gerrard had thought maybe Olarr really wanted, too.

So Gerrard took a deep, shaky breath, drew up his courage,

his truth. "And... to see you again," he added, barely more than a whisper. "This is... nice."

Nice. As if he'd been talking about good weather, maybe, or a decent night's sleep, rather than... this. But he'd said it, he'd said something, damn it—and Olarr's eyes had abruptly widened, looking surprised, and then pleased, or maybe even touched.

"Ach," he said, with a sharp little nod, a stroke of his claws to Gerrard's back. "This is nice."

Gerrard couldn't stop the hoarse laugh from escaping his throat, because it was so ridiculous, so preposterous. But he was still leaning against Olarr in the moonlight, his head tucked into Olarr's shoulder, and Olarr was still stroking his back like that. Wanting him. Caring for him.

"So you'll come back, then, captain?" Gerrard asked, a little steadier this time. "And until then, you'll stay the hell out of Slagvor's way? Be as prudent and cunning as you can?"

He tried to make it sound light and easy, but it still felt almost like a plea, like a request for some kind of... of promise. *Keep yourself safe. Come back to me. Don't betray me. Prove to me I'm not wrong, prove to me I can trust you...*

And oh, Olarr was nodding. Nodding, his eyes flashing with resolve, with certainty, with... with affection. With care.

"Ach, warrior," he said, a low, rumbling vow in his throat. "I shall."

20

For the next few weeks, Gerrard threw himself into his bizarre new double life. Playing the part of a loyal, wounded lieutenant—whose injuries had conveniently continued to persist—while also actively conspiring against his commanding officer, and regularly fraternizing with the enemy.

It helped that Livermore was so damned belligerent, with so little empathy for his own men's struggles. To the point where he'd openly raged over Head Command's reply to "his" last letter, because—much to Gerrard's surprise—Head Command had actually granted a few of the letter's requests. Including home leave for all the soldiers who were wounded or overdue, and a commitment to send out more supplies within the week.

But it had also meant that those costs would be cut from Livermore's own campaign budget, and therefore his own salary. And even worse—or better, to Gerrard's mind—it had meant that the outpost would be severely understaffed for the foreseeable future, making new offenses against the orcs even more impossible than before.

"I cannot fathom what Head Command was thinking, with this leave order!" Livermore had loudly barked to Gerrard, as they'd watched the group of tired but relieved-looking soldiers marching out of the gate, carrying multiple wounded men on stretchers between them. "It's making us unable to fill our mandate. Unable to pursue the orcs, and protect our home! It's a stupid, short-sighted decision, and I'm sending a very strongly worded response back to Duke Warmisham himself!"

Gerrard had exchanged a swift, meaningful glance with a nearby Cosgrove, who—bless him—had managed a glimpse at said letter earlier that day. And after a brief consultation on the matter, they'd decided to let this one go north as it was, knowing that Duke Warmisham was unlikely to appreciate being scolded by a subordinate, especially after so generously fulfilling that subordinate's previous request.

"Livermore is honestly his own worst enemy," Gerrard irritably told Olarr, later that evening. "It's fool enough for him to openly complain to his own men about giving them leave, but to grouse at Head Command? At Warmisham? At the filthy rich duke who's financing this whole mess in the first place?"

They were back down in that underground room again—it had become their de facto meeting place, these past weeks—and they were both sweaty and sated from another intensive round of fighting and fucking. Olarr had taken the win this time, and with it, Gerrard's arse—though Gerrard could admit that he hadn't at all minded. And there was something almost satisfying in the way Olarr was now cradling him close on the fur, his big hand reverently stroking over the distinctive swell he'd made in Gerrard's belly.

"Ach, this Livermore is a fool," Olarr replied, his voice sharp with contempt. "He shall build his own pyre for you, and you shall only need to keep lighting sparks, ach?"

Gerrard shot a brief, amused smile up at Olarr's hard face—his appreciation of Olarr's unapologetic cunning had only grown, these past weeks—but then he felt his smile fading as he shook his head. "I still haven't sorted out a way to actually get rid of the bastard, though," he said, with a sigh. "Fucking with his letters is a start, but it doesn't guarantee anything, right? I need something bigger. Something that'll bring Head Command down on him, with no chance of it coming back on me. Or my men."

He'd indeed spent far too much time creating and discarding plans around Livermore these past weeks—setups, blackmail, accusations, scandals—but his resources were so damned limited, and every viable plan he'd concocted so far risked exposing his own involvement, or endangering his men. And though he hadn't liked to think of it, he'd finally begun considering more... violent means, after all. Maybe a late-night swim gone wrong, or a sudden inexplicable disappearance...

But this wasn't the first time Gerrard had discussed this with Olarr—they'd gone through all his plans together, even his terrible old one of seducing Warmisham—and now Olarr was flashing him a rather devious-looking grin, and groping sideways for his pack. Drawing out what appeared to be a brown glass jar, the kind medics like Bassey used for salves and ointments. Except that it was full of... powder?

"Mushroom powder," Olarr said, his devious grin twisting higher. "A new treatment from your medic, I ken, for your stubborn wounds. But..."

Gerrard's brows were rising, his smile quirking, as Olarr thrust the jar into his hand. "But you must take great care with it," he continued, "for even a small pinch—in your soup or your tea, mayhap—shall grant you great and wondrous visions. Visions that none but you shall see."

This bastard. This brilliant, impossible bastard, and Gerrard couldn't help his sudden, loud crack of laughter, or his bright, disbelieving grin at Olarr's face. "You damned devious orc," he said, between chuckles. "Visions? Really? Like ghosts and faeries, that sort of thing?"

Olarr shrugged, but he was still grinning, too. "Ach, mayhap," he replied blandly. "You shall have to test it and see, ach? Mayhap where many others can see, also."

Gerrard laughed again, shaking his head, but the implications of it—the possibilities of it—were already unspooling eagerly through his thoughts. He'd never heard of anyone using mushroom powder for such a purpose before, right? So it wouldn't be familiar, or easy to pinpoint. And while such visions were a common enough ailment among soldiers in combat, Livermore had always treated sufferers with his usual threats and contempt, rather than the leave time and medical care they deserved. So along with undermining Livermore, this powder might well be a long-overdue lesson for him, too.

"You really are a diabolical genius," Gerrard told Olarr, giving a companionable nudge of his elbow into his side. "Thanks, captain. And"—his head tilted, his eyes studying Olarr's face—"please tell me you've been doing this with Slagvor, too?"

There was an instant's silence, hurtling out between them—and Olarr's eyes darkened, the smile rapidly fading from his mouth. "No," he said, far flatter than before. "Slagvor is not a fool, and well knows the visions mushrooms can bring. If he once fears that his food has been tampered with, he will seek out the orc at fault at once. And"—he sighed, even heavier—"even if he cannot learn the truth of this, he shall yet find someone to punish. Mayhap whatever poor orc who has been wounded of late, and thus has been forced to make Slagvor's food instead."

Right. Gerrard's own mirth had abruptly drained away too, because of course Olarr wouldn't set up one of his own kin to be punished. Olarr's fierce loyalty to his Bautul clan had become more and more apparent these past weeks, and it seemed to inform every one of his choices and actions—except, maybe, for this. For how he kept coming all the way out here, going to such obvious pains to keep seeing Gerrard, despite all the rubbish he was dealing with back home. Despite Slagvor.

"So what *are* you doing about Slagvor, then?" Gerrard asked now, his voice lower. "How are you using all your prudence and cunning for yourself? For your own kin?"

Olarr's mouth was still tight and thin, his eyes now gazing blankly at the earthen ceiling above them. "I do all I can to help my Bautul brothers amidst this," he finally said. "I make myself as strong as I am able, so I can wield my power for their sakes. And I seek to uphold Grimarr, as he seeks to defeat Kaugir, and end this war."

Right. This Grimarr and his goals had consistently come up these past weeks—it was clear that Olarr had a lot of respect for the fellow—but Gerrard still felt himself frowning, his fingers drumming against his swollen belly. Here Olarr was, blatantly encouraging Gerrard to plot against his commanding officer, while Olarr himself was still doing... what? Essentially nothing? Against a cruel despot of an orc who'd horribly killed many of Olarr's kin, including his own lover?

Olarr still wasn't meeting Gerrard's eyes, but his expression was heavy with sadness, or maybe even guilt. And Gerrard felt something catching, twisting in his own belly, because he knew what that guilt felt like. That... helplessness. And it had been Olarr who'd pulled him out of it, and helped him to start feeling... alive again. Himself again.

"How about another rematch, then?" Gerrard asked, waggling his brows at Olarr's grim face. "You wanna bet I can beat you this time?"

The warmth instantly flashed across Olarr's eyes, and he jerked a relieved-looking nod as he sat up, pulling Gerrard up with him. "Ach, we shall see, warrior," he said lightly. "Or mayhap you shall once again find yourself on your knees, screaming upon my stick."

Gerrard scoffed a bright, disbelieving laugh, but then blinked at the sight of Olarr reaching sideways, and gripping at Gerrard's own sword. Not the wooden practice blade, but his familiar sharpened, shining steel.

"But to make this more fair, this time," Olarr continued smoothly, "mayhap you shall wield *this* against me."

Gerrard frowned at the sword, and then at Olarr's face—even given Olarr's impressive healing abilities, he still didn't want to risk causing any lasting injury, right? But Olarr was gently smiling now, shaking his head. "I trust you, warrior," he said, husky. "I ken you shall not grievously wound me. And I wish to see you fight with this again. I wish to see what you can do with it."

He wanted to see Gerrard win, maybe, was the unspoken truth in that statement, and Gerrard rolled his eyes, even as he swiped the sword from Olarr's hand, and leapt to his feet. "You're gonna regret it, captain," he said lightly. "Especially once *you're* the one on your knees, yeah?"

Olarr had the audacity to look pleased by this, curse the calculating bastard, so Gerrard lunged forward as swiftly as he could, sweeping his sword across Olarr's chest. Close enough to make impact, damn it, leaving a bright line of red behind on Olarr's grey skin—but he hadn't even seemed to notice. And instead, he was fully grinning at Gerrard, flashing him all those sharp white teeth, as he swept his own wooden sword up into his hand.

The steel did give Gerrard a considerable advantage, he soon discovered, even more than he'd expected. Not only was the sword more familiar, more at home in his hand, but it made his swings faster and cleaner, with more power and weight behind them. And he could see Olarr working harder to stave him off, the sweat already beading on his brow, as Gerrard charged in again and again, gaining more ground every time.

"Sorry," he gasped, wincing, after wedging the steel deep into Olarr's shoulder, spurting out blood in its wake—but Olarr only shook his head, and swung again. And again and again, a little less precise every time, as Gerrard leapt and dodged and parried. Using his speed and stamina to his advantage, working to tire Olarr out, until...

Until Gerrard saw his opening, and shot forward. Not swinging for Olarr's sword this time, but instead slipping up beneath it, and—yes—shoving the flat of his blade against Olarr's neck.

"Got you," Gerrard gasped, grinning, between heaving breaths. "Regret it now, captain?"

For an instant, Olarr looked genuinely astonished, even angry—not a surprise, since Gerrard knew he still struggled with all that Bautul rubbish about losing, especially to a human. But he could already see Olarr working through it, his breaths deepening as his expression gradually cleared again, shifting into a wry, warm appreciation.

"Ach, I may have regrets upon this, warrior," Olarr replied, voice thick. "Though I ken this hangs most upon what you do with me next, ach?"

He'd even arched a taunting eyebrow, the prick, because he damn well knew Gerrard still couldn't risk going anywhere near him with his cock, or his seed. Which instead meant he'd had to keep finding creative uses for his hands, and his mouth, and his words. And no matter how much he meant to still take the advantage—to make Olarr pay for his audacity, to make him beg and plead—it always ended up like this. With Gerrard shoving Olarr down to the fur like this, looming up over him, and then...

Smiling at him. Spreading his hands wide against that

warm silver skin. And watching as Olarr's dark eyes shifted, shimmering with... gratitude. With trust.

"Gonna put you in your place, of course," Gerrard said, the words at laughable odds with how his hands were already stroking, slipping over all the hard lines of Olarr's bare body beneath him, smoothing over where some of those fresh wounds had already begun to heal over. "Gonna have my filthy way with my wise, clever, handsome captain, aren't I?"

Olarr's eyes shifted again, flaring with hunger, maybe even longing—because that was another thing Gerrard had learned these past weeks. Olarr's value to his clan—and perhaps to his past lovers—seemed to primarily lie in his strength and bravery in battle, rather than any other attributes he might possess. And Gerrard would perhaps never forget the way Olarr had blushed and moaned the first time he'd called him *clever*, or the way he'd startled at being called *handsome*.

"Ach, no, human," Olarr had protested, with a highly betraying twist on his mouth. "I am marked and scarred all over, and my face is hard and heavy and ill-pleasing, most of all to fair, well-formed men like you. Bautul are not—"

Gerrard had cut off that rubbish with a biting little kiss, a too-traitorous caress of his hand to Olarr's jaw. "Handsome," he'd insisted, into Olarr's mouth. "Love looking at you. More than any human I've ever met."

Olarr clearly hadn't believed it, but Gerrard had been vaguely surprised to find he'd meant it. And every time they'd met since, he'd made a point of saying it like this, saying it and meaning it to Olarr's disbelieving eyes, as his hungry hands roved all over that big, powerful body.

"So handsome," he said now, smiling again at Olarr's face, stroking both hands down his taut, trembling sides. "With your silver skin, and your gorgeous eyes, and your"—he bent down, gave that pointed ear a light little nibble—"your pretty elf ears.

You should see yourself in the moonlight. Just like a son of your goddess, yeah?"

Olarr's blush had already crept up his neck, darkly colouring his cheeks, and when he tried to shake his head, Gerrard caught it with another kiss, drinking up the warm, sweet taste of his mouth. "Don't you argue with me, captain," he murmured. "I won, remember? So now you need to listen to me. Accept your defeat."

Olarr's eyes were shining when Gerrard drew away, blinking at him with reverence, with worship, with... with affection. And yes, Gerrard wanted that, craved that, needed that look in Olarr's eyes. That promise that this wasn't about plots or treason, about pity or revenge. It was about trust, about friendship, about pleasure. About *care*. About enjoying this while it lasted, pretending it could last forever...

"And I say you're handsome, captain," Gerrard breathed again, just because he could, just because it made Olarr gasp and shiver like that. "You look so good. Feel so good. I love fighting you, and fucking you."

Olarr's gasp was more like a groan this time, his bare body bucking reflexively up against where Gerrard was straddling him. And against where—Gerrard fought down the instinctive embarrassment—his own previously filled arse was now leaking Olarr's own seed back out onto his grey cock, lying plump and swollen against his belly. A sight that Olarr was now watching with rapt attention, and Gerrard took a bracing breath, squeezed out a little more. Let it drizzle down between them, blatant and obscene, because Olarr liked it. Olarr wanted it. Wanted him.

"Love how much of this good seed you keep making for me," Gerrard continued, huskier now, as he stroked a brazen hand against his own rounded belly. "Love having this gorgeous fat cock of yours hard for me. Wanting to stab itself inside me."

Olarr bucked and groaned again, shamelessly grinding his slick shaft up between Gerrard's parted legs, and Gerrard huffed a breathless laugh, even as his damnable leaking body ground back, meeting it, wanting it. "You want to be inside me again, don't you, captain?" he breathed. "You want to open me even wider, pump me even fuller of you?"

Olarr shuddered all over, his head fervently nodding, his hips still bucking wildly upwards, and Gerrard smiled back, stroked up and down Olarr's sweaty flanks with creditable steadiness. "Then you'll need to ask me, captain," he purred. "Very nicely."

Olarr's eyes were almost frantic, now, but he was rapidly nodding, licking his long black tongue at his lips. "Ach," he croaked. "Ach, Aulis. Please, grant me this. By the goddess."

Gerrard made himself wait, raising his eyebrows, and Olarr shuddered again, his throat audibly swallowing. "Please, Aulis," he gasped. "You are—so stunning. So sweet. And you feel so soft and tight upon my prick, so—so—"

He broke off there, heaving for breath, because Gerrard had already shifted them together, settling that swollen, generously leaking tip against just where he wanted it. Against where he was still dripping that thick fluid out of him onto Olarr, coating him with it, just as Olarr kept pumping out more, too, feeding it back inside him, in a strange, surreal loop between them. And even if Gerrard hadn't already been soft and slack from last time, he was so open, so ready, and he had to fight to keep himself still, to keep waiting, holding Olarr's desperate eyes...

"I yet cannot fathom—why you wish for this—from me," Olarr choked, between dragging breaths. "Why you keep— welcoming me, and granting me—such gifts. There is naught more I long for than to bury myself deep within you, to fill you with my seed and my scent. To know you are mine, you are forever *mine*—"

His voice cracked, his head whipping back and forth, and

Gerrard desperately smiled through that impossible word *forever* as he finally sank downward. Swallowing that hard, straining head up inside him, and then taking in more, and more, and more. Consuming it breath by breath, making it his, only his, trapped firm and deep in his grip, in his thrall. While that captured flesh strove and shuddered, yielding to his command, spurting out more hot fluid with every milking clutch of Gerrard's body around him.

"Good, captain," Gerrard gasped, and now he was gripping his own straining cock, too, sweeping an easy hand up and down, while Olarr watched with stunned, blinking eyes. "Now, you're gonna give me what's mine, aren't you? You're gonna pour me full of you. Make me reek of you, fatten me up on you, until I can't possibly hold any more—"

Olarr writhed, wrenched, roared—and oh, that was it, his captured strength swelling again and again as he obeyed. Spraying out his bounty deep inside Gerrard, flooding his guts even fuller with fresh streams of orc-seed. And fuck, Gerrard could feel his belly swelling out further, plumping up more with every new spurt, and Olarr was watching too, his eyes fixed to the sight, to Gerrard's own rapidly pumping hand, so close—

Gerrard gasped as he leaned backwards just in time, his own pleasure screeching through him, driving out of him, spraying up all over his rounded belly. Painting it with glossy, dangling strings of his own mess, while Olarr moaned again, and ground up deeper inside, shuddering out even more. Making Gerrard's belly swell just a little fuller, while Olarr's wild eyes fluttered and stared, the sound from his throat almost like a sob.

Gerrard couldn't seem to move once they were done, couldn't seem to draw his eyes away from the sight. From his own swollen, spattered belly, and from how Olarr was still staring at it too, his black tongue blatantly curling at his lips.

"Someday, human," he rasped, "I shall lick you clean of your sweet seed. Every last drop shall be *mine*."

His voice sounded vicious, dangerous, but Gerrard twitched a shaky nod, flashed him an unsteady little smile. "Yeah," he whispered. "Someday."

It again felt almost like a promise, like a secret vow between them, especially once Gerrard had reluctantly extracted himself and dressed again, and headed for the door. Where he found himself abruptly being dragged into Olarr's tight, crushing embrace, as Olarr drew in a deep, shaky inhale against his neck.

"Stay safe, Aulis," he said, his voice a croak. "Be prudent, and cunning, and keep close watch around you, ach?"

Gerrard silently nodded against Olarr's shoulder, his hand spreading against his chest. "You too, Olarr," he breathed. "Especially with Slagvor. And with whatever you eventually decide to do about him, yeah? Whatever cunning vengeance you come up with?"

He wasn't quite sure what had made him bring that up again, or what made him draw away, searching Olarr's eyes. Where Olarr's eyes were almost... guarded, even as he nodded, and gave Gerrard a wavering smile. "Ach," he said thickly. "And I shall come to you again soon. Keep watch for me, and my sticks?"

They'd continued to communicate through sticks, of all things, and Gerrard managed a smile back as he nodded, and drew away. Trying to keep his expression steady, his steps light and easy, as he jogged up the stairs, and out into the cool night air of the forest.

But once he was deep in the woods again, he felt his steps slowing, his shoulders sagging beneath his uniform. That had been good... right? It had been so damned good, on all counts. And even if he was now staring down multiple days without Olarr, there was no reason for the strange little catch in his chest, the nagging whisper of something almost like unease. Like... foreboding.

But no. No. He'd already decided this. Committed to this. He wanted this, Olarr wanted this, they were in this together. Olarr cared about him, Olarr was helping him, Olarr had kept his word, again and again...

Gerrard repeated that certainty to himself as he crept back into the camp again, heading toward the med tent—but then he hesitated, and turned toward his own tent instead. He hadn't slept in it for weeks, and after a quick sweeping out, he sank down to his mat with a heavy sigh. One hand still gripping the jar of mushroom powder, the other slipping up under his tunic, spreading wide against his swollen, rounded belly. While his blinking eyes caught on the full moon, just visible through the flap in his tent.

He could do this. He could make this work. He could wield his cunning, and gain all that he wished. He *would*.

But even so, he couldn't seem to stop thinking about that urgency in Olarr's voice, that distinct guardedness in his eyes. And surely it hadn't meant anything, it hadn't, he could trust Olarr, he could...

But no matter how he tried, holding his bleary eyes to the light of the watching moon, sleep still didn't come for a long, long time.

21

The mushroom powder was an unqualified success.

Over the next few days after seeing Olarr, Gerrard had kept a close eye on Livermore, waiting for an opportunity to put the powder to the test. And his chance had finally come early one evening, when Livermore had first called for his supper in his tent, and then abandoned it in favour of berating his groom over his horse.

It had given Gerrard more than enough time to hop into Livermore's empty tent, on a pretense of seeking him out for a question. And it had only taken a moment to pull out the powder, dose Livermore's still-steaming soup, and hop away again.

Livermore's shouts began soon after nightfall, and they were full of wild, fantastical claims about his tent melting, and boiling into giant purple bubbles. A situation that soon had multiple intrigued soldiers standing and listening outside the tent, while Gerrard desperately fought to be on his best lieutenant behaviour, and called for Bassey to be fetched at once.

Bassey's verdict, loudly pronounced, was that Livermore was suffering from an acute but likely harmless fever, and only needed a good night's rest. And when Bassey gave Gerrard a too-piercing glance on the way out of the tent, Gerrard only smiled innocently back toward him, and went about his business.

He dosed Livermore twice more over the next few days—once in his breakfast tea, and again in his supper. Both times leading to highly satisfactory results, the first with Livermore seeing green fire in his tent, and the second—far more entertaining—with him being fully convinced that his bed was being swarmed by a vicious gaggle of wild, honking geese.

"I'm being attacked!" he hollered, his panicked voice ringing throughout the outpost. "Get them away! *Get them away!*"

Gerrard almost felt sympathy at that one, but any fellow feeling he might have possessed toward Livermore was rapidly banished by the way Livermore subsequently raged at him, and then at Bassey, and then threatened to have Gerrard flog anyone unfortunate enough to walk by his tent. Leaving the entire camp irritable and on edge, Gerrard very much included, and he spent the rest of the evening smiling and speaking kindly to all his wary-eyed men, before skulking into the armoury in the dark, digging out any remaining whips or canes, and hurling them all down the latrine.

He was far too late getting into his tent, but once again, sleep wouldn't seem to come. And instead, Gerrard found himself again lying there, gripping the jar of mushroom powder, and thinking, too strongly, of Olarr. Of how much he wanted to see Olarr, to talk to him, to tell him the success of his powder, and the whole ludicrous tale of the night's events. To make him laugh, to see the warmth in his eyes. And then, strongest of all, to hear his comfort and commiseration and approval. His reassurance.

Good, warrior, Olarr would surely say. *This was good work. This fool man is no match for your cunning, ach?*

And then he would touch Gerrard with his big hands, and draw him close, and fill him with warmth and hunger and pleasure. While Gerrard did the same to him in return, told him everything he'd ever wanted to hear, until they were both wild with it, writhing and shouting in each other's arms...

Gerrard ended up bringing himself off in the darkness—not for the first time that week—and then he stuffed the jar of powder into the hole he'd dug under his mat, and shoved over to sleep. Olarr would come soon. He had to come soon. It had already been a week, so maybe tomorrow, surely tomorrow...

But Olarr... didn't come. Not that day, or the next, or the next. And though Gerrard fought not to keep counting the days—ten, eleven, twelve—they seemed to drag slower and slower, no matter how he tried to fill them. Focusing on drilling with his men, surveying the ongoing repairs to the camp, reviewing the supply situation, sending out more men hunting. And then just running himself ragged with his own training, sparring and jogging and working, challenging his men to as many matches as they'd accept, all while fighting not to be bitter at how damned disappointing they were.

"Gods curse it, Lieutenant," gasped Corporal Ainley, one of Gerrard's best single-combat fighters, once Gerrard had again pinned him to the ground, his forearm thrust against his neck. "How did you get so much faster? What the hell have you been doing?"

Gerrard had worked to keep the easy smile on his face as he'd gripped Ainley's hand, yanking him up to his feet. "Just sparring with good strong fighters like you, brother," he'd said, as lightly as he could, as he'd clapped Ainley on the back. "Thanks for the match, yeah?"

Ainley had half-laughed and limped away, leaving Gerrard staring discontentedly after him, rubbing at his face. Damn, he missed Olarr. Sixteen days. Sixteen fucking *days*.

He pushed himself even harder over the next few days,

setting up an obstacle course outside the palisades to run and climb through, adding more and more challenges until he was the only one of his men left who could complete it. And then he joined in some of the game hunting, too, though it was tedious going, what with him constantly glancing around the forest, and jumping at movements and shadows, in pathetic hopes that Olarr might suddenly appear. And finally, after three days of increasing frustration, he gave up on the hunting altogether, in favour of staying up late into the night, so he could run his obstacle course alone until he was exhausted, without any of his men watching, or wondering at it.

Throughout it all, Gerrard had also kept being on his best lieutenant behaviour with Livermore, while regularly dosing him every few days with more mushroom powder. And while Livermore never made any mention of his new nighttime visions, he did roundly and repeatedly complain about how he hadn't yet received a reply from Duke Warmisham to his last letter, and was still awaiting a reversal of Head Command's previous irresponsible orders.

It at least meant they'd continued to stay put in the outpost, with no new orc attacks in sight—though by the twenty-third day without Olarr, Gerrard would have welcomed a scouting mission, a skirmish, even a full pitched battle. Anything to take his mind off Olarr, and the steadily rising foreboding that kept clouding his thoughts. Maybe Olarr had been caught by Slagvor. Maybe he'd been punished. Maybe he'd been hurt, tortured, *killed*.

Or maybe—maybe Olarr had just changed his mind. Maybe he'd come to his senses, and realized that this was too damned dangerous. Maybe he'd found someone else who called to him, another orc like Harja, perhaps. An orc he didn't need to travel for days to see, an orc he didn't need to hide from the Bautul kin he cared for so much. The Bautul kin he was putting at very real risk, by carrying on seeing Gerrard like this.

And it was that thought, that realization, that kept Gerrard lying awake long after dark that night, tossing and turning on his mat, frowning up at nothing in the pitch-blackness of his tent. Olarr cared for his Bautul kin more than anything else. And didn't that mean that at some point, he would need to make a choice? He would need to choose between Gerrard and the Bautul. And despite that discussion they'd had about someday, about making a life together, even adopting a son... would Olarr really choose that, over everything else he cared about? Would he?

Gerrard grimaced and rubbed at his eyes in the darkness, fought to steady his too-rapid breaths. He'd known this wouldn't last forever. He'd known. He was an adult, a lieutenant, it was wartime, he knew how these things went. So why the hell was he being such a damned mess over it, why was he nearly weeping in the darkness, what was—

What was—that. A sound. A movement. A rustle, quiet and close, just outside his tent.

Gerrard tensed all over, his eyes searching in the pitch-blackness, as his hand groped sideways for his sword. The noise was too quiet to be one of his men—they knew to call out if they needed something—and too heavy to be a wandering rodent or raccoon. And it was also far, far too purposeful, pausing just outside his tent door, drawing the flap back—

Gerrard was on his knees in an instant, whipping his sword up toward the looming shadow in his door—but before it could make impact, something grasped his wrists. Something big and warm and powerful, and... familiar.

Olarr.

22

Olarr was here. Inside the camp. Inside the palisades. Inside Gerrard's *tent*.

"The hell, captain!" Gerrard hissed, over his thundering heartbeat. "What the fuck are you *doing*?!"

His voice came out sounding both furious and relieved—Olarr was here, he'd come back, he was *alive*—but just as quickly there was alarm, surging cold and sickening through Gerrard's guts. Why was Olarr here. Maybe Slagvor had found out after all, maybe an attack was on the way, maybe they needed to run for their lives—

"Ach, naught to fear, warrior," came Olarr's voice, hot and rasping in Gerrard's ear. "I only came here earlier than I planned, and only longed—to see you. Should you—yet wish."

Oh. Oh. Gerrard felt his rigid shoulders sagging, his shaky breath abruptly exhaling. Olarr just—wanted to see him. Still wanted to see him. Still here, still alive, his big warm hands now gently prying the sword from Gerrard's stiff fingers, and setting it aside.

Gerrard's relief was still clanging against the uncertainty, or even anger—this was still a huge fucking risk, Olarr hated risk, he'd stayed away for more than three damned *weeks*—but even so, Gerrard was still leaning closer into Olarr's warm kneeling bulk, inhaling the familiar richness of his scent. "What the hell happened to prudence?" he breathed into the darkness, into the sweaty, sweet-scented curve of Olarr's neck. "And not being reckless?"

His traitorous mouth had already begun kissing at Olarr's skin, just needing to taste him, to know he was really here— and he could feel Olarr's answering full-body shudder, as sharp teeth scraped against his throat. "*You* happened, warrior," Olarr whispered, almost a groan. "Ach, I have missed you. It has been too long."

Gerrard refrained from pointing out that it had been Olarr who had stayed away all that time, and squeezed his eyes shut as his hands clutched against Olarr's waist, yanked him closer. His teeth now nipping against Olarr's neck, too, while his hips ground up against Olarr's front. Against where that familiar ridge was already jutting back toward him beneath the rough fabric, meeting Gerrard, missing him, wanting him, three *weeks*—

Gerrard hissed when Olarr gripped him tighter, spun him around—but he wasn't resisting, not in the slightest. Not even as Olarr roughly shoved him down onto his belly, and yanked off the undershirt he'd been wearing to sleep. And then—oh, hell—that slick, familiar cock was already there, seeking and nuzzling, burrowing its way down between Gerrard's taut arse-cheeks. Wanting in, and wanting in *now*.

Gerrard arched and gasped in the darkness, his frustration and his fear narrowing, funnelling fast and fierce into this. Into the truth of a huge, invading orc's body shoving him open, gouging into him with pain and pleasure, plunging itself further and further with every gasping breath. While Gerrard just kept taking it, needing it, needing to feel Olarr here, safe, alive, deeper, *more*. Until they were fully locked together, Gerrard's body clamped tight around Olarr's base, his strained breaths heaving into the mat beneath him.

"Ach," Olarr groaned, hot and breathless into Gerrard's ear, before he slowly drew out again, all the way, the sound slick and obscene—and then he snapped back in. The sensation so sharp, so stunning, that an audible moan escaped from Gerrard's throat, echoing into the darkness around them.

He winced, shaking his head, but Olarr's big hand had already clapped over his mouth, a very low growl rumbling into his ear. "Silence, human," he hissed. "You shall behave, whilst your captain ploughs you."

Gerrard's disbelief flared alongside his wheeling craving— this damned presumptuous prick, how dare he say that... and how dare it sound so damned *good*. And he even had to bite back another moan, inhaling and exhaling hard against Olarr's still-clamped hand, while Olarr ground hard and deep inside.

"Ach, thus," Olarr breathed, even hotter. "You shall stay pliant and quiet, whilst your captain favours you. Whilst you open your tight pretty rump wide, and welcome in his hungry prick."

Fuck. Gerrard gasped and bucked again, and Olarr instantly met it, his strength swelling even fuller inside Gerrard's grip, his hand tightening against his mouth. "Ach, thus, lieutenant," he growled, as his other hand slipped up, curled around Gerrard's *neck*. "You shall be a good, sweet little hole for your Bautul captain. You shall open wide for me, and seek with all your strength to milk me. And then"—his breath hitched—"you shall drink all my good orc-seed deep within you. Swallow up every last drop, and make yourself fat upon me. Make yourself *reek* of me."

The hell. Olarr had never gone off on Gerrard like this before, not even back in their earliest meetings—and why wasn't Gerrard protesting it, shoving back at it, at being used and commanded by an orc in his own camp, in his own damned tent. Maybe because of the darkness, covering them both like a thick heavy cloak—or maybe because of Olarr himself, still here, pressing Gerrard so powerfully into the mat, buried hilt-deep inside him.

Or maybe... maybe it was the blatantly obvious risk Olarr was taking in this. The very real possibility of being caught at any moment... but doing it anyway. Olarr was abandoning all his vaunted prudence and control, ignoring the multiple possible dangers, so he could sneak into his enemy's camp, and have his filthy way with a human.

The certainty of that thought only seemed to wrench Gerrard's craving higher, roaring in his breath and his ears and his groin. So strong he was rapidly nodding, his tongue even twisting out to kiss against Olarr's still-pressing palm against his mouth, his arse grinding up toward Olarr, needing more, more...

"Good, human," Olarr breathed, as his hips kept pumping, plunging deep again and again. "You take my deep ploughing all the way up your rump. You let me rut you, bind you, mark you, stretch you, *ruin* you, for all but *me*. And"—he dragged in a hoarse breath—"you shall feel me, and praise me, as my strong Bautul prick drives your own load out of you, and fills you instead with *mine*—"

And oh, damn, yes, Gerrard was silently begging, breaking, falling into the abyss, as his own cock finally spasmed, and spewed out onto his mat. His gasps groaning into Olarr's palm, his body quaking all over, while Olarr choked behind him, his hands clamping tighter—and then he was pouring out, too. His strength inside Gerrard jerking up again and again, spraying him full of hot fresh orc-seed, as his hips thrust deeper and deeper in, and oh it was good, so, so good—

"Lieutenant?" came a voice, *Cosgrove's* voice, just outside the tent. "You all right in there?"

Shit. *Shit.* Gerrard's heart blared in his chest, his body shot to sudden stillness, and behind him, he could feel Olarr freezing all over, too. Except for that swollen, spasming strength, still stabbed deep inside Gerrard's arse, still spurting out its seed into him, even now.

"Yeah, fine!" Gerrard's raspy voice somehow called back, once he'd shoved Olarr's hand away from his mouth. "Just was—having a fucked-up dream. Must be"—he drew in a shaky breath, racked his brain, please—"must be going around here these days, right?"

He was referring to Livermore's ongoing troubles, of course, and he was deeply relieved to hear Cosgrove's laugh, still far too close. Even as his own heartbeat kept thundering, as Olarr's rhythmic pulses inside him finally began to slow, his big body otherwise held stock-still over Gerrard, not breathing...

"Must be," Cosgrove's cheerful voice replied. "Hope you didn't get the geese, at least?"

Gerrard huffed a strangled laugh, and twitched a shake of his head Cosgrove couldn't see. "No geese, thank fuck," he called back. "Thanks for checking in, though, Corporal."

Cosgrove made a vague sound of assent, and Gerrard could finally hear him moving away again, back in the direction of his own tent. Which was indeed appallingly close to Gerrard's, and they'd been so damned stupid to risk this—so why was Gerrard almost *laughing* as he sagged heavily into the mat again, shaking his head against it.

"Some cunning you are, captain," he whispered, into the silence. "Aren't you supposed to be able to smell people that close?"

He could almost feel Olarr blanching, as sharp claws spasmed against his shoulder. "Ach," Olarr replied, his choked voice very quiet. "I ought to have scented this. But my breath was full of you, enough to drown out all else, and now I have put you in danger, and—"

Gerrard elbowed back up at him, breaking off his words mid-sentence. "Worth it," he whispered back. "No regrets, captain."

Olarr's breaths sounded ragged against Gerrard's neck, and now those were kisses, pressing softly down his shoulder. "You are sure, Aulis?" Olarr replied, so quiet. "Even with... how I... took you? How I... spoke to you? I ought not have..."

His voice trailed off, his hard swallow audible in Gerrard's ear, and it distantly occurred to Gerrard that Olarr's prudence—his cunning—had clearly failed him in this, too. That these weren't the kinds of things he'd ever meant to say or do to Gerrard. The kinds of things a proud human lieutenant might be reasonably expected to tolerate, from the enemy orc in his bed.

But even as Gerrard considered that, Olarr's heated words seemed to echo through his thoughts, sending something stirring again in his sticky groin. *You shall open wide for me. Make yourself reek of me. Let me rut you, bind you, mark you, stretch you, ruin you, for all but me...*

"I... don't mind," Gerrard heard himself say, and somehow, somehow, he meant it. "I'd really rather you didn't try to be... *prudent*, with me. Would rather you just... be honest."

He didn't miss the curious little shudder up Olarr's body over him, inside him, as his kisses seemed to press harder, almost desperate. But he didn't speak, and Gerrard took another breath, drew up the courage to just damn well say it...

"And not just in bed," he continued, very quiet. "But with the rest of it, too. Shit like—how long you'll be gone, this time."

The words seemed to hang there between them, bare and accusatory—and maybe horribly unfair, because it was Olarr doing all this travelling, wasn't it? Olarr putting himself at immediate risk of death, by having Gerrard's scent anywhere near him, and...

"Forgive me, Aulis," came Olarr's low, cracking voice. "I did not expect—ach. A moon or so ago, we killed a powerful orc—Kaugir's Left Hand, Skald. And though we have so far kept this secret safe, since then, Slagvor has grown... wary. Angry. Mistrustful. It has not been easy, to get away."

Oh. Gerrard's breath seemed stuck in his throat, because—wait. A moon or so ago was—before they'd met, last time. Before Gerrard had asked Olarr how things were going with Slagvor. And when he'd asked what Olarr was doing with Slagvor, Olarr had... dodged the question. Said some trite, secretive rubbish about being strong for his kin. And nothing, *nothing*, about what had clearly been his real plans. About targeting Slagvor's allies. About *assassinations*.

No. Instead, Olarr had told Gerrard something... prudent.

"So you didn't tell me any of this last time because... why?" Gerrard said, struggling to keep his voice low. "You didn't trust me, maybe? Thought I'd leak it somehow? Or maybe you didn't think I deserved to know?"

There was a horrible instant's silence, punctuated by the uncomfortable sensation of Olarr's now-soft heft fully retreating from Gerrard's body, bubbling out a surge of hot liquid behind it. "Ach, no, Aulis," Olarr replied, choked in Gerrard's ear. "Ach, this was only—selfish. So much of my life is tangled in this war, in this treason, this threat of pain and death from Slagvor. And when I am with you—*ach*. You are so full of life, of joy, of peace, and I am loath to... taint this. To allow Slagvor anywhere *near* this, even in thought or memory."

His voice was strained, earnest, and Gerrard fought down the strange, unsettling urge to laugh. Damn it, he wasn't full of life, or joy, or peace. He'd wanted to die, when they'd started this. And he'd spent the last three weeks in a towering dismal funk, over an orc. The orc whose big body was now squeezing

Gerrard all over, clamping him tightly to the mat, as if he was at grave risk of running off at any moment.

"I am sorry," Olarr said again, even quieter. "I missed you so, warrior. I thought of you so oft it ached. I grieved every endless day that passed, without you."

The fervency was almost visceral in his voice, in his taut heavy body. And though Gerrard knew he should keep arguing, pushing this—Olarr had still *lied* to him—he instead found his body sinking heavier into the mat, into the deep, undeniable relief of Olarr's crushing embrace.

Olarr had still come back. He'd apologized. He'd abandoned his prudence—was still abandoning his prudence—for this. For Gerrard. Choosing Gerrard over his Bautul kin, over Slagvor and the war, over everything else.

Olarr still—*cared*. Right?

"Missed you too, captain," Gerrard finally heard himself say, and he even felt his head lifting up, gently bumping against Olarr's. "And oh, do I have some tales to tell you, too."

Olarr's relief shivered through them both, his body's tension softening into a low chuckle, close in Gerrard's ear. "Ach?" he asked, warm, eager. "Mayhap we can meet again underground tomorrow, then, and you can tell me all of this? And I shall tell you"—a slow exhale—"all else you wish to know of Slagvor, also."

Gerrard instantly nodded, the relief settling even closer, deeper. And it felt easy, suddenly, so easy, so right, to twist his head up, to smile and kiss Olarr goodbye. And then to kiss him again, and again, and softly order him not to get caught on the way out, for the love of his goddess.

To his credit, Olarr seemed to escape the camp in passable silence, leaving Gerrard naked and sticky all over, and still smiling stupidly into the darkness. And firmly shoving down that distant nagging whisper—Olarr had *lied*—as he slipped off into sleep. Into a night of heated, hungry, satisfied dreams, of big powerful bodies pressing him down, whispering filthy forbidden orders in the dark.

Gerrard awoke early the next morning, and after a thorough bath in the creek, he tore through the day's list of tasks as quickly as he could. Drilling his soldiers, evaluating the newly repaired palisades, reviewing the much-improved state of the supply-wagon. And even managing to slip another few spoonfuls of mushroom powder into a fresh tin of tea while he was there, because Livermore was too damned greedy to share the tea with anyone else. And finally, after a quick word to both Cosgrove and Bassey—earning Bassey's now-typical, too-knowing look—Gerrard swiftly escaped the camp, slipping through the trees, making his way to Olarr's hidden underground room.

Olarr was ready and waiting by the trapdoor, his eyes lighting up as he dragged Gerrard roughly into his arms. And then he shyly tugged Gerrard into the larger room, to where the delicious smell of fresh cooked venison wafted through the air, and—Gerrard's brows rose—a few new wooden practice weapons were propped neatly along the wall. A larger sword, a halberd, even a massive *axe*.

"Mayhap first we eat, and speak?" Olarr asked now, that eager warmth still shimmering in his eyes. "And then a rematch?"

Gerrard readily agreed, and soon they were sitting across from each other on the fur, digging into the tender, succulent venison and greens Olarr had cooked. "These are delicious, captain," Gerrard told him, and he meant it. "Your cooking gets better every time, yeah?"

Olarr flushed and waved it away, but his smile was pleased, and he was eagerly eating, too. "Ach, it is naught," he said. "Now tell me all, Aulis. All you have done, this past moon."

So Gerrard willingly obliged, leaving out the bits about the loneliness and misery, and instead focusing on his work with his men, his improvements to the outpost, even his training, and his obstacle course. And finally, he launched into the full tale of Livermore's mushroom-induced visions, from the bubbles to the fire to the honking geese. And he was thoroughly gratified by Olarr's deep, helpless guffaws of laughter, his big hand repeatedly slapping his thigh.

"Ach, my clever warrior," he said between chuckles, wiping at his leaking eyes. "This is even better than I could have dreamt. And I have been pondering all day what you meant last eve about the geese! I shall be sure to bring you more powder, next time."

Gerrard grinned back, the warmth fizzing in his own chest—a sensation that swelled even higher when Olarr then began telling him, without prompting, how he'd spent the last few weeks, too. How he'd conspired with Grimarr and a handful of other orcs to support the secret assassination of this Skald orc, who was apparently a bastard just as vile as Slagvor. And though they'd successfully covered it up as a natural death, in a feat which had taken many months of planning, Slagvor had still rapidly descended into a furious state of suspicion and paranoia. Punishing and maiming his own orcs without cause, refusing to eat food he hadn't hunted himself, and demanding that a constant rotation of his strongest warriors be within reach at all times, Olarr among them.

"I ken he yet wishes to keep a close watch upon me, for he has not forgotten Harja," Olarr said, his voice gone quiet and grim. "I was also the only Bautul to witness Skald's death, and this has not helped, either. Slagvor would not have allowed me to leave at all, had Grimarr not claimed he needed me for a mission."

Wait. Gerrard sat up straighter, his eyes narrowing on Olarr's shadowed face. "Are you saying—you mean this Grimarr is *covering* for you right now?" he demanded, rather shrill. "Does that mean—does he know about me? About... us?"

Olarr grimaced, but then jerked a reluctant-looking nod, his eyes now dropped to the fur between them. "Ach, he knows," he said heavily. "I did not... offer this to him, or wish for him to know. But he is a clever orc, who keeps clever orcs around him, and I could no longer hide this truth from them. And I helped them against Skald, so..."

His voice trailed off, his eyes still fixed to the basket, and Gerrard's heartbeat lurched in his chest, his eyes intently searching Olarr's face. So the orcs... knew. Some of the orcs knew. And he'd known that was a risk, of course it was a risk, and was this going to lead to blackmail, or exposure, or him being compromised, all his own plans exposed and doomed...

And worst of all, Olarr had promised him that no other orcs would know. He'd sworn it. Hadn't he?

"Grimarr would not betray us to Slagvor," Olarr said, low and urgent, as he reached for Gerrard's hand, clasped it tightly in his fingers. "He knows he owes me a debt, and even without this, I know too many of his own deepest secrets. He would never wish to risk me proclaiming the truth of Skald's death to all our kin, ach? Or the truth of how he plots against his own father? He needs the Bautul for this. He needs *me*. And thus he seeks to help me, as I seek to help him."

Right. Gerrard's heart was still thumping, but he tried for a nod, his body sagging a little on the fur. Because it wasn't like he had a choice in the matter at this point, did he? And if Olarr, with all his prudence and his cunning, trusted this Grimarr that much, well—then surely Gerrard could try, too. Especially since by telling him this, Olarr was giving him all these secrets, too, and the power that came with them. Olarr was... trusting him. Being honest with him.

"So what if Slagvor does find out about us?" Gerrard finally asked, his voice thin. "What happens then?"

Olarr's jaw tightened, but his eyes were still on Gerrard's, glinting with dark, intent determination. "Then I run for you, and do my utmost to keep Slagvor from finding you," he said flatly. "And if Slagvor kills me first, or wrests any truth of you from me, Grimarr has sworn to send word to you at all speed, so you might choose what best to do next, and how to keep yourself *safe*."

Oh. So was Olarr really saying... he would die for this. For Gerrard. To the point where he'd made *plans* around it. He'd gained a debt from Grimarr, and used that debt to his advantage. To Gerrard's advantage.

"So might you next wish... for a rematch, then, warrior?" Olarr asked into the silence, with a smile that didn't quite reach his eyes. "Give me some good training with my axe?"

His gaze had flicked to the wooden axe still sitting innocuously against the wall, and at the sight of it, more comprehension flared through Gerrard's thoughts. So maybe they weren't doing this just for fun anymore, fooling around with sticks and swords. Olarr needed to be ready. Ready to face down Slagvor, and fight to the death.

Gerrard abruptly nodded, and attempted to smile back as he lurched to his feet. "Hell, yes," he replied, as smoothly as he could. "I hope you're prepared for a pounding, captain."

Olarr's grin back was instant, relieved—but that might have been a twinge of sadness in his eyes as he rose up too, and swung the huge wooden axe onto his shoulder. The sight of it doing strange, twisting things in Gerrard's belly, calling up vivid memories of the last time Olarr had wielded an axe against him—but he swallowed hard, and attempted another smile as he snapped his own sword up into his hand.

But despite Gerrard's best attempts to keep things light, the match still seemed heavier, harder than before. Both of them truly fighting for it, with all their strength and stamina, until Gerrard was bruised and aching all over, and Olarr's chest was criss-crossed with fresh bloody cuts from Gerrard's sword. And afterwards their lovemaking felt just as desperate, too, Gerrard showering Olarr with absurd earnest praises as he rode him, as Olarr gasped and begged beneath him, his blinking eyes oddly bright.

It turned out that Olarr had to leave again that night, a revelation that again sent Gerrard's belly plunging—but Olarr kissed him again and again, and vowed that going forward, if he was waylaid any longer than a fortnight, he would find a way to send word.

"And to help this, Aulis," he murmured, thick into Gerrard's neck, "I should like to... speak to my closest kin-brothers of you. The ones I trust most, who share my aims against Slagvor. I ken this brings us yet more risk, but"—his breath exhaled harsh against Gerrard's skin—"it shall bring more help, also. Not only in helping me slip away to see you, and send word to you, but in helping me hide this. In keeping you *safe*."

The foreboding was already rising again in Gerrard's thoughts—the more people who knew a secret, the less likely it was to stay a secret, right? Especially when Olarr's friends weren't at all likely to approve of him having a secret human lover to begin with? And what if Slagvor decided to punish or torture Olarr's friends, wring the information from them, and...

"My brothers shall not easily betray me, even under duress," Olarr said now, almost as if he'd followed Gerrard's thoughts. "Even if they do not agree with me upon you. They trust me, as I trust them. I swear this to you, before the goddess."

Gerrard's stomach was still twisting in his gut, his breaths too short and shallow. But this was clearly important to Olarr, it was clearly something he'd thought about at length, something he was being prudent and cunning about. And maybe—maybe it meant something, too, that Olarr wanted his most trusted brothers to know about this. That Gerrard was that important to him. That... he cared.

"Yeah, all right," Gerrard finally replied, muffled, into Olarr's shoulder. "If you really think it's best."

Olarr yanked back to grin at him, his eyes bright with relief—and then he leaned in again, kissed him again, again, again. "I thank you, my brave warrior," he murmured. "And I shall see you again soon. As soon as I am able. Ach?"

Gerrard nodded, kissed him back, even managed a grin as he left, and a cheerful squeeze at Olarr's arse. Olarr cared. Olarr was coming back. Olarr wanted this enough to tell his friends. Olarr was ready to die for this.

The renewed certainty of that did make the next few days easier, somehow, and Gerrard kept his focus on his men, on his own training, and his own goals. And especially on Livermore, who had now gotten into the fresh tin of tea, and had rapidly added faeries, giants, and swarms of flying orange beetles to his list of unwanted visions. A situation that Bassey had continued attributing to a stubborn infection—perhaps from insect bites—while also giving Gerrard amused, exasperated glances every time he walked past him out of the tent.

Together with Cosgrove, Gerrard had also continued to keep a close watch for Livermore's letters, and the day after the beetle incident, he finally intercepted the latest missive from Duke Warmisham himself, tersely requesting a complete budget update and campaign report. Which Gerrard promptly returned with another highly insubordinate letter of his own, this time quoting a few of Livermore's own favourite lines about his frustrations with this mission, and his inability to complete Warmisham's request, due to his ongoing compromised health.

To make matters even more promising, Olarr returned the very next day, alerting Gerrard with the usual stick outside his tent. And after Gerrard had joined him for an intensive round of fighting and fucking—with Olarr just squeezing out the victory, thanks to that wooden axe—Gerrard again regaled him with the tales of all his recent successes. While Olarr grinned and chortled and yanked him close, and then—as promised—handed over a brand-new jar of mushroom powder.

"Thanks, captain," Gerrard said, tucking the jar into his pile of nearby clothes. "And how... how did things go with you, this week? Did you end up telling your brothers about us?"

He'd tried to keep his voice light, but Olarr's eyes had gone suddenly wary, his sharp tooth biting his lip. "Ach," he said. "And I have brought... one I should wish you to meet."

Wait. He'd brought one of his brothers here? *Now*? But Gerrard was already jerking a nod, and he quickly dressed again, and followed Olarr up through the trapdoor. Out into the early evening twilight, where—there. Standing tall and armed and silent beneath a nearby tree, was indeed... another *orc.*

Gerrard hadn't set eyes on another orc since they'd begun all this, and he couldn't seem to make himself stop staring, comparing the differences between them. He'd perhaps begun to see Olarr as the default orc, the one that defined them all—but this new orc was noticeably leaner, his tightly coiled black hair neatly tied back, his skin a deep shade of rich pearly grey. And his black eyes on Gerrard looked just as wary as Gerrard felt, his full mouth pressed thin, his clawed hand clutching at the curved sword on his hip.

"Warrior, this is my Bautul brother Kalfr," Olarr said, with a genuine-seeming smile toward this Kalfr, as his hand stroked reassuringly up and down Gerrard's back. "I wished you both to meet, for Kalfr is likely to be the one to come to you if ever I am—delayed. And Kalfr, I have spoken to you of my—of Aulis. Aulis Gerrard."

This Kalfr's clawed hand hadn't moved from his sword-hilt, but he nodded and inclined his head toward Gerrard, his other hand briefly closing over his heart. "I have heard many praises of you, human," he said, in a low, accented voice. "It is an honour to meet Olarr's mate."

Olarr's mate. Wait, what the hell was a *mate*? And not only that, but Olarr had... spoken of Gerrard to this Kalfr? Praised him? Repeatedly?

It took Gerrard an instant too long to collect himself, but he kept his gaze on Kalfr, and even managed a nod and a smile back. "Good to meet you, too," he said, as easily as he could. "Olarr often speaks of his kin, and what brilliant fighters you are. I could never hope to measure up, yeah?"

There was an unmistakable flare of surprise—and then warmth—in this Kalfr's eyes, his hand's grip on his sword slightly relaxing. "Ach, if Olarr's tales are truth, I ken mayhap you could," he replied, with a shrug. "He says you are the best human warrior he has ever seen, and that you hold no fear of even his axe."

Gerrard huffed a wry laugh, a roll of his eyes toward Olarr. "Sure, because this stubborn Bautul never actually hits me," he said lightly. "I'd probably be pissing my trousers if he ever decided to really try."

Olarr's answering grin toward Gerrard was an odd blend of affection and relief, and maybe even appreciation. "Ach, warrior, and I ken you should yet kick off these trousers, and fight me anyway," he replied, husky. "And mayhap defeat me, also."

Gerrard's laugh came easier this time, his elbow jabbing into Olarr's side, while this Kalfr had begun to look curious, almost intrigued. Enough that Gerrard—perhaps foolishly— asked if Kalfr might like to come down and watch the two of them have a match, and judge for himself.

Kalfr instantly agreed to this, and Olarr was again looking appreciative, even grateful, as he ushered Gerrard back down into the underground room. To where Gerrard again stripped off—just to the waist this time—and then snatched up his sword, and handed Olarr the heavy wooden axe.

It was—different, at first, sparring against Olarr with an audience, because Gerrard perhaps hadn't realized how many little intimacies they'd allowed to grow into this, all their secret little touches and taunts and grins. But Olarr didn't seem to mind Kalfr seeing any of it, and to Gerrard's vague surprise, Kalfr even called out frequent praises and pointers, too. Telling Gerrard to aim for Olarr's left side or his groin, and whistling and cheering whenever Gerrard got in a good hit—and then finally shouting his delighted approval as Gerrard tackled Olarr to the floor, the flat of his blade shoved into his heaving throat.

"Ach, this was good," Kalfr said afterwards, flashing a broad grin toward Olarr's flushed, sweaty face. "Your mate well knows how to wield your weaknesses against you, brother. But mayhap"—his dark eyes flicked toward Gerrard, assessing now—"another opponent shall show us the truth of his skill?"

Wait. Kalfr was proposing that Gerrard—fight *him*? And beside Gerrard, Olarr's expression had gone suddenly, suspiciously blank, his shoulders stiff and square. But he didn't speak, didn't forbid or approve it, and it forcibly occurred to Gerrard that refusing such a request from a Bautul warrior was very possibly some kind of unforgivable social gaffe. But also— Gerrard's mouth pursed as he glanced back at this tall, well-rested orc—he damn well didn't want to lose, either. Didn't want to show himself a weak, imprudent human, before both these watching orcs.

"Yeah, sure, why not," Gerrard finally told Kalfr, who was still coolly eyeing him, awaiting his response. "But look, I'm already winded, and I've never even seen you fight before, so how about"—he half-smiled as he swiped for one of the weapons on the wall, and thrust it out—"you get a stick. And I'll use the wooden sword. Fair?"

Kalfr grinned again and grasped the stick, while Olarr's expression had again gone distinctly relieved, his shoulders sagging. Suggesting, thankfully, that Gerrard had properly assessed the situation, and come up with a reasonable solution. And this time, as Gerrard and Kalfr began circling one another, it was Olarr shouting out the orders, urging Gerrard to dodge and block and attack, to avoid that tackle, to never let a Bautul take the fight to the ground.

It was genuinely helpful, because Kalfr soon proved to be an excellent fighter, too. Faster than Olarr, with noticeably swifter strikes—and he was also far more willing to take risks, to do something unexpected, to pounce on an opening, a weakness. An experience that felt entirely new, impressing upon Gerrard the certain awareness that Olarr had indeed been taking it easy on him, all this damned time.

However, the contrast also made it clear that Olarr was still the more skilled fighter of the two, and that Olarr's typical way of watching and meeting and blocking—of being prudent, perhaps—also worked to his advantage. Allowing him to conserve and focus his energy, to make his attacks strong and clean and devastating. In Gerrard's experience, Olarr's technique only became sloppy when he was fully tired out, while this Kalfr was getting sloppier with every breath, getting impatient, landing a staggering strike across Gerrard's chest, but leaving his own side wide open...

Gerrard saw it, took it, rushed in fast and hard—and yes, *yes*, his wooden sword-tip made impact, gouging sharply into Kalfr's bare, undefended belly. "Got you," Gerrard gasped, between heaving breaths. "Gotta watch what you leave open, yeah? Never go for a hit that's going to break your own guard."

It was the kind of thing he'd say to one of his men, and he belatedly winced, shook his head. But wait, Olarr was already here at his side, his big arm clutching around Gerrard's sweaty waist, as his broad, gleeful grin lit up his face. "Ach, this is what

I always tell him, also," he informed Gerrard. "This was stunning, warrior. You are a true joy to watch."

Gerrard couldn't deny the heat pooling up into his already-flushed cheeks, and his uncertain glance toward Kalfr found him first looking nonplussed, and then grudgingly, reluctantly amused. Almost as if he now understood something he hadn't before.

"This was a well-met match, human," he said, with a brief bow of his head. "I should have expected no less, from Olarr's chosen mate."

The *mate* thing again. Gerrard smiled and nodded as politely as he could, while beside him Olarr was nodding too, and then blatantly waving Kalfr away, back toward the door. "Now leave us be, brother," he said firmly. "So I can reward my—warrior, as he deserves."

Kalfr didn't seem at all offended by this request, and even waved an easy goodbye before turning toward the exit. While Olarr had already spun and tackled Gerrard down to the fur, burying his face in Gerrard's sweaty neck.

"Ach, Aulis," he groaned between kisses, his sharp teeth dragging against Gerrard's skin. "This was so good. You are so good. A Bautul would *never* refuse a challenge for a duel, and not only did you follow this, but you faced it with such cunning and ease. Ach?"

Gerrard certainly wasn't about to argue, especially once Olarr's hands yanked down his trousers, so he could touch and caress him all over. Until Gerrard was trembling and shaking beneath him, opening up wide around him, clinging and clasping to him as they rocked and moaned together. Harder and faster and deeper, until Olarr shouted and poured Gerrard full of him, full of his life and pleasure and approval. His... care.

"So tell me, what's a *mate*?" Gerrard's breathless voice asked after, once they were both lying sprawled and sated on the fur. "An orc way of saying a fuck-buddy?"

He didn't miss the way Olarr's breaths stilled against him, those claws spasming on where they were caressing his rounded belly. "No," he replied, very slowly. "It is an orc way of saying... a... a husband."

Oh. Gerrard's stomach flipped, his heart lurching into his throat, and he jerked up on his elbow to look at Olarr, to search his suddenly guarded eyes. Kalfr had called Gerrard Olarr's mate, and Olarr hadn't argued it, and... a husband? Really? *Really*?!

But Olarr's bottom lip was jutting out, now, his eyes still distant, blank, careful. As if... well. Damn. And Gerrard couldn't seem to look at him anymore, could only seem to sink back down into the crook of Olarr's arm, bury his face into the warm strong safety of his shoulder.

"Well, yeah," he said, mumbled. "Makes sense, I guess. If you really think so."

Olarr's breath exhaled in a sudden, heavy shudder, his arms squeezing Gerrard so tight it hurt. "Ach," he whispered. "Ach, Aulis. I do."

The words seemed to resonate all through Gerrard's form, ringing low and powerful into his belly—because Olarr wanted him that much. He cared that much. Enough to make this... permanent. *Forever*.

And Gerrard wanted it too, he needed it too, with every breath of his being. They would make this work. They would find a way, and achieve their goals, together. They *would*.

It felt both harder and easier to say goodbye this time, with those impossible new words hovering between them. Mate. *Husband*. And Gerrard returned to the outpost with even more determination, more prudence and cunning, than ever before. He would protect his men. He would build his strength, and see

Livermore's defeat. He would get his promotion, and he would use every devious avenue at his disposal to end this damned war, and give soldiers a better life. To give himself that life with Olarr. With... his mate. His... husband. And maybe even, someday, a son.

And as the days turned into weeks, it almost began to seem... possible. The outpost's remaining soldiers looked to Gerrard more and more for guidance and leadership, as Livermore's wild visions continued unabated, and Gerrard continued sending increasingly combative missives off to Warmisham and Head Command. While Olarr kept coming by at least once a week, sometimes with Kalfr in tow—and then, one day, with two new Bautul orcs.

One of the new orcs was a broad, warily smiling hunter named Thorvald, whose raspy voice occasionally broke into coughs when he spoke, while the other was a massive, hideous brute named Silfast. Who made no secret of his furious contempt for Gerrard, blatantly snarling and sneering and flexing his claws—at least, until they spent the entire afternoon sparring together. And though the bastard nearly beheaded Gerrard with Olarr's wooden axe, Gerrard made a creditable recovery—luckily, this Silfast's stamina wasn't much better than Olarr's—and finally Gerrard even managed to squeak out a win, for their last fight of the day.

"I ken you could have chosen worse, brother," Silfast grunted at Olarr, as he stalked toward the door, while an amused, intrigued-looking Thorvald trailed along behind. "He has some promise, mayhap."

Olarr seemed far more delighted by this faint praise than was warranted, and afterwards explained to Gerrard—while kneeling and yanking off his sweaty trousers—that Silfast was among the Bautul's best fighters, and one of the few who could rival Olarr himself in battle.

"His defeat at your hands is a wondrous prize, warrior," Olarr breathed, from where he was still kneeling before

Gerrard's now-bared body. "It is a great, great feat, one of which you should be most proud. One most orcs in our mountain would never *dream* of gaining."

Gerrard flushed and waved it away, but willingly welcomed Olarr's slow, heated kisses against his thighs, and then around his hip, all the way to—he gasped—to his arse. That clever tongue seeking its way toward his crease, and then plunging in hungry and deep and shameless. Setting Gerrard moaning and staggering upon it, until his own bobbing, straining cock sprayed wildly across the room, while Olarr emptied out all over his feet.

"Ach, Aulis," Olarr groaned afterwards, his hands turning Gerrard back around to face him, his head bowing heavy against Gerrard's thigh. "Ach, my warrior. My mate. My own."

Gerrard's breath hitched, his hand finding Olarr's messy head, tilting it up. Holding those beautiful, worshipful eyes for a long, greedy breath, and then bending down, and pressing his lips to Olarr's. Tasting himself on them, and not caring in the slightest, because Olarr should taste like him. Olarr was his. His mate. His *mate*.

Gerrard repeated that still-strange, still-impossible word as he strode back to the camp in the twilight, the warmth still shimmering low in his chest. And for the first time in a long, long time, he let himself think about the other men he'd been close to, the other men who might have once held that place. There had been several, all of them years ago, all of them big powerful fighters like Olarr—but Gerrard had swiftly learned the bitter, lowering lesson that beautiful men like that had many, many options. And that there was little reason for them to become tied down to any one bed-partner, especially given the transient nature of soldiers' lives, and the secrecy—the looming danger—that such liaisons commanded.

The kinder men among them had been honest with Gerrard about their intentions, and thus sent him running toward the unkinder ones. The ones who would hide their other lovers, or their wives back home, and say whatever rubbish they could to get the pretty young soldier begging on his knees. And after far too many endless, sleepless nights, Gerrard had finally understood that none of them could be trusted. That he needed to take what pleasure he could, take as much control as he could—and in it, to try to be truthful, to be one of those kinder men he himself had rejected. And then to not care when it meant nothing. Because it meant nothing.

But—Olarr. Olarr, his enemy, an *orc*, had somehow gained Gerrard's trust. Had proven he could be relied upon. And he'd never once even hinted at walking away from the commitment, despite all the danger and inconvenience and time apart. Despite the very real risk of his cruel commander *killing* him over it.

It was a peculiar, buoyant feeling, bubbling bright and warm in Gerrard's chest, and it was enough, more than enough, to carry him through the next few days. To shove down those occasional nagging whispers, and to keep him focused on his work—and then, early the next evening, on the latest letter from Head Command. Which announced, in frigid tones, that Duke Warmisham himself was personally leading a contingent southward to review the outpost and Livermore's management in its entirety, and to expect their arrival in the very near future.

"This is exactly what we wanted, Lieutenant," Cosgrove whispered to Gerrard late that night, once a raging, hallucinating Livermore had finally shouted himself to sleep. "Isn't it?"

They were outside the palisades—both having ostensibly gone to wash up at the creek—and Gerrard was abruptly, deeply grateful for the clouds covering the moon above them. For how the darkness hid his face, his twisting mouth, his slightly trembling hands.

Because—yes. Yes, this was exactly what they'd wanted, exactly what Gerrard had spent so many weeks planning for.

Duke Warmisham coming to the camp in person was a very pointed omen, even a more promising outcome than he'd expected, and if Gerrard carried the thing off properly, he could not only get rid of Livermore, but take a major step toward that promotion he'd always wanted. Or maybe even gain it outright, and...

And wait, what had been his original grand plan, around that promotion? To get Duke Warmisham alone. And, if needed, to get him... in bed. To use what Gerrard knew—he *knew*—Warmisham had wanted from him, to gain his own goals. His chance to make the decisions, to give the commands, to wield power for himself, and his men. To fight for a better life for soldiers, for their families and children...

"Yeah," Gerrard told Cosgrove, over the rising taste of bile in his throat. "Yeah, exactly what we wanted. We just—need to show Livermore as his usual incompetent self, and let Warmisham see what we're dealing with, what he's been wasting his coin on. And then..."

"Then we get the hell out of this shithole," Cosgrove finished, his voice low and fervent. "Forever. I can finally go home, and see my family again. Thank *fuck*. And"—he drew in a breath—"thank *you*, Lieutenant. It's been absolute hell under Livermore, and we're all with you. All of us. Whatever you need, just give the order."

With that, Cosgrove lurched forward, and hurled his beefy arms tightly around Gerrard's shoulders. A blatant breach of protocol, but Gerrard clapped him on the back anyway, and managed a thin, croaky thank-you. And then, in lieu of anything better to say, he told Cosgrove that he'd keep him informed, and communicate any next steps as quickly as possible.

But once Cosgrove had rushed off, back in the direction of the camp, Gerrard's brain seemed curiously empty of plans, of goals, of even conscious thought. And instead he was just staring, staring at nothing in the darkness, while his heart wailed faster and faster against his ribs.

What... what was he doing? He'd made all these plans, all these vague goals of getting a promotion, going back north to the city. Using his status and his position for all the right reasons.

But now that he was facing it, the very real possibility of gaining it, all he could think of was... Olarr. The city was so much further away from Orc Mountain, well over a week's journey, and how the hell could an orc repeatedly travel through the city—through full-on enemy territory—without being caught and killed? And if Gerrard really did get that promotion, he'd be trapped right there in the middle of it, day in and day out—that, or stationed on a far larger military base somewhere, or leading far larger missions, with far fewer opportunities to sneak away. It would be so much harder, it would be damn near impossible...

Gerrard rubbed at his hot face, at his prickling eyes—and then he froze, sudden and rigid, as a sharp, strange chill swept up his spine. As he strained, sought to listen in the darkness... and heard the sound. A footfall, here in the darkness behind him.

Gerrard whirled around, his heart hammering, his sword already in his hand—and just at that moment, the full moon slipped out of the clouds above, and shone down around them. Revealing—oh. A big familiar figure. With a sharpened curved axe-blade, flashing over its shoulder.

"Olarr?" Gerrard said, blinking his bleary eyes—and yes, yes, it was Olarr. But it wasn't—right, it was off, it was wrong. It was Olarr, but it wasn't, his eyes empty and unblinking, his big body swaying and staggering as he jolted toward Gerrard, his silver skin painted with thick streaks of flat blackness...

"What is it?" Gerrard asked, demanded, as he lurched forward, no, no, no. "What the fuck is it, Olarr!"

But he knew, he knew, even before Olarr opened his mouth. Knew, from the look in his eyes, and from... the blood. The dark dried blood on his hands, spattered across his chest, his face...

"Slagvor has scented you," Olarr gasped. "And he is coming."

<h1 style="text-align:center">23</h1>

Slagvor was coming.

Gerrard's heart skipped a beat—and for a breath, everything... stopped. The world wrenched to sharp, strange stillness all around him, as a cold, empty dread pooled into him, flooded him with rot and darkness.

Slagvor had scented him. Slagvor was coming.

"How?" Gerrard's voice finally asked, from very far away. "And how much time do we have?"

Olarr's breath was still heaving, his eyes squeezed shut, as his bloody hand spasmed against his bloody chest. Against— Gerrard's wide eyes searched it—no, not an injury, not his own blood. But... someone else's. Another orc's, surely. A Bautul.

"And who's taking the fall for you?" Gerrard asked now, sharper than before. "Who's keeping Slagvor away from here right now?"

Olarr's hand spasmed again, his mouth working, and oh, hell, that was actually a tear, streaking from his eye. "Silfast," he rasped. "He was not yet dead when—when I left. He can bear great pain, he has always taken great pride in this, but—"

Fuck. Fuck. Visions of the snide, snarling Silfast were

flooding Gerrard's brain, roiling in his gut. Because no, Silfast hadn't been kind in the slightest, but Olarr had trusted him, and clearly cared for him, and now, now—

"But—*how*?" Gerrard demanded, his voice cracking. "How did Slagvor find out? Did your brothers..."

Did they betray you, he wanted to ask, but couldn't, couldn't—and Olarr shook his head, rubbed the back of his hand on his mouth. "We were—careless," he croaked. "Or—I was. Your scent—a drop of your seed—landed upon my pack, our last night together. But I had borrowed this pack from Silfast, and Slagvor turned first upon him, whilst Kalfr pulled me away. Before"—Olarr's throat convulsed—"Slagvor could link the scents, and find you all over me."

Damn it. Damn it to fucking hell and back, and Gerrard's hands dragged at his face, his throat. "And what—what was Silfast's story," he gulped, and he didn't want to know, he didn't. "Couldn't he just say—fuck, I don't know—the scent was just from a stupid prank by a human, or just some fool getting off in the woods, and not realizing the pack was there? If Silfast left it behind while he was off hunting or something?"

He was grasping, he well knew, clutching at a fantasy world where vile captains didn't immediately jump to the worst conclusions—but Olarr was already shaking his head, his mouth even grimmer than before. "Mayhap," he replied, "had we not just come back from scouting, scenting of... *here*. And one of Slagvor's orcs—one of his most loyal warriors—remembered you from our battles here. Remembered your scent and your face and your rank, because"—his voice cracked—"you are so fair. So beautiful."

Of fucking course. Of course some random awful orc would remember Gerrard's fool face, would link it to a drop of spunk on a fucking borrowed pack, and it would ruin his life. Would ruin Olarr's life. And would no doubt take the life of Olarr's friend, his loyal Bautul brother, one of the orcs he'd most trusted. And Olarr would never forgive himself for that, it would weigh on him forever, just like Harja, and...

"And you couldn't just attack Slagvor?" Gerrard demanded. "Why couldn't you and Kalfr and Thorvald and Silfast jump the bastard, and just fucking kill him?!"

His voice was piercing, almost pleading, and Olarr's own voice made a strange, choked sound, his eyes squeezing shut. "You forget the guards Slagvor keeps around him," he replied thickly. "You forget the dozens of strong Bautul warriors that your whole human band could not defeat, in spite of your higher numbers, and better weapons."

Fuck. Gerrard had begun pacing now, his head shaking, his hand clutched painfully to his sword. "What about challenging Slagvor to a duel, then," he snapped. "The way Harja did. You told me that not even Slagvor would refuse a challenge for a duel, right? No Bautul would?"

Olarr's mouth twisted, and his pained, glimmering eyes opened again, found Gerrard's. "Ach, Slagvor would be bound to meet this call," he croaked. "And mayhap I should have sought this, before I came here. But Slagvor is yet the strongest warrior amongst us, and if I fell to him"—his voice cracked— "he yet knows your scent and your name, Aulis. He knows you welcomed pleasure with an orc. And he—he knows where to find you. How to hunt you. And if I am killed, and then my trusted brothers fall after me, and none of us remain to protect you—"

He broke off again, rubbing his eyes, whipping his head back and forth. "Slagvor shall not grant you an easy death, Aulis," he said, his voice a whisper. "If he even grants you death at all. There are other ways he should wish to... use you. To *destroy* you."

The horror cut through Gerrard's ribs like a blade, the multiple sickening visions of it roiling in his gut, and he had to choke back the vomit lurching into his throat. Fuck, they'd been so stupid. So, so stupid to risk this, for either of them, for the people they cared about. They should have walked away long ago, they should never have kept going. Meeting kin-brothers, having picnics and sparring-matches, fucking all over the damned place, pretending they were *mates*. Pretending everything was fine, when in truth…

"And you said Slagvor's coming here, now?" Gerrard somehow asked, through the foul taste of bile still in his mouth. "How many Bautul are with him? Your whole band?"

Olarr shook his head, dug his palms into his eyes. "Kaugir called for the band to return home, just before this," he replied, thin. "So it is mayhap a dozen."

A dozen. Only a dozen. And Gerrard was clinging to it, he had to cling to it, please, please. "And how many of those orcs are—on your side," he breathed. "How many would be—against Slagvor. Or could be—convinced."

But Olarr was still shaking his head, damn it, damn it. "Not enough," he rasped. "Kalfr. Thorvald. Gaelfr. Mayhap Egil."

Four. Four orcs, of a dozen. "And you," Gerrard replied, rapid, desperate. "And me. And Silfast. That's seven. Over half."

Olarr barked a bitter, broken laugh, jerked another shake of his head. "Not enough," he said again. "Not against Slagvor, and any orcs yet loyal to him. And Silfast shall not be a help to us now, and mayhap never shall be again. And *you*…"

Olarr's jaw flexed in his cheek, his eyes again squeezing shut, as visible pain spasmed across his face. Pain, and something… guarded. Something…

Something like *guilt*.

And Gerrard had… seen that look before, on Olarr's face. Had seen it again and again and again. And suddenly the awareness was charging, flailing, dragging up that old nagging voice. The voice he'd so often sought to quell these past weeks. The voice he ought to have listened to, long ago…

But Gerrard was... listening, now. Listening, gasping for harsh, ragged breaths, as he blinked up at the night sky, at the round silver light of that full moon. Gazing down upon them, almost like an eye, like something bearing witness, seeing everything they'd tried to hide away...

"Yeah, me," he heard his voice say, distant and cold, just like the silver light of that cruel, all-seeing eye. "Because now it's on me, isn't it? It's on me to go face Slagvor, and try to fight him to the death. Just like Harja. Just like..."

He drew in breath, dropped his gaze, met Olarr's empty eyes. Eyes just as empty as his voice, as the moon, showing only the guilt behind them...

"Just like you wanted, Olarr," he whispered. "Just like you... planned."

24

*J**ust like you planned.*

The words seemed to ring out all around them, loud and final and impossibly powerful. Bringing all Gerrard's darkest, most secret fears to horrible, sickening life, and marching them out into the open, like soldiers doing one last hopeless rally, before charging to their deaths.

And Olarr… didn't try to fight them. Didn't even take out his fucking axe. Just stood there and gazed at Gerrard in the all-seeing moonlight, with such empty, hollow, guilty, *guilty* eyes.

"Yeah, you don't need to bother denying it," Gerrard's voice said, full of useless bravado, cracking with the spreading, sickening grief. "Trained me up real good, didn't you? You found a doomed human soldier, a decent single-combat fighter, seeking out a respectable death—and you thought you could find a better use for me. You thought you could wind me up, and send me marching toward your enemy instead."

The words kept escaping Gerrard's mouth, sounding so damned certain, like part of him had always known this—while another part of him was screaming, raging, wailing and weeping in the corner, and frantically shoving pieces together.

Olarr had wanted to kill Slagvor for years. Olarr wanted vengeance for Harja's death, wanted to finish what Harja had started. Olarr had tried, researched, made multiple attempts against Slagvor, and he'd kept coming up short. He hadn't been able to find a way to do it, without drawing blame onto himself, without risking the brothers he cared about.

Until he'd found Gerrard.

And Olarr hadn't killed Gerrard, in that battle. Olarr hadn't killed Gerrard when he'd hunted him the next day, either. Olarr had been unreasonably generous, irrationally patient, far kinder than any orc—any sensible living being—ought to have been, when facing off against a sworn enemy who'd wanted his death.

And when Olarr had first fucked Gerrard, had that been part of the plot, too? Had that been Olarr scenting what Gerrard had wanted from him, and then—and then bending him over, taking him from behind, so he didn't need to see him, or smell him? So he could grit his teeth and bear it, get it over with as quickly as possible, and do whatever it took to keep the foolish human attached? To keep him coming back?

But no, no, it had always been Olarr coming back, hadn't it? Olarr pushing it, again and again. Olarr so often putting Gerrard on his knees, so he didn't need to see his face. And Olarr helping him plot and plan against Livermore, giving him a silly little project to keep him amused, to give him hope. To keep him constantly training, and fighting, and learning how to defeat a Bautul. Learning how to fight a huge Bautul with an axe. Learning how to fight multiple different Bautul with axes. Learning how to fight Slagvor.

And then, surely—when Olarr had decided Gerrard was ready—he'd have sent Slagvor after him. He'd have set him up, somehow. Maybe he'd have even put out his damned sticks, and when Gerrard arrived at that cozy underground room, it would have been Slagvor waiting there instead.

And if Gerrard had won, Olarr would have had his revenge, without the slightest risk or cost to himself, or his allies. And if he'd lost? Well, then Olarr could move to his next clever plan, maybe his next so-called *mate*, and forget Gerrard had ever existed.

And all that time, Olarr had told Gerrard to be prudent, and cunning. He'd fed him so, so much rubbish. Puffed up his contentment and his pride, let him think he was in control, told him they were mates, *husbands...*

The bile burned higher in Gerrard's throat, and he wiped a shaky hand at his trembling mouth, fought to breathe the too-thin air. "So I bet Harja was your real mate, wasn't he?" he whispered, and why was he saying this, with all the far more crucial things he should be shouting right now. "He was your real husband, right? I bet you did the thing properly with him, too. Didn't just casually bring it up after a fuck, and expect him to just fucking *believe* you?"

And no, no, Olarr hadn't done that. Or had he, he had, he *had*—and before Gerrard could possibly catch it, he buckled to his knees, and vomited onto the earth between them. The taste and the sensation just as agonizing as the vile bitter poison flooding his thoughts, his memories, tainting everything he knew with grief and pain and death.

"I *did* believe you," he whispered, broken, wiping at his mouth with his sleeve. "That was some damned impressive cunning, you prick. I really thought—I thought—"

Another surge of vomit rose, spewed out of his gasping mouth. And once the foulness had finally abated, Gerrard was left gasping and shivering, staring at the rancid, reeking mess he'd made. "I thought you were different," his fool voice choked toward it, all on its own. "I thought—I thought—you *cared.*"

It sounded so weak, so plaintive, so foolishly fucking pathetic, but Gerrard couldn't even lift his head, couldn't stop the water escaping from his eyes. "Would've been kinder," he gulped, "to just kill me from the start, yeah?"

There was a strange rasping croak, grating too loud in his ringing ears—and suddenly—Olarr was here. Olarr was here, kneeling beside Gerrard, his big powerful arms clamping tight around Gerrard's body, his familiar rich scent flooding Gerrard's heaving breaths.

"No, warrior," came his voice, slicing into Gerrard's already-screaming skull. "No. Please. Do not scent thus, do not *think* thus. It was not all—I did not mean—"

But Gerrard wrenched away from him, shoving backwards, scrambling up to his feet. And somehow his sword was in his hand, and he was gripping it like a dying man, and ramming the blade hard and vicious against Olarr's throat.

And Olarr... didn't resist. Didn't fight it. Just stayed there on his knees, staring up at Gerrard with his guilty eyes, while Gerrard's trembling sword-blade dug deeper into the sweaty silver skin of his neck. Deep enough that a trickle of blood was already escaping, streaking down Olarr's heaving chest, but Olarr still wasn't moving. As if he was going to just let Gerrard go ahead and kill him...

But he knew Gerrard wouldn't. Of course he wouldn't. Gerrard was weak, he was a coward, he was guilty of fucking high treason with Olarr, and now all those orcs knew it. His career was over, his plans were over, his goals for going north, helping soldiers and orphans like him—over. Done.

And now—Slagvor was still coming for him. Olarr had sent Slagvor after him. Slagvor, who'd tortured Olarr's real mate to death, was now coming for Gerrard, because of Olarr. Because of this Olarr, who Gerrard had trusted, who he'd touched and kissed and praised and worshipped. *My wise, clever, handsome captain. You look so good. Feel so good. I love fighting you, and fucking you...*

The vomit was again surging in Gerrard's throat, but he

coughed it down, spat out some of the foul taste in his mouth. "So was it fun for you, manipulating me like that?" he choked, prodding his blade harder into Olarr's broken skin. "A nice little reward for all your clever cunning, to have me kneeling and praising you like I did? Being kind to you? *Caring* about you?"

Olarr's eyes briefly closed, and Gerrard barked a hoarse laugh, jabbed the blade even harder. "Real entertaining, I bet," he continued, his voice cracking. "Just as entertaining as fucking me from behind, putting me on my hands and knees for you, so you didn't need to see my face. Secretly laughing at me while I begged for you. Maybe thinking about Harja the whole time, so you could actually stay hard and blow your load with a human?"

Olarr's mouth spasmed, and then opened, as if to speak, but Gerrard barked back down at him, shoved the blade so hard that blood spurted across his knuckles. "Did you think about Harja the whole time?" he demanded. "Or wait, maybe better to think about Slagvor, yeah? Maybe you liked to imagine the day when you'd set me up against him. You'd have locked me in with him somehow, wouldn't you? Hoped we'd end up killing off each other, maybe, or I'd at least give him some decent wounds on my way down. And then you'd have gotten rid of my body afterwards, so my scent wouldn't come back to bite you. That would be the prudent, cunning thing to do, yeah?"

Olarr's mouth spasmed harder, a harsh noise rasping from his mouth, but Gerrard cut it off with another reckless thrust of his sword. "Is that what you thought about, when you fucked me?" his relentless voice pressed on, shouting, lost. "Did that give you comfort, Olarr? Did you like to think about Slagvor breaking me, using me, making me scream and beg for death? Did that make it all worthwhile for you?"

He was feeling sick again, ready to hurl up his guts again, his eyes hazy and stinging, so strong he could scarcely see.

Couldn't see how Olarr was—how he was—shaking, and choking, and—

Weeping. Olarr was... *weeping*. The water streaking freely
from his guilty eyes, as his head jerked back and forth, and
ugly sounds like broken blows heaved out of his throat.

"No, Aulis," he gasped. "Please. Please, do not say such
things. Please let me speak, and tell you the full of it. *Please*."

Gerrard was furiously shaking his head too, his stomach
still wildly churning, but fucking Olarr was still talking, still
weeping, *weeping*. "Ach, I shall not deny to you," he gulped,
"that I... thought of this, at first. Slagvor's cruelty to our kin had
grown deeper and deeper, and I begged the goddess to bring
me help, to guide me to a new way. And then—then came *you*."

Gerrard was not listening to this rubbish, he was not, he
was going to kill Olarr, he was. "You were so beautiful," Olarr's
gasping voice continued, over another wrenching sob in his
throat. "You were as a pure doomed son of the goddess, your
light dying before my eyes. I could see this in your face and
your scent, and I thought—ach. I thought mayhap this was the
goddess' gift, the goddess' last hope. You were the strongest
human warrior I had ever met, and you wished for death—so
ach, I thought mayhap you could gain this against Slagvor. And
if you could not kill him, mayhap you could yet weaken him,
for all our gain. And"—another sob heaved from his throat—
"when you hunted me again, after I spared you, I first
thought—I thought this was a sign. I was *sure* of this."

The water was still streaking from his eyes, almost making
it seem like truth, almost—but Gerrard knew better now, didn't
he? And he should just be killing the cruel devious bastard,
should be swinging his blade back, slicing off these lies once
and for all...

"But then we fought, and spoke," Olarr choked, speaking
faster now, "and the light came back to your eyes. You heard my
words, you knew my clan, you showed yourself quick and

clever. You told me the truth of how you sought your death from me, you begged me with your beautiful eyes, and then"—he drew in a dragging breath—"then you kissed me. You hungered for me. Your taste and your scent and your touch were as naught I had ever, *ever* known. And then you welcomed my own touch, in return. You took me into your beauty, granted this so freely to me, without fear or shame."

Gerrard shouldn't still be tolerating this, listening to this, wanting to hear this—and damn him but Olarr was still saying it, still with that wetness pouring from his eyes. "And amidst this, I was already lost, ach?" he croaked. "Already fallen at your feet. And that first day when I took you, I only turned you away from me because I could not bear to see the pain or loathing in your eyes. And if I could not see this, then I could—I could keep doing this, even when I knew I had no right to this. I could drink of your beauty and bravery, if only for a moment. I could make you *mine*."

Mine. The word too familiar, too horribly, viciously painful, but Olarr was rapidly nodding, even as it scraped his neck against Gerrard's sword. "And I did make you mine," he continued, his voice breaking. "Against all my well-thought plans, all my cunning. I granted the goddess' son my scent, and my seed. And amidst this, I entwined my fate with yours, from that first day. You would never face Slagvor, without him knowing my treason. Without him knowing you were *mine*."

That damnable word scraped even harder this time, enough to finally jerk Gerrard to life again, to cough a bitter, mocking laugh from his throat. "Oh, how *noble* of you, orc," he snarled. "You'd still decided to train me up as your puppet—your *weapon*—but in exchange for a bit of extra danger, now you'd get a warm body to fuck along the way, too. And if I did somehow manage to defeat Slagvor—if you'd have come up with a good enough story to tell me afterwards—maybe you'd have even gotten to keep at it too, yeah? Keep lying to me?

Coming to see me whenever you felt like having an easy fuck?"

Olarr's eyes squeezed shut again, his face contorting in the moonlight, and Gerrard laughed again, not a laugh in the slightest. "You were probably still even fucking around the whole time, too," he gritted out. "So *convenient*, that I couldn't smell it on you, right? But you knew that was what I wanted from you, so you *lied* to me, just like all the other—"

He caught himself there, clamping his fool mouth shut far too late, because what the hell was he saying, why was he giving this prick *anything* right now—and Olarr's eyes were blinking open, his head shaking again, his raw red skin slicing itself harder against Gerrard's sharpened steel.

"*No*, Aulis," he said, almost pleaded, his eyes glimmering too bright in the moonlight. "No. I did not. I would not. I knew what a gift your fealty was, and ach, I longed for this too. I should have raged and wept to find other scents upon you. I ken I should have gladly rushed off and killed any others you had touched, and then you should have never spoken to me again. As you should have done, long before."

He was speaking too rapidly, blinking too hard, his breaths sharp and shallow from his mouth. "But you kept welcoming me," he continued, even faster. "You kept meeting me. You kept granting me such beauty, such joy. You were so generous, so alive, and you returned my failings with such kindness. Such... goodness. You trusted my word. You told me your truths, and made me laugh as I had not done in many, many summers. You were so free with your warmth and your forgiveness. You were as light itself, Aulis. As the goddess' own favoured son, in my arms."

Olarr's still-streaming eyes had snapped up to the moon, to where it was still shining down from above, washing his blood-streaked skin rust and silver. "And the longer this went," he gasped, "the deeper I fell, and the more I wished to forego this fool plan I had made. I wished to forget I had ever thought of this, or risked such great harm upon one I loved so deeply. I wished to only care for you, and cherish you, and keep you safe."

Gerrard attempted a scoff, a furious shake of his head, but Olarr was still gazing at the moon, the water still streaking down his cheeks. "But by granting you my scent," he rasped, "I had already brought great danger upon you, ach? I had marked you for Slagvor, for my enemies. And together with this"—he drew in a great, shaky breath—"I had granted you a Bautul's strength. I had fed you full of it, again and again. Even more than we knew, ach?"

There was a strange, heavy foreboding in his words, and Gerrard twitched, waiting, as Olarr kept blinking at the moon, heaving for air. "There are old, foolish tales," he said, hitching, "of the human men who lie with orcs. Of... their power. Their... skill. Oft well beyond that of the men around them."

Gerrard kept staring, listening, his heart now erratically thumping, and Olarr's eyes squeezed shut. "In the tales, these men became... swifter," he croaked. "Stronger. More hearty and hale. Some grew taller, or gained more seed in their loins. Others gained... great gifts. Some even learnt to see in the darkness, near as well as any orc."

And—wait. Fucking *wait*. Because right now, this very moment, Gerrard was standing here in the darkness, moving about easily and confidently, without a lamp, with only the moonlight above. But there were rocks and trees all around, and the occasional cloud passing over the moon, but it hadn't seemed to matter... had it? Just like it hadn't mattered most other times these past weeks, all those times they'd travelled and spoken and fought in the dark? Fuck, all the times Gerrard had gone out alone in the dark himself, skulking about the outpost, running his damned obstacle course?

"I carried not a thought of this, at first," Olarr said, speaking faster now, "for I pay little heed to tales, and I had never before witnessed such a change in a human man or woman. But"—he drew in a shaky breath—"I have known no other orc who has lain with one man thus, as we have, over many moons, ach? And our Bautul women do not oft fight or spar against us, so this is not so easy to see upon them—and with a woman, I ken the seed's strength oft goes first to... the sons. With a man, there is no son, and thus—"

He waved a shaky hand at Gerrard, at his belly, oh hell, oh *fuck*. "And thus," Olarr continued, his mouth twisting, "I had made—a true *weapon* of you, warrior. Far beyond what I had ever dreamt."

Those impossible words hovered there, clanging back and forth between them, echoing with Gerrard's thundering heartbeat. That wasn't possible. It wasn't. Was it...

"And one day," Olarr said, on a heavy breath, "Grimarr came to me. He told me he had sent two of his closest orcs to spy upon us, and they had seen how I had sought you out, and trained you, and strengthened you, for my vengeance upon Slagvor. He... applauded me, and my cunning plan, and swore to help me when the time was right. And once I had followed this, I raged at him, and we fought, until he swore to leave this be, and keep you secret. And—"

His voice choked off again, his shoulders visibly slumping, the misery drawing down his mouth. "And this was when I stayed away from you," he said. "For those twenty-three days. I saw what I had done, and I wished to keep you away from me. To keep you safe. But I could yet—*feel* you, Aulis. I could scent your pain and your grief, and I could scarce eat or sleep for missing you. So when I came to you again, I swore to the goddess I would—"

Gerrard's whole body was frozen, waiting, as Olarr hauled in another breath. "I swore I would do all within my power to protect you," he rasped. "So ach, I then—I trained you. I pushed you to become even swifter and stronger, to learn to fight Bautul orcs, to become as strong a warrior as any Bautul I have ever met. For if Slagvor—or any other—yet learnt of you, I wished you to be ready. I wished you to have all the safety—all the hope—I could grant you. I wished you to *live*."

Gerrard's heartbeat was still thudding in his ears, his breath strangled in his throat. He didn't want to hear this rubbish, didn't want to believe it, couldn't possibly believe Olarr had unintentionally made him into some kind of—of—preposterous overpowered *orc-man*. And even if these unthinkable claims were somehow true, Olarr had still never—he'd *never*—

"But," Gerrard finally said, and suddenly he just felt cold, and wretched, and so, so tired. "But you could have just—*told* me, Olarr."

His own eyes were leaking again, because that was the crux of it, the worst of it—and he gulped down a breath, shook his head. "You had so many chances, you lying prick," he continued, blank and bitter. "Fuck, I even asked you, and you gave me such rubbish back. I knew you were keeping secrets from me, I knew your plans around Slagvor didn't add up. I knew I shouldn't trust you. I *knew*, Olarr."

Olarr's empty eyes were back on Gerrard's face, and now he was nodding, the movement scraping his raw throat harder against Gerrard's still-pressing blade. "Ach," he whispered. "I… I wished to speak this truth to you, again and again and again. But"—his throat audibly swallowed—"I also hoped and prayed, with all my strength, that this would never come to pass, ach? And the more I had come to know you, the more I saw your deep care for those around you, and what you would give for them. And I thought—I feared—"

He was dragging for breath, gulping it down as though he was starving, his eyes still pure misery on Gerrard's face. "I feared you would yet do this," he choked. "I feared if you knew you were a match for Slagvor, you would rush forth, and call him to a duel, and seek to defeat him. I feared you would do this"—his voice cracked—"for your men, and for my kin. For... *me*."

For him. Gerrard's bark of a laugh scraped painfully through the air, but the sword in his hand was suddenly shaking, jostling on its own against Olarr's raw neck. Olarr hadn't told him, because he'd thought Gerrard would be—imprudent. Reckless. He'd thought Gerrard would throw himself on his sword, throw away his life and his goals and his future, for—

Gerrard was shaking his head again, whipping it back and forth. No, no, no, Olarr was wrong, he was so wrong, he had no idea what Gerrard would have done, and...

Fuck. He would have done it. Fuck Olarr and his cunning, fuck the whole cursed world, Gerrard would have done it. If he'd known Olarr had thought he even had a *chance* of defeating Slagvor, he would have done it. He still would. He... he *was*.

His sword was still trembling against Olarr's neck, now flashing fresh bright pain across Olarr's eyes—but Olarr still hadn't moved, hadn't even tried. As if he hadn't even noticed the thick stream of blood now seeping down his front, staining his silver skin even darker than before. And Gerrard had done that, he'd put that there, and he'd even done it—on *purpose*. Just like—like—

Gerrard blinked, flinched, shuddered all over—and with a sudden jerk of movement, he wrenched his sword back, and hurled it away. Watched its bloody blade twirl end over end, until it caught on a bush, and clattered sideways against the earth.

Fuck, what was he doing. What was wrong with him. Why the fuck was he standing here raging and weeping over all this rubbish, and not just—just—

"*Do* you really think I could beat Slagvor?" he asked, his voice hoarse, hollow. "You really think I have a chance?"

Olarr's eyes squeezed shut, his shoulder jerking up. "Mayhap," he replied, just as hollow. "You bear great strength and skill, warrior, enough to defeat me, and every Bautul I have brought before you. And whilst Slagvor is yet stronger than any of us, you…"

Gerrard waited, his heart still thundering, his mouth gone dry. "You are human," Olarr said, on a sigh. "And if you called Slagvor to a duel, before all his kin, in the way of the Bautul—I ken he would accept this, for he would never wish to be seen as fearing a human. But"—another raw, shaky breath—"he would also never fathom a human to be a match for him, ach? So he may well be… reckless. Careless. Far more than he would be, against an orc."

Gerrard might have laughed again, but his thoughts were tumbling too fast now, racing behind his unseeing eyes. He still had a chance. A small chance. And no matter what, Slagvor was still coming here, now. Coming for him, for Olarr—and even worse, for Gerrard's severely understaffed camp. For Gerrard's men. When they'd been so close to finally escaping here, so damned close…

And now Bassey's words from months ago were swarming up, circling like vultures in Gerrard's gut. *We had to retreat and leave the wounded behind. Our commander at the time ordered them killed, for their own sakes…*

"How much time do we have," Gerrard abruptly demanded, at where Olarr was still kneeling, the blood still streaking down his chest. "How far away can we get from here—from my camp, and my men—before we meet your band. Before I challenge Slagvor."

Olarr's kneeling body twitched, and his eyes blinked at Gerrard, speaking suddenly of surprise, and then disbelief, or maybe despair. "We have yet a little time, but—*no*, Aulis," he croaked. "I did not mean—I should not have said—*ach*. There is no need for you to do this. No need to place yourself in such grave danger. Slagvor is yet the most fearsome Bautul fighter in the realm, and if you lose, he shall—*destroy* you. You ought to—you ought to run, Aulis. As far north as you can. Now. *Please.*"

Gerrard blinked back at him—what the hell did he mean, *run?*—and Olarr fumbled in his pockets, brought out something glinting, something *gold.* "I have brought you," he gulped, as he shoved his hands out toward Gerrard, "as much as I could beg or borrow, ach? It should be enough to—to gain you horses, mayhap, or hire a coach. Or should you yet wish for my guarding, I should be glad to come with you, as far as you can bear this. For only this night, or for as many nights as you wish."

Wait. Wait, wait, *wait.* After all Olarr's cunning plans, after all his damned devious lies, after spending all that time and effort training Gerrard up to fight Slagvor—now Olarr was proposing—he wanted to *run?* To run from Slagvor, from the Bautul, from his precious kin and his home? And he wanted *Gerrard* to run? To desert the army? To leave everything? Together? For as long as Gerrard wanted?

"Fuck, no," Gerrard snapped, over the peculiar new plunge in his belly. "What the fuck, Olarr! I'm not running off and leaving my men to be attacked by fucking *Slagvor*! And you said Silfast was almost dead, after taking that hit for you! You can't honestly mean to just turn around and *abandon* him? What the hell kind of Bautul brotherhood is that?!"

He was shouting again, his voice sharp with fury and disbelief, and he whirled around, away, and stalked over to snap up his sword. Feeling the familiar weight of it, the steady certain strength of its steel, as he clutched it tight, and turned his face up to the watching, all-seeing moon.

He'd failed, yet again. He'd lost his plans. He'd surely lost his livelihood, his reputation, his goals, his future. He'd lost Olarr.

But this time, he wasn't giving up. He would do his damnedest to save his men, to give them as much help as he could. And he would sure as hell try to take Slagvor down with him. To keep Slagvor from hurting anyone else, ever again.

"So I'm going to go wrap up my affairs," Gerrard said, his eyes held to the moon. "And then I'm going to fight Slagvor. To the death."

25

It didn't take Gerrard long to pack up his life, and ready himself to leave the outpost for good. Again.

He had very few personal effects to deal with, beyond his clothes and his sword, and the half-full jar of mushroom powder, still tucked in the hole under his mat. And after a long moment's weighing it, he crept over to Cosgrove's nearby tent, and shook him awake in the darkness.

"Lieutenant?" Cosgrove's strained voice whispered in the darkness. "What is it?"

"I've been called away," Gerrard told him, his voice creditably steady, "on an important job, and I'm not sure when I'll be back. Or if I'll be back at all. So in case you need it—"

He thrust the jar of powder into Cosgrove's hands, and explained its properties as quickly as he could. "I need you to keep using it on Livermore," he said, under his breath, "especially when Warmisham and his lackeys are here. I need you to be careful, and cunning, and do whatever the hell you can to get our men out of here. And if you happen to get caught"—he swallowed—"you blame it on me. You say it was a direct order from me, and I told you it was for Livermore's health. Got it?"

Cosgrove attempted to protest, his voice rising dangerously in the silence, but Gerrard swiftly shut it down, and said a firm, decisive farewell. Followed by a brief, impulsive embrace to Cosgrove's solid form—he'd been such a good brother, such a gift—before lurching back into the darkness, and wiping at his stupidly prickling eyes.

Next he went for the med tent, drawing a wary-looking Bassey out into the moonlight. And in contrast to Cosgrove, Bassey remained perfectly silent throughout Gerrard's explanations, his eyes cool and assessing, his arms folded tightly over his chest.

"Does this have to do with the orc?" he finally asked, his voice very even, once Gerrard had finished. "The one you've been seeing, all this time?"

Gerrard startled all over, his mouth falling open—Bassey *knew*?!—and Bassey shrugged, gave a grim little twitch of a smile. "That bite you had," he said. "Orcs don't do that to their enemies. They do it to their lovers. Their *mates*."

Their *mates*. Gerrard couldn't stop staring at Bassey, and Bassey shrugged again, his eyes not quite meeting Gerrard's, now. "You aren't my only patient who's ever gone there," he said. "Plenty of orcs seem to like human men—at least, when they're not trying to kill us. But"—his too-aware eyes flicked back to Gerrard's—"you know they can't be trusted, either, right, Lieutenant?"

Gerrard fought down the sudden, irrational urge to laugh, and then gave a shaky-feeling nod, and tightly clasped Bassey on the shoulder. "Yeah, I know," he said thickly. "Thanks for all your hard work and help, brother. It's been an honour."

He suddenly couldn't bear to hear Bassey's response, and he spun away, strode into the darkness. His steps quick and jerky, his hand clamped on his sword-hilt, his gaze fixed straight ahead. This was it. He was leaving here, finished here, probably forever. And he could only pray he'd done enough.

That his men would survive this, and stay safe, and go home again.

He gritted his teeth tighter, walked a little faster—and then winced at the sight of Olarr's familiar silver bulk shifting through the surrounding trees, and falling into step beside him. His big body nearly silent as they walked, except for the sound of his too-loud breaths, rasping through the still night air.

"You are yet... sure of this, Aulis," Olarr's low voice finally said, slicing into the heavy darkness. "Should you wish to turn around, I could—"

"No," Gerrard snapped back, as something dark and bitter surged in his chest, almost too powerful to be borne. "I'm not leaving my men to this, and you damn well know it. You"—his voice cracked—"you *knew* it, the entire fucking time."

Olarr's breaths were heaving louder, but he didn't reply, and Gerrard's mouth made a harsh, frustrated sound, much like a growl. "And I was so damned close to getting them out of here," he continued, harder. "So close to getting rid of Livermore for good. Enough that I was even back there worrying about *leaving* you, worrying about how I would keep seeing you—and meanwhile, you were lying to me, again and again. Pretending to want to see me, and spar with me, while training me up to fight your battles. To face my own *death.*"

A choked laugh grated from his mouth, ringing through the trees, while beside him, Olarr was rubbing at his face, his eyes. "I ken you do not wish to hear me, Aulis," he croaked, "but I have never wished for your death. I have done my utmost to help you, and strengthen you, and keep you alive. You are—my *mate.*"

Gerrard laughed again, shook his head so hard it hurt. "Oh, fuck off with that, Olarr," he hissed. "I am not. Harja was your mate. The one you really loved, the one whose death you're avenging with all this. I'm just—just like your axe. A tool you use and sharpen and keep nearby, until you break it, use it up, and find another one."

But now that was Olarr's laugh, or maybe a sob, grating out harsh between them. "No, warrior," he insisted. "My axe is part of me. It grants me strength, and bravery, and keeps me safe from my enemies. It defends those I care for most. And ach, I sharpen it, polish it, spar with it, and care for it as well as I can. For I should be lost—*lost*—without it."

Gerrard grimaced and shook his head—so maybe that had been a rubbish comparison, but his point still stood—until a hand, Olarr's hand, grasped his arm, yanked him to a stop. "You are—so much more to me, Aulis," he said, his eyes bright and miserable in the moonlight. "You have become part of me, and I have never—*never*—longed for another, as I have longed for you. And ach, I ken I did not swear the vows of matehood to you, as I ought"—his still-reddened throat convulsed—"but I yet marked you. I granted you my mating-bite. I covered you with my scent and my seed, and touched no other. I even took you beneath the moon, face to face, upon the goddess' altar, as is her wish."

That caught Gerrard short for a moment—did Olarr mean that night he'd spread the fur on the stone, and afterwards they'd sat together in the moonlight, and talked about their future? About... a son?

"I claimed you in our deepest ways," Olarr continued, between heavy breaths. "In the ways of the Bautul, and our goddess. I made you *mine*."

His voice had deepened, his bottom lip jutting out, the challenge flaring in his eyes. So familiar, and so damned painful, clutching tight in Gerrard's belly. And somehow he laughed again, shaking his head, clamping his shaky hand against his sword-hilt.

"You don't get to say that, Olarr," he countered. "You don't. You lied to me, the whole time. You didn't tell me any of this!

You didn't tell me *shit* about this so-called 'claim' of yours, or what it meant to you—let alone your secrets, or your plans! You put me at risk, you fucked up my goals, you put my men in danger. And"—another bitter laugh in his throat—"you never even once sucked me off, or let me fuck you. This all went one way, Olarr. This all went *your way*! To benefit *you*!"

But Olarr was still looking like that, shaking his head, his hand squeezing tighter on Gerrard's arm. "You ken I did this for my *gain*?" he demanded. "You ken I ever wished to grieve you, or harm you, or see you face my cruelest enemy? You ken I wished to live in such fear for you, praying and praying, with all my strength, for the goddess to spare you? And"—his eyes shimmered, bright with misery and pain—"you ken I wished to go all these moons without knowing your scent upon me? Without even *once* tasting the sweetness of you?"

Gerrard bitterly laughed again, shook his head. "Well, you made your choices, didn't you?" he said, clipped. "And whatever the hell you say to me, it still doesn't change what you *did*. You lied to me. You hurt me. You put me and my men at risk. You *never* saw me as your equal, even when you pretended you did. And you didn't go there in bed, not even close, not *once*—"

When without warning, Olarr... sank downwards. Sank to his knees before Gerrard, his molten eyes held to Gerrard's face, as his hands clutched for—Gerrard's trousers. Fumbling at them, yanking the front fall down...and suddenly revealing Gerrard's groin, his slack dangling cock. Exposing him to the cool air, the white light of the watching moon.

And curse him, but Gerrard—didn't move. Didn't protest. Just stood there, staring, breathing hard, as Olarr leaned forward, and... inhaled. Inhaled, slow and deep and reverent, the way he'd done so, so many times. But he'd never gone further than that, he'd never, he'd never—

Touched Gerrard there, with his lips. Kissed him. Tasted

him, that hot slick tongue already slipping eager against his slit, and... seeking. As if... as if...

"The hell, Olarr!" Gerrard gasped, as he lurched backwards, far too late—but damn it, he was half-hard now, and Olarr was still just kneeling there before him. Gazing at him with those shimmering eyes, as his tongue blatantly swept across his lips.

"It's—too risky," Gerrard choked, even as he winced at the sound of the words, coming from his mouth. "Slagvor will smell it, and he'll—"

But Olarr just kept looking at him like that, with too much meaning, too much grief, in his watching eyes. "I told you, Aulis," he whispered. "My fate is entwined with yours, and always has been, since that first day I touched you. The moment Slagvor scents you, I have met my own doom, ach?"

His voice sounded steady, curiously calm, as if he'd been awaiting this, expecting this, as if he'd known it all along. And for perhaps the first time, blinking down at Olarr's upturned face, Gerrard fully considered how Olarr... had done that. He'd marked Gerrard as his own, and thus he'd marked himself, too. And had it been some kind of fucked-up double suicide mission, or had it been... had it been...

"I never wished for you to face," Olarr continued, between heaving breaths, "aught that might come, without me. Never wished to ask you to bear what I would not bear alongside you. And I have prayed each night and each day that this would not come, this fate would not find us. That the goddess would see us, and keep us safe."

But she wasn't, she hadn't, and now they were doing this, walking straight toward Slagvor, toward their doom. And Olarr was still on his knees, still looking at Gerrard with such agony, such adoration, in his eyes. As his big hand reached forward, found Gerrard's hip, drew him closer again...

And then sucked him deep. Swallowed Gerrard's ever-hardening length all the way down, enclosing it in his hot mouth, his tight throat. As that slick, clever tongue flicked and twirled at his too-sensitive tip, and Gerrard staggered, gasped, swelled up to full, dizzying hardness in an instant. While that hot sucking mouth easily stretched to accommodate it, to keep him held tight and safe and full, oh, oh—

It was unlike anything, any mouth, any hole, Gerrard had ever felt before—and the moan ripped from his throat on its own, hitching out low and hungry between them. As his hips reflexively bucked forward, gouging himself deeper... and finding only more warmth, more approval. More dark, dizzying pleasure as Olarr moaned too, the sound rumbling all around them, through them, through Gerrard's very skin, into the swollen pulsing craving beneath.

Olarr's big hands were here now too, clutching at Gerrard's hard arse, caressing his full bollocks, drawing him closer. And sucking him even deeper, harder, just on the perfect edge of pain, as that sinuous tongue swirled, and that hot throat audibly bobbed and clenched. Working Gerrard over with frantic, single-minded dedication, with appalling skill, and Gerrard would never forget the sight of it, the feel of it, the visceral obscene sounds of it. The truth of this huge powerful orc salivating on his knees, all but gagging himself with Gerrard's rigid leaking cock, as if he would never, ever get enough...

Gerrard's hand had somehow sunk into Olarr's messy hair, maybe to steady himself on his shaky feet. Or maybe just to see this, to know this, to remember what this finally looked like... or maybe, maybe, to touch him. To caress him. To keep himself from...

"Good, captain," Gerrard croaked, before he'd even thought it. "Fuck, you're so good, aren't you? With such a sweet mouth, and such a deep tight throat?"

Olarr's groan was utterly unfeigned, the rumble vibrating Gerrard from the inside out, his eyes so wide, so worshipful, on

Gerrard's face. And Gerrard even tilted Olarr's head back a little, gave himself a better view of the powerful deceitful warrior, working on his knees, with a leaking human cock jammed through his lips, stuck down his throat.

"Yeah, that's it," Gerrard gasped, as his own head tilted back, his blinking eyes fixed to the moon. "You're such a good orc, aren't you? Such a good Bautul. Just where your goddess wants you, on your knees, sucking out your—"

His voice choked, wrenched, his hips hitching forward, plunging even deeper into that eager glorious heat—and yes, fuck, that was it. His release catching, cresting, and—flying. He was flying, crying out, as the unthinkable euphoria whipped and whirled all through him, emptying him in pulse after screaming, shattering pulse. Pouring him out into Olarr, into Olarr's mouth, down Olarr's desperately sucking throat, while Olarr himself moaned and shuddered, his lashes rapidly fluttering, his rapt, moonlit face covered with a sheen of sweat. And Gerrard only distantly noticed that Olarr had also shoved his own trousers downwards, and his own release was spurting around Gerrard's feet, spattering white and sticky across his leather boots.

And even as Gerrard's pulses slowed, faded, Olarr kept sucking. Tasting. Caressing. The sensation already too strong, too sensitive, but Gerrard couldn't seem to pull away, either. Couldn't stop watching this orc licking him, lavishing him, rolling him around in his mouth, on his tongue. As though Gerrard were a priceless delicacy, a stunning perfect morsel, even as soft as he was, even as he knew—he knew!—how it tasted.

But when Olarr finally drew away, let Gerrard fall from his mouth—still slow and reluctant, as if he couldn't bear to let go—he was still licking his lips, his eyes still hungry and half-lidded, his throat convulsing again and again. "Ach, Aulis," he breathed. "Even sweeter than all my dreams of it. I... I thank you, for honouring me with such a gift."

He looked so serious, so worshipful, and then, then, so sad. "I am so sorry, my brave one," he whispered, as another tear streaked down his hard cheek. "I ought to have spoken all these truths to you. I sought with such fervour to keep you safe, but in this, I lost sight of what *you* wished. I placed my own aims—my prudence, my cunning, my longing for you—above your own selfless need for justice. Your kindness. Your care."

Gerrard couldn't speak over the rising spasm in his throat, and he only distantly noticed that his hand was still sunk in Olarr's hair, his thumb absently stroking. And Olarr was leaning into it now, his sad eyes fluttering, his breath exhaling unsteady and slow. "It is just like Harja, all over again," he croaked. "And just like Harja, you show yourself a far braver warrior than I have ever been, ach? You again show yourself a true son of the goddess, willing to offer yourself on her altar, for those she most loves. Whilst I"—his eyes squeezed shut—"I have been the coward, Aulis. A failure of a Bautul. Just as you saw, just as you said, from the start."

He huffed a strange, broken little laugh, the sound catching in Gerrard's belly—enough that he swallowed hard, shook his head. "You know I was talking rubbish, Olarr," he said thickly. "You're the furthest thing I know from a failure, yeah? You're devoted to your clan and your people, you're a brilliant fighter, you're clever and cunning and prudent. And you're thoughtful, and generous, and a spectacular fuck. And I really thought—I would have—"

His voice cracked, his hand spasming in Olarr's hair, because what the hell had he been about to say? *I would have stayed forever, I would have done anything you asked, I would have never stopped loving you—*

And suddenly Gerrard couldn't stand it anymore, couldn't—and he lurched away, away, fastening up his still-hanging trousers with shaky fingers. Fuck, what was he doing. What were they doing. Slagvor was coming, Slagvor was about to kill them, and here they were, getting off in the woods, and making stupid, useless confessions? And Gerrard was again offering up his own kindness, his own care, to the cruel, calculating orc who'd lied to him since the first day they'd met?

Gerrard didn't look at Olarr as he started walking again, but he could feel him already falling back into step beside him, his breaths still rasping too loud in the silence. And the further they walked, making their way along a path that seemed very familiar to Olarr, the darker and heavier it all felt. Gerrard was going to fight Slagvor. He was probably going to die in the attempt. And amidst it, he would betray Olarr to Slagvor, too, and then...

"I think you should—stay back," he finally said, hoarse, into the oppressive silence. "Let me meet Slagvor alone. And that way you can run, or hide, make new plans, and—"

He broke off at the harsh, abrupt sound from Olarr beside him, something like a laugh, or maybe a sob. "You cannot—ask this of me, Aulis," he choked. "Not now. Not when you would not run or hide for me, ach? I shall not leave you. Not until the very end."

Oh. Maybe Gerrard should have expected that, but it still clutched and curdled in his belly, roiled into his throat. "Right," he managed. "Thanks."

There was more silence beside him, more empty unbearable misery, and he drew in another deep, shaky breath. "So what's the best way to do this, then?" his thin voice asked. "What's going to keep Slagvor—or your Bautul kin—from killing me on sight? Or killing *you*, once they smell me on you?"

Olarr's hand was rubbing at his face, his breaths still heavy and harsh. "I ken my brothers would not attack me on first sight, even over a human," he said. "I have upheld them to the best of my strength, for many, many summers. I have won them countless battles, and fed them countless meals, and gained many debts. This ought to be enough to grant us a chance to speak, ach? And once we gain this…"

His voice trailed off, and Gerrard drew in breath, squared his shoulders. "Then I challenge Slagvor to a proper Bautul duel," he said. "Before your clan, before the goddess."

Olarr was sighing, nodding, glancing sideways with dark, miserable eyes. "Ach, just thus," he said, quiet. "And if Slagvor accepts, the rest of us are then bound to watch, and witness this, without help or hindrance."

Right. "And if I lose," Gerrard said, tentative now, "and Slagvor decides to start having his fun with me… what then?"

His heartbeat had been slowly rising throughout this, but now it was drumming in his ears, calling up painful visions of that day he'd knelt before Olarr on the battlefield. The depth of that shameful, visceral fear. Goddess, he would ask nothing else, but he wanted an easy death. He wanted it to be swift, merciful, like that axe-swing Olarr had almost, almost taken…

"Then I shall do all within my power to—help," Olarr said, through his thick breaths. "To grant you death, as kindly as I can, before I meet my own."

Gerrard's throat convulsed, his belly plunging, because yes, that would be the next outcome, wouldn't it? "And you couldn't challenge Slagvor next?" he ground out. "Couldn't try for a duel of your own?"

But Olarr was shaking his head, rubbing his hand at his eyes. "As I am your mate, this would yet be seen as… help," he replied, his voice rough. "As vengeance. Slagvor would never honour this, and he would at once cast claims of treason upon me. He may yet claim this from the start, but I hope"—he exhaled—"I hope his greed shall be stronger, ach? His hunger to mock and destroy a weak human, before all his kin. Most of all a human he knows I… care for, so deeply."

Fuck, Slagvor was a piece of stinking carrion, and Gerrard spat on the ground beside him, and clutched at his sword. "So what does Slagvor fight like," he hissed. "Tell me everything. As much as you can."

Olarr readily obliged, though his voice was blank as he spoke, the words dull and hollow. Telling Gerrard of Slagvor's speed, his strength with his axe, his fearlessness, his cruelty. How he enjoyed dragging out his fights, taunting his opponents and watching them suffer. How he used their fear to his gain.

Gerrard listened in silence, as the darkness weighed heavier and heavier, his hand gone clammy against his sword-hilt. Until finally Olarr's voice stopped, and then his body stopped too, his hand gripping at Gerrard's arm.

"I can—scent them, up ahead," Olarr breathed. "You are sure you do not wish to turn back. You could yet run, and escape, and—and live."

His voice cracked, his eyes pleading on Gerrard's face, but Gerrard gritted his teeth, shook his head. While Olarr's trembling hands came up to touch his face, cupping it, cradling it, as though it were something prized, something precious.

"You are—so good, Aulis," he croaked. "So brave, and so beautiful. It has been a true joy to know you, and to know your kindness and your care. You have brought me—such hope. Such peace. And with the goddess as my witness, I—"

He broke off there, his inhale shaky and thick, his eyes blinking hard. "I pledge you my troth, Aulis Gerrard," he whispered. "I grant you my axe, and my favour, and my fealty. I shall honour you, and care for you, and keep you safe. For as long as I bear breath."

It was goodbye, it was, it was—but it felt like something deeper, too. Something that drew Olarr's grieving, glimmering eyes up to the watching moon, as his fist closed against his heart. Making a promise. A... vow.

And Gerrard wasn't fighting it anymore. Was just—

nodding, agreeing, his mouth quivering, as he blinked back the wetness pooling behind his eyes. "Y-you too, Olarr of Clan Bautul," he choked back. "Still gonna haunt you after, yeah?"

And why had he said that, bringing that up again, because it felt like an age had passed since then. Since Gerrard had looked at Olarr on another moonlit night, and made yet another promise, another vow. *If you kill me, I'm haunting you forever, with your goddess as my witness.*

But Olarr was nodding too, rapid and fierce, his eyes flickering between warmth and despair. "I should be—most honoured, warrior," he breathed. "Most glad to meet you again, in the goddess' realm."

Gerrard nodded too, jerking his head against Olarr's still-cradling hand, as the water finally escaped, streaked down his cheeks. This was it. It was goodbye. And it was—

"Ach, what is this?" came a deep, contemptuous voice, far too close. "Is this a—*man?*"

It was Slagvor.

26

Gerrard turned to face Slagvor with slow, guarded steps, with dread and darkness boiling in his gut.

The bastard was gigantic. Bigger than Olarr, than even Silfast, with huge sloped shoulders, a powerful barrel chest, and a massive shining axe, gleaming sharp and deadly on his back. And while his grey-skinned face bore the usual heavy Bautul cragginess, it was also spattered all over with brown streaks and splotches. With... blood. Not just fresh blood, surely, but old blood, too.

The dread surged higher in Gerrard's belly, and his gaze darted beyond Slagvor's huge shoulders, to the group of orcs behind him. A dozen-odd Bautul orcs, just like Olarr had said. All of them armed, and all of them staring at Olarr and Gerrard. And the only orc Gerrard recognized was Kalfr, standing at the very rear of them, his face a shadow in the moonlight.

"What is this, Olarr," Slagvor's deep voice demanded, reverberating in the moonlit silence. "Why is this human here. And why does he *reek* of you!"

There was an instant's quiet, and Gerrard could feel Olarr

inhaling beside him, about to speak—but then Gerrard jerked forward. Walked straight toward his destiny, his doom, even as his gaze darted up, caught on the watching white light of the moon above them. He was doing this. He was.

"I'm Lieutenant Gerrard of Preia," his voice said, quiet but steady. "And I'm here because Olarr—won me. He converted me, and conquered me. Gained me as his war-prize, with the blessing of the goddess."

More silence thudded through the empty air, and Gerrard could almost taste the sudden confusion from Olarr behind him, and from the Bautul orcs behind Slagvor. But Gerrard's eyes were only on Slagvor, on where Slagvor was still watching, still listening, for now...

"After Olarr routed my regiment in battle," Gerrard continued, faster now, "he came back to finish me off. He defeated me in single combat, and put me on my knees. And then he ploughed me into the dirt with his strong Bautul prick, until I begged and screamed for his mercy."

Slagvor's beady eyes darted beyond Gerrard toward Olarr, his heavy brows furrowing—so Gerrard kept talking, spitting out the words as fast as they would come. "And since Olarr is such a wise, cunning Bautul," he said, through his rapid breaths, "he saw this as a gift from the goddess, and decided to use it to his advantage. He used me to spy on my regiment. He used me to stop any further attacks against you. He even used me to poison my commander. He used his cunning for your gain, for his clan's gain. And yeah, he took his pleasure with me along the way, too, because why the hell wouldn't he?"

Slagvor's eyes were still fixed on Olarr, and something ugly curled on his bloodstained mouth—but behind him, the assembled Bautul were shifting on their feet, their eyes wary, uncertain, surprised. Curious. Maybe even... impressed.

And at the sight of it, something almost, *almost* like hope caught, kindled up in Gerrard's chest. Because yes, yes, he knew he was still facing certain death here tonight—but he could at least try to keep Olarr from coming with him. Could keep Olarr alive, keep intact the respect from his clan that he'd worked so many years to gain. Olarr needed another chance, another day, another cunning plan to save his kin—and Gerrard was doing his damnedest to give it to him.

"And the longer I served Olarr, the more I wanted to stay with him," Gerrard continued, as steadily as he could. "I wanted him to recognize me, and take me as his full Bautul mate. But he told me I wasn't worthy of this yet—but that he would give me a chance. A chance to prove myself, by defeating a powerful Bautul in single combat."

He could feel that he had the orcs now, could feel their curiosity, their full attention. And though Slagvor was still glowering at Olarr behind Gerrard, he also wasn't moving, cutting in to speak, not yet...

"So therefore, Captain Slagvor," Gerrard announced, lighter now, aiming for flippancy, for foolishness. "I've decided to come here tonight and meet *you*, beneath our goddess' full moon. And"—he drew out his sword with a smooth, silken shirr—"in the name of the goddess, I challenge you to a Bautul duel."

The silence echoed out after Gerrard's words, resonating all around them—and then, suddenly, laughter. Laughter, deep and mocking, from many of the assembled Bautul orcs, and from Slagvor most of all. The sight contorting his blood-streaked face into something even crueler, something alight with ridicule and rage.

"Is this truth, Olarr!" he roared, between loud, scraping guffaws. "You sent your piddling man to *duel* with me!"

Gerrard had been fighting very hard to keep from looking at Olarr behind him, but he couldn't seem to help it now. Couldn't stop himself from finally glancing backwards, to where Olarr was standing a few steps away, his big body very still. His eyes fixed to Gerrard's, almost frozen, and Gerrard felt his own eyes sharply narrowing back, his mouth tightening. He was doing this, he was doing this for Olarr, and Olarr had to see it, had to meet him in it. Had to wield his prudence and his cunning, for all his kin. Please, goddess, please—

He could almost taste Olarr's reluctance, his rebellion—but then, yes, *yes*, his capitulation. There in the shift in his eyes, the half-amused, half-aggrieved look on his face, and then the cool, careless shrug of his bulky shoulder.

"Ach, I have brought Preia's most promising lieutenant here to duel with you," he told Slagvor, his voice steady, calm. "I have long wished to grant you such a surprise, in return for... past deeds. So when this man came into my debt, I thought"— another careless shrug—"you might... welcome this challenge, Captain."

In another moment, another world, Gerrard might have admired the easy, duplicitous delivery of those words—not only was Olarr suggesting that he'd planned this as an amusing prize for Slagvor all along, but he hadn't said enough to turn off his worshipful lover, either. Or had he, because Slagvor's suspicious beady eyes had flicked back to Gerrard, awaiting his response...

"What do you mean, you thought he might *welcome* it?" Gerrard said, the sharpness coming easy to his voice, as he spun back to frown at Olarr. "I thought you said I was good enough to defeat him!"

There were a few snickers from the assembled Bautul, and goddess curse Olarr, bless Olarr, he was giving Gerrard a soft, crooked little smile, and then even stepping forward, grasping his face, and—kissing him. Kissing him on the mouth, hard and hungry and urgent, and Gerrard didn't even need to feign his groan, or the instant press of his body back into Olarr's solid, familiar bulk.

Olarr drew away with a tight grasp at Gerrard's arse, a

gentle pat at his cheek—and another soft, indulgent little smile. "Ach, I ken you are very good, *litli maður*," he purred. "But to show yourself a true Bautul, you cannot refuse now, ach? True Bautul are never cowards, most of all before our goddess."

The words were so light, so affectionate, accompanied by an easy wave of Olarr's hand up toward the moon. And it was too easy to sink into it, to nod and smile back in return. To ignore the low whistles of the assembled Bautul behind Slagvor, the quiet murmurs of *fífl* and *fokk-drukkinn*.

And once Olarr pulled away, Gerrard kept the dazed smile to his mouth, the hazy look in his eyes, even as he turned to face Slagvor again. As he raised his sword again, letting it visibly waver in his hands.

"So we're doing this, then, right?" he asked, allowing a slight slur into his voice. "I'll give you a damn good fight, cap'n."

Slagvor's sneer was heavy with mockery and contempt, and he barked a harsh, scornful laugh. "Ach, fool human," he replied, as he drew the massive axe from his back, and swung it in a smooth, easy arc before him. "I shall meet your duel. I ken I shall revel in the sound of your screams, and the taste of your blood."

Fuck, he was such a vile ugly maggot, and Gerrard gritted his teeth, and reflexively tilted his face up, toward the cool silver light of the moon. Drinking in its brilliance, its purity, its goodness. Its gift of light, in the deepest, deadliest darkness.

"Then let's do it, orc," he said. "And may the best warrior win."

27

Gerrard didn't hesitate. Didn't waste a breath. Just rushed in, and attacked.

He'd wanted to take Slagvor by surprise, to gain the upper hand—and in his now-considerable experience, those axes were slow, enough to at least give him a chance to duck in and out again. But even so, his sword-strike barely touched Slagvor's arm, and the answering axe-swing was dizzyingly fast, sharp, and vicious. Enough that Gerrard had to stagger and drop backwards, the axe-blade slicing close enough over his head that he could feel it skimming his hair.

"Falling already, little man," came Slagvor's deep, taunting voice, as he lurched forward and swung again, nearly enough to catch Gerrard across the waist this time. "Or is this running?"

Gerrard was indeed still scrabbling backwards, distantly thanking the goddess that this clearing was relatively large and flat, with few rocks and sticks scattered about. But his full attention was otherwise on Slagvor, because fuck, this bastard was fast. Faster than Olarr or Silfast or Kalfr, or maybe even anyone else Gerrard had ever fought, either in practice or in battle.

And combined with the axe, it meant that every single swing could mean instant death, and it only took one misstep, one tiny mistake...

He was already out of breath, clutching his sword and watching that blade, while Slagvor laughed aloud, flipped the axe in his hand, and lunged in again. "You thought this man was good, Olarr?" he called, to where—Gerrard spared it the briefest of glances—Olarr was now standing with the other Bautul, his eyes intent, his body very stiff. "Your judgement has failed you again, I ken. He is even more useless than your last pretty pet, ach?"

If Olarr replied, Gerrard didn't hear it, and he sucked down air, kept watching that axe in the moonlight. Trying desperately to learn it, to follow Slagvor's patterns, to discern his habits and tendencies—but the bastard was good at this, too. Easily alternating between swings, backwards and forwards, up and down and sideways, with no obvious pattern, no noticeable preferences. It was exhausting, and fucking enraging, especially since Gerrard couldn't keep running like this, couldn't risk having Slagvor claim a victory because he wasn't even fighting...

So with a breath and a prayer, Gerrard darted sideways, waited for the next swing—and then he ducked close beneath Slagvor's upraised arm, dodging straight through behind him. It was a close thing, but it worked, and Gerrard grunted with relief as his sword made impact against Slagvor's bare back, drew up a line of dark red blood.

Slagvor snarled and swung around again, very nearly catching Gerrard straight across the neck with that huge gleaming blade—but Gerrard again danced forward and under, mixing up his own patterns, too. This time getting in a good hit to Slagvor's knee, enough that his big bulk jerked sideways, giving Gerrard another chance to duck in, swing, get out again.

"You ken you are clever, little man," Slagvor sneered, barely out of breath, as he charged forward again. "We shall see how clever you are when you are screaming for death beneath my claws, ach?"

His charge had been fast enough that Gerrard just needed to focus on running again, staying out of the way, while Slagvor laughed, the sound cruel and deadly between them. "I shall savour this, little human," he hissed. "I shall laugh as I peel the skin from your bones, and lick off the blood beneath. You shall not be running then, shall you? You shall not be waving around your piddly little sword like a drunken orcling?"

Gerrard didn't justify this rubbish with a reply, but maybe his distaste had shown on his face, because Slagvor kept spewing out more commentary, listing all the horrifying things he wanted to do to Gerrard, while charging at him again and again. And though Gerrard knew this was another tactic—and one he'd expected, thanks to Olarr's warnings—it was considerably worsened by the awareness that this bastard would no doubt follow through with all of it, and thoroughly enjoy it. And when Gerrard again took a calculated lunge forward, he very nearly made it all truth, because instead of swinging the axe, like he'd expected, Slagvor's other arm pummelled him powerfully in the back, and sent him flying forward into the dirt.

Gerrard could vaguely hear the Bautul's gasps and murmurs as he fought to roll into the impact, taking the worst of it on his left shoulder. And leaping back up to his feet just in time, as Slagvor's axe slammed down into the earth, just where his neck should have been.

It took Slagvor an instant to wrench the axe back, but by then Gerrard was behind him again, dragging for air, rolling out his now-screaming shoulder. But he couldn't stop, had to keep going, keep moving, please, goddess, please—

Slagvor rushed for him again, swinging the axe with staggering force, while spouting more horribly detailed vitriol about how he was going to prolong Gerrard's death as much as possible, cut him apart piece by minuscule piece, on and on and on. But Gerrard doggedly kept going, dodging and ducking, making his attacks as calculated as he could. Keeping Slagvor going, too, swinging that axe, shooting off his mouth, as sweat finally beaded on his heavy brow, and streaked down his bloodstained face.

"Ach, I shall enjoy breaking you, even more than Olarr's last fool pet," Slagvor snarled, between more furious deadly swings. "You wish to hear how he died? How he begged and screamed beneath my claws?"

Gerrard fought to keep ignoring it, to focus on avoiding that swing, and that one, and that one. Stamina was the way he'd always won these matches, and it was the only way now. He just had to stay upright, stay the course, breathe duck dodge, as the swings kept coming, kept coming, closer, closer—

But Slagvor kept charging in, and kept raging on. Now reminiscing in detail about how long it had taken for Harja to die, how he'd needed six orcs to hold Olarr back. Saying things Gerrard couldn't dream of openly saying about someone on his own side, someone who was a loyal, brilliant fighter. Someone who was standing there watching this, listening to every word.

But it had to mean that Slagvor... suspected. That he was starting to realize this could be a setup on Olarr's part. Which meant that if Gerrard lost, there would be no getting out of this for Olarr, either. No chance of saving his kin, of making Gerrard's sacrifice worthwhile...

No. No. And Gerrard dragged down more harsh, desperate breaths as he kept moving, kept swinging, kept ducking and dodging. One more, one more, one more...

But Slagvor just didn't stop, and Gerrard knew he was finally slowing. Flagging. Losing ground. Losing focus, losing his attention on that ever-swinging blade. And that was even worse than losing his footing, it only took one wrong turn, one slight miscalculation, the panic now rising cold and vicious through his heaving chest. He was almost done, he was nearing the end, if he didn't salvage this, he was, he was...

He was going to die, and that was all.

So when Slagvor raised his axe again, Gerrard didn't move. Didn't lift his own leaden blade. And instead he just stood there, tall and proud and praying, as Slagvor's axe swung straight for his throat.

28

If Slagvor had kept swinging, Gerrard's death would have been quick. Quick, and clean, and relatively painless, his head sliced straight from his shoulders in one sharp, decisive stroke.

But it was as if time had—skipped. Skipped, and flashed backwards, to another hopeless battle, another bitter defeat. Another day, when another orc hadn't wanted to kill him. When another orc hadn't wanted to grant him a swift, easy death.

And on that day, just like this one, the orc's huge axe-blade—wrenched up. Sideways. The sharp edge spinning away, so the flat of it would land instead. So it would crash into Gerrard's shoulder like a hammer, sending him screaming into the dirt.

But this time, Gerrard... expected it. Expected it, lunged from it, braced for it. Not in time to avoid it entirely, no, but just enough that he stayed upright as the wall of steel met his shoulder, as the pain flashed and bloomed, blared behind his eyes. And as the sharp edge of Slagvor's blade shot upwards, wild and uncontrolled, slicing toward the moon.

It was a moment Gerrard had missed, last time. A moment he hadn't seen, because he'd been too shocked, too lost in the pain. But afterwards, when he'd lain in the med tent brooding over it, he'd realized there must have been a moment. A moment where the orc had lost his control, had lost his momentum, just... just like this.

And this time, Gerrard was watching. Waiting. Fighting through the agony, gritting out another prayer, shoving up to his feet. Driving his own sword forward, plunging with all his strength, into...

Into Slagvor's bare, undefended belly.

There was a breath of jolting, jarring stillness. An instant where Slagvor startled, staggered, blinked downwards. His eyes widening, his breath catching—and then his hand flailed downwards, swiping for the blade. Surely about to yank it out, to keep going. To wield that impossible orc healing against Gerrard, too. To use his own unthinkable gift from the goddess, to bring about more death and pain and suffering.

So with one more breath, one more prayer, Gerrard again lunged forward. Not for his own blade, no—but for that huge, gleaming axe, now held slack in Slagvor's other hand. Slack enough that Gerrard could wrench it away with two hands, as his foot hooked behind Slagvor's knee, and pulled. The same move he'd used on Olarr a dozen times, and yes, yes, it sent Slagvor flying backwards, his huge body careening toward the earth—

And when he landed, Gerrard was there. There, with a massive Bautul axe in his hands, heaving it up to the sky, bathing it in the moonlight, begging the goddess' blessing...

It fell with sharp, decisive purpose, a single deadly blade from the heavens, dropping toward Slagvor's straining neck. And slicing through with startling ease, sinking with a staggering thud into the earth beneath.

It was done.

29

The next breath felt like an eternity. Like silence, stillness, screaming through Gerrard's ears, resounding from somewhere deep within him, shuddering its way out.

Slagvor was dead. Dead.

Gerrard didn't even need to look, he could smell it in the air, could hear the steady gurgle of blood feeding the hungry earth. Could just make out those jolting final twitches as the body beneath him spasmed, sinking into its inevitable end.

And even as a dim distant part of Gerrard wanted to shout, dance, spit down upon Slagvor's twitching body—*that's for Harja, you foul prick*, he might have hollered—he just found his eyes... rising. Rising to the still-shining light of the moon above him. The light that had shown him the way, kissed his blades, offered him its blessing.

And standing here beneath its radiance, its impossible generous beauty, breathing, *alive*, Gerrard could only seem to bow his head toward it, and bring his hand to his frantic, hammering heart. "Thank you," he choked, through his dry, rasping throat. "Thank you."

There was another whisper of stillness, of silence that felt almost alive, near enough to touch—until it was broken by a shout. And another one, and another one. And when Gerrard blinked blankly toward them, it was—the Bautul. The group of watching Bautul, hollering not as if in pain or rage, but almost like... victory.

Gerrard wasn't following it, wasn't believing it, not even at the sight of Kalfr grinning at him, and another unfamiliar orc clapping Olarr on the shoulder. Olarr who hadn't seemed to notice in the slightest, because he was still... staring at Gerrard. Staring, and blinking, his eyes stunned and blank, almost as if Gerrard had sliced him across the neck, too.

Gerrard swallowed hard, attempted a quivering little smile toward him—and that, somehow, seemed to snap Olarr awake again. And suddenly he was shoving away from his kin, and pitching forward. Closing up the space between them with large, loping steps, and dragging Gerrard into his hot, shaky embrace.

"Ach, my warrior," Olarr's hoarse voice gulped, strained and wavering in Gerrard's ear. "Ach. You have done this. You have *done* this."

It was like he still didn't believe it, still couldn't understand it was real, and Gerrard sagged heavily into his strength, and huffed a shrill, shaky laugh into his shoulder. "Didn't think I was going to," he gulped, and fuck, suddenly he was dangerously on the verge of sobbing, the breaths quaking hard in his throat. "But you were right. Bastard was greedy. Too greedy to give me an easy death."

Olarr made a thick, choked sound into Gerrard's ear, and yanked him even tighter, rocking him back and forth. "This was so wise, my brave one," he croaked. "So strong, so prudent and cunning. So—*reckless*."

But it didn't sound disparaging this time, it sounded like awe, like wonder. And Olarr roughly yanked away again, so he could cradle both hands around Gerrard's face, and look him in the eyes. "You are a true son of the goddess, Aulis," he rasped. "You have won a fair victory, and proven yourself as a brave and worthy Bautul, beneath the goddess' eye."

A strange, shimmering warmth was thudding in Gerrard's chest, radiating into his limbs, into his slow, tentative smile. "Yeah?" he heard himself ask, almost shy. "You really think so?"

Olarr's nod was jerky, frantic, as his hands gave Gerrard a fierce little shake. "Ach, I know this," he said, his voice hard, utterly certain. "And all my kin now know this also. Ach, brothers?"

Gerrard followed his eyes, and then twitched at the sight of all those orcs, here. Standing in a loose circle around them, watching them. And while some of them were indeed smiling and nodding—Kalfr among them—a few of them still looked uneasy, confused, maybe even fearful. But none of them, Gerrard's distant thoughts pointed out, seemed even slightly saddened by Slagvor's passing, and one was even darkly frowning at his immobile body, while also warily kicking at it, as if to make sure he was dead.

"Ach, brothers?" Olarr asked again, with an edge of command on his voice. "You cannot claim that this was not a fair duel, in the way of the Bautul. This human won by his own hand, and had no aid in this, but from the goddess herself."

None of them seemed inclined to argue—and if Gerrard wasn't mistaken, Olarr's easy assumption of authority here wasn't new, either. These orcs were used to listening to him, following him, clearly more than he'd let on—and now his words from what felt like an age ago were echoing in Gerrard's skull.

I have upheld them to the best of my strength, for many, many summers. I have won them countless battles, and fed them countless meals, and gained many debts.

Was Olarr—was he aiming for *captain* of the Bautul? Had

he been working toward making himself captain, this entire time?

But curse it, of course he was, and Gerrard should have known that all along. Or maybe—maybe he even *had* known, with how he'd done his damnedest to set Olarr up after this, to make sure he didn't face any repercussions from this, whether Gerrard won or lost. But part of that setup had been Gerrard selling himself as a foolish lovestruck weakling, and not a calculating enemy who could take down an all-powerful Bautul captain in single combat.

And yes, yes, if Gerrard wasn't mistaken, that was suspicion, now glinting in several of the orcs' eyes—and one of them was fully frowning at Gerrard, his mouth pressed thin. "Ach, this human fairly won this battle," his deep voice said, "and we ken he scents of you, brother. But even if you have claimed him as your mate, this does not mean he has gained our trust. He is yet human, and a lieutenant in Preia's army. He is not a Bautul. He is our *enemy*."

There was more silence flanking the words, followed by more uneasy glances, and then a few brief nods. Agreeing with this, agreeing that Gerrard still couldn't be trusted—and Gerrard had to bite back his curse, the rising twitching frustration. Damn it, he hadn't just killed Slagvor to get Olarr strung up over this. To fuck up his chances of being made captain. But a good captain surely wouldn't cavort with the enemy against his clan's wishes, right? Let alone claiming one as his mate?

So Gerrard somehow took a breath, pasted on his most affronted expression—and then he spun and pouted up at Olarr, and even slapped him irritably across the chest. "What do they mean, I haven't gained their trust?" he demanded, in his sulkiest voice. "I thought you said if I beat Slagvor, that would be enough! And your clanmates would see how worthy I am, and let me be your proper Bautul mate!"

He could see Olarr's confusion, swiftly followed by

comprehension—and then his effort to shift his eyes, to jerk a dismissive shrug. But the affection in his eyes on Gerrard was real, almost painfully so, as he slowly shook his head. "The Bautul must yet agree upon such matters," he said. "I cannot force them to my will, upon this. And most of all upon an enemy human."

"But," Gerrard protested, and he didn't even need to bring the whine to his voice. "But this captain of yours was so horrid to you! Why does he get to be Bautul, and I don't? All those things he said about you! About Harja! I would have *liked* Harja, I'll have you know, and"—he let his pout deepen—"I bet he'd have liked me too. And you know he'd be right here cheering beside me, and probably setting this ugly prick's body on fire, so we don't need to look at him anymore!"

There was yet more fraught silence, a few more exchanged glances that said Gerrard wasn't wrong on this—and before any of them could speak, Gerrard slapped at Olarr again. "I almost died at least a *dozen times* just now," he continued. "You can't just cast me off over that! There must be something else I can do, right? I mean, I told you I'd keep spying for you, didn't I? And keep the human forces away from you, as much as I can?"

There were more shifting eyes and exchanged glances around them, but Olarr's eyes were only on Gerrard, his big hands now settling heavy to his shoulders. "You have done well, *litli maður*," he replied, his voice low, almost achingly tender. "You have done far more than I could have dreamt. But you ken my first fealty must always be to my kin, and my goddess."

He even glanced up at the moon as he spoke, and a jerk of sudden sinking misery pulled at Gerrard's belly, at his unsteady mouth. Because—because that was still true, wasn't it? Whatever the hell Olarr was saying right now, or not saying, that was still true. In the end, this was always going to come down to this choice, between Gerrard and the Bautul.

And Olarr had already made that choice, long before they'd come here. He'd lied to Gerrard. He'd planned to use him for the Bautul's gain. And now that he had, now that Gerrard had actually gone and done his bidding, fulfilled all Olarr's cunning plans, his own goals—Olarr didn't need Gerrard anymore. Did he?

"Right," Gerrard said, through the sudden burning in his throat, in his eyes. "Yeah. I see. I'm sorry I thought—right. I'll just—"

He dropped his eyes, jerked his head to the north, to safety—and then he shoved away, moving as quickly as his still-shaky legs would take him. But then he whirled back around, showing all these silent watching bastards his water-streaked face as he swiped unseeing for his sword, still stabbed in Slagvor's gut. He was not fucking leaving it behind this time, if this was it, then it was fucking *it*, and—

And then he reared back again, because he was facing—a wall of Bautul. All of them clumped together just before him, with Olarr at the front. And Olarr was wildly clutching for Gerrard's free hand, his own eyes suddenly molten too, because maybe—maybe he hadn't meant it. Maybe he hadn't wanted Gerrard to leave, after all. And Olarr was even shaking his head, bringing Gerrard's trembling hand to his own quivering mouth, kissing it as though Gerrard was some fine lady at a ball, and...

A—crash. Loud, crunching and crackling, from the south. And Gerrard and the Bautul all whipped to look in unison, at where a—a huge, hairy beast had emerged from the line of trees. Running on all fours at full speed toward them—*shit*—and Gerrard instantly snapped into his fighting stance, his eyes intent, his bloody sword raised. As the beast reared up toward him, and Gerrard braced for a strike, for—

For nothing. For nothing—nothing?—because the beast was now just standing there, and scowling at him. And Gerrard twitched as he stared back, as recognition finally flashed through his frantic brain. It was—an orc. A vaguely familiar orc. It was—*Silfast*?

But yes, yes, surely it was, except that Silfast was covered all over in mud and blood and horrifying fresh wounds. Including a vicious gash in his nose, a massive cut across his chest, and a visible head wound, causing a tuft of bloody hair to stand straight up from his skull. But he was alive, he was upright and moving, when Olarr had thought he might not survive at all. And Gerrard couldn't help his choked laugh of relief, especially once he caught sight of the second orc now running over after Silfast, and coughing between his deep, ragged breaths. Thorvald.

"Silfast!" Gerrard heard his voice say, as he lowered his sword again. "Didn't recognize you. But glad to see you're all right, yeah? Thank the goddess."

Silfast grunted, and then nodded at Gerrard—and his sword—with what almost seemed to be approval in his eyes. "Ach, Slagvor could never kill me," he said scornfully, with a sharp kick of his booted foot at Slagvor's body between them. "But I am most pleased to be greeted by his corpse, brothers. This was well done."

Gerrard gave a wan half-smile back, and a nod toward Thorvald, too. But Thorvald was blinking blankly down toward Slagvor, at where that axe was still standing upright in his neck, its curved blade buried deep into the earth. "Who did this, then?" Silfast continued, his voice echoing through the clearing. "Mayhap all of you together, as vengeance for Slagvor's great sins toward me? I yet cannot fathom that he sought to kill *me*, for ploughing a human! As if"—Silfast loudly scoffed, waving his bloody hand toward the group of assembled Bautul—"every one of our fathers has not also done this!"

There was another instant's echoing silence, heavy with something much like shame—until behind Gerrard, Olarr cleared his throat. "Aulis killed Slagvor, alone," he said thickly. "He challenged him to a Bautul duel, before the goddess."

Yet more silence rang behind his words, as Silfast's eyes widened, and then dropped toward the sword in Gerrard's hand. The sword that was still streaked with fresh red blood. Slagvor's blood.

"Then I—thank you, human, for avenging me," Silfast finally said, into the stilted silence, with a brief little bow toward Gerrard. "And I commend you, also. There are not many Bautul brave enough to face this. Or"—his lip curled as he glanced between Gerrard and the rest of the Bautul—"to next seek to keep safe all his kin, when he sees a new threat before them."

Oh. Damn. Gerrard darted a glance over his shoulder, wincing at the belated realization of how this must look—one single human standing poised before a dozen huge Bautul warriors, ready to foolishly take on an unknown beast, on their behalf. And though he abruptly lowered his sword, he could feel his face again burning, his head twitching back and forth.

"Thanks, but I actually—was just leaving," he gritted out, with a jerky shrug. "But I—hope this helped. It was—good meeting you all."

He'd already turned away again, about to push back through the cluster of Bautul—but wait, they were all blocking him again, Olarr nearest of all. Olarr still with that pure molten misery in his eyes, while behind Gerrard, there was a loud scoffing noise, and then the sound of something being wrenched from the earth.

"You cannot yet leave without this," came Silfast's hard voice, and when Gerrard glanced backwards, Silfast was holding Slagvor's axe, and thrusting it out toward him. "It is your fairly won battle-prize, human. And also"—his eyes narrowed—"why must you now leave us?"

His gaze had sharply flicked to Olarr, whose big warm hand now slipped around Gerrard's side, drawing him close. "I have shared my wish," Olarr supplied, his voice stilted, "to welcome Aulis amongst us, and claim him not only as my mate, but as a full Bautul, also. But"—his gaze slid toward the first orc who'd argued it—"not all our kin are in accord, upon this."

Silfast's scoff was instant, his lip curling, his arms crossing over his bloody chest. "Why is this?" he snapped back. "Why can we not welcome this man? Most of all after he has avenged me, and thus done our clan a great service, as any new Bautul warrior ought? Even when the rest of our clan was too weak and fearful to do this?"

He'd again cast a pointed glance down toward Slagvor's body, while the orc who'd originally protested was purposefully avoiding any of the others' eyes. At least, until another unfamiliar orc spoke, waving his clawed hand up toward the sky.

"This human has not yet been taken on an altar before us," he said flatly. "In the way a Bautul mate ought to be claimed, before the goddess."

Gerrard blinked, cast an uneasy glance at Olarr, while beside them, Silfast's expression briefly cleared, before glowering back toward Olarr. "Ach, has this not yet been done, Olarr?" he demanded. "Why have you not first offered this? There is an altar near here, and the goddess now grants us her blessing!"

He'd waved imperiously at the full moon, and again frowned at Olarr—but Olarr was looking at Gerrard again, his hand clenching against his side. His expression gone uneasy, nervous, even pained.

"This is a long-standing Bautul custom," Olarr told Gerrard, under his breath. "Any mate wishing to join our clan must freely seek the goddess' favour upon an altar, with their Bautul orc. They must be... bared, and opened, and offered before the clan, and offer a gift of fresh Bautul seed in return."

Oh. Wait. Olarr sure as hell hadn't mentioned anything like that before, had he? And at Gerrard's disbelieving stare back toward him, Olarr winced, and clasped him even tighter. "I did not wish to expect this of you, warrior," he choked. "Not after all else you have done."

Right. Of course. More secrets, more important things Olarr hadn't told Gerrard, ostensibly for his own damned good. And he couldn't have said whether it was fury, or recklessness, or just sheer fool stubbornness, that made him spin back toward Silfast, his chin lifted, his hand again gripping tightly at his sword.

"Then take us to the altar, brother," he snapped, "and let's do this. Now."

30

As promised, the goddess' altar was close. Close enough that Gerrard still hadn't quite digested what he'd agreed to, even as Olarr drew him to a halt before it. As Olarr slowly turned to face him, his eyes uneasy, uncertain, maybe even sad.

The rest of the Bautul had already followed them, now standing in a loose circle around the flat, fur-topped stone. Ready to watch this, to judge this, to weigh Gerrard by another scale he hadn't even known existed.

Gerrard swallowed, shot another glance up at the moon—and then began undressing, yanking at his uniform's buttons with numb, fumbling fingers. He'd agreed to this, he was going to do this, he was going to fucking get Olarr out of this, and then...

Olarr's hand closed over his, warm but firm, and when Gerrard shot a glance up at his face, he was still looking—miserable. His mouth drawn thin, his eyes heavy and shadowed in the moonlight. "Ach, Aulis," he said, a low rasp between them. "There is no—"

"No reason not to do this, yeah?" Gerrard cut in, fighting to keep the sharpness out of his voice. "Goddess knows I could use a good proper pounding, after all that! I need you to put your brilliant Bautul prick to good use, and erase that vile scum from my memory, all right?"

He hoped it sounded like something a lovestruck minion would say, complete with an entirely genuine grimace behind him. Toward where he could just still make out Slagvor's body, lying with unnatural stillness beneath the silvery moonlight.

Olarr had followed Gerrard's eyes, his throat convulsing—but then, thank the goddess, he nodded. Nodded, and drew Gerrard close, folding him into his arms.

His kisses were gentle at first, lips brushing soft again and again, but Gerrard could feel the intensity simmering behind them, behind the slow stroking touches of Olarr's hands. The way he was touching Gerrard as if he was made of glass, or of gold, the reverence whispering without a word through his lips and his fingers.

It did make it easier, better, and Gerrard could feel his heartbeat slowing as he willingly sank into it, into the familiar reassurance of Olarr's body, his touch. Enough that he only twitched a little when Olarr gently lifted him, setting him down onto the altar, and then began working at his buttons with one hand, while the other cupped his face, slid into his hair. Keeping Gerrard's focus fully on him, and not on the band of orcs watching them—but Gerrard could still feel them, could still hear them, the shifting feet and breaths, the occasional quiet cough from Thorvald's direction.

But despite it all, Olarr was still here, still stronger, as his hands gently drew off the jacket of Gerrard's uniform, and then his undershirt, baring his upper body to the moonlight, to his touch. To where his hands were already stroking again, sliding harder and faster, the hunger bleeding into his fingers, shimmering in his too-bright eyes as he drew away, searched Gerrard's flushed-feeling face.

"You are yet sure, Aulis," he whispered, so quiet—and this time, Gerrard groaned his frustration, rolled backwards, and yanked Olarr downwards over him. So they were both lying on the altar, now, Gerrard slightly shivering on his back, Olarr held up on his elbows over him. Still looking at him like that, with all that miserable regret shouting in his eyes, and Gerrard pulled him down further, crushed their mouths back together.

Olarr didn't protest again after that, just kept kissing and touching and caressing, worshipping Gerrard with his mouth and his hands. As Gerrard's body kept responding, kept welcoming that painfully familiar touch, his own desperate craving kindling higher and hotter with every breath. Until he was almost grateful when Olarr finally tugged off his uniform's trousers, and freed his rigid, straining cock into the open air.

There were a few distant murmurs at the sight, enough that Gerrard's eyes did dart sideways, toward where all these Bautul orcs were still watching, many with unmistakable interest—or even greed—glinting in their eyes. But Olarr was here again, drawing Gerrard's face back again, consuming his mouth with his own, tasting him with his long, hungry tongue.

"They have only never before seen a man thus, so rich and full with hunger," Olarr murmured, between kisses. "They only envy me, you ken."

Gerrard fully expected to hear protests from the watching Bautul, or maybe laughter or mockery, but nothing came. Only more caresses from Olarr's hands, more heated kisses from his mouth, as he finally kicked off his own trousers, too. Pressing the full length of his bared, heavy body down against Gerrard on the altar, the ponderous shaft at his groin already dropping deep between Gerrard's thighs, streaking slickness against his crease.

"They only wish to know—the joy of this," Olarr's hitching voice continued, as his knees spread Gerrard's wider, and that slick, delving head swiftly found what it was seeking.

Shuddering as it settled there, spurting out more hot hunger against it, into it. While Gerrard gasped and clutched back, feeling it, kissing it—and then... welcoming it. Opening for it, while a dozen orcs stood there, and watched. Watched Olarr's hard, straining body sinking into him, opening him up with smooth, familiar ease, while he shook and spasmed upon it.

"They only wish to know what it is," Olarr murmured, between gasps, as he pressed deeper, deeper. "To have a brave, powerful human warrior freely offer up such a gift. Such favour. Such *power*."

His fluttering eyes had even flicked up toward the goddess again, holding there with palpable gratitude, with worship. As his strength inside Gerrard swelled even fuller, giving Gerrard even more, offering more in return.

And though it should have been humiliating, mortifying, being splayed out, plugged up and put on display before all these watching orcs, Gerrard found himself almost—nodding. Agreeing. Because yes, he could admit now, this was strength. This was a gift. This was him making the choice to do this, to find pleasure in this, and maybe even power. To have a huge, deadly orc worshipping on his knees over him, offering up his body, his fealty, his surrender. Giving it all to Gerrard, freely and publicly, before all his clan, for Gerrard to use and wield however he damn well wished.

"More, captain," Gerrard breathed, ordered, snapping Olarr's eyes back to his. "Give me more."

Olarr's breath choked, his groan rumbling through his throat, and yes, yes, that was more. His strength inside Gerrard obligingly swelling fuller, sinking deeper, and Gerrard pulled his head down again, gave him a sharp, biting kiss this time. "Told you, I want a proper Bautul pounding," he breathed. "Want you fucking *working* for me on this altar, captain."

Olarr groaned again, but yes, yes, he was doing it. His hips rocking now, grinding against Gerrard's arse with compulsive purpose, swirling out swarms of sensation all around it, sparkling it up Gerrard's spine. And Gerrard was meeting it, clinging to him, spurring him on faster, faster. "Good, captain," he breathed. "You're gonna open me up wide for you, aren't you? Gonna make me swallow up every last drop of that good orc-seed?"

There were a few more murmurs from the watching Bautul around them, but Olarr's groan was far louder, vibrating into Gerrard's ear. His body pumping even harder, his hips levering himself in and out, while Gerrard arched and met it, drank it deep inside him. "Yeah, just like that," he gasped. "You're gonna fatten me up on you, aren't you? Gonna make me reek of you, and your good Bautul seed?"

The watching orcs murmured again, one of them even letting out a low whistle, while Olarr plunged faster, his movements jerky and frantic, his eyes wide on Gerrard's face. Shimmering with shock, with fervour, with pure blatant devotion, and Gerrard twitched a little smile back, and slipped his hand up into Olarr's messy hair. Guiding his head downward, down into his neck, into that scar he'd made, so many moons ago...

"Good, captain," Gerrard breathed, his head tilting up, his eyes fluttering, as Olarr's hungry teeth scraped against his skin. "You take your human however the hell you want. You rut me, bind me, mark me. Ruin me, for anyone but you."

Olarr's body was trembling and straining all over, mindlessly driving into Gerrard, worshipping him, obeying him. Those teeth seeking harder, sharper, as the furious craving whipped closer, coiling and condensing, lurching for the edge...

"Yeah, just like that," Gerrard gasped, his eyes rolling back, again finding the light of the moon above. "Taste me, take me, *love* me. Fill me with yourself, with your worship, until I'm too full to hold it all in—"

And fuck, yes, Olarr's shout roaring into his ear, into his skin, as sharp teeth sank deep, and that cock inside Gerrard jerked, and released. Pumping out with so much force that he could feel the flood of fresh heat slamming inside, could feel the pain and the pressure, flashing bright and dazzling with the crush of teeth in his skin. It was so, so good, so perfect, so right, everything Gerrard had wanted, everything he'd asked for, such a good obedient orc, worthy of blessing, of gifts, and—

His own pleasure caught, quivered—and then capitulated, spraying out of his straining cock with fierce, aimless abandon. Painting his bare chest all over with it, and oh, Olarr had yanked back to watch, his eyes hazy and bright, his mouth streaked with red, streaming slick and messy down his chin. But it looked good on him, he was so fucking good, and Gerrard arched and moaned beneath him, let the ecstasy and the rightness wash over him, raw and rugged and pure beneath the watching light of the moon.

When the pleasure finally twined away, ebbing into trembling little shudders, Gerrard found himself sprawled wide and debauched on the altar, his belly visibly swollen, and painted all over with astonishing amounts of his own spend. While Olarr was still caught inside him, his half-hard cock still spasming as his shoulders heaved, and his greedy eyes drank up the sight of Gerrard beneath him. And as his tongue licked again and again at his red lips, as if he'd never tasted anything so glorious, except, perhaps...

Gerrard's hand smeared against his rounded belly on its own, sliding itself into his own slick—and then he raised his hand to Olarr's mouth. Another silent order, or maybe an offering, or both—but Olarr instantly took it, groaning harsh and guttural as his tongue snapped out, curled against Gerrard's fingers. Licking them off with urgent, single-minded hunger, until he'd caught every drop—so Gerrard did it again. And this time, he didn't miss the audible groans from the orcs around him, or—he glanced again toward them—the vivid, undeniable craving in their eyes.

And now that Gerrard's own craving was mostly sated, it abruptly occurred to him that this, too, was power. This attention, this longing, this hunger. *They only wish to know what it is,* Olarr had said, *to have a brave, powerful human warrior freely offer up such a gift. The fresh seed of a human man is the richest, sweetest, most wondrous taste in all the realm...*

And Gerrard wasn't thinking this, he wasn't, rash, reckless, *cunning,* as his hand again streaked in his own copious mess, and then held itself... up. "Do you think, captain," he whispered, his heart suddenly thrumming in his ears, "that your warriors might want a taste, too?"

There was a beat of taut, stunned silence, Olarr's eyes shot wide and disbelieving—and then, oh, a groan. Multiple groans. Multiple glittering, hungry eyes staring at Gerrard, at Olarr, awaiting Olarr's decision, his own gift to his clanmates. And Gerrard was bracing himself now, brittle and breathless, because what if this was some kind of horrendous error in judgement on his part, what if it was an insult, or Olarr considered it a betrayal, or...

Or wait. Wait. Because behind the shock, that look in Olarr's eyes was... approving. Appreciative. And maybe even— awed. Just like the day Gerrard had met Kalfr's duel, and the day he'd beaten Silfast. As if Olarr couldn't believe his good fortune, couldn't possibly believe a human had followed this, was doing this, offering him this.

Olarr's nod was rapid and fervent, his hands spasming at where they'd been gripping on Gerrard's hips—but Gerrard could see him attempting to smooth it over, to find his familiar authority again, as he glanced sideways, toward the nearest orc. The one who'd first protested Gerrard's being Bautul, and who was now looking at his still-upraised hand with blatant longing in his eyes.

"Ach, I should be honoured to grant my warriors such a gift, human," Olarr said, his voice only slightly wavering. "Matuk, should you wish to be first?"

The orc—Matuk—flinched all over, but then jerked a nod, and lurched forward. Standing over Gerrard now, near enough to touch—but then stilling, glancing uncertainly toward Gerrard's upheld hand. And what was Gerrard doing, oh goddess, bringing his dripping fingers to this Matuk's mouth, brushing them against his hot grey lips...

Matuk instantly groaned, his tongue slipping out, curling swift and slick against Gerrard's fingers. Feeling so foreign, so strange, so similar to Olarr's tongue, but so unlike it, too—but Gerrard's glance at Olarr found him still watching with unmistakable approval glinting in his eyes. Or maybe even hunger, hunger that was echoed by an unmistakable swelling of his half-hard strength, still buried deep inside Gerrard's arse.

"My mate tastes good, ach?" Olarr's cool voice said to Matuk, tinged through with pride, maybe even triumph. "He pleases you?"

Matuk's hazy eyes fluttered as he nodded, as he sucked Gerrard's finger fully into his hot mouth—but at that, Olarr gave a low hiss, and plucked Gerrard's hand away. "Enough," he said. "Who shall be next?"

It turned out that Thorvald was next, eyeing Gerrard with something between fear and abject craving, but Gerrard half-smiled back, and slid his hand back into his mess, getting more. Not minding nearly as much as Thorvald reverently licked off his fingers, one by one, and Olarr didn't seem to mind either, watching Thorvald with mild, indulgent eyes.

But Thorvald, too, needed to be nudged away, and then came another orc, and another. Working their way around the circle, Gerrard realized, taking turns, though Silfast only bowed his head toward Olarr when his turn came, and Kalfr visibly hesitated, glancing toward the bulky, cool-eyed orc beside him. But the orc waved him forward with an impatient hand, and soon it was Kalfr kissing at Gerrard's fingers, his eyes fluttering, his mouth warm and gentle.

Kalfr's companion was far less so, even allowing his teeth to scrape against Gerrard's fingers, but somehow Olarr had caught it—perhaps in the look on Gerrard's face—and hissed the orc away, waving the next one forward. But by now Gerrard's rounded belly was sticky, almost dry, and Gerrard didn't miss Olarr's brief, seeking glance, his silent question, before he waved the orc toward Gerrard's belly.

"You may lick my mate clean, Arne," he said, with the air of one making a great concession. "And should he be so kind to allow this, mayhap I shall fuck out another load of his sweet seed for the rest of you."

Olarr was already fully hard again, grinding deep inside, though his eyes were again searching Gerrard's, again with a twinge of uncertainty, as if he was sure this would be the line too far. But Gerrard was already too deep in this now, damn it, and it certainly wasn't a hardship to have an orc's mouth gently licking at his belly like this, while Olarr's jutting cock swelled even further, sent more pleasure spiralling through his groin.

"Whatever you want, captain," Gerrard murmured, gasping as the next orc's tongue slipped into his navel, and Olarr's grinding began hardening into smooth, steady thrusts. "I'm your mate, yeah? Yours to use however you please."

Olarr's growl was low and velvety, deepening as the orc's licking tongue brushed dangerously close to Gerrard's own rapidly swelling cock. "Careful, Thrand," Olarr hissed. "My mate's prick is mine alone. I only share his seed with you, ach?"

This Thrand instantly obliged, moving back to safer territory, but he didn't stop licking, either. And soon the next orc had joined in on the other side, scattering out more spinning, staggering sensation, especially once Olarr's hand closed around Gerrard's swollen cock, drawing it up. Almost fully concealing it, protecting it in his slowly pumping grip, so the Bautul could keep tasting him beneath, swirling their tongues against his skin and even into his coarse hair, until he was licked entirely clean.

But wait, now there was more for them to taste, seeping out smooth and clear from Gerrard's slit, and Olarr squeezed it out onto his rounded belly, watched with hazy eyes as it was immediately licked away. And then there was more, more, oozing out drop by drop as Olarr kept driving in, his hand steadily working, making more. And oh, the Bautul were still taking turns, but now two—three—four—at once, the fourth just kissing at Gerrard's chest, tonguing at his nipple, because maybe he was waiting, watching, for—

Gerrard shouted as the relief consumed him again, as his body contracted all over, as the hot release sprayed from within Olarr's fist. Spattering Gerrard's belly all over again, and catching a few of the orcs, too—not that they seemed to mind, because they were groaning, jostling for position, seeking out more. While Olarr—somehow, even as he kept going— directed it all, ordered them to take turns, and viciously snarled when Kalfr's friend got too close to Gerrard's still-raw-feeling neck.

It felt like Gerrard was just swimming in the sensation of it now, rolling with the impossible giddy unreality of it. With Olarr still pumping into him, still pumping every last straining drop out of him, while hot, slippery mouths kissed and caressed him, cleaned him, bathed him, blessed him beneath the moon's watching eye.

And when Olarr finally gasped and sprayed out again, too, plumping Gerrard's already-full belly even fatter and rounder beneath those licking tongues, it felt even more unreal, more unimaginable. More like a frantic, far-away fever dream, like a bizarrely sweet battle-frenzy consuming Gerrard whole—especially when Olarr drew himself out, leaving hot seed bubbling and gurgling in his wake. And then his own hot mouth dropped to Gerrard's half-hard cock, enveloping it full and safe inside, caressing its wildly sensitive head with his slick seeking tongue. The feeling too much, so much, joining the overpowering truth of all those other licking tongues, but resonating so much stronger above it all, as if staking out its claim, its conquest, its...

Its worship. Its blessing. And in a brief, dangling glimpse of clarity, Gerrard saw all the orcs bowed over him on the altar, honouring him, anointing him in the moonlight. While he squeezed out one final shudder of seed, the very dregs of all he had—and in return, his mate reverently swallowed, and gave him one last, lingering kiss. And then rose to his knees on the altar, his hand over his heart, his craggy face lifted toward the moon.

"Goddess of Bautul," he breathed, the words hushed, awed, reverberating with the waiting, shining forest all around. "I bring my brave, beloved Aulis here before you this night. I beg your blessing upon him. I beg you to grant him your favour, and welcome him here amongst us. To welcome him as my own bonded Bautul mate."

His words hung there in the silence, waiting for an answer—and after another instant, it seemed to... come. Shimmering softly around them with the rustle of the trees, the steady silver gleam of the moon. A light that almost seemed to brighten as it smiled down upon them, as it saw Gerrard's offering, and accepted it. Welcomed it. Drew it into its bosom, its secret hallowed home, and flowed out light and favour in its wake.

He was blessed. He was brave. He was... Bautul.

"Oooooh," cut in a voice, a new, unfamiliar, human-accented voice. "It's Slagvor's head! Does this mean it's time for a party?"

31

It was, it turned out, time for a party.

The new arrivals turned out to be a band of reinforcements from Orc Mountain, and among them were multiple new Bautul, along with a gruff, heavily scarred orc from the Ash-Kai clan who was apparently a healer. And close beside the healer was the first orc who'd spoken, a lean, long-haired, excessively handsome orc who beamed between Olarr and Gerrard with unmistakable glee.

"Oh, this is perfect," he said brightly, casting an appreciative eye up and down Gerrard's still-bared body, now seated on the altar. "Oh, *look* at him, Eft. And smell him! I only wish we'd gotten here in time to see Slagvor's face before you chopped his ugly head off. Absolutely brilliant work, sweetheart."

Gerrard couldn't recall the last time he'd been called *sweetheart*—if ever—but he gave a polite nod and smile back, despite Olarr's distinctly disgruntled grunt beside him. "My mate is called *Aulis Gerrard*, of Clan Bautul," Olarr said repressively. "And Aulis, this is Kesst, and our mountain's Chief Healer, Efterar. Who is also Kesst's *mate*."

Gerrard gave a polite nod toward this Efterar too, even as a distant part of his brain was still whirling to catch up. Because Olarr was—he wasn't *jealous*, was he? After he'd just gone and let a dozen orcs *lick* Gerrard, and taste his fresh spunk?

This Kesst seemed to share Gerrard's confusion, because he rolled his eyes, and tossed his long black hair over his shoulder. "Oh, get over yourself, Olarr," he snapped. "The only one around here losing his head over a handsome human is *you*. Well"—he wrinkled his nose, and glanced around at all the Bautul now milling about—"you, and your entire band! You didn't actually *share* your gorgeous killer man with them, did you?"

An unmistakable redness was creeping up Olarr's neck, and he jerked his head back and forth, his own lip curling with distaste. "Only his seed," he said stiffly. "And only amongst my closest Bautul warriors, to aid in his offering before the goddess. But this is *all*, for he is *mine*."

There was a surprising hostility in Olarr's voice, as if he suspected this Kesst might well make an attempt to seduce Gerrard away from him at any moment. To which Kesst rolled his eyes again, and unceremoniously pushed Efterar toward Gerrard, before stalking off toward Slagvor. "Who's going to help me light this old ghoul on fire?" he called out. "Anyone got any really flammable fuel?"

Beyond an affectionate look over his shoulder toward Kesst's back, this Efterar looked thoroughly unperturbed by any of this, and was already holding up a hand, hovering it up and down over Gerrard's bared body. "Mind if I touch you, Bautul, to help deal with some of this?" he asked Gerrard, nodding toward some of his cuts and bruises. "It won't hurt, I promise."

Gerrard shot a questioning glance toward Olarr, but he was nodding, his eyes steady again, clearly far more approving of this Efterar than of Kesst. And when Gerrard nodded too, Efterar settled his warm hand to the bruise on

Gerrard's shoulder. Holding there for a long, hanging moment, as something seemed to prickle beneath the touch—and when his hand drew away again, the bruise was—gone?

Gerrard twitched and gaped at it, but Olarr again didn't look slightly alarmed, and waved Efterar toward a gash in Gerrard's thigh. To where it soon was miraculously healed too, followed by multiple more cuts and bruises, most of which Gerrard had entirely forgotten about during the proceedings. Until the only stinging left was in Gerrard's neck, where Olarr had again bitten him, in what felt like the exact same place as before.

"Do you want this addressed?" Efterar was asking now, his eyes glancing between Olarr and Gerrard. "Or your abdomen? I could probably make it so the seed doesn't swell you quite as much, going forward. The trimmer you are, the more likely it is to show like this."

Now it was Gerrard's face rapidly heating, and he jerked a quick, dismissive wave of his hand. "No, it's fine," he said, as steadily as he could. "It'll sort itself out eventually, it always does."

As he'd spoken, Olarr's hand had even slipped over to spread against his rounded waist, as if to protect it from Efterar's unwanted interference. And once Gerrard had managed a thank-you, Efterar shrugged and went off to join Kesst, where a small but growing fire was already crackling away in the clearing.

Olarr had cleared his throat, obviously about to speak— when up ahead, even more orcs suddenly crashed into the clearing. All of them calling out greetings and questions, accompanied by loud exclamations about Slagvor—though again, none of them seemed particularly disappointed by his demise. While beside Gerrard, Olarr was looking both aggrieved and relieved, and finally he groped for Gerrard's uniform and helped him dress, before drawing him over to meet the newcomers.

There were at least a dozen more new orcs, most of them more Bautul, but one of them was Olarr's longstanding ally Grimarr, too. He turned out to be a big, serious, capable-looking fellow, also from the Ash-Kai clan, and he greeted Gerrard with what seemed to be genuine warmth, before loudly congratulating him on his victory in such a fairly won Bautul duel. Making it all sound very natural and above-board, as though there could have been no other possible outcome— and that there was nothing bizarre whatsoever about having an enemy lieutenant standing here in his bloody, ragged uniform, watching as a half-dozen Bautul orcs dragged their former captain's heavy body onto the now-roaring fire.

Someone had brought out a set of drums, ostensibly as a send-off to Slagvor, but if anyone else noticed that Grimarr spat on the fire afterwards—followed by a few other Bautul—they didn't let on. And as the drumbeats thrummed through Gerrard's feet, he felt himself slightly relaxing again, sinking into the certainty that the mood had shifted decisively in their favour. Perhaps because of this Grimarr's decidedly authoritative presence, and his obvious desire to smooth over the situation—but surely also because of what had happened with Gerrard on the altar. Because of how the Bautul had kissed him, and tasted him. Welcomed him.

And Gerrard could still feel it, even now, glancing around the fire. Several of them were still watching him, some with unmistakable warmth in their eyes, and Kalfr was even smiling softly toward him—at least, until his sharp-eyed companion knocked him in the shoulder. Several more were looking toward Olarr, some with envy in their eyes, some with something almost like cunning. As if they were slyly plotting ways to gain another taste of Gerrard's spunk, or maybe even to steal him away from Olarr altogether.

But that sure as hell wasn't part of Gerrard's plan, and he cleared his throat, leaned in a little closer to Olarr. "So, now that Slagvor's gone," he said, too loudly, "who gets to take his place as captain?"

He hadn't quite expected the jolt of sudden watchfulness around the fire, the way multiple orcs' heads instantly swivelled toward him, and even the drummer had fallen silent again. But Gerrard again fought to keep the bland innocence in his eyes as he vaguely smiled back, and then grinned up at Olarr beside him. "I just think you'd do a brilliant job of it, captain," he said lightly. "You've been working yourself ragged caring for your kin for years, yeah? And you're so strong and cunning, too."

He punctuated this with an eager caress of his hand to Olarr's bulging bicep, stroking appreciatively up and down, while Olarr swallowed, and cast him a look he couldn't at all read. "This is not a choice that is made in one night," he replied, his voice low. "Or even amongst only us here. This is upon all the Bautul to choose."

Right. But Gerrard hadn't missed how the Bautul were glancing at each other again, how the idea of appointing Olarr as their captain clearly wasn't an unwelcome one—when Olarr swallowed again, twitched a shake of his head. "And mayhap I should not be the one best suited for this," he said, heavier. "I ken I have oft been too... prudent. Too careful, too cunning, at the cost of those I care for most."

His eyes were very steady on Gerrard now, glimmering with that familiar sadness, with regret. And then he shot a pained-looking glance toward Silfast, too, who—despite how Efterar was currently working over him—was still visibly bleeding from multiple wounds, his gaze now very intent on the light of the moon above them.

Gerrard could see the other orcs' eyes glancing toward Silfast too, clearly remembering the obvious danger Olarr had brought upon his clanmate and friend. And curse Olarr, he was not about to fuck up all Gerrard's efforts over his damned unhelpful guilt, and Gerrard desperately fought to keep the ease in his eyes, the blithe smile on his mouth. "Well, maybe you just need a good co-captain, then," he said, as smoothly as he could. "Someone who balances out your cunning with a little more recklessness."

He'd given a purposeful nod toward Silfast as he spoke, earning a brief nod from Silfast in return, his eyes glinting with unmistakable appreciation. But when Gerrard glanced back at Olarr, Olarr's eyes were still firmly fixed on him, as something wavered on his smiling mouth. "Ach, warrior," he said thickly. "I ken you are right, in this."

It was very clear Olarr wasn't just talking about Silfast, and though Gerrard kept smiling back, he knew it didn't reach his eyes this time. And he was distantly grateful to hear this Kesst's cool voice cutting in, dryly pointing out that the Bautul could do a damn sight worse than Olarr and Silfast as co-captains, and also, did anyone have any fresh meat to roast over the fire?

There were a few choked laughs at that, and then the murmur of drums and conversation rose again, sounding even more relaxed and relieved than before. A few orcs even came over to congratulate Olarr and Gerrard on the evening's gains, and Gerrard greeted their well-wishes as gratefully as he could, though he couldn't quite seem to look at Olarr anymore. Not even when he could feel Olarr studying him, and bending down to inhale against his still-raw neck—and finally Olarr was making excuses, saying farewells. While Gerrard just kept nodding and smiling, even as Grimarr came over, and thrust something soft into his chest.

"A mating-gift," he said firmly. "We shall speak again soon, brothers."

Brothers. Again as if Gerrard really was one of them now, and he again fought to nod and smile, and to thank Grimarr for the gift. Which, at first glance, seemed to be some sort of women's shawl, coloured a garish bright yellow. But by this point, Gerrard was well beyond trying to understand any more bewildering orc customs, and he made a show of politely patting the shawl before slinging it over his shoulder, and then blithely waving goodbye as Olarr steered him away.

"Should you wish to rest for the night, Aulis?" Olarr said, quiet, as the sounds of the voices and drumbeats gradually faded behind them. "There is a cave near here, and—"

"No," Gerrard cut in, his voice tired but certain. "I want to go back to my camp."

He hadn't at all meant to say that, hadn't even thought it, but now it seemed like what he'd always meant to do. Because the part of him that he'd locked away throughout all that—the part of him that was still distantly screaming—was suddenly pacing in its cell, grabbing and shaking at bars. Needing Gerrard to finally see it again, to hear it again, to face all its damning, devastating truths.

Olarr had still lied to him. Olarr had still betrayed him. Olarr had still planned for him to kill Slagvor, at the start, and now Gerrard had gone and done it. He'd done it, and he'd even wrapped it all up in a clean, pretty little package to hand back to Olarr, too. At the cost of his own pride, his own submission, his own brazen public debauchery on that altar.

And the more his imprisoned conscience clawed its way out, the more Gerrard understood that the altar had, surely, been the crux of it, even more than his defeating Slagvor. Because on that altar, Olarr had demonstrated to all his clan, very clearly, that Gerrard wasn't a threat. He'd proven that Gerrard was his to wield, to use, to command and share as he pleased. He'd proven his strength, by crushing Gerrard's own beneath it...

But curse it, no, no. Gerrard had already worked through this, already come to terms with this, and he drew in breath, raised his eyes to the still-watching moon. He'd made that choice, on that altar. He'd given Olarr that gift, of his own free will. Even if Olarr didn't deserve it, or even realize it, Gerrard had done it. Because it was the right thing to do. Because the Bautul deserved better, and Harja deserved vengeance.

And because—Gerrard's eyes prickled as he blinked up at the moon—because he loved Olarr. He loved Olarr, he loved him like he couldn't remember loving anyone but his parents. Loved him so much that it had torn a raw, jagged, leaking wound in his chest, just like the one in his neck.

"Ach, Aulis," came Olarr's voice beside him, cracking into the heavy, bitter silence. "Should you only wish to go back, and never again see me, or speak to me, I fully follow this. I shall honour this. But I only wish to say—"

His voice broke, his breaths dragging, but Gerrard just kept walking, numb, waiting. Because he couldn't bear to stop, to look, he couldn't...

"I wish to—thank you," Olarr croaked. "Thank you for your great kindness toward me. Thank you for wielding your strength and your cunning—and ach, your recklessness—on my behalf. Thank you for your care of my kin. Thank you for— avenging Harja, in my stead. In the face of all my failings."

Gerrard swallowed hard, let out a shaky breath. "Happy to help," he said, though it felt so trite, so hollow. "Glad it worked out."

There was more heavy silence beside him, but Gerrard still couldn't look. Could only keep his eyes on the moon, on the distant quiet whisper of hope in its silvery light. The reminder of why he'd done this. What it meant. One small step toward ending this war.

"But actually, I do have one request for you, in return," Gerrard heard his voice add, flatter than before. "I want you to—to *use* this, Olarr. To do everything within your power to make yourself captain of the Bautul, whether that's with

Silfast or not. You won't just sit there and watch while another piece of carrion like Slagvor crawls out of the mire, and tries to drag the rest of your clan back down with him. Fucking *no*, Olarr."

The silence beside him seemed to stretch, quivering, trembling out in a slow, hitching sigh. "Ach, warrior," Olarr replied, very quiet. "I shall do this. I swear this to you, before our goddess."

Gerrard's eyes finally darted toward Olarr, taking in his upturned head, his eyes fixed to the moon, his hand over his heart. Making another vow, and Gerrard's thoughts flicked back to his last vow, the vow he'd made when he'd thought Gerrard was about to die.

I pledge you my troth, Aulis Gerrard. I grant you my axe, and my favour, and my fealty. I shall honour you, and care for you, and keep you safe. For as long as I bear breath.

Gerrard wanted to laugh, or maybe weep, but instead he just kept walking, gazing blankly at the dim path up ahead. While Olarr kept perfect pace with him, his heavy breaths now audible in the silence.

"I also wish you to know, Aulis," Olarr abruptly said, "how sorry I am. I am sorry for breaking my first vow to you, when I swore not to harm you. I am sorry for hiding my truth from you. I am sorry for all the grief and pain I brought you. And I am sorry"—he drew in a shaky breath—"if ever I led you to believe that you were not my... equal. That I saw you as weaker. As... less."

Gerrard couldn't hide his reflexive flinch, his eyes cutting brief and searching toward Olarr beside him. Toward where Olarr was again looking at the moon, drawing in more deep breaths, as if seeking for courage.

"But in truth, Aulis," he continued, on another heavy exhale, "I have *never* seen you as less. You have always been— more. So much more. So much stronger and brighter than any other I have known. I have admired you, and envied you, and longed to be near you, from the first night we met."

Oh. Gerrard's dry mouth swallowed, his throat constricted and hot, and Olarr let out another unsteady breath, rubbing both hands at his eyes. "And now, this night," he choked. "I shall never forget all you have done tonight, Aulis. How you faced my kin with such bravery and cunning. How you offered me the gift of your surrender before them, and then the gift of your seed—the one gift they could not refuse. The one gift that would bind them to you, and bring them alongside me, to share my fate, and defend me against the rest of our kin. And Slagvor—"

He broke off there, whipping his head back and forth, as a low, strangled growl scraped from his throat. "I have never known fear such as this, in any battle I have ever fought," he rasped. "But you, Aulis—you faced my greatest enemy with such strength, and such wisdom, and such ease. You fought as though you were a god yourself. The goddess' blessing burned upon you, warrior, and we all saw this. We all knew this. But you made sure of this, upon that altar. You bound us, and uplifted us, with your care, and your light."

His voice was hushed now, his eyes again glimmering on Gerrard's face, his hand spreading wide over his heart. "I ken you may no more wish for my vow of matehood," he croaked. "But should you allow this, I should yet be honoured to serve you. I should be honoured to follow you, and stay with you, and keep you safe, with all my strength. Whether as only your vassal, or your guard, or your... bedmate. Aught that you might wish, aught within my power. No matter where you are, or upon which side of this war you now stand."

Gerrard stared at him again, his stomach twisting, his heart thundering in his chest. Because not only was Olarr saying he'd meant that vow of matehood he'd made, but he was also offering up—power. Command. Recognition of what Gerrard had done, what Gerrard had given him. And goddess, it would be so easy for Gerrard to take it, to wield it, to use it as his own vengeance, for all he'd borne...

But his head was already shaking, his hand gripping tightly at his sword-hilt, and he desperately fought for breath, courage, bravery, cunning. Fought his way through the mess, through his own selfishness and pride, to where...

"Look, Olarr," he replied, his voice steady but resigned. "You just promised me—and our goddess—that you'll make yourself captain of the Bautul, and be a good leader to your kin. And you're not very well going to do that if I've got you either trapped up in Preia with me, or running all over the realm on random missions, yeah?"

There was more heavy silence from beside him, and then another slow sigh. And when Gerrard shot another glance toward Olarr, he couldn't tell if that was pain, or unease, or dread, shimmering so dark and strange in his eyes.

"So you would not then ponder, mayhap," Olarr ventured, very quiet, "staying with us? You ken you would now be welcome amongst the Bautul, even if I would not yet risk taking you to the mountain. Mayhap we could seek out—our own cave, or a cottage. Or both. If you wished."

He sounded so tentative, so damnably hopeful, and Gerrard squeezed his eyes shut, hauled down more air. If he wished. And yes, yes, curse him, he did still wish it, all of it, so much it hurt—but. But.

"Look, I'm not saying I don't ever want that," he finally replied, around a shaky exhale. "But I've just gone and thrown over all my own goals, my own kin, to help yours. Even after you lied to me, and used me, and—and betrayed my trust. So now, I just want"—he found another breath—"I want to go back to my goals. I want to finish what I started. This war's still happening, and we might've paused a tiny piece of it, for now—but unless we do something about it, it's going to keep coming back. It's going to keep sending us at each other's throats again and again, killing each other at the whims of senseless greedy *fools*, until it tears us all apart."

Olarr was still looking at him, still with such bright, shimmering eyes, and it still hurt, but it felt right, too, it felt like the only way. "We need to fix this, Olarr," Gerrard continued, harder now. "We can't just hide our arses in a cottage and hope this all goes away. We can't wait for someone else to come along and deal with it for us."

It came out sounding more pointed than he'd meant, and he didn't miss Olarr's flinch, the twitch of misery on his mouth. But wait, he was already nodding, jerky and quick, and his mouth wavered as it pulled up into a slow smile, as he drew them to a halt, and settled both his big hands firmly against Gerrard's shoulders.

"I would expect no less of you, warrior," Olarr said, his voice hoarse. "I ken you shall have the goddess' greatest blessing, in this."

It was just the kind of thing he would say, the kind of thing he always said, most of all when he was saying goodbye—and there was a sudden, sharp pang of alarm, flaring up in Gerrard's gut. Because yes, he'd just said all that, he'd meant it, but he also—he just—

But now Olarr was swinging something down from his back, thrusting it out toward Gerrard, and it took a moment's blinking to realize that it was—Slagvor's axe. Olarr had somehow brought Slagvor's axe, and Gerrard hadn't even noticed. And though his hands had instinctively caught the handle, its metal cold and unfamiliar against his fingers, he was already recoiling at the feel of it, the weight of it. The memory of it, swinging at him again and again, while all those vile words had spewed from Slagvor's mouth.

"Look, I don't want this," he said, shoving it back, shaking his head. "I won't use it, I don't need it, I—"

"You do need it, warrior," Olarr's rough voice cut in, as he gave another firm, reassuring clasp to Gerrard's shoulder. "If even only for this day, ach? You need to flaunt it to your kin, and tell them how bravely you won it from the fearsome captain of the Bautul. You must keep your sights on your own aims. On gaining this place of General, and stopping this war."

Damn it, Olarr was right, of course he was. Gerrard needed the axe. Needed to be prudent, cunning, focused on his goals. And even as he was nodding, gripping the axe again, he couldn't stop looking at Olarr, feeling that prickle in his eyes, the tightness in his throat. The sudden, dizzying gratitude, swarming him from the inside out.

Because Olarr had done this so, so many times. Uplifted him. Encouraged him. Given him strength and hope and purpose—and yes, even cunning—when Gerrard had been at his lowest. When he'd so desperately needed the help.

And beyond that, Olarr *had* given Gerrard all that training, too. He'd gone to all that effort, he'd kept coming back, when he hadn't needed to. He'd kept offering Gerrard his support, and his pleasure, and his care.

And even now, Olarr was attempting to smile again, and clasping back at Gerrard's shoulders, as he jerked his head toward the outpost. Because wait, they were already almost there again, that was the creek rippling away just ahead, and this couldn't be it already, could it...

"I can now scent these new men, from the north," Olarr continued, with another bracing little shake to Gerrard's shoulders. "With this Duke mayhap amongst them. So you shall go, and greet them, and amaze them all, ach? You shall show them what a strong, able General you shall make. You shall show them"—his throat convulsed—"how deeply blessed they shall be, to have you fighting by their side."

Gerrard couldn't speak, not with the growing lump in his throat, the heat pooling behind his prickling eyes. But he nodded, and even attempted a wan little smile of his own, a curt twitchy nod. Because this was goodbye, it was, and Gerrard was doing this, facing this, he had to, oh goddess, he had to...

So he yanked that yellow shawl—that mating-gift—off his shoulder, and thrust it into Olarr's slack hands, before turning and jerking away. Lurching out into the cold empty darkness, desperate and alone, where he could pretend he'd never heard the sounds of Olarr weeping in his wake.

32

It took Gerrard far too long to pull himself together, to deal with his swollen eyes and leaking nose. To make his own sobs stop coming, escaping out his choked, blocked throat.

He was doing this. He had to do this.

A quick wash of his face and hands in the creek's ice-cold water helped, and so did the steadily rising hubbub of voices and activity, emanating from the outpost. It sounded far too loud for this late at night—it was nearer to dawn than dusk, now—and as Gerrard broke out of the line of trees, his searching eyes caught on the new group of clean, well-kept coaches and wagons, clustered closely around the camp's palisades.

So Olarr had been right, then. Head Command's envoy had come. And they'd come even earlier than they'd indicated, no doubt hoping to find the camp unprepared, so they could make a more accurate assessment of its current state. And there—Gerrard squinted through the darkness, and broke into a jog—yes, there was Duke Warmisham himself, standing near a group of guards with his arms crossed, while an agitated-looking Cosgrove fluttered about before him.

"What do you mean, you don't have any accommodations prepared for us?" Warmisham was asking Cosgrove, in clipped, carrying tones. "Did you not receive word of our impending arrival?"

Cosgrove was wringing his hands, glancing helplessly toward Livermore's tent, which still had its door-flaps firmly closed, and several men hovering uncertainly outside it. All of them clearly still unwilling to risk violating Livermore's previous enraged orders around not entering his tent without permission, or disrupting his much-needed rest, lest they wanted to be flogged and discharged.

On any other night, Gerrard might have laughed at the absurdity of it all, but he was doing this—he'd promised Olarr he was doing this—so he propped Slagvor's axe on his shoulder, and closed up the remaining distance as quickly as he could. Not missing Cosgrove's startled glance toward him in the torchlight, and Gerrard cheerfully clapped him on the back, before turning to face Duke Warmisham.

Preia's vaunted, appallingly wealthy leader looked even smaller than Gerrard remembered, but he was just as richly attired, even for a days-long military jaunt. His crisp uniform looked new and freshly laundered, his silver-streaked hair was neatly combed back, and his handsome face was clean and freshly shaven, if rather too pretty for Gerrard's tastes.

"Welcome, Your Grace," Gerrard said to Warmisham, with a polite bow—at least, as much as it was possible to bow, what with the huge axe still propped on his shoulder. "Glad you arrived safe and sound. And if you can just give us a moment, we'll get you settled as fast as we can."

Warmisham was already looking somewhat mollified, his slim shoulders relaxing, though his assessing eyes were now running up and down Gerrard's form. "Lieutenant Gerrard, isn't it?" he replied, with a faint little sniff. "I presume we've arrived at a rather... inopportune time? Has some... mishap occurred?"

His watchful gaze was now lingering on Gerrard's chest, and when Gerrard glanced downwards, he belatedly recalled that his uniform was slashed wide open, showing off his still-bloody bare skin beneath it. And not just there, but down his arms and legs too, and—Warmisham's eyes narrowed as they flicked up toward it—that bare, exposed skin at his neck, with that fresh orc-bite still marked deep into it.

Right. There was no point trying to dance around it, and Gerrard was doing this, he was. "Nothing to worry about now," he replied, with what he hoped was a reassuring smile. "We did have an orc band coming for us earlier tonight, but I've gone and dealt with it."

Warmisham's manicured brows rose, his head tilting with unmistakable interest, or perhaps incredulity—and since no one else spoke, Gerrard took a breath, and plunged onward. "We've had a lot of attacks down here, on Slagvor's orders," he said. "And today I got some reliable intelligence that Slagvor himself was on his way here. But we don't have the men or the resources for another pitched battle at the moment, so I went out to meet him alone instead."

There were a variety of shocked gasps and murmurs all around them—Slagvor's reputation most definitely preceded him—and Warmisham's guards exchanged uneasy glances, while beside Gerrard, Cosgrove's round face had gone pale. "You didn't—you didn't actually fight Slagvor, did you, Lieutenant?" Cosgrove demanded. "*Captain* Slagvor?!"

But his wide eyes were now staring at Gerrard's new axe, giving him a clear opening—so Gerrard attempted another reassuring smile, and obligingly brought the axe down off his shoulder. Swinging its massive weight as smoothly as he could, showing off the sharp, blood-stained blade in the torchlight.

"Yeah, Captain Slagvor," Gerrard replied, the weight of truth ringing in his voice. "But lucky for me, the Bautul clan has a long tradition of single-combat duels, and the rest of them will stay out of it, if a challenge is fairly made. Let's just say Slagvor didn't expect a human to win his weapon, and then chop his ugly head off with it."

There were more buzzing murmurs all around, now, and even Warmisham looked reluctantly impressed, his eyes darting between Slagvor's axe and Gerrard's exposed chest. "How very valiant of you, Lieutenant," he said smoothly. "But I don't recall ordering General Livermore to authorize any assassinations, even on targets like Slagvor. Do I?"

There was an instant's uneasy silence, but it was again broken by Cosgrove, loudly clearing his throat. "General Livermore has been—unwell, for quite some time," he said quickly. "Lieutenant Gerrard has been running this place and keeping us all fed for weeks. And he's right, we didn't have the manpower or the resources for another attack, as we've been *severely* understaffed and under-supplied since the day we got here, so—"

But Warmisham was looking at Cosgrove's stout body with far less favour than he'd looked at Gerrard, his lip curling higher with every word—and Gerrard abruptly clasped Cosgrove's shoulder, cutting him off mid-sentence. "No, General Livermore didn't authorize me to go," he said, his voice flat, his eyes narrowing on Warmisham's face. "But I did what needed to be done, to protect our men from the monster coming to torture them in the dark. If you need to sanction me over that, I'll fully accept it—but none of my men were involved, or even aware of it. At any time."

More silence rang out after his words, and even Warmisham seemed at a loss for a response, now glancing uneasily at the dark forest all around them. Until finally Gerrard turned back to Cosgrove, and purposefully nudged him toward Livermore's tent. "Go wake the General, and get him over here to greet our guests, will you?" he said, under his breath. "And then divide the tent and put up a fresh cot, so the Duke can use it, and we can all get some sleep."

Gerrard could again feel multiple eyes on him, prickling, assessing, judging. But he did his damnedest to ignore it as he called for a proper meal for their guests, and a decent fire, while the tent was prepared. And soon he was ushering Warmisham and his men toward the fire, settling them on the best stools the camp had, and then asking the usual polite questions about their trip, and why they'd travelled so late, rather than setting up camp for the night, and waiting until morning to finish their journey.

"Our scouts encountered several signs of... *enemy activity* around our planned stop," Warmisham supplied, his mouth thinning with distaste. "Along with a sighting of several armed orcs, as well."

This revelation was met by more echoing silence, and even more uneasy glances and obvious fidgeting from Warmisham's men. Who were thinking, no doubt, of Gerrard's tale about Slagvor, and how they themselves might very well have ended up facing Slagvor firsthand, had Gerrard not gone off and addressed the situation.

Gerrard let that awareness hover there for another long, unpleasant moment, and then he cleared his throat, and ordered his men to bring over the last keg of Livermore's ale. A development that was greeted with genuine relief, and soon their guests were all rapidly downing frothing mugs of ale, no doubt with visions of death by Slagvor's axe marching behind their eyes.

It all seemed to be going well, perhaps even better than Gerrard had dared to hope—and for a brief moment, as he stood guard over the drinking, chatting men, he let himself consider the possibility that maybe, maybe, this would be enough. He'd singlehandedly rescued Warmisham and his men from a genuine threat, and now he was showing himself a competent lieutenant, keeping them comfortable and safe. And even if he'd ruffled Warmisham's feathers a bit, it also meant he'd been clear about his priorities, and his commitment to his men. And surely any reasonable commander would see that, and appreciate it, and yes, Warmisham was even glancing over at Gerrard again, his tongue brushing his lips—

When of course, at that very moment, Livermore emerged from his nearby tent, and stalked over to join them. He too was impeccably dressed, much in the manner of Warmisham himself, and he didn't hide his disdainful glance toward Gerrard as he halted before Warmisham, and gave him a deep, flourishing bow.

"We are most delighted to welcome your exalted presence to our humble outpost, Your Grace," he said, in his silkiest, most simpering voice. "We have been most eagerly awaiting the favour of your blessed presence for *days* now, and Lieutenant Gerrard here *repeatedly* assured me that he had made all the arrangements I requested for your comfort and protection."

Gerrard stared at Livermore for an instant too long—the hell, this lying prick had never *once* mentioned such a thing—while Livermore's mouth curled into a cool, contemptuous little smile. "But instead," he continued blandly, his cold eyes flicking toward Gerrard, "I've been informed, Lieutenant, that tonight you have once again flouted my direct command, abandoned our base without permission, and run off to play the part of the lone conquering hero. Leaving your men without the support and direction they sorely need, most of all with multiple enemies lurking about our gates, and threatening our esteemed guests!"

Oh, curse it. Gerrard shot a brief, reflexive glance at Warmisham, whose expression had decidedly darkened—no, no, *no*—but even as Gerrard opened his mouth to speak,

Livermore cut him off with a light, tinkling laugh. "But as usual, you betray yourself, *Lieutenant*," he drawled. "Next time you supposedly 'kill' an 'orc captain', why don't you actually prove your outrageous tale, and bring back his head? Instead of just waving about a useless, rusty old memento that anyone might find lying around anywhere?"

Gerrard's disbelieving gaze dropped to the axe he was still holding—that was *blood*, not rust, and an orc-forged axe like this would sell for a hefty price, and Livermore damn well knew it. But the bastard was already lightly laughing again, and waving one of the men away so he could sit down beside Warmisham, primly crossing one leg over the other. "Or," he continued, waving a hand at Gerrard's chest, "why don't you actually give yourself the wounds, too, rather than just arbitrarily tearing up your perfectly good uniform? The uniform our very generous guest *paid* for, at that?"

Gerrard gritted his teeth, glowered down at Livermore's vile smug face—but curse him, he couldn't seem to find a single damned response. Because that Efterar orc had gone and healed all his wounds, and the rips in his uniform indeed only showed smooth clear skin, fuck, *fuck*—

"And the uniform," Livermore went on, smirking at Gerrard's visibly rounded belly, "that you're even growing out of, Lieutenant. No wonder we've been short on food stores lately, with you lazing about and putting on weight like *that*."

Goddess fuck this lying piece of reeking *offal*, and Gerrard's next attempt to speak was blocked by a forceful signal from Livermore's imperious gloved hand, as his icy gaze turned back to Warmisham. "I dislike discussing such matters publicly, Your Grace," he said archly, "but as I've *repeatedly* written, Lieutenant Gerrard has been an ongoing and ever-worsening problem. He's failed to follow major orders on multiple crucial occasions, along with multiple counts of recklessness, ingratitude, disrespect, and insubordination. And once again, I am officially requesting his demotion, if not his removal from service altogether."

The horrified fury flashed behind Gerrard's eyes—no, no, this couldn't be happening, not now, not when he'd been so damned close. And he was one breath away from hollering, from hurling all his rage straight in Livermore's face, when something grasped him from behind. And when Gerrard whirled around to face it, it was Cosgrove, his eyes wide and alarmed.

"Sorry to interrupt," he said, high-pitched, "but could you please come help with the tent, Lieutenant?"

Gerrard still wanted to start shouting, or better yet, to slam Slagvor's axe down on Livermore's pompous head, but Cosgrove was already jabbing him hard in the back, and yanking him toward the tent. And finally Gerrard followed, after another brief bow toward Warmisham, who still looked far more forbidding than before.

"Fuck that odious little swine," Gerrard hissed at Cosgrove, once they were safely in Livermore's tent. "He still wants to demote me? After I killed fucking *Slagvor*?"

But even Cosgrove had cast an uncertain glance down at Gerrard's nonexistent wounds—damn it, *damn* it—and Gerrard waved a furious hand at his neck, still with that fresh orc-bite in his skin. "Do you think I did this on purpose?" he demanded. "Or that I just picked up a massive orc-forged axe on the side of the fucking *road*?!"

Cosgrove looked almost frantic, now, flapping his hands, and shaking his head. "No, Lieutenant," he said, in a hoarse whisper. "But we can't think of that now, all right? I need to tell you—"

"The powder!" Gerrard cut in, as a bright, staggering relief blazed through his chest. "We can still salvage this, if we can slip Livermore some powder before he goes back to bed. They'll both be here in this tent, with just the partition between them, so Warmisham will see all of it firsthand! He'll see how Livermore behaves in an emergency, and realize that he's not fit to be General!"

And yes, yes, that was the answer, it was, it had to be. They could still spike Livermore's drink, they could still make this work, they could. Livermore would show his true raging self to Warmisham, and Warmisham would realize he'd been fed a passel of lies, and then...

"But that's what I'm trying to tell you!" Cosgrove hissed, though he sounded afraid, his voice on the verge of breaking. "I'm so, so sorry, Lieutenant—but the powder is gone. It's over. We're *lost*."

33

The powder was gone. Gone?

Gerrard stared at Cosgrove, aghast, while Cosgrove wrung his hands, dragged them against his flushed face. "Livermore tried to find you, after you left tonight," he gulped. "And once he saw you were gone, and your tent was empty, he went on a rampage! Demanded we all turn out our tents, and prove we hadn't aided and abetted you! So I dumped out all the powder under my sleeping mat, and pretended I'd just been using the jar as a cup!"

No. No. Damn it, no, and Gerrard had to force his eyes shut, and bite back his furious string of curses. No. This wasn't Cosgrove's fault. It wasn't, and they could still keep trying, keep thinking, something...

"And there's no powder left at all?" Gerrard croaked, blinking back at Cosgrove's agitated face. "You couldn't salvage even a little? Dig it out from under your mat?"

"I tried!" Cosgrove replied, his whisper nearly a wail. "I went back to look after, but it was all sunk in! And you can't put mud in Livermore's food, he's going to notice it, right? And then he'll realize what's really been happening, this whole time!"

Right, right, and why couldn't Gerrard think, why was there only the fear and rage and exhaustion, clashing together behind his eyes. What the hell was he supposed to do now. Livermore was surely over there regaling Warmisham with even more tales of Gerrard's recklessness and insubordination, and by morning, he would be officially discharged, and everything would be ruined. All his grand plans, all his goals, gone, forever, just like that.

"There must be something we can do, Lieutenant," Cosgrove said, his wide eyes pleading on Gerrard's face. "There must be. Right?"

But Gerrard's sluggish brain was uselessly grasping, fighting to drag up alternatives, and finding nothing. Nothing, because whatever he did, Duke Warmisham would be right there, watching it, witnessing it. While already believing that Gerrard was erratic and unreliable, or maybe even a risk to his men. Any kind of offense from him would be suspect, any kind of target or attack, and Gerrard couldn't risk putting that on someone like Cosgrove, goddess knew he'd already done enough...

But Cosgrove's too-perceptive eyes were rapidly blinking now, his head whipping back and forth. "Fuck, I'm sorry," he gulped. "I'm so, so sorry, Lieutenant. If I've fucked this up for all of us, if we're stuck with Livermore for years because of this, if I never get to go home again, I—"

He looked genuinely pained, contrite, even terrified. And as Gerrard stared at him, his own rage and fear seemed to coil, burning up into determination in his throat.

No. *No.* He couldn't let Livermore get away with this. He couldn't let this happen to his men, after all they'd borne. He needed to try. He needed to do everything within his power to end this war. He needed...

"Just—give me a moment," he said, rushed and thin, his

heart thumping in his ears. "Take deep breaths, and hold things here for just a little longer, yeah?"

He didn't wait for Cosgrove's response, just ducked out the back of the tent, and sprinted along the palisades in the darkness. Moving as quietly as he could, slipping out of the gate, and then running at full tilt toward the creek. Toward the only thing he could think of. Toward cunning. Toward—hope.

Toward Olarr.

"Olarr," he called, his voice a strained croak in the moonlit darkness. "Olarr! Are you still here? Please, I—"

His voice cracked, broke, and he sprinted faster, leaping over rocks and roots, his breaths burning in his chest. Olarr had to still be here, he had to be, he wouldn't have left yet, what if he'd left...

"Olarr!" he called again, as loudly as he dared. "Olarr, if you're still here, I need to talk to you, please—"

Goddess, he was already breaking, already losing it, because he'd all but told Olarr to go, he'd told him it was over. And Olarr should have gone, he should have, why the hell would he have stayed...

"Please," Gerrard rasped, as he caught sight of the creek up ahead, the silver moonlight shimmering on the still, quiet water. "Please, goddess, I—"

But wait. Wait. The water was breaking, splashing, rising—

And oh, thank fuck, it was Olarr. Olarr, standing there with water pouring off his face and hair, his skin gleaming wet and silver in the moonlight. And his eyes on Gerrard looked blank, bewildered, his head tilting, his brow creased.

But Gerrard had already gasped and lurched toward him, the relief screaming through his skull. And it was all he could do to keep from charging straight into the creek, and hurling his arms around Olarr's neck.

"Olarr, please," he choked. "I need your help."

It was so pathetic, so weak and foolish and reckless, he'd

just flounced off in some kind of grand statement, and now he was already back here again, begging. And Olarr should reject him, he should leave and walk away forever...

But instead, Olarr was... striding forward. Wading out of the creek toward Gerrard with big, purposeful steps, the water streaming down his bare body. And he didn't falter, didn't once hesitate, as he strode straight up to Gerrard, and yanked him into his arms.

"Ach, warrior," he said, gruff, into his hair. "I am here."

34

It only took Gerrard a few moments to pour out the entire sordid tale. Telling Olarr of Warmisham's arrival, Livermore's accusations, the missing powder. Of his certain looming defeat.

But Olarr had seemed entirely undaunted, and had listened with his usual calm attentiveness. And he'd even dunked Grimarr's garish yellow shawl in the water, and used it to gently wipe off Gerrard's sticky, grimy face.

"You forget all the kinds of power you wield, warrior," Olarr crisply told him, as he set aside the shawl, and began running his damp claws through Gerrard's hair, sweeping it back from his face. "I could scent that duke's deep hunger for you from here, ach? He should yet be most pleased to gain you to his side."

Oh. Gerrard blinked at the steady matter-of-factness in Olarr's words, betrayed only by a glimmer of pain in his eyes. Because wait, he was implying—was he implying—

"I'm not going to fuck Warmisham for this, Olarr," Gerrard said, over his tangled tongue. "I wouldn't."

It took Olarr a moment to reply, his eyes still intent on his claws combing Gerrard's hair. "This would be the cunning thing to do," he finally said. "You told me how you had planned for this before, ach? And you—you ought to do what you wish, warrior. What shall gain you your own aims. Without thought for—aught else."

His voice had gone very low, very even, and Gerrard's throat spasmed, even as he defiantly lifted his chin, and held Olarr's eyes. "I wouldn't," he said, and he meant it. "I already—I already have a mate, yeah?"

Olarr stilled for an instant, his hands hovering over Gerrard's hair—but then he seemed to catch himself again, his mouth wavering, his eyes very bright. "Ach, then," he said, choked. "Then we shall—find another way. But it may yet help you to tempt this foul little duke with this, ach? Show him how much he has to gain, by bringing such a strong, lusty, beautiful warrior to his side."

Gerrard flushed and rolled his eyes, but somehow they were smiling at each other, shy but true. And then Olarr cleared his throat, and suggested a possible alternative plan. One so ridiculous—and so appallingly dangerous—that Gerrard refused to believe it, at first.

"You can't, Olarr," he countered, wildly searching his hard, determined eyes. "It's risky, it's reckless, it's—it's *imprudent*."

But Olarr's smile back was equal parts challenge and affection, his brows raised, his shoulder shrugging. "More reckless than you calling Slagvor to a duel?" he asked. "Whilst I had to stand there, and watch this?"

He had a point, the bastard, and it wasn't as though Gerrard had any better ideas, so he finally, reluctantly relented. And then he headed back to the outpost as quickly as he could, fighting down his racing heartbeat, taking deep, shaky breaths. And even sending a few silent prayers to the goddess, still watching him from above.

He was doing this. He could trust Olarr in this, just how Olarr had trusted him. He would.

The determination kept circling as he slipped back into camp, where he first stopped by the supply-wagon—on Olarr's suggestion—and scrounged up a new uniform. It was a bit too tight and short, but it was still a sight more presentable than his old shredded one, which he tossed over the palisades, again at Olarr's request. Along with a few other items Olarr had asked for, including a stubby little candle.

Once that was done, Gerrard took a brief glance around at the camp—luckily, Warmisham and his men were still by the fire with Livermore—before quietly skirting around them in the darkness, and ducking back into Livermore's tent. Where Cosgrove had finished setting up Warmisham's bed behind the canvas partition, and was now pacing back and forth with obvious agitation.

"Lieutenant!" Cosgrove gasped, once he'd caught sight of Gerrard. "Where have you been? Did you find more powder?"

His expression was hopeful, pleading, and Gerrard winced as he shook his head. "No powder," he replied, fighting to ignore the way Cosgrove's face crumpled. "But look—I've got something else in mind. I'll just need you to trust me, and follow my lead, yeah?"

Cosgrove didn't look even slightly convinced, his eyes fearful on Gerrard's face, but Gerrard was doing this now, and he herded Cosgrove out of the tent, and back toward Warmisham's group by the fire. Where he interrupted as politely as he could, and informed Warmisham that his accommodations were ready.

Gerrard ignored Livermore's snide comment about how long it had taken, and didn't miss how Warmisham still looked him up and down, despite whatever drivel Livermore had been pouring into his ears this entire time. And when Gerrard offered to escort Warmisham to the tent, the bastard didn't refuse, either, and even had him move the bed further away from the partition, his eyes prickling on Gerrard the entire time.

Olarr definitely hadn't been wrong, then, and Gerrard clung to that hope, that possibility, as he headed not for his own tent, but for the med tent instead. Where there would be plenty of witnesses as to his whereabouts, and after a brief nod toward a curious-looking Bassey, he sank down onto his old cot, and blinked up at the tent's canvas ceiling in the darkness. Waiting, waiting, his heart pounding louder with every shaky breath.

He had to trust Olarr. Had to trust the goddess. They could do this, together. They would...

The scream rent the air like a knife, tearing through the quiet darkness. A scream of pure terror, of abject misery, of sure and certain death.

"Help!" screeched Livermore's shrill, carrying voice. "There's an orc in my tent!"

35

Gerrard leapt out of bed, and ran. Ran as fast as he possibly could, pelting across the camp. And catching, there in the darkness behind Livermore's tent, a brief, distinctive flash of yellow, before it vanished into the trees.

"General!" Gerrard bellowed, as he burst into the tent. "Where's the orc!"

Livermore was crouched and trembling on his cot, his blanket pulled up to his nose, and he pointed a shaky finger toward the empty space beside his cot. "There!" he wailed. "Here, in my very tent! Just waiting to gut me in my sleep! He might still be there!"

Gerrard cast a cursory glance around the tent—it was, of course, devoid of orcs—before realizing that Livermore's eyes were still unfocused, unseeing in the darkness. So he swiped for the lamp, lighting it as quickly as he could, before thrusting it up, waving it back and forth. Showing only the empty tent, while Livermore's streaming eyes squinted to see in the bright light.

"There's nothing here, General," Gerrard said, as firmly as

he could. "Did you see which way he went? I didn't see anything out in the camp, but—"

Livermore cut him off with another wail, and now here was Warmisham himself, lurching through the canvas partition in his nightclothes. Followed quickly by several more of his own men, still dressed in uniform, and then by Cosgrove, too.

"Corporal, go pull together a party," Gerrard told Cosgrove. "Search the entire camp for orcs, and report back as quickly as you can. Arm yourselves, and be *careful*. Holler at your first sign of anything suspicious."

Cosgrove instantly nodded and rushed off, and Gerrard returned his attention to a still-flailing Livermore. "What did the orc look like?" he demanded. "Could you identify any details in the dark? His clan? His weapon?"

Livermore frantically nodded, his eyes wide and terrified. "He had a big stick!" he replied, between panting breaths. "A big pointy stick! And he was wearing a bright yellow cape, and a tall beaver hat, and—and—a Preian *uniform!*"

His voice rang through the tent, through the entire listening camp, and Gerrard desperately fought to keep his expression as bland as possible, his eyes on Livermore's wild face. "The orc was wearing a *uniform*," he repeated, deadpan. "And a beaver hat, and a yellow cape. And he had a... big stick."

"Yes!" came Livermore's sharp, shrill reply. "And he was standing *right there*, and *leering* at me! Waiting to jab me with his stick!"

He flailed his shaky hand toward the spot where Gerrard now stood, several steps away from Livermore's cot. And Gerrard looked down at the ground, and then back at Livermore, and then at the nearby Duke Warmisham, who was watching all this with bewildered, disbelieving eyes.

"Er, forgive me, General," Gerrard ventured, carefully now, "but how... how *did* you see all this, in the dark? There was no light in here when I came in...?"

He let the question delicately hang there, its implication ringing louder with every breath—but Livermore didn't let it go, the affronted fury flashing across his face. "The orc was lit up!" he shouted back. "He must have been carrying a light, so I could see him!"

The words again seemed to echo out around them, reverberating with damnable finality, and Gerrard couldn't stop his mouth from twitching as he raised his eyebrows. "The orc who came in here to attack you," he said blandly, "didn't just... do so, in the dark? You *do* remember orcs can see in the dark, right?"

Livermore sputtered and glared at Gerrard, perhaps finally following how his claims might be construed, and Gerrard exchanged a brief, meaningful glance with a still-staring Warmisham. "And orcs carry real weapons, too," Gerrard continued. "Almost always axes, and curved swords. Not... *sticks.*"

There was more hanging, echoing silence, but of course Livermore was already babbling again, demanding that Gerrard go hunt down the foul invading beast at once—until Cosgrove slipped back into the tent, sidling over toward Gerrard, and shaking his head. "Nothing, Lieutenant," he said, with a discreet little cough. "Gate's closed, we checked all the tents, every last corner and wagon. No orcs in yellow capes and top hats. With—big sticks."

His voice had quivered at the last bit, his eyes alight on Gerrard's face, and Gerrard had to bite the inside of his cheek, and clear his throat. "Then search outside the palisades, just in case," he said, under his breath. "And maybe go fetch Bassey too, will you?"

Livermore had clearly heard that, and he jerked upright in his bed, glaring viciously toward Gerrard. "I do *not* need treatment," he snarled. "The orc was here! I saw him! He was *here!*"

But thankfully, no one seemed inclined to listen at this point, and Warmisham had even nodded at Cosgrove, and waved him out of the tent with an imperious flick of his hand. Only to earn himself another round of increasingly shrill justifications from Livermore, until Cosgrove soon returned with Bassey. Who was wearing his best calm medic's face, and carrying a large bottle in his hand.

"This again?" he said coolly, striding across the tent toward Livermore in the bed. "Not to worry, General. Just have a drink of this, it'll help, like always."

Livermore blanched, staring open-mouthed at Bassey, before launching into another furious tirade that no one listened to. Until finally Warmisham himself stalked over, plucked the bottle from Bassey's hand, and thrust it in Livermore's face.

"Drink it, General," he snapped. "Now. We've had enough of this nonsense for one night."

Livermore clearly wanted to keep arguing, but perhaps he'd realized who he'd be arguing with, and he grudgingly snatched the bottle, and drank. "This is ridiculous, Your Grace," he said, plaintively, once he'd lowered the bottle again. "This is some kind of setup, or—or a misunderstanding! It's Gerrard's fault, he sent the orc to me, he's been..."

But with that, his eyes went hazy, unfocused, and his body slowly slumped down onto the bed. While Bassey promptly went to collect the bottle, and then appeared to conduct a brief examination before turning back to Gerrard and Warmisham. "That should keep him sedated for the night," he said smoothly. "My professional recommendation would be to keep him sedated until you can take him back to the city with you, where he can be sure to rest, and have the best possible care. This posting has been a difficult one, and many of our men have similarly struggled."

Bassey didn't wait for Warmisham's answer, and swept out of the tent with haughty, devastating dignity. Leaving even Warmisham looking decidedly discomfited, glancing uneasily at Livermore in the bed, and back at Gerrard again. As if uncertain what to do next, or how to handle the situation from here.

And Gerrard was doing this, he was, so he flashed Warmisham what he hoped was his most reassuring smile. "Thanks for your help, Your Grace," he said, as steadily as he could. "Livermore's not an easy fellow at the best of times. If you'd be willing, I'd love to get you another drink, and tell you all that's been going on down here."

He sent up another silent prayer as he waited, as he watched Warmisham's eyes flick up and down his form. Judging, weighing, and please, goddess, please...

"Very well, then, Lieutenant," Warmisham finally replied. "Come into my tent, and tell me everything."

36

By the time Gerrard was able to escape camp again, the sun was rising over the outpost, flickering its dappled orange light through the palisades.

And even as Gerrard tilted his face up toward its warmth, drawing in deep breaths as he slipped out of the gate toward the forest, he found himself thinking, oddly, of the moon, and its cool silver gleam. Of all the light and guidance and safety it had given him, all these past months.

He walked faster through the trees, following the familiar narrow path, his heartbeat quickening in his chest. It had taken so much longer than he'd intended to get away, and what if Olarr had gone. What if he'd given up, or been called elsewhere. What if he'd changed his mind, or...

There. There. The stone trapdoor was just up ahead, opening, crunching upward—and Gerrard sprinted forward, straight toward it. Nearly tripping on his way down the stairs, and hurling himself into Olarr's warm, waiting arms.

"You're—still here," he gasped, into Olarr's chest, and suddenly he was blinking hard, fighting back the wetness pooling behind his eyes. "Wasn't sure you'd—stay."

But Olarr yanked him even tighter, swaying him back and forth, his low growl rumbling into Gerrard's ears. "Ach, I am here," he croaked back. "Bautul do not leave our kin behind."

Our kin. The relief bubbled up bright and convulsive in Gerrard's chest, escaping in a thick, high-pitched laugh. Because not only had Olarr not left him behind, but he—he'd saved him. He'd come up with that reckless, ridiculous plan last night, and saved Gerrard's livelihood, saved his men, saved all his goals. At great risk to Olarr's own goals, his own clan's future, his own damned life. And Gerrard couldn't bear to think what might have happened if Olarr had been caught, if he'd been killed, if he'd been lost to him, forever.

"It was such a brilliant plan, captain," Gerrard said now, muffled into his chest. "A fucking triumph of Bautul cunning and recklessness. The cape, the hat, the uniform? The stick?"

He drew back a little so he could see Olarr's face, and flashed him a rather weepy-feeling grin. "That stick is gonna become legend, you know," he informed him. "It was all my men talked about all night. '*A big pointy stick! Waiting to jab me!*'"

Olarr was grinning back too, his eyes dancing on Gerrard's face. "A strong orc-stick would do this foul man much good, I ken," he said lightly. "But I am most glad it did not come to this, ach?"

Gerrard laughed again, shaking his head, even as Olarr's expression sobered, his head tilting. "So this all went well, then, Aulis?" he asked, more carefully than before. "How did you fare with this duke?"

That was definitely unease in Olarr's eyes, now, surely in regards to what Gerrard had done last night with Warmisham, or promised to do in the future. And it was a fair question, one Gerrard wanted to answer fairly, too—so he took a breath, and drew Olarr over to the fur. To where Olarr had apparently pulled together another picnic for them, the brilliant bastard, and after a fervent thank-you, Gerrard sat down across from him, and launched into the full tale of the night's events. Telling Olarr how Livermore had raved and raged about the orc in his tent, how Cosgrove and Bassey had helped drive it home, and how Warmisham had invited Gerrard in, and given him a chance to speak.

"You were right about Warmisham, because he was definitely interested in more than just talking," Gerrard told Olarr, around a mouthful of tender, succulent venison. "But I pretended I didn't notice, and kept it to the point. Didn't even need to get into Livermore's powder-induced visions at all, either—just talked about all the mismanagement, the food and supplies, the useless offenses, the deaths. And I especially focused on how keeping this outpost staffed is a waste of Warmisham's valuable time and coin, and how we'd all be of much better service to him elsewhere."

He could see Olarr stiffening at that mention of *elsewhere*, and Gerrard squared his shoulders, and drew in a breath. "So yeah," he said, around a dry-feeling swallow. "That means... I'm going north. We're all going north. Shutting down the camp, starting today."

Olarr's body betrayed a faint flinch, his eyes gone still—but he didn't speak, so Gerrard pulled in another breath, kept going. "I also made a good case for how Warmisham would need better protection on his way back home, with Slagvor's orcs possibly running around, seeking revenge," he said. "And he agreed to that, too, and even congratulated me on defeating Slagvor last night, and asked me how it went. By the end of it, he sounded like he was pretty interested in keeping me around, going forward. Maybe even giving me that promotion, if I play it right."

Olarr's eyes were still entirely blank, unreadable, his body frozen and unmoving on the fur. But Gerrard had been thinking about this constantly since last night, and he was committed to seeing it through. To being brave, and cunning, and honest with Olarr, even if it ached like this in his gut.

"I still don't trust Warmisham in the slightest," he continued. "Even if he's outwardly less awful than Livermore. But if I'm up north with him, in the midst of it all—and especially if I can get myself that promotion—I can keep pushing toward my own goals. I can do my damnedest to help my men, and their families—and even the Bautul, too. I can keep trying to end this endless war."

Olarr audibly swallowed, but something had shifted in his eyes, and he twitched a firm little nod, and even a faint, crooked smile. "Good," he said, hoarse. "I am most glad of this, warrior. I am sure you shall gain all you aim for, and I wish you—all the goddess' favour, in this."

But Gerrard could almost taste Olarr's misery, his grief, coiling deep and heavy between them. His certain awareness that this was goodbye, after all, that Gerrard was leaving him for good. But even amidst that, he was still... encouraging Gerrard. Supporting him, strengthening him, the way he always had.

Gerrard's eyes were blinking hard, now, and he held Olarr's gaze, and drew up breath. "But—I've also been thinking," he said slowly, weighing every word. "About how we're such a good team, yeah? And how we—we both want the same things, and we've helped each other do things we could never have done alone. And how it would help both of us, and all the people we care about, if we could still keep—working together. Keep... seeing each other. Maybe even keep being... mates."

Something else shifted in Olarr's eyes, maybe doubt, maybe astonishment—so Gerrard drew in another breath, kept going. "I know it won't be easy," he continued, faster. "It'll mean a hell of a lot of time apart, and more distance to travel, and all the rest of it. But"—more breath, more truth—"if this was ever going to work with us long-term anyway, I need—to trust you,

Olarr. I need you to show me I can trust you. I need you to keep coming back to me, even when it's not easy. I need you to decide to tell me the full fucking truth, and keep your word to me, again and again and again, until I can believe you'll always do it. Until I can trust you enough to make a full life with you. And if you can't do that, or you won't, then—"

He jerked a shaky-feeling shrug, but he couldn't move his eyes from Olarr, couldn't stop searching his face. "So you can take it or leave it," he said, his voice a little hollow, now. "It's up to you. But I'm still going. No matter what."

His heart thudded faster, his breaths shallow in his chest, his eyes still searching Olarr's face. Waiting, waiting, as Olarr's throat spasmed, his mouth twisting, and...

Olarr lurched forward with a gasp, his huge body tackling Gerrard's back to the fur, his hot face shoving deep into Gerrard's neck. "Ach, Aulis," he croaked, muffled, into Gerrard's skin. "Ach, I should be most honoured. I shall prove this to you, and regain your trust in me. No matter how long this takes."

Oh. Oh, goddess. Gerrard's relief swarmed him all over, fizzing through his belly, escaping in a strangled little laugh. And his arms and legs were already wrapping around Olarr, drawing him closer, harder, as his body arched up, his neck willingly pressing into the threat of those seeking, hungry teeth. Inviting it, ordering it, oh fuck, and Olarr's groan might have been a sob as he took it, obeyed it, flashed Gerrard full with his pain and his pleasure.

"And it'll be—only me," Gerrard gasped, as his hand pressed Olarr's head closer, his fingers spreading, sinking deep into his messy hair. "Only my scent on you. Only me fucking you."

Olarr's gulping, greedy swallows abruptly choked off, the sound loud and betraying in Gerrard's ear. Enough that Gerrard caught on it too, considering it—and when he nudged Olarr upwards again, Olarr jerked back, his mouth rimmed with red, his eyes stunned and hazy on Gerrard's face.

"Because that's gotta be part of it too, captain," Gerrard said, lifting his chin, holding those eyes. "Goddess knows I've waited long enough, yeah?"

And oh, hell, the way Olarr groaned. The sound rumbling down the full length of his body, fluttering his eyes, flushing his cheeks. Sparking Gerrard's own simmering hunger higher, into a shivering dizzying craving—and before he could think better of it, he shoved himself up, and pushed Olarr over onto his back. Not missing how easy he went, how his long tongue hungrily licked his red lips, how he was already fully hard in his trousers.

"Good, captain," Gerrard breathed, as he began yanking at those trousers, pulling them down and off over Olarr's hips, his legs, his feet. "You're gonna let your man undress you? Let me take care of you?"

Olarr groaned again, his bare swollen cock already bobbing up, streaking white against his belly. And Gerrard gazed at it, feasted on the sight of it, as he rapidly shucked off his own clothes, and knelt between Olarr's big, hair-dusted thighs. "So good, captain," he continued, as his hungry hands stroked those thighs, slowly spread them wide apart. "You're gonna be so good for me, aren't you? Gonna let me finally learn how good you feel?"

Olarr nodded and moaned, his gaze rapt and almost pained on Gerrard's face—and it was enough to stop Gerrard short again, to drag his frenzied thoughts backwards. Back to many weeks before, when they'd talked about this, to the darkness Olarr had hinted at around this...

"Only if you're sure, though," he said, quieter now, holding Olarr's eyes. "If it's not going to..."

But Olarr's hands were already reaching down, clasping at Gerrard's hips, drawing him in closer. "Ach, I am sure, Aulis," he replied, his voice hoarse, his eyes glimmering. "It shall be a great honour, to gain such a gift from you."

The heat was swarming Gerrard's face, pooling in his groin, and he gave Olarr a smile that felt almost shy as he stroked up and down that gorgeous silver body, felt it shudder and flare beneath his touch. And when his seeking hand found Olarr's cock, smoothing up easy and gentle, Olarr gasped and rocked to meet it, his thighs falling open wider, welcoming Gerrard in.

So Gerrard kept touching, kept stroking, now slicking one hand with Olarr's slippery, spurting seed, and slipping it down-wards. Caressing Olarr with it, coating him with it, nudging it into that smooth pulsing heat with hungry, trembling fingers. And then also slathering the seed all over his own cock, until he was liberally dripping with it, and seeping fresh from his own slit, too. Because fuck, this felt so good, it looked so good, this vicious powerful orc on his back for him, spreading for him, opening for him. And then shivering all over at the very touch of Gerrard there, at his slippery head kissing against that slick soft heat.

Gerrard kept it there for as long as he could bear, his gasps deepening into groans as he settled closer, closer—and then, oh, fuck, he was easing inside. Sinking into Olarr's tight, glori-ous, clamouring warmth, feeling it clutch and spasm around him. Feeling it take him, caress him, welcome him, more, more...

Gerrard's head arched back as he cried out, and he plunged himself the rest of the way, fully to the hilt. He was in Olarr, he was finally *in Olarr*, and Olarr looked just as frantic as Gerrard felt, his cheeks red, his eyes shocked wide and bright. While his own straining, leaking shaft bobbed up again and again, as if trying to gain the attention of Gerrard's rapidly fluttering eyes.

"Fuck," Gerrard gasped, as his shaking hand again found that shaft, gripped it tight in his tingling fingers. "Fuck, you feel good, captain. So damn good."

Olarr choked and nodded, his bright eyes worshipful on Gerrard's face, and Gerrard smiled back, tender and painfully affectionate, as he stroked his beautiful orc, revelled in the truth of this impossible, unthinkable moment. Of opening him, being inside him, finally getting to have him, oh goddess, *oh*.

"So good," Gerrard breathed, as he gave his first small, careful thrust, his hand moving in time with his hips. "So gorgeous, captain. Been dreaming of this for so damn long."

Olarr fervently nodded again, his body grinding down to meet Gerrard's hips, so Gerrard kept going, drinking up every flutter of those eyes, every stunning spasm of that silken heat around him. "You're such a big, powerful, generous captain, aren't you?" he gasped. "Such a good, brave Bautul. Taking your human's prick like this. Letting it fuck you wide open, and fill you with good sweet man-seed."

Olarr's groan sounded more like a howl this time, and oh, how Gerrard adored him, caressing him, worshipping him, plunging his hips in again and again, filling them both with sparking streams of pleasure. "You're gonna be a good strong Bautul, and take all of it," he gasped, moving faster, faster, the compulsion driving him, consuming him. "You're gonna suck your man's seed deep, and make it your own. You're gonna prove to me how much you want this, how much you want me, and it's gonna reek on you, and shout it to every Bautul you meet. You won your enemy's seed, and his loyalty, and his *heart*, and you made him *yours*—"

And fuck, yes, the relief and the truth flashing out in furious, juddering flares, pumping Gerrard's release deep into that perfect clutching heat, milking him dry. And wait, that heat was suddenly softening, opening even wider, as Olarr's body thrashed against the fur, his hips bucking up—

And before Gerrard had even caught it, followed it, he'd yanked himself out, and lurched down to suck Olarr's spraying head deep into his throat. Gulping and guzzling it out of him, sucking as hard as he could, while Olarr's bellows echoed through the room, his body a flailing wild thing beneath Gerrard's tongue. And pitching even wilder when Gerrard slipped his fingers down, filled that messy hole again, keeping his own seed inside. Feeling how the hole was lax and stretched, now, because Gerrard had fucked it open, and filled it with himself.

But Olarr was filling him too, still sputtering out into his mouth with slowing, lengthening pulses, while Gerrard sucked and licked and adored, and caressed his mate's insides with his gently stroking fingers. Until Olarr finally sagged heavily beneath him, his breath escaping in a shuddery heave, his big hands skittering over Gerrard's hair, his shoulders, his face.

"Ach, Aulis," Olarr rasped, as he tilted Gerrard's head up, met his blinking eyes. "Ach, my mate, my heart, my prize. This was—such a gift. Such a great, great blessing."

Gerrard's mouth twitched into a shaky smile, and Olarr blinked at it, once—and then his entire body flailed up again, clutching at Gerrard's shoulders, dragging him down to lie close against his chest. "Such a blessing," he croaked, as his fervent hands caressed Gerrard's hair, his face, his back, his sides. "Ach, I deserve none of this. I had not *dreamt* that you would yet offer it to me. That you would yet allow me to come to you, to see you and touch you and speak to you, and—*love* you. To come alongside you, to help end this war. To yet be— your mate."

He sounded hushed, reverent, almost reckless, and he clutched Gerrard even tighter as he rolled them sideways on the fur, and buried his face in Gerrard's neck. His teeth scraping sharp against Gerrard's already-raw skin, but Gerrard didn't care, not even a little, and he willingly tilted his head away, and pressed Olarr's head down harder. Feeling those sharp teeth clamp down, the snap of pain almost instantly shifting into pleasure, as Olarr's greedy, desperate gulps filled the air between them.

Gerrard let him go as long as he wanted, gently stroking Olarr's hair again and again, his own breaths gone slow and deep. And the longer Olarr drank, the more Gerrard felt the frenzy in that familiar body against him shifting, settling, finding its ease again. Until Olarr finally gasped and twitched all over, and then jerked back, away, his eyes wide and strange on Gerrard's face.

"Ach, I am sorry, Aulis," he said, rushed and hoarse in his throat. "I did not mean—I ken this was too much, I—"

But Gerrard shushed him with a hard, purposeful kiss, with a blatant taste of the iron and salt on his mate's lips. "All good, captain," he murmured. "I want my mate wanting me. Want you thinking about how good I taste. And how much you want to come back to me."

His eyes had sobered a little on Olarr's, because he might not yet realize what he was agreeing to, and just how difficult this could be—but Olarr was already nodding, licking his lips, giving Gerrard a slow, red-rimmed smile. "I yet always thought this," he murmured back. "But I shall gladly think of you even more, ach?"

Oh. Well, then. Gerrard's own smile slowly pulled up too, feeling a bit jaunty now, maybe even triumphant. "Good," he said, husky. "Especially because now"—he waggled his eyebrows—"now you finally have *my* seed-ling, yeah?"

He shot a satisfied smirk down at where his hand was stroking Olarr's belly, caressing at where it was just slightly more rounded than before. Not much, not enough that anyone would have even noticed, if they weren't looking. But Gerrard was sure as hell looking, and grinning broadly back at Olarr's stunned, watching face.

"Even did it from both ends," he said smugly. "How's it feel,

Bautul? To fall for a human? And to be so thoroughly conquered?"

There was an instant's stillness, a quiver on Olarr's mouth—and then he laughed. Laughed, the sound bright and booming, sparkling in his eyes, shaking in his big hands, drawing Gerrard close and safe. Making him his. Making him home.

"It feels good, warrior," Olarr whispered, his heart in his beautiful, worshipful eyes. "It feels good."

EPILOGUE

Aulis Gerrard was going to be defeated by a four-year-old.

"Augggghhhh!" he groaned theatrically, as he fell back onto the carpet, flailing beneath the felling blows of said four-year-old's weapon—a bright yellow parasol. "I've been destroyed by a monster! Noooo!"

Little Molly Cosgrove grinned broadly back toward him, and gave him one more decisive whack with the parasol. "I destroy you!" she exclaimed, with contagious glee. "I win the victory!"

Gerrard laughed again, and then propped himself up on his elbow as Susie came over to sweep Molly up into her arms. Susie was Cosgrove's wife, just as plump and cheerful as he was, and she beamed down at Gerrard as she bounced Molly on her hip. "She's a ferocious little warrior, aren't you, lovey?" she asked Molly. "Going to be such a good protector for your new little sister or brother?"

Molly eagerly nodded, patting Susie's visibly rounded belly with a reassuring little hand, before beaming proudly over toward Cosgrove. Who was fondly watching all this from the sofa, and now waving Molly and Susie over, so he could yank them both into his arms.

It was a scene Gerrard had often witnessed over the past eighteen months, since they'd all packed up the outpost, and moved back north again. Cosgrove had successfully obtained an administrative position within Warmisham's ranks, a role which not only suited him very well, but also allowed him to live at home in the city with his wife and daughter. And whenever Gerrard was in town, the Cosgroves invariably invited him over for dinner, and a recurring sparring-match with Molly, too.

"Are you sure you don't want one of your own yet?" Susie asked Gerrard, now, with a teasing grin. "Find a nice woman, and finally settle down?"

Gerrard didn't miss Cosgrove's alarmed look toward him, or his meaningful jab at Susie's side—because while Gerrard had never gone into detail with Cosgrove on such matters, he'd clearly gotten the idea, at least. But Gerrard easily grinned back and waved it away, shoving himself up to his feet. "Nah, no kids yet," he said lightly. "Still too busy, with too much to do. But maybe I'll think about it someday, yeah?"

It wasn't even slightly a falsehood, because Gerrard did still think about it, probably more than he should—but the past year and a half had proven to be even busier than he'd expected. Requiring him not only to tramp all over the realm upon command, but also to collaborate with his fellow generals, develop training regimens, and support the improvement of military processes and policies—especially the ones that affected soldiers' families—all while also serving as the leader of Duke Warmisham's powerful household guard.

But Gerrard had wanted the guard position, had angled for it for months—and a well-orchestrated orc "attack" on one of Warmisham's carriages had finally helped to settle the thing. Thrusting Gerrard into a frequently tedious but also highly enviable position in Warmisham's closest circle, which granted him copious amounts of inside information on Preia's current government, and the military's major projects and priorities. And which also allowed him to pass on said information to the orcs, so Olarr—and more often, Grimarr—could make decisions from there.

And the more Gerrard had gotten to know of Grimarr, and the extent of his many sprawling schemes, the more he'd gotten drawn into it all. Not only spying and sending intelligence, but making bargains and deals, disseminating false information, and trading land—and sometimes lives—back and forth between them. It wasn't always easy, and it had given Gerrard many close calls and sleepless nights—but he'd still felt the rightness in it, too. The goddess' blessing. And with every day, every deal, Gerrard could feel them moving a bit closer, making another gain. Preventing another battle. Sabotaging another public punishment or execution. Targeting more of the orcs—and human men—who were driving the war the hardest, who were responsible for the most deaths, on both sides.

It had meant Gerrard had taken on several more Bautul duels over the past year, too. One against the clan's other previous Captain Borek—only slightly less vile than Slagvor—and another against an odious creeping vermin deep in the south. It had turned out that the swine had been the leader of a ring that had targeted younger orcs—Olarr among them—many years previously, and Gerrard had taken a rather vicious joy in killing the bastard, and making sure he damn well stayed dead.

Of course, Gerrard had also needed to manage Warmisham throughout it all, keeping his primary employer satisfied and safe. But while Warmisham was indeed still as selfish and spoiled and careless as any other noble, he'd also proven to be far less volatile than Livermore, with a passable sense for military and administrative matters, and a far greater eye to his own comfort, reputation, and pleasure. Which meant that he not only preferred having capable help around him, but he also preferred that help to be brawny, well-dressed, and ready to warm his bed at a moment's notice.

It had made for a few decidedly awkward moments at first, but finally Gerrard had just breathed a prayer to the goddess, and told Warmisham something not unlike the truth. "Look, Your Grace, I'm flattered," he'd said, "but I've already got a steady guy twice my size, and he'd tear me a new arsehole if he knew I was at it with you. He's already hard enough on me as it is, yeah?"

Thankfully, it had perhaps been the best possible solution, because not only had it given Gerrard a convenient and lasting excuse, but it had spared Warmisham from being too offended, while also offering him a highly compelling little vision to ponder, whenever he set eyes on Gerrard. And it also meant that Gerrard didn't need to bother hiding it anymore when Olarr got a little rough with him, when there were visible scratches and fingerprints on his neck, or when he ended up limping around after a night's hard ploughing.

And thankfully, it also meant that Gerrard could still look Warmisham's wife in the eyes, too. She was a young, eager, increasingly miserable woman named Maria, who deserved far better than a cheating, self-absorbed noble like Warmisham. And Gerrard had already sent word to Grimarr that Maria was someone he might want to keep an eye on, as part of one of his larger ongoing schemes—and Gerrard hadn't been at all surprised to see one of Grimarr's favourite spies lurking around more often afterwards, hanging in windows, and snatching food off plates when no one else was looking.

And speaking of which—Gerrard's gaze flicked to the window behind Cosgrove's sofa—that was a *stick* in the window, bobbing with unnatural purpose above Cosgrove's head. A stick that was being held by a distinctly grey hand, with long black *claws* attached.

"Well, sorry to say, but I should probably head out for the night," Gerrard told his hosts, making a show of yawning, and stretching his arms over his head. "Thanks again for having me, you two. And as for *you*"—he pointed an imperious finger at Molly—"we'll have a rematch next time, yeah?"

Molly giggled excitedly in her mother's arms, and after another round of thanks and farewells, Gerrard headed out into the bustling city street. It was nearly nightfall, but there were still multiple pedestrians and vendors and wagons milling about, enough that Gerrard almost missed the familiar sight of the stick, lying on the street just in front of Cosgrove's garden. And pointing carefully north, straight in the direction of Warmisham's house.

A smile twitched at Gerrard's mouth, and he obligingly began walking toward the house, rather than stopping at Head Command on his way home, as he'd originally planned. There were multiple projects and policy revisions currently on the go, and a diplomatic trip scheduled for Warmisham next week, but the sticks were always more important. Olarr was more important.

That certainty had only deepened this past year, as Gerrard and Olarr had settled into their unconventional relationship, their unconventional life. Working primarily with their own people, on their own goals, but making room for each other, whenever they possibly could. Making that room count, building and strengthening each other, trusting each other, enjoying each other, to the fullest extent possible.

But it had been a long time since Olarr's last visit—almost three weeks—and Gerrard still felt that familiar rising patter of his heartbeat as he strode up the street, his eyes sweeping over the dark alleys and increasingly manicured lawns around him.

Until he squinted toward a nearby hedge, which now had a familiar messy head poking up behind it.

"Evening, Joarr," Gerrard said with a grin and a nod toward Grimarr's favourite lurking spy, who Olarr often travelled with these days, too. "Anything urgent going on? Olarr at the house?"

He could see Joarr's shadow keeping pace with him on the other side of the hedge, though like most orcs from the Skai clan, he moved in perfect silence, as if his feet scarcely touched the ground. "Ach, naught urgent, and Olarr is there, and Thorvald also," came Joarr's smooth reply over the hedge. "But Grimarr wish to know first when Council next meet, and whether Lord Norr come. And if yes, where he stay, and whether he bring wife."

Gerrard didn't even try bothering to ask for explanations from Joarr anymore—he was an endlessly tricky orc—and instead just answered the question, speaking as quietly and comprehensively as he could before reaching the end of the hedge. Earning in return a toss of a shiny red apple over the hedge, and Gerrard grinned as he caught it, and gave a companionable wave farewell.

He'd almost reached his destination, now, and he swiftly polished off the apple as he approached. Warmisham's city house was a grand, imposing place, looming over the surrounding neighbourhood, but at the moment it was mostly empty, thanks to Maria's being stuck at the country house, Warmisham's being out at an event, and it being the staff's usual night off. But even so, Gerrard walked up the back lane and slipped through the side door as quietly as he could, glancing around in the darkness, listening for any signs of life.

And yes. There. What sounded like a growl, coming from the direction of the downstairs drawing-room. So Gerrard headed toward it, listening and glancing around as he went.

But fortunately, the house indeed seemed to be empty, except for—he swung open the drawing-room door—except for this.

Gerrard halted in the drawing-room's open doorframe, and blinked at the sight confronting him in the firelit darkness. At none other than *Bassey*, sitting sprawled by the fire in Warmisham's favourite brocade chair, with his trousers around his knees, and a familiar orc's head bobbing and slurping over his groin. *Thorvald's* head.

Gerrard knew Thorvald and Bassey had met a few months previously, and the meeting had in fact been his own doing—Thorvald had travelled here with Olarr, as he often did, but had ended up suffering a cough so severe that he'd struggled to breathe. And finally, Gerrard had gone to fetch Bassey, who—after a fair bit of advocating on Gerrard's part—had recently been appointed as Warmisham's personal physician. A post that Bassey had well deserved, because he was still a brilliant medic, as insightful and unflappable as ever—and he'd taken one look at Thorvald, coolly informed him that he was a chronic asthmatic, and demanded whether he'd been exposed to any smoke or other airborne pollutants on his journey here.

Thorvald had looked instantly chastised, and not a little intrigued, while Bassey had sighed, mixed up a prescription, and ordered Thorvald to drink it whenever he had an exposure. And as far as Gerrard had known, that had been the end of it, except... well.

Thorvald had taken no notice whatsoever of Gerrard at the door, in favour of remaining fully focused on the potential feast in his mouth, but Bassey had angled Gerrard a warning look, his mouth pursed. "He needed a new prescription," he said flatly, with impressive steadiness. "Why he thinks it's a good idea to keep lighting fires in those poorly ventilated caves, I cannot begin to comprehend."

Gerrard's mouth quirked, but he nodded as gravely as he

could, and glanced sideways, toward where he'd felt Olarr waiting. Toward where Olarr was already quirking an amused smile of his own as he strode toward Gerrard, and drew him tightly into his arms.

"Ach, my warrior," he breathed, heated and husky, into Gerrard's neck. "Ach, it is so good to see you. I have missed you."

Gerrard nodded and exhaled, sinking gratefully into Olarr's safe, wonderful arms, while Olarr's hot mouth eagerly nudged at his throat. Finding its usual place, settling against Gerrard's now-heavily scarred skin—and then hesitating, seeking permission. But as always, Gerrard willingly gave it, his head tilting back as he drew Olarr's head down, and gasped at the truth of those sharp teeth sinking deep.

He could feel Bassey watching it, and briefly considered taking Olarr into the adjoining room—but Bassey could make his own choices, and if he wanted to fuck around with a Bautul, well, he'd soon be realizing what that meant. So Gerrard didn't fight back his steadily rising groans, or the way his hands were already running over Olarr's bare chest, unfastening both his axes from his back, and letting them fall to the floor with a thud. One of the axes was of course Olarr's old familiar one, while the second was the one Gerrard had won from Slagvor—and though Olarr had hesitated about keeping it at first, Gerrard had insisted, until Olarr had agreed. Because it was a good strong weapon, well suited to a warrior of Olarr's size and strength—and more importantly, it also reminded everyone Olarr met who it had last belonged to. Who it had killed.

And that constant reminder, Gerrard knew, had been a considerable help in finally making Olarr co-captain of the Bautul, several months before. A position that Olarr and Silfast had indeed sought out together, since they were both the strongest remaining warriors in their clan. And, just as Gerrard had expected, it had turned out that they did make a very good team. Olarr was the cunning one, the thoughtful responsible one, while Silfast lived for the reckless brutal chaos, for hurling himself repeatedly at danger and death, obeying what he felt was the clear command of the goddess. And while Gerrard knew that wasn't always easy for Olarr, he also knew how much Olarr appreciated Silfast's stubborn steadfastness, too—and especially how freely Silfast wielded it to support Olarr's plans, and Olarr's priorities.

And those priorities, of course, always included Gerrard. Meaning that Olarr frequently was obliged to leave his clan behind, in Silfast's care, so he could come here and do this, with Gerrard. Tasting Gerrard, drinking him, grinding up hungrily against him, and finally shoving down his trousers, and tackling him down to the drawing-room's plush expensive carpet.

"Fuck," Gerrard gasped, his back arching as Olarr drew his mouth away from his neck, so he could kiss down Gerrard's belly, and latch onto his now-bared cock instead. "Fuck, that's good, captain. So good. Just like that."

Olarr's groan vibrated all through Gerrard's body, so loud that he almost didn't hear Bassey's low gasp—but a sideways glance showed Bassey still watching this, his dazed eyes darting between Olarr and Gerrard, and then back to his own still-sucking orc. But he wasn't making the slightest effort to protest, either, and he'd even sunk his hands into Thorvald's hair, much the way Gerrard was now doing with Olarr. So Gerrard dismissed it, forgot it, because Olarr was finally here, and this was his, this was *everything*.

"So good, captain," Gerrard gasped again, guiding Olarr faster, his fingers gently tugging at his hair, his leg hooking around his back. "You're gonna suck up every drop of me, aren't you? Gonna milk out everything I've been making for you? Saving for you?"

Olarr's growl was pure hunger, pure palpable pleasure, and

Gerrard drank up the dizzying sensation of it, the clustering coiling ecstasy, the worshipful shimmer in Olarr's watching eyes. "Yeah, just like that, captain," he breathed. "You keep kneeling for me, behaving for me. Drinking your sweet human milk like a good Bautul should, fuck, fuck—"

His voice had been rising, his body almost fully off the carpet—and he shouted as he poured out, sprayed deep into Olarr's hot, sucking, all-encompassing mouth. And oh, there was nothing in the world like emptying into Olarr, like having his seed swallowed, wanted, worshipped by his own devoted, adoring orc.

Gerrard was still gasping once he'd finished, still spasming out into Olarr's hot lingering mouth. And this was where Olarr would usually pull off, and offer a taste of Gerrard's seed to whatever orc was with him—a bit of a reward, Gerrard knew, for making the journey, and staying the course beside him. But Thorvald was most certainly gaining a taste of his own right now, loudly groaning as Bassey's head tilted back, his chest heaving, his brown hands fluttering in Thorvald's hair.

But it was just as well, because it meant Gerrard got to enjoy this to its fullest, got to revel in his brilliant mate lingering on him, sucking him dry. A sensation that would once have been too strong to bear, but over the past few months, Gerrard had begun to suspect that this was part of Olarr's seed-induced strength, too. Making it easier to control his body's responses, somehow, to draw things out or speed things up, or even to go for another round, far sooner than he'd ever been able to before. Just one more miracle to add to all the rest, alongside the unnatural strength and speed, the much-improved night vision, the ability to go longer and longer without sleep—and even the surprising ability to sense when Olarr was nearby, or to sniff him out in a dark forest, or across a crowded room.

They were all incredible, unspeakable gifts, gifts that had

vastly improved Gerrard's ability to excel at his chosen work, and to push for his goals. But—he softly smiled at Olarr as he stroked his hands through his hair—he'd perhaps given Olarr a few gifts of his own, too. Because not only was Olarr noticeably faster on his feet in their sparring-matches these days, but he also seemed increasingly sensitive to touch, texture, and taste. He'd even developed a marked preference for cooked food, and he unabashedly adored the sweet treats Gerrard brought him from the city's bakeries and markets. And maybe it was all just coincidence, all Gerrard's imagination, but he liked to think of him and Olarr influencing each other, strengthening each other, expanding their abilities and world-views and experiences, deepening their pleasure together.

And oh, hell, the pleasure was deepening now, because Olarr was shifting further downwards. Slipping Gerrard's bollocks into his mouth one at a time, rolling them on his tongue, before yanking off Gerrard's trousers the rest of the way, and kissing lower. And lower, and lower, until that stunning, slippery tongue was easing itself deep into Gerrard, opening him wider and wider, while he shuddered and shouted and keened upon it.

But wait, Bassey and Thorvald were still here, still witnessing this—and Gerrard's brief, searching look sideways showed them both blatantly watching, now. Watching a fully bared Preian general writhing and moaning on an orc's invading tongue, in a highly revealing, highly compromising scenario. And it distantly occurred to Gerrard that maybe he should care, maybe he should hide this. Because his past self would most certainly be shoving Olarr away right now, and then launching into a round of furious self-loathing, inwardly bleating on about pride and power and shame...

But maybe this was part of Olarr's gift too, or maybe it was a gift from the Bautul, or the goddess. Or maybe—maybe even just from Gerrard himself, with all he'd learned these past months, all the choices he'd made. Because he wanted this. He *was* this. He was a warrior, a killer, a spy, a revolutionary—and also a hungry, lusty, reckless man who wanted to use and enjoy his body, wield it to honour himself, his goddess, his mate. And right now he had his mate's glorious mouth fastened to him, his mate's tongue twisting inside him, and oh, nothing was this good, nothing had ever been this good.

"If you haven't tried it yet," he heard himself gasp to Bassey, pulling his thighs up higher so Olarr could go deeper, "it's fucking spectacular. And he'd absolutely go for it, no question."

Bassey's wide eyes shot a shocked glance down at Thorvald, who was currently giving Gerrard a deeply grateful look, and then plucking hopefully at Bassey's trousers. While Olarr still hadn't taken the slightest notice of any of it, because he was busy yanking at his own trousers, and shifting his way up again. Settling his swollen, dripping head against Gerrard's wet, willing, wide-open heat, and slowly, surely, piercing him deep.

Gerrard writhed and hollered, arching up to meet it, scraping his fingernails hard against Olarr's back. And if Bassey was staring slack-jawed again, while Thorvald eagerly spread his now-bared thighs wide, Gerrard truly didn't care. Because there was only this, only the rioting reeling pleasure of his mate finally here, finally inside him, ploughing him wide open, breaking him apart upon his altar.

"Goddess, yes, captain," Gerrard gasped, clutching Olarr tight and close, clamping around him as hard as he could. "Fuck me. Make me feel that good Bautul prick, ploughing all the way up my arse."

Olarr was growling now too, plunging harder and faster, as his hands swiped for Gerrard's arms, and firmly pinned his wrists to the carpet above his head. "Ach, I shall, my pretty human," he hissed back, his sharp teeth snapping close against Gerrard's ear. "And you shall beg and squeal beneath your strong Bautul captain, ach? You shall be a good, snug, sweet little hole for me. You shall let me rut you, bind you, mark you all over, open you so wide you shall never close *again*."

Gerrard was rapidly nodding, fighting for it, begging for it, as Olarr kept pounding into him, conquering him, his sharp teeth bared, his eyes blazing with raw, ravenous greed. "And"— Olarr's voice dropped deeper, into a vicious, thrilling rasp— "you shall welcome my triumph, my beautiful warrior mate. You shall whimper and weep and wail for me, as my strong Bautul prick fucks you, and feeds you, fills you, floods you only with *me*—"

And yes, yes, it was this, it was shrill screaming wonder, flying all through Gerrard's body, lighting him up from the inside out. And surging him full of Olarr's worship, his offering, his fierce unflinching care. While Gerrard kept thrashing and shouting and pleading for it, until his own seed again spurted out, streaking across his chest, his breaths breaking into something almost like sobs.

But Olarr was still here, Olarr was still with him, rocking gently into him, kissing softly at his lips again and again. And then carefully slipping out of him, easing downwards again, so he could kiss Gerrard's seed-spattered chest, could taste him, could lavish and lick him all over, not wasting a single drop. Until Gerrard's breaths were slow and steady again, his sweaty body sprawled lax and languid on the carpet. And his belated hazy glance over at Bassey showed him looking just as stunned as he felt—until without a word, Bassey yanked up his trousers, prodded Thorvald to his feet, and strode toward the adjoining room, his head held very high.

Thorvald's expression as he followed looked both rapt and gleeful, as if a priceless, long-awaited gift had just been dropped in his lap, and Gerrard let out a breathless laugh as the sliding door slammed shut behind them. But Olarr still hadn't even spared them a look, and instead he was sliding to his side on the carpet, and gathering Gerrard's boneless body into his arms.

"Ach, this was so good, Aulis," Olarr murmured now, stroking at Gerrard's back, his arse, his hair. "All I could have dreamt of, all these weeks apart."

Gerrard huffed a contented sigh and curled closer, breathing in a slow, deep breath of Olarr's rich-scented skin. "Goddess, yes," he whispered back. "Missed you so damned much, captain. And now"—he shot a shy, teasing smile up at Olarr's face—"talk to me, yeah? Tell me everything."

Olarr chuckled and nodded, and kept stroking his big hand up and down Gerrard's back as he began speaking. Indeed telling Gerrard everything that had gone on since they'd last seen each other, including Grimarr's ongoing plots against his vile father, as well as his latest target—none other than Lady Norr, apparently. And then on to the orcs' perspective on the newest battles and raids and victories and deaths, what the repercussions had been among them, what they expected to come next.

It was a decidedly heavy discussion, so at Gerrard's prodding, Olarr then told him all the latest Bautul gossip, too. How two opposing captain candidates in the south had settled their differences by mating the same woman. How Silfast had decided that the goddess wanted to grant him a mate, but only after he'd worshipped at an unspecified number of Bautul altars, all over the realm. And how, most surprising of all, Kalfr had recently discovered he had a one-year-old *son*, after a short fling with a woman had apparently gone very wrong, many moons before. To the point where even now, this woman refused to see Kalfr, or to allow him—or any other orc— anywhere near her orcling.

"I can't imagine Kalfr mistreating a woman," Gerrard said at that one, frowning up at Olarr's face. "Enough that she'd hide a son from him for that long, and keep Kalfr from even seeing him? From doing his part, and being a decent father? Making his son part of his clan?"

Olarr grimaced, looking genuinely pained, because Gerrard well knew how glad he would have been to welcome any son of Kalfr's to the clan. "No, this was not Kalfr's doing alone, I ken," he said heavily. "But Gaelfr was mixed up in this also, ach? They will not say what went amiss, but they have fought bitterly over this, and now Gaelfr has gone south, and says he will never again return."

Gerrard had now met this Gaelfr multiple times—he was the cool-eyed orc who'd tasted him with Kalfr at the altar—and he also knew that Gaelfr was Kalfr's bond-brother. It was a kind of pact young Bautul often made with one another, often when their families were already tied in some way, and it generally extended to caring for each other's future sons and mates, also. And while Gaelfr had never seemed like a particularly friendly fellow, to have broken his bond, and deprived his bond-brother and clan of a son, seemed like a damning development indeed.

"I'm so sorry, Olarr," Gerrard said, quiet, stroking his hand up and down Olarr's side. "I know how much a new Bautul son would have meant to you. Maybe they'll still work it out, yeah? Or maybe Silfast will have some luck with the altars?"

Olarr huffed a short laugh and shook his head, but his eyes on Gerrard were still sad, glimmering with genuine grief. Calling up the many conversations they'd had about this, about how the future of the Bautul was one of Olarr's greatest growing concerns as captain. How every son lost, every life lost, was a blow that might never again be overcome.

It was enough that Gerrard had tentatively asked Olarr, months ago, whether he wouldn't prefer to find a woman after all—but thank the goddess, Olarr had been aghast and offended, and Gerrard had needed to spend the entire night working him over, reassuring him that he hadn't wanted that, either. That he only feared for their clan, and wanted Olarr to be content with his own contributions, and his own choices.

But Olarr had kept roundly insisting he was content, and he hadn't even hinted at their discussion from months and months ago. That unforgettable conversation they'd had about possibly adopting a human son, someday. Being fathers to a kid who needed it, while also bringing new blood into the clan.

But Gerrard had known Olarr had been thinking it, at the time—and surely he was thinking it now, too. And Gerrard swallowed hard as he met Olarr's eyes, as his hand stroking Olarr's side stilled, in favour of gripping tight against him, drawing up strength.

"Look, I know we've still got a lot to do yet," Gerrard said, his voice thick. "But—do you still want to try to adopt a son of our own, someday? When we're ready?"

Olarr's eyes widened, his breath held in his chest, and it belatedly occurred to Gerrard that the question wasn't just about the son. It was about... them. It was about their commitment, their bond to each other, their willingness to keep seeing this through.

And maybe—maybe it was also about that ultimatum Gerrard had given Olarr, after they'd dealt with Slagvor and Livermore. *I need you to show me I can trust you. I need you to keep coming back to me, even when it's not easy. I need you to keep your word to me, again and again and again, until I can believe you'll always do it. Until I can trust you enough to make a full life with you.*

Olarr still wasn't breathing, wasn't even blinking, but finally he twitched a small, cautious nod. "Ach, Aulis," he whispered. "I yet—wish for this. But I know you may yet—not. Trust me. Most of all enough to—raise a son, with me."

But Gerrard was studying him now, his steady, solid, supportive mate, who'd kept his word, and kept coming back, again and again. Who'd consistently given Gerrard his openness and honesty, who'd offered him such ready generosity, who'd welcomed him into his clan and his faith and his life. Who'd more than made up for his secrets. And who'd somehow become Gerrard's true partner, in bed, in battle, in war, and—he hoped—in peace. His best friend.

"Yeah, I want it," Gerrard said, steady, certain, to Olarr's blinking eyes. "It would be—an honour, captain. A gift from the goddess."

Olarr kept staring at him, unblinking, and Gerrard drew in breath, fought through the rising thud of his heartbeat. "And it would be—a victory of our own, yeah? Our own promise of making peace, together. Overcoming all our differences, learning to love our enemies. Making a life together. Making—home."

His voice hitched at the end, gone raw with longing, with hope. And Olarr was still staring, blinking hard, something shifting, lighting, behind his eyes—

When suddenly, oh goddess, Olarr yanked Gerrard close. Clutching him so tightly it hurt, rocking them fiercely back and forth. Conquering him, caressing him, saving him.

"Ach, my warrior," Olarr whispered, his voice breaking, breathing, like an orc fallen, and risen again. "This I vow, before the goddess. Home."

BONUS EPILOGUE

There was naught else in the realm like coming home.

Olarr halted just within the edge of the forest, blinking toward the familiar sight of his beloved little home before him. Toward where Aulis and the younglings were sparring in the clearing again, shouting and laughing as they snapped their sticks together, the sounds and scents of their joy bubbling bright through the air.

It was a sight Olarr oft saw these days, for nine-year-old Alfie lived for fighting, and had long ago decided that he would someday become a great Bautul warrior, just like his fathers. And whilst his six-year-old sister Ophelia had claimed no such wish, she also wished to do all Alfie did, and thus threw herself into their sparring-matches with unchecked glee.

Olarr's mouth drew up as he watched Ophelia swing and kick and shout, her little blonde braid whirling through the air behind her. A daughter had not been part of his plans, not in the slightest—for he and Aulis had been prepared to adopt a son, and only a son. But Aulis had grown deeply fond of Alfie, whose father had been a soldier beneath his command, and Alfie had refused to leave the orphans' home without his sister.

And Aulis had despaired at leaving them there, in a cold grimy house with stale air, weary masters, and little food.

"We'll make it work, yeah?" Aulis had told Olarr, his beautiful blue eyes wide and beseeching. "We're already living at the mountain through most of the winter anyway, so they can both go to school there, and there are plenty of women around to help us. We can make sure to ask their advice, ask them to come visit. And if it's not working after a few months, we'll revisit it, and sort out something else. *Please*, captain."

Olarr had never been able to withstand Aulis' pleading, and in truth, he had loathed the thought of leaving Ophelia behind, also. And he had been doomed at their very first meeting, during which the small, grubby girl had first stared at him, and hidden behind her brother—but when Olarr had offered her one of his sweet-cakes, she had eaten it with unabashed delight, and had then begun plying him with a stream of eager questions. Asking after his axes, and his thick gold wedding-ring, and even his claws and teeth.

And now—Olarr's smile pulled higher as he watched Ophelia wrench away Aulis' stick, and toss it across the clearing—he could not dream of life without her, or without Alfie. It was such deep joy to watch his son and daughter learn and grow, to teach them all he knew, and bask in their sweetness and their life. To know he was giving back to his clan, giving the Bautul new blood and new hope for the days to come.

And mayhap, most of all, it was joy to share this with Aulis. To be a father together with Aulis, and build the home they had always longed for. And even after seven full summers as mates, Aulis still made Olarr's heart race, and stirred the hunger in his loins. Mayhap even stronger than their early days together, for—Olarr choked a husky laugh as Aulis careened back onto the earth, howling—he was such a kind father. Such a warm, worthy mate.

And ach, Aulis had even twitched up again, his eyes

narrowing, scanning the line of trees. Searching for Olarr, sensing him there, as he so oft did. And Olarr's smile drew even higher, softer, as Aulis' eyes lit up, and he jumped up to jog toward him. Whilst both younglings looked round, and then shouted and raced after him—and within a breath, Olarr was piled upon with warmth and laughter, with his kin's beloved scents swarming his breath.

"Pabbi's home!" Ophelia exclaimed, as she threw her squirmy little body into his arms. "Why did you go so long? Did you bring pie? I beat Alfie in sparring, Pabbi!"

"She did not!" Alfie protested, muffled, from where he had crammed himself in between Olarr and Aulis. "I *tripped*! That's all!"

Olarr heartily laughed, and rustled his hand against Alfie's tousled brown curls. "Ach, I am sure it was a good match, with strong fighting on all sides," he said firmly, as he leaned in to briefly meet Aulis' kiss, drinking up the taste of his mate's warm succulent sweetness on his lips. "And I did bring pie, ach? One for each of us—and I was sure to gain apple for you, *litli kjúlli*."

Ophelia crowed with delighted joy—apple had always been her favourite—and after a quick peck to Olarr's cheek, she scrambled down from his arms, in favour of grasping his hand, and dragging him across the clearing toward the cottage. Toward... home.

It was a humble little house, made of logs and stone, but it was solid, and safe, and *theirs*. And best of all, the Ka-esh had helped them choose the place, so they might dig out a dry little tunnel beneath, leading to two underground rooms—one larger, for sparring and training, and one for Olarr and Aulis' bedroom. It was near enough to the house above that Olarr could yet scent the younglings, but far enough that they could not hear any shouts or curses or moans from their fathers below.

The house also stood in the forest amidst a large clearing, with ample room for playing and sparring, and Aulis had built another of his *obstacle courses* to run through, full of ropes and ladders and tricky balancing tests. And whilst Olarr could finish this course—with effort—he took far more joy in watching Aulis and Alfie do this, throwing their lean bodies from one trial to the next, laughing and chattering together all the while.

It had turned out that Ophelia also held little care for the course—and in a rare divergence from her brother, she had eagerly joined Olarr in his own outdoor project. His own garden. It had taken much effort at first, and much help and guidance from their kin-brother Joarr, who had his own far larger garden at Orc Mountain. But Olarr now found a deep, quiet contentment in tending to his little plot with his daughter, and growing good food to keep his kin hearty and hale.

"So what else did you bring?" Alfie asked, as they tumbled into the cozy kitchen together. "Did you visit the Bautul fighting-pit? Was there lots of good matches?!"

The Bautul pit was Alfie's favourite place in all of Orc Mountain, and Olarr chuckled and nodded as he slung his heavy pack down onto the table, and began unloading. First carefully lifting out the pies and treats and bread he had gained from Orc Mountain's kitchen, and then a few new books from the library. But then he paused, meeting Aulis' gaze across the table, and he could see the awareness, and then the excitement, kindling across his mate's eyes.

"Did you get it?" Aulis asked, and now he was digging into the pack also, and drawing out a long, wrapped item. An item their son had been asking after for many moons now, and Alfie was now bouncing on his toes, his dark eyes gone very wide as they darted between Olarr and Aulis.

"Get what?" he asked, his voice shrill. "What, Papa?"

Aulis smiled down toward him, swift and almost

unbearably fond, and thrust out the wrapped item toward him. "A gift, son," he said, husky. "Brand-new, just for you. Just like the one you kept eyeing all winter, yeah?"

Alfie's small hands trembled as he snatched the package, and carefully unwrapped it. And whilst Olarr well knew what was within, it was yet a warm, wondrous delight to hear Alfie's gasp, and then his shout of sheer unfettered joy, as he drew out the dagger.

It was bright and gleaming, new from the Skai forge, which made the best weapons in all the realm. And whilst the dagger was larger than was best for a youngling Alfie's size, he would soon grow into it, and it would well serve him for all his days. And he was blinking as he stared at it, as he traced a reverent finger against its sharp edge—and with a gulp, he lurched into Aulis' side, squeezing him tight.

"Thank you, Papa," he choked, blinking worshipfully up toward him, before rushing over into Olarr's waiting arms, too. "And thank you, Pabbi. Though"—he drew back to aim a gap-toothed smile at Olarr's face—"Papa made you do it, didn't he?"

Olarr shot a tolerant smile over at Aulis' dancing eyes, and bent his head to kiss Alfie's curls. "Ach, mayhap," he said thickly. "But I ken how much you wished for this, *litli maður*. And I ken you shall take great care with this, ach?"

Alfie solemnly nodded toward him, and Olarr felt his smile deepening, the fear and the fondness a low mingled ache in his chest. If he had learnt aught from the end of the war, five summers past, it was how deep the wounds of war went, and how those scars had broken and betrayed his kin. How even in the war's end, amidst this new peace between orcs and men, the Bautul had barely begun to find a way beyond this. A way beyond weapons, and fighting, and pain.

And ach, Olarr could admit, he wished to spare his younglings this pain. Wished to teach them the softer, kinder ways of their clan—their care for their kin, their unmatched food and gardens, their deep love for the earth and the forest and the goddess' night sky. And whilst Olarr knew Ophelia would mayhap follow his will in this, Alfie had always longed for the thrill of sparring and adventure, and sought to gain the strength to keep his kin guarded and safe. Just as—Olarr angled another fond glance toward Aulis—just as his human Bautul father did, also.

"We'll be careful with it, son, won't we?" Aulis said now, with a gentle little shake to Alfie's shoulder. "We'll learn how to clean and care for it, and you still won't be using it in any sparring against anyone for a long, long time. We don't want to give Pabbi anything else to worry about, yeah?"

He flashed a jaunty grin toward Olarr, and Olarr gave a slow, grateful smile back before dropping his gaze back to Ophelia. She had gone unusually silent amidst this, her eyes downcast, and though the sight of it plummeted in Olarr's chest, there was no realm in which he would grant his excitable six-year-old youngling a deadly new Skai dagger, no matter how she or Alfie or Aulis begged. And instead—Olarr breathed a silent prayer to the goddess—he had sought out another gift. Another gift he had thought—he had hoped—she might welcome.

His Bautul kin-sister Gwyn had helped him pack it up in a little carved box, each piece carefully wrapped in cloth, and Ophelia's eyes widened as Olarr held the box out toward her. "And now for you, *litli kjúlli*," he said, his voice soft. "This is also a good Bautul gift. Our sister Gwyn oft uses these, herself."

Ophelia's eyes brightened upon hearing of Gwyn, who was, Olarr had been decisively told, *the most marvellous woman in the mountain.* Mayhap due to Gwyn's good work as the mountain's midwife and herbalist, or mayhap—Olarr was less eager to admit—due to her being mated to Joarr, who despite his great gardening skill, was just the sort of sly, flighty orc Olarr should least wish to fix in Ophelia's mind as an ideal mating-prospect.

Ophelia ought to have a steady, steadfast mate to support and protect her, and Olarr had already set his eye upon Kalfr's elder son Svein, who at seven had already begun to show himself a good, kind, stable Bautul son, in spite of the tumult of his parents' early estrangement.

Of course, Aulis had only merrily laughed when Olarr had told him of this clever plan, and ordered Olarr never to speak of it to Ophelia, so long as he lived—lest he wished her to do the reverse, if only out of spite. And whilst Olarr had well seen the wisdom of this, it had not stopped him from oft inviting Kalfr and his kin to visit, and welcoming Svein to help him and Ophelia in the garden, also.

But mayhap his wisdom had not failed him in this, at least. For Ophelia was quivering with anticipation as she placed the box on the table, and opened its lid with eager, careful fingers. Showing all the smaller gifts inside, wrapped in a rich array of cloth in Ophelia's favourite colours, bright reds and purples and blues. And when she picked up an odd shape, and drew off the blue cloth, she revealed a stoppered green bottle, with dried leaves inside.

"It is—a set for readying herbs," Olarr told her, his voice only slightly strained, whilst his eyes rapidly searched her face. "There are bottles and jars, and tools such as scissors and stirrers, and even a little burner. Gwyn has also sent some of the herbs she most oft uses, so you can learn from these, and mayhap prescribe them, to anyone in need."

Olarr had made very certain that they were harmless herbs—nettle and chamomile and the like—and he kept watching, his breath stilled in his chest, as Ophelia pulled out the bottle's stopper, and sniffed at the herbs inside. "Lavender!" she exclaimed, holding it out toward Olarr. "She sent lavender, Pabbi!"

Olarr felt his smile drawing up, the relief rising in his chest, and he nodded his approval toward her, and waved toward the box. "Can you name the others, also?" he asked. "If you can find them?"

Ophelia excitedly nodded back, her little face alight, and she snatched up another item. This one turned out to be a small steel scale, meant for weighing and measuring herbs, and Ophelia gasped and marvelled at it before unwrapping more herbs—the chamomile and nettle—and then a mortar and pestle, a sieve, and a variety of stirring and chopping tools. Until the table was covered with shiny little items of glass and stone and steel, and Ophelia bobbed with excitement as she stared at them all, her little hands clasped to her chest.

"It's *wonderful*, Pabbi," she breathed, her voice hushed, her blue eyes shining on his face. "The best present ever. Even better than a silly old dagger."

This was said with a brief, scornful look toward Alfie, who was pouting as he clutched his dagger close—but behind him, Aulis was smiling at Olarr too, with just as much gratefulness glinting in his eyes. "Yeah, Pabbi always gets the best presents, doesn't he?" he said, hoarse, and then he lurched over toward Olarr, and hooked his arm around his neck. "Thanks, captain. It's perfect."

Olarr sank into Aulis' touch, his warmth, his approval—and then shuddered all over at the scent and feel of his mate, so close, after three full days apart. And whilst three days ought to have been naught, after all the time apart they had borne, Olarr found he was far less able to bear it, these days. Now that he had finally gained the great gift of living with his beautiful hungry man, and having him whenever he wished.

Aulis' mouth was still at Olarr's throat, his blunt teeth giving a gentle little nip—enough that Olarr had to bite down his growl, and shift to cover the swell in his trousers. And when he drew back to look at Aulis, he could see him fighting it, too, his long lashes low over his blue eyes, his tongue brushing his plump lip...

"You bring me anything, Pabbi?" Aulis murmured in Olarr's ear, his voice firing straight to Olarr's prick. "Anything hidden in your trousers, maybe?"

Olarr almost groaned this time, amidst a choked little laugh—but thank the goddess, both Ophelia and Alfie were well absorbed in their new gifts, and paying no heed to their fathers. And before he could lose himself further, Olarr shoved up to his feet, and gave a sharp, warning nip back at Aulis' scarred throat. "Soon," he breathed, into his sweet-scented skin. "I hope you are well rested, my warrior, for you shall not be sleeping this night."

Aulis' grin back was bright and full of promise, and Olarr had to hold his breath and force himself away, over to the iron stove. He had also brought a good store of spices and vegetables from the mountain, and he already had a good meal in mind, to go along with the pies.

"Oh, *Pabbi's* cooking," came Ophelia's excited voice from behind him. "Thank the goddess. Do you need any nettle, Pabbi?"

Aulis' affronted scoff rang through the room, but they were all laughing as Olarr waved Ophelia over, and told her that mayhap he could use some nettle, and mayhap she could weigh this for him on her new scale. And soon they were chopping and working side by side, whilst Aulis and Alfie fussed over the new dagger together.

Olarr's meal of spiced poultry and sweet roasted nuts and vegetables proved to be a very tasty one, and it was a true gift to watch his kin eagerly eating it, and then feasting on apple pie, until all their bellies were full. And afterwards, they sprawled on the furs before the crackling fireplace, whilst Aulis plucked out one of the new books Olarr had brought, and read them a tale. It was a rousing new one of heroes and battles—Orc Mountain's librarian always tucked such books away for them—and Aulis read it with his usual warm, eager enthusiasm, acting out each voice, and switching a few of the humans into orcs, also.

By the end of it, night had fully fallen, and Alfie and Ophelia were both sleepy and content, yawning on the fur. So after the usual nighttime rituals—snacks, washing up, prayers of thanks to the goddess—Olarr and Aulis tucked them into their beds, and bade them goodnight. And once Olarr had checked the door and windows, making sure all was tight and safe, he finally headed underground. Toward where his mate had already gone ahead, and—Olarr groaned, the hunger blooming in his groin—he was already naked, with his favourite sparring sword in hand.

"Finally, captain," Aulis said with a grin, tossing Olarr's own sword over toward him. "Been waiting for this for three damned *days*."

Olarr readily agreed, shunting off his own trousers—this just made it easier, after—before settling into his own stance. Watching his beautiful bared mate watching him, his lean body taut and alert—and then flying straight toward Olarr with all its usual speed, grace, and ease. So stunning that it swallowed Olarr's breath, blunted his own sword's parry, and ach, this was just what his cunning mate had wished, shouting his triumph as his sword struck against Olarr's bare side, ringing pain out in its wake.

Olarr hissed and shook his head, fought to draw his mind back to his blade, to the match. To meeting his mate's strikes, making him dance and work for it, drawing out his curses and his laughter.

But ach, Aulis was good. Quick, and strong, and clever. And in truth, he had seemed to grow yet stronger with every summer that had passed, until he could easily meet any man or orc in battle. Until Olarr could almost—almost—forget the ever-lurking fear of this, of his mate's slim neck breaking, or his delicate skull cracking open, or a sword gutting into his pale belly. Of his beautiful man being maimed, weakened, lost, the light fading from his eyes.

But Olarr fought never to speak of this to Aulis, never to betray his doubt or fear, and risk Aulis questioning Olarr's steadfast faith in him. Just as he had always fought never to speak of his own weaknesses, or his own defeats, even at Aulis' own hands. He had never told Aulis of the true wounds he had gained in their battles. He had never spoken of the pain he still felt in his shoulder, from where Aulis had cut the bone, in their first match together. And unless Aulis asked, Olarr rarely spoke of Harja, either, for he would never forget Aulis' deep hurt when he had first learnt of Harja. When he had learnt that Olarr had taken Harja as his mate, when he had not rightly done this with Aulis.

It had been one of many failings on Olarr's part, and he had sworn to the goddess that he would not fail his mate thus again. He would uphold Aulis, and cherish him, and show him no doubt or weakness or fear. Aulis deserved only Olarr's best. Olarr's faith, his strength, his cunning. His care.

But ach, Olarr's strength was failing him this eve, with each strike of his clever mate's sword, with the speed and ease of his dancing feet. And with how Olarr's greedy eyes wished not to watch Aulis' blade, but to drink up the beloved sights of his fair form, his smooth pretty prick, his flushed handsome face. His quick, stunning smile as he rushed in again, and—Olarr cursed, even as he knew it was too late—tripped him from behind, and tackled him to the fur below.

"My win, orc," Aulis gasped, still grinning, as his lean body dropped down onto Olarr's, his wooden sword thrusting into Olarr's neck. "Even slower than usual, I see."

Olarr's fond smile was already pulling at his mouth, despite the pain of the blade jamming into his throat. "Ach," he croaked. "Only—diverted, I ken."

His voice had barely been audible, and he winced as Aulis

twitched and tossed the sword away, his brow furrowing, his eyes searching and intent. And within a breath, Aulis' mouth was on Olarr's aching throat, kissing and licking with gentle, wondrous sweetness. Whilst Olarr's tired body sank into the softness of the fur, the warmth of his mate's mouth, the deep relief of his touch and his scent. His mate was here, alive, safe, in his arms, in his home.

And ach, Olarr would never grow weary of his mate's touch. Would never not welcome this, however his mate wished to give it. And these days, it was even easy to spread his legs wide for his mate thus, and to welcome those clever fingers, delving deep inside him. And to gasp and marvel at the sight of his human's other hand gripping his own pretty pink prick, and pumping out thick bursts of his own early seed. It was another of the goddess' great gifts, that Aulis could now make enough of his own for this—and ach, how he looked, how he scented, as he spread it down his shaft, stroking himself to a smooth, slick shine. And when he leaned forward, and gently pressed his dripping head to Olarr's spasming hole, Olarr shuddered and groaned and opened, and welcomed its slow, sweet glide inside.

It was only pleasure, now, only Olarr's beautiful mate taking him, finding joy with him. Fucking into him with swift, singleminded hunger, his lashes fluttering, his cheeks flushed, his little pink tongue sweeping against his lips. Whilst his clever hands roved all over Olarr's skin, sparkling warmth inside and out, drawing up Olarr's gasps and moans with startling ease. And there was naught in the realm like this, naught like being taken by a hungry devoted man, a man whose beautiful body arched as he shouted, as his sweet seed spurted out into Olarr, making him his own.

It was enough to tip Olarr into release also, his own body jerking, his bollocks yanking tight—and ach, ach, it was Aulis' mouth. Aulis' hot, sweet, wonderful mouth, latching onto his spewing prick, sucking his seed into his throat, into his belly. The truth and the feel of it crashing across Olarr's awareness, striking his body to writhing thrashing madness, as he poured out with all his strength, all his heart, all his devotion. Filling his worthy mate, feeding his hungry belly, cherishing him with all he had. With his very best.

He was still shivering when Aulis pulled off again, licking at those plump pink lips, flashing Olarr a smug, satisfied grin. And then even leaning back on his knees to take a good long look at the mess he had made of Olarr's hole, at how his sweet seed was already oozing out, anointing the fur beneath them.

"So handsome, captain," Aulis murmured, with another blatant lick at his lips. "And so sweet and tasty for me, too. Got myself a nice fat seed-ling, this time."

He had given a firm little slap to his now-rounded belly, the sound much like that of a deep contented drum, and Olarr choked a laugh as his shaky arms clutched for his mate, and dragged him down onto his chest. A demand that, thankfully, Aulis did not resist in the least, his pliant body sprawling warm and willing over Olarr's, his grin still pulling up his mouth, lighting up his eyes.

But then his smile slightly faded, his head cocking sideways, his brow slowly furrowing. "So are you gonna tell me, then, captain?" he asked, very steady. "What's going on?"

Olarr blinked and swallowed, caught in the suddenness of the question, the certain awareness in Aulis' eyes. Awareness that was shifting into stubbornness, his jaw clenching, his expressive mouth thinning. "You were gone for a whole extra day," he said flatly. "And you brought the kids those gifts, when there was no real reason, and I *know* how you felt about that dagger. And, you keep looking at me like that, and"—with a jerky movement, he bent his face into Olarr's hairy armpit, inhaling deep—"your scent is off, too."

In another day, another moment, Olarr might have revelled

in his impossible man brazenly scenting him thus, drawing out his truth thus—but today, he could only gaze up at Aulis' face, his heart thudding strange and stricken in his chest. He needed to uphold Aulis. Needed to cherish Aulis. Needed to be strong. To show no fear. To keep him safe, to care for him, to grant him his best, to—

"Fuck, Olarr," Aulis said, harder now, as something new flashed in his eyes and his scent, something alarmingly close to hurt. "You're not gonna make me drag it outta you, are you? We're not still really doing this?"

A thick sound wrenched from Olarr's throat, and his arms around Aulis spasmed, yanking him tighter, closer. "No," he gulped, and was it a falsehood, mayhap, mayhap. "I only—it is—"

He was breathing too hard to speak, his eyes wide and blinking on Aulis' face, and he could see the twitch of unease across Aulis' eyes now, the faintest whisper of fear in his scent. And no, no, this was what Olarr wished to prevent, what he needed to prevent, his mate needed the best, only the best, and ach, he had failed. He had failed.

"It is—the men," he finally rasped, forcing the words out, making them into harsh, bitter truth. "The Council. In the north. Most of all Lord Culthen and the new Lord Rikard. Last week they held a summit amongst them, and in this, they began again calling—for war."

His voice cracked, breaking on the sudden sharpness in Aulis' eyes, the surge of emotion in his scent. But Olarr had begun this now, and he needed to finish it, to grant his mate the answer he sought. "As of yet, Lords Otto and Anton and Warmisham have spoken naught against this," his choked voice continued, "and naught against the Council's claims against us. They have said that we are poisoning the fields, and tainting the markets with our gold and goods. Drawing good human women—and men—and *children*—away to our mountain."

Aulis' mouth had sunk into a frown as Olarr spoke, and now he fiercely shook his head, spreading a hand against Olarr's clammy chest. "So yeah, that's utter *rubbish*, and those pricks are such vile little vermin," he snarled, his voice thin and scathing. "But—we knew they were stirring this up, yeah? They want an easy excuse for their own fool mistakes. They've done shit all to deal with that grain shortage, all these years, and it's a hell of a lot easier to blame it all on the orcs, yeah? Especially with all the success we've been seeing? The legal rights, the new camps, the land we've gained? All those humans willingly moving to the mountain, and joining the clans?"

It was all truth, and ach, none of it was new, it was naught they had never spoken of before this. And Olarr could see that awareness darkening Aulis' eyes, thinning his mouth even tighter. "So what else?" he demanded. "Tell me, Olarr. All of it."

But it was again too hard to speak, the words strangled and sickening in Olarr's throat, his breaths juddering through his chest. And that was more fear, shifting into Aulis' eyes and his scent, and for a breath, Olarr thought he might vomit, or weep.

"Grimarr asked me," he choked, between his heaving breaths, "if you might wish to—go back. Back north, to Duke Warmisham's household. To spy for us again, and help keep away this war."

There. There, he had said it, he had been honest, he had hurled this out between them. This question, this obligation. This doom.

For Olarr knew that Aulis would do aught that he could for his kin. He would give all, and offer all. And Olarr had always known this, and he would honour this, honour all that Aulis wished—but in his selfish, broken heart, he so longed to keep Aulis. To protect his dear mate, to cherish him, to live with him, to raise their younglings together. To witness him growing old, to meet their Bautul grandsons together, to mayhap someday see Ophelia's smile on a Bautul orcling's face. To keep this life they had made. To keep this home.

But now—now Olarr would need to forego this. To offer this up once again, on the altar of the men's greed, and the men's war. And he would do this, he would force his way through this, but—but—

He was blinking hard, fighting back the water now prickling behind his eyes, and bracing himself against the fur. Waiting, aching, as he searched Aulis' unreadable face, and dreaded his doom...

When Aulis grasped Olarr's face, and kissed him. Kissed him hard and wild and urgent, his teeth biting, his breaths ragged and short. "Oh, *captain*," he breathed, between kisses, and he yanked back again, searching Olarr's eyes. "You didn't think I would, did you? You can't honestly think I would—"

But mayhap Olarr's face betrayed it, or his scent, or his sudden certain confusion—what did Aulis mean, he would not?—and Aulis' breath caught in his throat, his head jerking back and forth. "I gave them almost *five years*, Olarr," he said, his voice cracking. "I put up with that foul little duke's rubbish for five fucking *years*. I lived on the other side of the *realm* from you, I missed you every damn day, and we ended the damn war, we *did*. And like hell am I going through that again. Like hell am I putting our kids through that. What, did you think I would just run off and leave them? Leave *you*?"

Olarr's voice had failed him, his eyes yet blinking at Aulis' face, for—ach. Ach, he knew Aulis, he knew his fierce care for his kin, he knew how he would give all. And Olarr had sworn to honour this, had sworn it to Aulis and the goddess and himself, so—

So why was Aulis staring at him like this. Staring, and now he was the one blinking, and dashing his palm at his eye. "Goddess damn you, Olarr," he said thickly. "You—you really thought I would."

Olarr's breaths were heaving so hard it hurt, dragging through his chest. "I only know what you—will give," he croaked. "For your kin. For my kin. Ach, with Slagvor, with Borek and Ulfgast, with all those five years apart. And I know how you would never wish to—sit back, and do naught, and wait for others to save our kin on our behalf. And I have sworn to uphold you, and to honour you in—all. All you might wish. All I can ever grant you."

His voice cracked again, his prickling eyes fixed to Aulis' stunned face. To how Aulis was shaking his head, rubbing harder at his eyes, as a hoarse sound hissed from his throat. "But—*you're* my kin now, Olarr," he rasped. "You, and Alfie, and Ophelia. You're my family. My *home*. And there is nothing—*nothing*—that will make me walk away from you. Not Grimarr, not a war, not even you. *Nothing*, Olarr."

Ach. Olarr's chest was cracking, breaking, his eyes finally brimming over, streaking water down his cheeks. Ach. This could not be truth, this could not be his, it could not be glinting thus, flashing in his mate's stubborn eyes. But he knew that look, he knew that scent on his mate, he could not mean, he could not—

"I'm not leaving, Olarr," Aulis insisted, now with a twinge of frustration in his voice. "I'm fucking *not*. I'm a father now, yeah? And we built this house here on purpose, remember? We wanted to be able to get away, and have some space from it all. We wanted to finally focus on each other. On being a *family*."

Ach, this was truth, but it was one Olarr had hoarded close and shameful to his chest, in all those many moons since. As a good Bautul captain, he ought to have accepted his clan's wishes after the war, and moved Aulis and his kin into the mountain for good. It was safe there now, and Aulis was well liked amongst the Bautul, many of whom yet shamelessly angled for a taste of his sweet seed. But Aulis had yet wanted the house, had insisted upon the house, even if only for the summers. And this had made it easy, too easy, for Olarr to support this, and welcome this…

"And look, if you really want to talk about leaving," Aulis continued, his voice sharpening, "then why don't we talk about you still being a Bautul captain right now, yeah? Why don't we talk about you being away at Orc Mountain for three whole days? While I'm out here alone with the kids, telling them over and over that you'll be back at some point, even if I don't exactly know when? While also listening to them whinge about my cooking, and about how they can't sleep when you're not here? And Ophelia complains every time we run the obstacle course without her, but Alfie complains every time I try to do some garden rubbish with her, and I hate leaving them in here alone when I'm out hunting for game, and it's just—we miss you, yeah?"

Olarr blinked up at Aulis, whilst his heart knocked loud and harsh and strange in his chest. Aulis had truly—thought this, and faced this, all this time? He had never once complained, had he? But ach, no, he would not, he was such a good brave mate, he—

"And look, I know how important our clan is to you," Aulis said, on a heavy sigh. "And you—you've given me so much, yeah? Given me so many concessions and sacrifices. All those years, all that travelling, this house, even Ophelia. And I knew if I asked, you'd do it just for me, and I don't want you—resenting me. Don't want you—regretting me."

The water was again streaking from Olarr's eyes, for he could never regret Aulis, could never regret Ophelia or Alfie, could never regret aught of this, in all his days. And ach, even the thought of staying here, spending each blissful day here at his home with his kin, was heating and sparking in his belly, in his heart…

"And shit, now I've gone and said it, so now we're fucked, aren't we?" Aulis added, his mouth twisting into a bitter little grimace. "But look, Olarr"—more determination flared in his eyes—"you're not as young as you used to be either, yeah? You're past forty now, and you don't heal as fast as you used to. And even if Silfast's forgotten how to feel pain, that doesn't mean *you* need to keep breaking yourself apart in that fighting-pit every time you're there. You don't think I haven't noticed how you favour your left shoulder these days? Or how much longer you need to sleep, every time you come back? While the kids are up here clamouring to get at you, and whinging about my cooking, again?"

Ach. Olarr could not speak, could not think through the grief and the hope and the fondness now careening through his body, shrieking in his chest. Ach, he had failed his mate, his mate had known his weakness and his defeat, all this time, and he yet wished—to stay? Aulis wished to stay? Aulis wished—*Olarr* to stay?

And before Olarr could stop this, or catch this, he had tackled Aulis to his back on the fur, and pinned him hard beneath him. His swift dancing man could yet not escape him thus, was yet no match for Olarr's sheer size and strength, not with Olarr's arms and legs holding him down thus, not with Olarr's good strong prick already seeking at his mate's hot clutching hole, and shoving its way inside. Skewering him at his very core, trapping him here upon Olarr, beneath Olarr, where he could never again escape, or hide aught from him.

And Olarr held those wide blue eyes as he furiously fucked his beautiful wonderful man, as he rutted and growled and bared his teeth. Aulis was *his*, and Aulis would never leave him again, for Olarr was his kin, Olarr was his home. And Olarr was fully overcome with it, lost with it, with his need to prove this to his mate, to make this truth. To mark it into his mate's soft pale skin, to bite and tear at his neck, his ears, his shoulder. To not falter as his man kicked and moaned beneath him, caught and held in his strength, bound to his yoke and his prick and his teeth.

Olarr's release pounded through him, poured out of him with desperate strength, flooding his mate in stream after stream of good hot Bautul seed. Whilst only a part of him noted Aulis' teeth seeking at in his own neck, scraping with strange new purpose—until they too clamped down hard and sharp and deep. And Aulis had betrayed a low, guttural moan, his mouth sucking, latching, catching hold. Just the way an orc would, just the way Harja always had, and Olarr quaked all over as he gave it, as he poured out his very best for his beautiful mate, for his heart, his home.

It felt vague and dreamy afterwards, like naught else Olarr could ever recall, and he tended to his shivery mate with a dazed, distant intent. Sucking and kissing at his mate's bitten ears, at his ragged throat, until he could no more taste blood or pain. Only smooth soft healed skin, just as he wished, just as it ought to be. And then he moved to his mate's trembling mouth, licking and cleaning off the taste of his own lifeblood, before gently guiding that sweet mouth back to his own wounded throat. Purring his approval at the first careful lick of a tongue, tentative at first, but then growing stronger, surer, hungrier. Until those teeth bit down yet again, flaring out pain and pleasure, and Olarr moaned and fucked him through it, lost in the hot hazy wonder, in the raw roaring need to keep filling his mate. Keep holding him here, keep supporting him, giving to him, offering all he had.

Aulis cleaned the wound properly before pulling away this time, enough that Olarr could feel the familiar healing prickle in it—and afterwards he kissed Aulis for it, again tasting himself on his mouth, deep in his scent. Deep in a way that felt strong and new, thrumming low and content in his belly. His. *His.*

He could not have said how long they stayed there together,

kissing and tasting and scenting one another. But when Aulis finally twitched and drew away, Olarr could feel his own awareness returning, and with it a sudden, rising alarm. Ach. They had just—they had—

"Well, that was new," came Aulis' hoarse voice, his smile on Olarr's face careful, mayhap uncertain. "Drinking each other's... yeah. I take it that's a thing... orc mates do?"

Olarr jerked a nod, his own eyes searching Aulis' face. "Tastes and scents so good, ach?" he breathed, before he could stop it. "Sinks our scents even deeper upon one another, makes a bond that shall not be broken. I only had never thought you might wish to—"

He swallowed hard, drew in air, drew up strength. Despite all his own failings, his mate deserved his truth. His care. His best.

"I am sorry, my warrior," he whispered. "I am sorry I did not speak to you of this. And more than this, I—I am sorry I doubted you. I am sorry I did not have faith that you would... stay with me. With us."

Aulis' eyes had gone flinty again, his tongue brushing at a smudge of red yet on his lip. "Yeah, well, why didn't you, though?" he shot back. "I mean, I swore vows to you. I gave you an orc-forged wedding-ring. I joined your clan. Moved here with you. Adopted kids with you. What the hell else do I need to do, Olarr? Honestly?"

He was searching Olarr's eyes, truly seeking an answer, demanding it. "Is it because I'm not an orc?" he continued. "Because I'm not—Harja?"

Olarr winced, shook his head, but he could feel Aulis' sharp fingernails in his back, now, could taste his stubbornness wheeling in the air. "Because yeah, maybe I'll never be able to compete with Harja, yeah?" he demanded. "I can never compete with your dead, brave, valiant Bautul mate. With your

first love, with an orc, who fought beside you, who *died* for
you—"

A thick, hoarse sound barked from Olarr's throat, and
though he whipped his head back and forth, the darkness was
yet there again, sick and cold and bitter. And mayhap it was the
pain in Aulis' scent, or the truth of the blood on his mouth, or
the wonder of all they had just done together—but Olarr could
not hold the darkness back. Could not wall it away, block it in,
keep it from escaping...

"No," he gasped. "No, Aulis. For Harja—he *betrayed* me. He
spurned my counsel. He refused all my plans, all my pleading,
all my offerings. He refused, and he yet turned from me, and
left me!"

He had never before spoken this aloud, never even to the
goddess herself, but it was yet breaking from him, near
shouting from his mouth. "Harja left me behind to bear Slagvor
alone," he choked. "He left me behind to face my grief, and to
avenge his death, and carry my clan, without him! For I was not
enough for him, and I ken he"—his voice cracked—"he *wished*
for his death. He sought it just as—just as *you* did, Aulis."

His betraying voice scraped jagged and painful between
them, spewing aloud all Olarr's most bitter regrets, his deepest,
darkest griefs. He had sought with all his strength to save
Harja, to grant Harja hope and peace and comfort, to seek
other ways, other answers—and it had meant naught, in the
end. It had meant naught, and Olarr had failed. And he would
never stop grieving this, never stop wondering what more he
could have done.

And beneath him, Aulis looked and scented—shocked.
Stricken. And then saddened, as his strong hands stroked up
Olarr's back, drew his head down into his neck. "Oh, captain,"
Aulis whispered, into his hair. "Fuck, that explains so much,
and I should have—I should have guessed. You—you know it

wasn't about *you*, yeah? You know there's nothing you could have done?"

They were impossible words, spilling so easy from his impossible mate's mouth, and Olarr could not bear it, he could not—and ach, he was weeping into his mate's strong shoulder, shuddering beneath those strong stroking hands.

"I'm sure he loved you," Aulis went on, with that sureness ringing in his voice, his touch. "And I know he didn't do it to hurt you. He just couldn't—"

His voice faltered, mayhap caught in his own memories of his own darkness, his own despair—and somehow Olarr found his breath, dragged it into his gulping throat. "But *you* did," he croaked. "You listened to me, Aulis. You welcomed my comfort, and my counsel. You came beside me to avenge Harja, and helped me save my kin. You did all this in the face of my weakness, and my falsehoods to you. My—cowardice. And this was such a great gift to me, it was hope and kindness beyond all measure, and I have always longed to—repay this. To grant you all you might wish."

It was the full truth, now, bare and shameful in his cracking voice, and he could hear Aulis' swallow, could feel his slow, shaky sigh. "Look, Olarr, I would say you don't have a damned thing to repay," he replied. "But since I know what a stubborn Bautul you are, then—yeah. You want to repay me, you can step down as captain, and stay the fuck home with me. Forever."

Forever. That beautiful, wonderful word rippled through Olarr's body, sagging him heavily down onto Aulis, enough that Aulis' breath escaped in a sharp, sudden grunt. And then a thin, shaky chuckle as he heaved Olarr over onto his side, and shoved up onto his elbow to look at him. To look at Olarr's wet face, his trembling mouth, and mayhap his—hope. His longing.

"You really don't mind?" Aulis asked, soft again, as the

awareness flickered across his searching blue eyes. "You're sure?"

Olarr drew in a slow breath, and again fought to find truth, to speak it to his mate's eyes. "No, you ken I should—welcome this," he said. "I have missed you also, warrior, more with each passing day I am parted from you. And I have grown so weary of all this war and fighting, and to hear of it come again was—*ach*. I should be most glad to leave it to Silfast, and spend my days here, tending to my kin and my garden."

Aulis' grin was sudden and swift, lighting up his face, sparkling in his eyes. "Yeah?" he asked, almost shy. "I'd like that too, captain. And you know"—he grasped Olarr's shoulder, gave it a reassuring squeeze—"Silfast would love it too. He'll love getting to pick out a new co-captain or two to boss around, yeah? None of them will give him near as much trouble as you have."

Olarr couldn't help a low chuckle, for ach, though he yet loved Silfast like a blood-brother, they remained oft at odds over many, many clan matters. And whilst the thought of handing the clan fully into Silfast's care was not an easy one, he also well knew that Silfast *would* care. He would work and fight until the end, and give them his very best.

And Olarr could give his best... here. Here, to his beautiful man, and his sweet younglings, and his cozy little home. And his man was still grinning at him, and suddenly tackling him back to the fur, pinning him firm and safe beneath his lean, strong body. "And you won't even need to worry about staying in shape," he said, with a smug little grin. "Because you know I'll keep you going, yeah?"

Olarr smiled back at him, so broad it ached in his face, and in his chest. Ach. Ach, he was so blessed. So blessed to have such a fierce, faithful mate. The most stunning man in all the realm, with the warmest eyes, and the sweetest scent, and the greatest, swiftest strength. And even—Olarr's hungry hands slid on their own to caress it—the roundest, plumpest seed-belly.

"Oh, good goddess," Aulis groused, darting a brief, baleful glance down toward it. "What the fucking hell, captain! It might as well be a real damned orcling! It's never been that—"

But his voice broke there, for his eyes had wandered to... Olarr's neck. To where he had finally bitten Olarr, like the lusty goddess' son he was, and drunk out his mate's lifeblood, along with a full belly of seed, and a full rump of it, too. And Olarr was still smiling proudly toward it, caressing it with hungry greedy hands, whilst Aulis groaned and rolled his eyes, and then... shifted backwards. So he could find Olarr's already-hard prick, and slowly, surely, seat himself down upon it.

Olarr kicked and moaned, already caught, already lost. Lost in such awestruck wonder, in such pride and pleasure and peace. In the staggering truth of his beautiful man eagerly clamping upon him, reeking of him, milking out even more of him. And smiling so sweetly toward him, flashing him a mouthful of sharp, red-rimmed teeth.

"Good, captain," Aulis murmured, so soft, so bright, so alive. "You're such a good strong Bautul, aren't you? You're gonna do such a good job of filling me? Taking care of me?"

It was all Olarr had ever asked for, all he had ever prayed for, all his greatest longings brought to life, dropped here upon his lap, in his own sacred home. And he could only nod and breathe and adore his goddess' beautiful son, and forever praise the day he had fallen at his feet.

"Ach, my brave warrior," he whispered, with all his heart. "I shall."

THE END

THANKS FOR READING!

Thank you so much for joining me for Aulis and Olarr's tale! I've been wanting to write their story for years, and it was such a joy to finally be able to bring it to life.

And for even more Olarr and Aulis, they show up throughout my Orc Sworn series! We first meet them in *The Heiress and the Orc*, and Aulis plays an important background role in *The Duchess and the Orc*, helping Duke Warmisham's wife Maria to escape her horrid husband.

I know we'll keep seeing more of Olarr and Aulis in the future, too... along with Bautul friends like Kalfr (who will definitely be getting his own story!). If you have thoughts on what you're most excited for, I'd love to hear from you at my Facebook group, on my Discord server, or on my Patreon (which has even more exclusive Olarr bonus chapters and artwork!). You can find them all linked on my website at finleyfenn.com.

Plus, on my website you can also find my mailing list, which has all kinds of free bonus content for you—including artwork from this book, and a free Orc Sworn story about how Silfast finally found himself a sweet mate. I'd love to stay in touch with you!

Thank you again for joining me on this adventure! Your support means so much to me, and I'm so grateful to you. Hugs!

ACKNOWLEDGMENTS

As always, I'm just so, so grateful to my truly awesome community of readers, supporters, and friends. Your kindness and enthusiasm is what makes it possible for me to write these books, and I cannot express how much it means to me.

But for this book in particular, I especially need to thank my incredible Orc Sworn supporters on Patreon. Not only did they overwhelmingly vote for me to finally write this book, but they literally made it possible through their ongoing generosity, and cheered me on all the while! I would not have been able to take the time to write this without them, and I am just so thankful. May all the goddess' greatest blessings be upon you, my dear Orc Mountain kin!

I also need to thank the beta readers, proofreaders, and subject matter specialists who supported and strengthened this book: Amy F., Ari, Cookie, Driznar, Erin, Jen M., Jen R., Judi Szabo, Kahaula, Lauren Mauchley, Lexi K. Jordan, Mary Lynne Neilsen, MK, Otto, Serena, and Þórey H. And I'm especially grateful to my fabulous author friends in this genre who took the time to share their invaluable insights and expertise with me: Lillian Lark, V.C. Lancaster, Goddess Ruby Dixon, and the utterly brilliant Eris Adderly/Octavia Hyde (who also served as this book's editor). They are all wonderful, and I cannot recommend their own books highly enough!

I also want to say a special thanks to the fierce friends who have so generously shared their gifts with the entire Orc Sworn community. My heartfelt gratitude to my best Bautul sister Marykate, for managing so many details, and always granting me such wise counsel; to Amy and Elizabeth, for always being here, and helping to make my Discord such a fun and welcoming community; to Erin, fearless leader of the Skai Mafia PR Team, for all the awesome artwork and true Skai fealty; to our dear Grisk galdr-spinner Morning Dove for the tales, laughs, and friendship; to Coco for the perfect character designs and illustrations; to EJ and the Skai sisters for my all-time favourite podcast, *Tales from the Orc Den* (highly recommend!); to my fantastic audio publishers at Podium for making my audiobooks possible; and to Katie at Romantically Inclined Reviews for all the laughter and enthusiasm, including her encouragement on writing this book in the first place.

And finally, my deepest gratitude to my own brave mate, who feeds me all his delicious cooking, and always keeps me guarded and safe. I am so blessed, my warrior.

ALSO BY FINLEY FENN

THE SINS OF THE ORC

He's fallen too far to save... but his enemy is going to try.

In a world of warring orcs and men, Kesst of Clan Ash-Kai is a pawn. A pretty, pliant plaything, bound to the cruelest orcs in the realm.

Until the new healer storms in.

He's huge, hostile, and hideous, with a powerful scarred body and terrifying ancient magic. And it only takes one disastrous meeting before he and Kesst are bitter enemies, and Kesst vows to see the vile brute destroyed...

And then **a sudden, deadly attack** hurls his helpless body straight at the healer's feet.

Kesst fully expects to be mocked, belittled, abandoned to his doom — **but instead, his new enemy picks him up.**

Soothes his wounds.

And carries him home...

Soon Kesst is trapped in a tiny sickroom beneath Orc Mountain, caught in the thrall of the healer's impossible magic. In the surprising gentleness of his touch. In the strength of his stubborn, seductive safety...

But with his horrid handlers close on their scent, Kesst can't possibly be falling for his forbidden foe... can he? **Can a healer save him from his sins... or destroy him?**

ALSO BY FINLEY FENN

THE HEIRESS AND THE ORC

Once, he was her dearest friend... but now he's a brutal, terrifying monster.

In a world of recently warring orcs and men, Ella Riddell is determined to ignore it all. She's the wealthiest heiress in the realm—and soon, she's to wed a lord, and become a real lady.

Until the night her engagement-party ends in utter *disaster*, and Ella runs for the forest—**and straight into the powerful arms of a hulking, deadly orc.**

And it's not just any orc. It's *Natt*. The orc Ella made a secret, foolish pledge to, many years past...

He's huge and shameless and vicious, not at all the gangly, laughing daredevil Ella remembers. **And he's here with one shocking, scandalous aim: to wreak vengeance on Ella's betrothed. With *her*.**

With her hunger.

Her surrender.

Her undoing.

Ella knows she should run, even if this deadly enemy was once a friend. Even if his scent drags up a dark, forbidden longing. Even if his kisses are the sweetest, filthiest thing she's ever tasted in her life...

But will Ella truly risk her perfect future, for an orc? Will she face the bitter truths of the past, and brave the terrifying Orc Mountain, before more war rises to destroy them all?

ALSO BY FINLEY FENN

THE DUCHESS AND THE ORC

He's a massive, mocking, murderous monster. And there's only one thing he wants from her...

In a world of recently warring orcs and men, Maria is desperate for escape. She's trapped in an opulent prison, tainted by rumours of madness, and wed to a cold, vindictive duke who hungers only for war.

But with no family, no funds, and no hope, there's nowhere left to run — except for the one place even a duke can't reach. The place where women almost always meet their doom...

Orc Mountain.

It's a grim, deadly fortress, filled with fierce, bloodthirsty beasts — **and the first orc Maria meets is the most terrifying of them all.** A huge, hostile, hideous brute, hardened by hatred and war, who instantly accuses her of foul trickery, and threatens her with death —

But this orc also wants something. Something that kindles deep in his gleaming black eyes, in his rough, rugged scent, in the velvet heat of his voice. Something that just might grant Maria his safety... but only if she grants him *everything* in return.

Her defeat.

Her dignity.

Her devotion...

And surely, a duchess wouldn't dare make such a shameful deal with the devil — or would she? Especially when surrender might spark yet more war... **or bring the mighty Orc Mountain to its knees?**

ABOUT THE AUTHOR

Finley Fenn is "the queen of dark orc romance" (Virgo Reader), and her ongoing Orc Sworn series has been praised as "sexy, romantic, angsty, and captivating ... utter brilliance" (Romantically Inclined Reviews).

When she's not obsessing over her stories, Finley loves reading, drooling over delicious orc artwork, and spending time with her incredible readers on Patreon, Discord, and Facebook. She lives in Canada with her beloved family, including her very own grumpy, gorgeous orc husband.

For free bonus stories and epilogues, special offers, and exclusive Orc Sworn artwork, sign up at www.finleyfenn.com.